Muse and Reverie

By Charles de Lint from Tom Doherty Associates

Muse and Reverie

Charles de Lint

TOR®

A Tom Doherty Associates Book
New York

The city, characters, and events to be found in these pages are fictitious. Any resemblance to actual persons living or dead is purely coincidental.

MUSE AND REVERIE

A Tor Book
Published by Tom Doherty Associates, LLC
175 Fifth Avenue
New York, NY 10010

www.tor-forge.com

Tor® is a registered trademark of Tom Doherty Associates, LLC.

Library of Congress Cataloging-in-Publication Data

De Lint, Charles, 1951–
 Muse and reverie / Charles de Lint. — 1st ed.
     p. cm.
 "A Tom Doherty Associates book."
 ISBN 978-0-7653-2340-8
 1. Newford (Imaginary place)—Fiction.   2. City and town life—
Fiction.   3. Fantasy fiction, Canadian.   I. Title.
 PR9199.3. D357M87 2009
 813'.54—dc22

                                                      2009034713

First Edition: December 2009

Printed in the United States of America

0 9 8 7 6 5 4 3 2 1

Copyright Acknowledgments

This volume of stories
goes out to the late
Johnny Cash & Joe Strummer,
two musicians who are much missed
but whose music
continues to enrich my life.

Contents

Author's Note

Five collections in now, I'm at a bit of a loss as to what to say about these stories set in Newford because I'm sure I've said all there is to say in previous introductions. But one thing I can do is thank you, the readers, for your continued support over the years.

I'm sure the fact that the previous four collections are all still in print is not unique to me (there must be collections by other authors with long shelf lives), but it does owe everything to your going out and buying them, and talking them up to your friends. As does the fact that in these trying economic times Tor is publishing yet another one—for which I thank Patrick Nielsen Hayden and Tom Doherty, my editor and publisher, respectively. And I would certainly be remiss if I didn't send a shout-out to all the bookstores that carry them.

But mostly it's because of you.

That said, I do want to add individual thanks to my wife, MaryAnn, who came up with the title for this collection, as she has for so many of my books. She continues to make astute suggestions, both before and after the stories are written, and busy as her life is with her own work and art, she still finds the time to handle so much of the business side of my career, which lets me concentrate on the writing. This year she gets an added thanks for her persistence in visiting the Humane Society, which netted us the most recent addition to our family, our pup Johnny Cash.

His boundless energy is a perfect counterpoint to our cat Clare's regal calm.

Thanks as well to Rodger Turner, who makes me look good on the Web with the site he maintains for me (check out his review/info site at www.sfsite.com), and my agent, Russ Galen, who takes such good care of me in the big world of business.

And of course my appreciation goes out to the individual editors who first commissioned some of these stories: Ellen Datlow, Terri Windling, Martin H. Greenberg, Janet Pack, Al Sarrantonio, Kealan Patrick Burke, Andrew M. Greeley, Christopher Golden, Mike Mignola, and Kerrie Hughes.

I'm taking a break from Newford, but it's nice to know that the characters can go on about their business in this collection while I move on to other things. And there are enough completed short stories on file for one more collection, so I might well be writing another of these introductions in a year or two.

Until then, take care of each other.

Lastly, some notes on a couple of the stories.

With "Refinerytown" I've gone and broken a long-held rule for my writing and put a couple of real people in the story as actual characters. Sharyn November is my Young Adult editor at Viking, a magnificent woman who really does have chicken puppets, though I've yet to see them. Nina Kiriki Hoffman is my good pal, a wonderful writer, a talented musician, and a fellow lover of silly things and toys.

They're here because "Refinerytown" started as a joke at a convention. We kept trying to convince Sharyn to buy the idea as a series of picture books, and the more serious we appeared to be, the more horrified she became. There were others involved in the creation of "Refinerytown," most prominently Charles Vess.

He didn't make it in because the story already has a comic book artist in it, but he does get a mention. I don't even get that.

And you can blame MaryAnn for telling me I should actually write the story. I think she meant the *real* "Refinerytown," but I'm leaving that in Mona's and Nina's capable hands.

In "Newford Spook Squad": Special thanks to my pals Dave Russell and Mark Finn for vetting this.

If any of you are on the Internet, come visit my home page at www.charlesdelint.com. I'm also at MySpace, Facebook, and Twitter, so you can drop in and say hello to me there as well.

CHARLES DE LINT
Ottawa, Winter 2009

Take, if you must, this little bag of dreams;
Unloose the cord, and they will wrap you round.

—W. B. Yeats, from "Fergus and the Druid"

Muse and Reverie

Somewhere in My Mind There Is a Painting Box

Such a thing to find, so deep in the forest: a painter's box nested in ferns and a tangle of sprucey-pine roots, almost buried by the leaves and pine needles drifted up against the trunk of the tree. Later, Lily would learn that it was called a pochade box, but for now she sat bouncing lightly on her ankles admiring her find.

It was impossible to say how long the box had been hidden here. The wood panels weren't rotting, but the hasps were rusted shut and it took her awhile to get them open. She lifted the lid and then, and then . . .

Treasure.

Stored in the lid, held apart from each other by slots, were three 8×10 wooden panels, each with a painting on it. For all their quick and loose rendering, she had no trouble recognizing the subjects. There was something familiar about them, too—beyond the subject matter that she easily recognized.

The first was of the staircase waterfall where the creek took a sudden tumble before continuing on again at a more level pace. She had to fill in detail from her own memory and imagination, but she knew it was that place.

The second was of a long-deserted homestead up a side valley of the hollow, the tin roof sagging, the rotting walls falling inward. It was nothing like Aunt's cabin on its sunny slopes, surrounded by wild roses, old beehives, and an apple orchard that she and Aunt were slowly reclaiming from the wild. This was a place that would only get sun from midmorning through the early after-noon, a dark and damp hollow, where the dew never had a chance to burn off completely.

The last one could have been painted anywhere in this forest, but she imagined it had been done down by the creek, looking up a slope into a view of yellow birches, beech and sprucey-pines growing dense and thick as the stars overhead, with a burst of light coming through a break in the canopy.

Lily studied each painting, then carefully set them aside on the ground beside her. There was the hint of another picture on the in-side lid itself, but she couldn't make out what it was supposed to be. Perhaps it was just the artist testing his colours. Looking at it made her feel funny, as though the ground under her had gotten spongy, and she started to sway. She blinked. When she turned her attention to the rest of the box, the feeling went away.

The palette was covered in dried paint that, like the inside lid, almost had the look of a painting itself, and when lifted from the box revealed a compartment underneath. In the bottom of the box were tubes of oil paint, brushes and a palette knife, a small bottle of turpentine, and a rag stained with all the colours the artist had been using.

Lily turned the palette over and there she found what she'd been looking for. An identifying mark. She ran a finger over the letters that spelled out an impossible name.

Milo Johnson.

Treasure.

"Milo Johnson," Aunt repeated, trying to understand Lily's ex-citement. "Should I know that name?"

Lily gave her a "you never pay attention, do you?" look and went to get a book from her bookshelf. She didn't have many, but those she did have had been read over and over again. The one she brought back to the kitchen table was called *The Newford*

Naturalists: Redefining the Landscape. Opening it to the first artist profiled, she underlined his name with her finger.

Aunt read silently along with her, mouthing the words, then studied the black-and-white photo of Johnson that accompanied the profile.

"I remember seeing him a time or two," she said. "Tramping through the woods with an old canvas knapsack on his back. But that was a long time ago."

"It would have to have been."

Aunt read a little more, then looked up.

"So he's famous then," she asked.

"Very. He went painting all through these hills and he's got pictures in galleries all over the world."

"Imagine that. And you reckon this is his box?"

Lily nodded.

"Well, we'd better see about returning it to him."

"We can't," Lily told her. "He's dead. Or at least they say he's dead. He and Frank Spain went out into the hills on a painting expedition and were never heard from again."

She flipped towards the back of the book until she came to the smaller section devoted to Spain's work. Johnson had been the giant among the Newford Naturalists, his bold, dynamic style instantly recognizable, even to those who might not know him by name, while Spain had been one of a group of younger artists that Johnson and his fellow Naturalists had been mentoring. He wasn't as well known as Johnson or the others, but he'd already been showing the potential to become a leader in his own right before he and Johnson had taken that last fateful trip.

It was all in the book which Lily had practically memorized by now, she'd read it so often.

Ever since Harlene Welch had given it to her a few years ago, Lily had wanted to grow up to be like the Naturalists—especially Johnson. Not to paint exactly the way they did, necessarily, but to have her own individual vision the way that they did. To be able to take the world of her beloved hills and forest and portray it in such a way that others would see it through her eyes, that they would see it in a new way and so understand her love for it and would want to protect it the way that she did.

Aunt considered her endless forays into the woods with pencil and paper in hand a tall step up from her earlier childhood ambition, which was simply to find the fairies she was convinced lived in the woods around them. Lily had pursued them with the same singular focus that she now devoted to her drawings of trees and stones, hillsides and hollows, and the birds and animals that made their homes in the forest.

"That was twenty years ago," she said, "and their bodies weren't ever recovered."

Twenty years ago. Imagine. The box had been lying lost in the woods for all that time. She must have passed by it on a hundred occasions, never noticing it until today when pure chance had it poke a corner up out of its burrow of leaves just as she was coming by.

"Never thought of painting pictures as being something dangerous," Aunt said.

"Anything can be dangerous," Lily replied. "That's what Beau says."

Aunt nodded. She reached across the table to turn the box towards her.

"So you plan on keeping it?" she asked.

"I guess."

"He must have kin. Don't you think it should go to them?"

Lily shook her head. "He was an orphan—just like me. The only people we could give it to would be in the museum, and they'd just stick it away in some drawer somewhere."

"Even the pictures?"

"Well, probably not them. But the painting box for sure . . ."

Lily hungered to try the paints and brushes she'd found in the box. There was never enough money for her to think of being able to buy either. They lived on whatever they could grow or gather from the woods around them, augmented by the small checks that Aunt's ex-husband sent every other month or so. So Lily made her brushes with wild grasses, or by crimping locks of her own hair with bits of tin and pliers, attaching them to the end of hardwood sticks. For colour she used anything that came to hand—old coffee grounds and teabags, berries, fine red mud, the hulls of nuts, and onion skins. Some, like the berries, she used as she found them. Others she'd boil up to get their colour. But their faint washes lent only a ghost of colour to her drawings. These paints she'd found would be like going from the gloom of dusk into the bright light of day.

"Well," Aunt said. "You found it, so I guess you get to decide what you do with it."

"I guess."

Finder's keepers, after all. But she couldn't help feeling that she was being greedy. That this find of hers—especially the paintings—belonged to everyone, not just some gangly backwoods girl who happened to come upon them while out on a ramble.

"I'll have to think on it," she added.

Aunt nodded, then got up to put on the kettle.

The next morning Lily went about her chores. She fed the chickens, sparing a few handfuls of feed for the sparrows and other birds that were waiting expectantly in the trees nearby. She milked the cow and when she was done poured some milk into a saucer for the cats that came out of the woods, purring and winding in between her legs until she set the saucer down. By the time she'd finished weeding the garden and filling the woodbox, it was midmorning.

She packed herself a lunch and stowed it in her shoulder satchel along with some carpenter's pencils and a pad of sketching paper made from cutting up brown grocery bags and tying them together on one side to make a book.

"Off again, are you?" Aunt asked.

"I'll be home for dinner."

"You're not going to bring that box with you?"

She was tempted. The tubes of paint were rusted shut, but she'd squeezed the thin metal of their bodies and found that the paint inside was still pliable. The brushes were good, too. Milo Johnson, as might be expected of a master painter, knew to take care of his tools. But much as she wanted to, her using them didn't seem right. Not yet, anyways.

"Not today," she told Aunt.

As she left the house she looked up to see a pair of dogs come tearing up the slope toward her. They were the Schaffers' dogs, Max and Kiki, the one dark brown, the other white with black markings, the pair of them bundles of short-haired energy. The Schaffers lived beside the Welchs, who owned the farm at the end of the trail that ran from the county road to Aunt's cabin—an hour's walk through the woods as you followed the creek. Their dogs were a friendly pair, good at not chasing cows or game, and showed up every few days to accompany Lily on her rambles.

The dogs danced around her now as she set off through the orchard. When she got to the Apple Tree Man's tree—that's what Aunt called the oldest tree of the orchard—she pulled a biscuit she'd saved from breakfast and set it down at its roots. It was a habit she'd had since she was a little girl—like feeding the birds and the cats while doing her morning chores. Aunt used to tease her about it, telling her what a good provider she was for the mice and raccoons.

"Shoo," she said as Kiki went for the biscuit. "That's not for you. You'll have to wait for lunch to get yours."

They went up to the top of the hill and into the woods, the dogs chasing each other in circles while Lily kept stopping to investigate some interesting seed pod or cluster of weeds. They had lunch a couple of miles farther on, sitting on a stone outcrop that overlooked the Big Sinkhole, a two- or three-acre depression with the entrance to a cave at the bottom. The entrance went straight down for about four feet, then opened into a large cave. Lily had climbed down into it the first time she'd come here and found old bits of rotting furniture and barrels and such scattered around the dank interior. Stories abounded as to who'd been living there in the old days—from mountain men and runaway slaves to moonshiners hiding from the revenue men—but no one knew the real history of the place.

Most of the mountains around Aunt's cabin were riddled with caves of all shapes and sizes. There were entrances everywhere, though most only went a few yards in before they ended. But some said you could walk from one end of the Kickaha Hills to the other, all underground, if you knew the way. There was even a cave entrance not far from the cabin. Aunt had built shelves inside this smaller cave and they kept their root vegetables and seed potatoes for next year's planting on the wooden planks, keeping them safe from the animals with a little door made of wood and tin. It was better than having to bury them in the ground to keep them away from the frost the way some had to do.

Lunch finished, Lily slid down from the rock. She didn't feel like caving today, nor drawing. Instead she kept thinking about the painting box, how odd it had been to find it after its having been lost for so many years, so she led the dogs back to that part of the woods to see what else she might find. A shiver went up her spine. What if she found their bones?

The dogs grew more playful as she neared the spot where she'd come upon the box. They nipped at her sleeves or crouched ahead of her, butts and tails in the air, growling so fiercely they made her laugh. Finally Max bumped her leg with his head just as she was in midstep. She lost her balance and fell into a pile of leaves, her satchel tumbling to the ground, spilling drawings.

She sat up. A smile kept twitching at the corner of her mouth but she managed to give them a pretty fierce glare.

"Two against one?" she said. "Well, come on, you bullies. I'm ready for you."

She jumped on Kiki and wrestled her to the ground, the dog squirming with delight in her grip. Max joined the tussle and soon the three of them were rolling about in the leaves like the puppies the dogs no longer were and Lily had never been. They were having such fun that at first none of them heard the shouting. When they did, they stopped their roughhousing to find a man standing nearby, holding a stick in his upraised hand.

"Get away from her!" he cried, waving the stick.

Lily sat up, so many leaves tangled in her hair and caught in her sweater that she had more on her than did some of the autumned trees around them. She put a hand on the collar of either dog, but, curiously, neither seemed inclined to bark or chase the stranger off. They stayed by her side, staring at him.

Lily studied him for a long moment, too, as quiet as the dogs. He wasn't a big man, but he seemed solid. Dressed in a fraying broadcloth suit with a white shirt underneath and worn leather boots on his feet. His hair was roughly trimmed and he looked as if he hadn't shaved for a few days. But he had a good face—strong features, laugh lines around his eyes and the corners of his mouth. She didn't think he was much older than she.

"It's all right," she told the man. "We were just funning."

There was something familiar about him, but she couldn't place it immediately.

"Of course," he said, dropping the stick. "How stupid can I be? What animal in this forest would harm its Lady?" He went down on his knees. "Forgive my impertinence."

This was too odd for words. From the strange behavior of the dogs to the man's even stranger behavior. She couldn't speak. Then something changed in the man's eyes. There'd been a lost look in them a moment ago, but also hope. Now there was only resignation.

"You're just a girl," he said.

Lily found her voice at that indignity.

"I'm seventeen," she told him. "In these parts, there's some would think I'm already an old maid."

He shook his head. "Your pardon. I meant no insult."

Lily relaxed a little. "That's all right."

He reached over to where her drawings had spilled from her satchel and put them back in, looking at each one for a moment before he did.

"These are good," he said. "Better than good."

For those few moments while he looked through her drawings, while he looked at them carefully, one by one, before replacing them in her satchel, he seemed different once more. Not so lost. Not so sad.

"Thank you," she sad.

She waited a moment, thinking it might be rude of her to follow a compliment with a question that might be considered prying. She waited until the last drawing was back in her satchel and he sat there holding the leather bag on his lap, his gaze gone she didn't know where.

"What are you doing here in the woods?" she finally asked.

It took a moment before his gaze returned to her. He closed the satchel and laid it on the grass between them.

"I took you for someone else," he said, which wasn't an answer at all. "It was the wild tangle of your red hair—the leaves in it and on your sweater. But you're too young and your skin's not a coppery brown."

"And this explains what?" she asked.

"I thought you were Her," he said.

Lily could hear the emphasis he put on the word, but it still didn't clear up her confusion.

"I don't know what you're talking about," she said.

She started to pluck the leaves out of her hair and brush them from her sweater. The dogs laid down, one on either side of her, still curiously subdued.

"I thought you were the Lady of the Wood," he explained. "She who stepped out of a tree and welcomed us when we came out of the cave between the worlds. She wears a cloak of leaves and has moonlight in Her eyes."

A strange feeling came over Lily when he said "stepped out of a tree." She found herself remembering a fever dream she'd once had—five years ago when she'd been snakebit. It had been so odd. She'd dreamt that she'd been changed into a kitten to save her from the snakebite, met Aunt's Apple Tree Man and another wood spirit called the Father of Cats. She'd even seen the fairies she'd tried to find for so long: foxfired shapes, bobbing in the meadow like fireflies.

It had all seemed so real.

Aunt hadn't said a thing as Lily had babbled on about her adventures. She'd only held her close, held her so tight it was hard to breathe for a moment. Tired from her long day, Lily had gone to bed as soon as they returned to their cabin and not woken for two days when she found Beau Welch sitting in a wooden chair by her bed. His features broke into a grin when he saw her open her eyes.

"Em," he said over his shoulder. "She's back."

And then Aunt joined him, Beau's wife, Harlene, beside her.

"You gave us a right scare, you did," Aunt said, stroking Lily's brow with her fingers. "But I guess the Lord heard my prayers and He didn't take you away from me."

"There was a snake . . ." Lily began.

Harlene nodded. "You got bit bad. But you fought off that poison like a soldier. There's nothing wrong with you that a little rest won't cure."

"It was magic," Lily tried to tell them. "I got to see the fairies."

Beau chuckled. "I don't doubt you did. Folks see every sort of thing in a fever."

Lily was too tired to try to convince them that what she'd seen was real.

She'd gone to the Apple Tree Man's tree in the orchard when Aunt finally allowed she was fit enough to get out of bed.

"Thank you, thank you," she'd told him.

But he didn't step out of his tree to talk to her. She didn't see the Father of Cats again either. Or the fairies. And though she tried to hold the whole of it fast in her mind, it all began to fade the way that dreams do.

That was when she finally put aside the fancies of childhood and took up drawing—a different kind of fancy, she supposed, but at least you could hold the paper in your hands and look at what you'd drawn. The drawings didn't fade away. They were always there when you went back to look at them.

She blinked away the memories and focused on the stranger again. He'd gotten off his knees and was sitting cross-legged on the ground, a half-dozen feet from where she and the dogs were.

"What did you mean when you said 'us'?" she asked.

Now it was his turn to look confused.

"You said this lady showed 'us' some cave."

He nodded. "I was out painting with Milo when—"

As soon as he mentioned that name, the earlier sense of familiarity collided with her memory of a photo in her book on the Newford Naturalists.

"You're Frank Spain!" Lily cried.

He nodded in agreement.

"But that can't be," she said. "You don't look any older than you do in the picture in my book."

"What book?"

"The one about Milo Johnson and the rest of the Newford Naturalists that's back at the cabin."

"There's a book about us?"

"You're famous," Lily told him with a grin. "The book says

you and Mr. Johnson disappeared twenty years ago while you were out painting in these very hills."

Frank shook his head, the shock plain in his features.

"Twenty . . . years?" he said slowly. "How's that even possible? We've only been gone for a few days . . ."

"What happened to you?" Lily asked.

"I don't really know," he said. "We'd come here after a winter of being cooped up in the studio, longing to paint in the landscape itself. We meant to stay until the black flies drove us back to the city, but then . . ." He shook his head. "Then we found the cave and met the Lady . . ."

He seemed so lost and confused that Lily took him home.

Aunt greeted his arrival and introduction with a raised eyebrow. Lily knew what she was thinking. First a painting box, now a painter. What would be next?

But Aunt had never turned anyone away from her cabin before and she wasn't about to start now. She had Lily show Frank to where he could draw some water from the well and clean up, then set a third plate for supper. It wasn't until later when they were sitting out on the porch drinking tea and watching the night fall that Frank told them his story. He told them how he and Milo had found the cave that led them through darkness into another world. How they'd met the Lady there, with Her cloak of leaves and Her coppery skin, Her dark, dark eyes and Her fox-red hair.

"So there is an underground way through these mountains," Aunt said. "I always reckoned there was some truth to that story."

Frank shook his head. "The cave didn't take us to the other side of the mountains. It took us out of this world and into another."

Aunt smiled. "Next thing you're going to tell me is you've been to Fairyland."

"Look at him," Lily said. She went inside and got her book, opening it to the photograph of Frank Spain. "He doesn't look any older than he did when this picture was taken."

Aunt nodded. "Some people do age well."

"Not this well," Lily said.

Aunt turned to Frank. "So what is it that you're asking us to believe?"

"I'm not asking anything," he said. "I don't believe it myself."

Lily sighed and took the book over to him. She showed him the copyright date, put her finger on the paragraph that described how he and Milo Johnson had gone missing some fifteen years earlier.

"The book's five years old," she said. "But I think we've got a newspaper that's no more than a month old. I could show you the date on it."

But Frank was already shaking his head. He'd gone pale reading the paragraph about the mystery of his and his mentor's disappearance. He lifted his gaze to meet Aunt's.

"I guess maybe we were in Fairyland," he said, his voice gone soft.

Aunt looked from her niece's face to that of her guest.

"How's that possible?" she said.

"I truly don't know," he told her.

He turned the pages of the book, stopping to read the section on himself. Lily knew what he was reading. His father had died in a mining accident when he was still a boy, but his mother had been alive when he'd disappeared. She'd died five years later.

"My parents are gone, too," she told him.

He nodded, his eyes shiny.

Lily shot Aunt a look, but Aunt sat in her chair, staring out into the gathering dusk, an unreadable expression in her features. Lily supposed it was one thing to appreciate a fairy tale but quite another to find yourself smack-dab in the middle of one.

Lily was taking it the best of either of them. Maybe it was be-cause of that snakebite fever dream she'd once had. In the past five years she still woke from dreams in which she'd been a kitten.

"Why did you come back?" she asked Frank.

"I didn't know I was coming back," he said. "That world . . ." He flipped a few pages back to show them reproductions of John-son's paintings. "That's what this other world's like. You don't have to imagine everything being more of itself than it seems to be here like Milo's done in these paintings. Over there it's really like that. You can't imagine the colours, the intensity, the rich wash that fills your heart as much as it does your eyes. We haven't painted at all since we got over there. We didn't need to." He laughed. "I know Milo abandoned his paints before we crossed over, and to tell you the truth, I don't even know where mine are."

"I found Mr. Johnson's box," Lily said. "Yesterday—not far from where you came upon me and the dogs."

He nodded, but she didn't think he'd heard her.

"I was walking," he said. "Looking for the Lady. We hadn't seen Her for a day or so and I wanted to talk to Her again. To ask Her about that place. I remember I came to this grove of sycamore and beech where we'd seen Her a time or two. I stepped in be-tween the trees, out of the sun and into the shade. The next thing I knew I was walking in these hills and I was back here where every-thing seems . . . paler. Subdued."

He looked at them.

"I've got to go back," he said. "There's no place for me here. Ma's gone and everybody I knew'll be dead like her or too changed for me to know them anymore." He tapped the book. "Just like me, according to what it says here."

"You don't want to go rushing into anything," Aunt said. "Surely you've got other kin and they'll be wanting to see you."

"There's no one. Me and Ma, we were the last of the Spains that I know."

Aunt nodded in a way that Lily recognized. It was her way of making you think she agreed with you, but she was really just waiting for common sense to take hold of you so that you didn't go off half-cocked and get yourself in some kind of trouble you didn't need to get into.

"You'll want to rest up," she said. "You can sleep in the barn. Lily will show you where. Come morning, everything'll make a lot more sense."

He just looked at her. "How do you make sense out of something like this?"

"You trust me on this," she said. "A good night's sleep does a body wonders."

So he followed her advice—most people did when Aunt had decided what was best for them.

He let Lily take him down to the barn where they made a bed for him in the straw. She wondered if he'd try to kiss her, and how she'd feel if he did, but she never got the chance to find out.

"Thank you," he said and then he lay down on the blankets.

He was already asleep by the time she was closing the door.

And in the morning he was gone.

That night Lily had one of what she thought of as her storybook dreams. She wasn't a kitten this time. Instead, she was sitting under the Apple Tree Man's tree and he stepped out of the trunk of his tree just like she remembered him doing in that fever dream when the twelve-year-old girl she'd been was bitten by a snake. He looked the same, too, a raggedy man, gnarled and twisty, like the boughs of his tree.

"You," she only said and looked away.

"That's a fine welcome for an old friend."

"You're not my friend. Friends aren't magical men who live in a tree and then make you feel like you're crazy because they never show up in your life again."

"And yet I helped you when you were a kitten."

"In the fever dream when I *thought* I was a kitten."

He came around and sat on his haunches in front of her, all long gangly limbs and tattered clothes and bird's nest hair. His face was wrinkled like the dried fruit from his tree.

He sighed. "It was better for you to only remember it as a dream."

"So it wasn't a dream?" she asked, unable to keep the eagerness from her voice. "You're real? You and the Father of Cats and the fairies in the field?"

"Someplace we're real."

She looked at him for a long moment, then nodded, disappointment taking the place of her momentary happiness.

"This is just a dream, too, isn't it?" she said.

"This is. What happened before wasn't."

She poked at the dirt with her finger, looking away from him again.

"Why would it be better for me to remember it as a dream?" she asked.

"Our worlds aren't meant to mix—not anymore. They've grown too far apart. When you spend too much time in ours, you become like your painter foundling, forever restless and unhappy in the world where you belong. Instead of living your life, you lose yourself in dreams and fancies."

"Maybe for some, dreams and fancies are better than what they have here."

"Maybe," he said, but she knew he didn't agree. "Is that true for you?"

"No," she had to admit. "But I still don't understand why I was allowed that one night and then no more."

She looked at him. His dark eyes were warm and kind, but there was a mystery in them, too. Something secret and daunting that she wasn't sure she could ever understand. That perhaps she shouldn't want to understand.

"Your world is no less a place of marvels and wonders," he said after a long moment. "That's something humans too often forget and why what you do is so important."

She laughed. "What *I* do? Whatever do I do that could be so important?"

"Perhaps it's not what you do now so much as what you will do if you continue with your drawing and painting."

She shook her head. "I'm not really that good."

"Do you truly believe that?"

She remembered what Frank Spain had said after looking at her drawings.

These are good. Better than good.

She remembered how the drawings had, if only for a moment, taken him away from the sadness that lay so heavy in his heart.

"But I'm only drawing the woods," she said. "I'm drawing what I see, not fairies and fancies."

The Apple Tree Man nodded. "Sometimes people need fairies and fancies to wake them up to what they already have. They look so hard for the little face in the thistle, the wrinkled man who lives in a tree. But then they start to focus on the thistle itself, the feathery purples of its bloom, the sharp points of its thorns. They reach out and touch the rough bark of the tree, drink in the green of its leaves, taste of its fruit. And they're transformed. They're *in* their own world, fully and completely, sometimes for the first time since they were a child, and they're finally appreciating what it has to offer them.

"That one moment can stop them from ever falling asleep again. Just as the one glimpse such as you had can wake a lifetime of imagination. It can fuel a thousand stories and paintings. But how you use your imagination, what stories you decide to tell, will come from inside you, not from a momentary glitter of fairy wings."

"But it wakes an ache, too," Lily said.

He nodded. "That never goes away. I know. But if you were to come into our world, it still wouldn't go away. And then you'd also ache for the world you left behind. Better to leave things as they are, Lillian. Better the small ache that carries in it a seed of wonder than the larger ache that can never be satisfied."

"So why did you come to me tonight? Why are you telling me all of this?"

"To ask you not to look for that cave," he said. "To not go in. If you do, you'll carry the yearning of what you find inside forever."

What the Apple Tree Man had told her all seemed to make perfect sense in last night's dream. But when she woke to find Frank gone, what made sense then didn't seem to be nearly enough now. Knowing she'd once experienced a real glimpse into a storybook world, she only found herself wanting more.

"Well, it seems like a lot of trouble to go through," Aunt said when Lily came back from the barn with the news that their guest was gone. "To cadge a meal and a roof over your head for the night, I mean."

"I don't think he was lying."

Aunt shrugged.

"But he looked *just* like the picture in my book."

"There was a resemblance," Aunt said. "But really. The story he told . . . it's too hard to believe."

"Then how do you explain it?"

Aunt thought for a moment, then shook her head.

"Can't say that I can," she admitted.

"I think he's gone to look for the cave. He wants to go back."

"And I suppose you want to go looking for him."

Lily nodded.

"Are you sweet on him?" Aunt asked.

"I don't think I am."

"Can't say's I'd blame you. He was a good-looking man."

"I'm just worried about him," Lily said. "He's all lost and alone and out of his own time."

"And say you find him. Say you find the cave. What then?"

The Apple Tree Man's warning and Aunt's obvious concern struggled against her own desire to find the cave, to see the magical land that lay beyond it.

"I'd have the chance to say goodbye," she said.

There. She hadn't exactly lied. She hadn't said everything she could have, but she hadn't lied.

Aunt studied her for a long moment.

"You just be careful," she said. "See to the cow and chickens, but the garden can wait till you get back."

Lily grinned. She gave Aunt a quick kiss, then packed herself a lunch. She was almost out the door when she turned back and took Milo Johnson's painting box out from under her bed.

"Going to try those paints?" Aunt asked.

"I think so."

And she did, but it wasn't nearly the success she'd hoped it would be.

The morning started fine, but then walking in these woods of hers was a sure cure for any ailment, especially when it was in your heart or head. The dogs hadn't come to join her today, but that was all right seeing how oddly they'd acted around Frank yesterday. She wondered what they knew, what had they sensed about him?

She made her way down to that part of the wood where she'd first found the box, and then later Frank, but he was nowhere about. Either he'd found his way back into fairyland, or he was just ignoring her voice. Finally she gave up and spent awhile looking for this cave of his, but there were too many in this part of the forest and none of them looked—no, none of them *felt* right.

After lunch, she sat down and opened the painting box.

The drawing she did on the back of one of Johnson's three paintings turned out well, though it was odd using her pencil on a wood panel. But she'd gotten the image she wanted: the sweeping boughs of an old beech tree, smooth-barked and tall, the thick crush of underbrush around it, the forest behind. It was the colours that proved to be a problem. The paints wouldn't do what she wanted. It was hard enough to get each tube open they were stuck so tight, but once she had a squirt of the various colours on the palette it all went downhill from there.

The colours were wonderfully bright—pure pigments that had their own inner glow. At least they did until she started messing with them and then everything turned to mud. When she tried to mix them she got either outlandish hues or colours so dull they all might as well have been the same. The harder she tried, the worse it got.

Sighing, she finally wiped off the palette and the panel she'd been working on, then cleaned the brushes, dipping them in the little jar of turpentine, working the paint out of the hairs with a rag. She studied Johnson's paintings as she worked, trying to figure out how he'd gotten the colours he had. This was his box, after all. These were the same colours he'd used to paint these three amazing paintings. Everything she needed was just lying there in the box, waiting to be used. So why was she so hopeless?

It was because painting was no different from looking for fairies, she supposed. No different from trying to find that cave entrance into some magic elsewhere. Some people just weren't any good at that sort of thing.

They were both magic, after all. Art as well as fairies. Magic. What else could you call how Johnson was able to bring the forest to life with no more than a few colours on a flat surface?

She could practice, of course. And she would. She hadn't been any good when she'd first started drawing either. But she wasn't sure that she'd ever feel as . . . inspired as Johnson must have felt.

She studied the inside lid of the box. Even this abstract pattern where he'd probably only been testing his colour mixes had so much vibrancy and passion.

The odd feeling she'd gotten the first time she'd looked inside the lid yesterday returned, but this time she didn't look away. Instead, she leaned closer.

What was it about this pattern of colours?

She found herself thinking about her Newford Naturalists book, about something Milo Johnson was supposed to have said. "It's not just a matter of painting *en plein air* as the Impressionists taught us," the author quoted Johnson. "It's just as important to simply *be* in the wilds. Many times the only painting box I take is in my head. You don't have to be an artist to bring something back from your wilderness experiences. My best paintings don't hang in galleries. They hang somewhere in between my ears—an endless private showing that I can only attempt to share with others through a more physical medium."

That must be why he'd abandoned this painting box she'd found. He'd gone into fairyland only bringing the one in his head. Frank had said as much last night. Unless . . .

She smiled as the fancy came to her.

Unless the box she'd found was the one he carried in his head, made real by some magic of the world into which he and Frank had strayed.

The pattern on the lid of the box seemed to move at that moment and she thought she heard something—an almost music. It was like listening to ravens in the woods when their rough, deep-throated croaks and cries all but seemed like human language. It wasn't, of course, but still, you felt *so* close to understanding it.

She lifted her head to look around. It wasn't ravens she heard. It wasn't anything she knew, but it still seemed familiar.

Faint, but insistent. Almost like wind chimes or distant bells, but not quite. Almost like birdsong, trills and warbling melodies, but not quite. Almost like an old fiddle tune, played on a pipe or a flute, the rhythm a little ragged, or simply a little out of time like the curious jumps and extra beats in a Kickaha tune. But not quite.

Closing the painting box, she stood. She slung her satchel onto her shoulder, picked up the box, and turned in a slow circle, trying to find the source of what she heard. It was stronger to the west, away from the creek and deeper into the forest. A ravine cut off to the left and she followed it, pushing her way through the thick shrub layer of rhododendrons and mountain laurel. Hemlocks and tulip trees rose up the slopes on either side with a thick understory of redbud, magnolia, and dogwood.

The almost-music continued to pull her along—distant, near, distant, near, like a radio signal that couldn't quite hang on to a station. It was only when she broke through into a small clearing, a wall of granite rising above her, that she saw the mouth of the cave.

She knew immediately that this had to be the cave Frank had been looking for, the one into which he and Milo Johnson had stepped and so disappeared from the world for twenty years. The almost-music was clearer than ever here, but it was the bas-relief worked into the stone above the entrance that made her sure. Here was Frank's Lady, a rough carving of a woman's face. Her hair was thick with leaves and more leaves came spilling out of her mouth, bearding her chin.

Aunt's general warnings, as well as the Apple Tree Man's more specific ones, returned to her as she moved closer. She lifted a hand to trace the contours of the carving. As soon as she touched it, the almost-music stopped.

She dropped her hand, starting back as though she'd put a finger on a hot stove. She looked around herself with quick, nervous glances. Now that the almost-music was gone, she found herself standing in an eerie pocket of silence. The sounds of the forest were muted—as the music had been earlier. She could still hear the insects and birdsong, but they seemed to come from far away.

She turned back to the cave, uneasy now. In the back of her mind she could hear the Apple Tree Man's voice.

Don't go in.

I won't. Not all the way.

But now that she was here, how could she not at least have a look?

She went as far as the entrance, ducking her head because the top of the hole was only as high as her shoulder. It was dark inside, too dark to see in the beginning. But slowly her eyes adjusted to the dimmer lighting.

The first thing she really saw were the paintings.

They were like her own initial attempts at drawing—crude stick figures and shapes that she'd drawn on scraps of paper and the walls of the barn with the charred ends of sticks. Except, where hers had been simple because she could do no better, these, she realized as she studied them more closely, were more like stylized abbreviations. Where her drawings had been tentative, these held power. The paint or chalk had been applied with bold, knowing strokes. Nothing wasted. Complex images distilled to their primal essences.

An antlered man. A turtle. A bear with a sun on its chest, radiating squiggles of light. A leaping stag. A bird of some sort with enormous wings. A woman, cloaked in leaves. Trees of every shape and size. Lightning bolts. A toad. A spiral with the face of the woman on the entrance outside in its center. A fox with an enormous striped tail. A hare with drooping ears and small goat horns.

And more. So many more. Some easily recognizable, others only geometric shapes that seemed to hold whole books of stories in their few lines.

Her gaze travelled over the walls, studying the paintings with growing wonder and admiration. The cave was one of the larger ones she'd found—easily three or four times the size of Aunt's cabin. There were paintings everywhere, many too hard to make out because they were lost in deeper shadows. She wished she had a corn shuck or lantern to throw more light than what came from the opening behind her. She longed to move closer, but still didn't dare abandon the safety of the entranceway.

She might have left it like that, drank her fill of the paintings and then gone home, if her gaze hadn't fallen upon a figure sitting hunched in a corner of the cave, holding what looked like a small bark whistle. She'd made the same kind herself from the straight smooth branches of a chestnut or sourwood tree—Beau had showed her how. You rubbed the bark until it came loose, then cut the naked stick to make stoppers for either end of the bark cylinder, the one by the mouthpiece having a slice taken off the front. When the stoppers were put in you could play a tune if you were musically inclined. She hadn't been bad, but she'd never been able to whistle nearly so well as what she'd been hearing Frank play earlier.

But the whistle was quiet now. Frank sat so still, enveloped in the shadows, that she might never have noticed him except as she had, by chance.

"Frank . . . ?" she said.

He lifted his head to look at her.

"It's gone," he said. "I can't call it back."

"The other world?"

He nodded.

"That was you making that . . . music?"

"It was me doing something," he said. "I don't know that I'd go so far as to call it music."

Lily hesitated a long moment, then finally stepped through the entrance, into the cave itself. She flinched as she crossed the threshold, but nothing happened. There were no flaring lights or sudden sounds. No door opened into another world, sucking her in.

She set the painting box down and sat on her ankles in front of Frank.

"I didn't know you were a musician," she said.

"I'm not."

He held up his reed whistle—obviously something he'd made himself.

"But I used to play as a boy," he said. "And there was always music there, on the other side. I thought I could wake something. Call me to it, or it to me."

Lily raised her eyes to the paintings on the wall.

"How did you cross over the first time?" she asked.

He shook his head. "I don't know. That was Milo's doing. I was only tagging along."

"Did he . . . did he make a painting?"

Frank's gaze settled on hers.

"What do you mean?" he asked.

She pointed to the walls. "Look around you. This is *the* cave, isn't it?"

He nodded.

"What do you think these paintings are for?" she asked. When he still didn't seem to get it, she added, "Perhaps it's the paintings that open a door between the worlds. Maybe this Lady of yours likes pictures more than She does music."

Frank scrambled to his feet and studied the walls as though he was seeing the paintings for the first time. Lily was slower to rise.

"If I had paint, I could try it," he said.

"There's the painting box I found," Lily told him. "It's still full of paints."

He grinned. Grabbing her arms, he gave her a kiss, right on her lips, full of passion and fire, then bent down to open the box.

"I remember this box," he said as he rummaged through the paint tubes. "We were out painting, scouting a good location—though for Milo, any location was a good one. Anyway, there we were, out in these woods, when suddenly Milo stuffs this box of his into a tangle of tree roots and starts walking. I called after him, but he never said a word, never even turned around to see if I was coming.

"So I followed, hurrying along behind him until we finally came to this cave. And then . . . then . . ."

He looked up at Lily. "I'm not sure what happened. One moment we were walking into the cave and the next we had crossed over into that other place."

"So Milo didn't paint on the wall."

"I just don't remember. But he might not have had to. Milo could create whole paintings in his head without ever putting brush to canvas. And he could describe that painting to you, stroke for stroke—even years later."

"I read about that in the book."

"Hmm."

Frank had returned his attention to the paints.

"It'll have to be a specific image," he said, talking as much to himself as to Lily. "Something simple that still manages to encompass everything a person is or feels."

"An icon," Lily said, remembering the word from another of her books.

He nodded in agreement as he continued to sort through the tubes of paint, finally choosing a colour: a burnt umber, rich and dark.

"And then?" Lily asked, remembering what the Apple Tree Man had told her in her dream. "Just saying you find the right image. You paint it on the wall and some kind of door opens up. Then what do you do?"

He looked up at her, puzzled.

"I'll step through it," he said. "I'll go back to the other side."

"But why?" Lily asked. "Why's over there so much better than the way the world is here?"

"I . . ."

"When you cross over to there," Lily said, echoing the Apple Tree man's words to her, "you give up all the things you could be here."

"We do that every time we make any change in our lives," Frank said. "It's like moving from one town to another, though this is a little more drastic, I suppose." He considered it for a moment, then added, "It's not so much better over there as different. I've never fit in here the way I do over there. And now I don't have anything left for me here except for this burn inside— a yearning for the Lady and that land of Hers that lies somewhere on the other side of these fields we know."

"I've had that feeling," Lily said, thinking of her endless search for fairies as a child.

"You can't begin to imagine what it's like over there," Frank went on. "Everything glows with its own inner light."

He paused and regarded her for a long moment.

"You could come," he said finally. "You could come with me and see for yourself. Then you'd understand."

Lily shook her head. "No, I couldn't. I couldn't walk out on Aunt, not like this, without a word. Not after she took me in when no one else would. She wasn't even real family, though she's family now." She waited a beat, remembering the strength of his arms, the hard kiss he'd given her, then added, "You could stay."

Now it was his turn to shake his head.

"I can't."

Lily nodded. She understood. It wasn't like she didn't have the desire to go herself.

She watched him unscrew the paint tube and squeeze a long worm of dark brown pigment into his palm. He turned to a clear spot on the wall, dipped a finger into the paint and raised his hand. But then he hesitated.

"You can do it," Lily told him.

Maybe she couldn't go. Maybe she wanted him to stay. But she knew enough not to try to hold him back if he had to go. It was no different from making friends with a wild creature. You could catch them and tie them up and make them stay with you, but their heart would never be yours. Their wild heart, the thing you loved about them . . . it would wither and die. So why would you want to do such a thing?

"I can," Frank agreed, his voice soft. He gave her a smile. "That's part of the magic, isn't it? You have to believe that it will work."

Lily had no idea if that was true or not, but she gave him an encouraging nod all the same.

He hummed something under his breath as he lifted his hand again. Lily recognized it as the almost-music she'd heard before, but now she could make out the tune. She didn't know its name, but the pickup band at the grange dances played it from time to time. She thought it might have the word "fairy" in it.

Frank's finger moved decisively, smearing paint on the rock. It took Lily a moment to see that he was painting a stylized oak leaf. He finished the last line and took his finger away, stepped back.

Neither knew what to expect, if anything. As the moments dragged by, Frank stopped humming. He cleaned his hands against the legs of his trousers, smearing paint onto the cloth. His shoulders began to slump and he turned to her.

"Look," Lily said before he could speak.

She pointed to the wall. The center of the oak leaf he'd painted had started to glow with a warm, green-gold light. They watched the light spread across the wall of the cave, moving out from the central point like ripples from a stone tossed into a still pool of water. Other colours appeared, blues and reds and deeper greens. The colours shimmered, like they were painted on cloth touched by some unseen wind, and then the wall was gone and they were looking through an opening in the rock. Through a door into another world.

There was a forest in there, not much different from the one they'd left behind except that, as Frank had said, every tree, every leaf, every branch and blade of grass, pulsed with its own inner light. It was so bright it almost hurt the eyes, and not simply because they'd been standing in this dim cave for so long.

Everything had a light and a song and it was almost too much to bear. But at the same time, Lily felt the draw of that world like a tightening in her heart. It wasn't so much a wanting as a need.

"Come with me," Frank said again.

She had never wanted to do something more in her life. It was not just going to that magical place, it was the idea of being there with this man with his wonderfully creative mind and talent. This man who'd given her her first real kiss.

But slowly she shook her head.

"Have you ever stood on a mountaintop," she asked, "and watched the sun set in a bed of feathery clouds? Have you ever watched the monarchs settled on a field of milkweed or listened to the spring chorus after the long winter's done?"

Frank nodded.

"This world has magic, too," Lily said.

"But not enough for me," Frank said. "Not after having been over there."

"I know."

She stepped up to him and gave him a kiss. He held her for a moment, returning the kiss, then they stepped back from each other.

"Go," Lily said, giving him a little push. "Go before I change my mind."

She saw he understood that for her, going would be as much a mistake as staying would be for him. He nodded and turned, walked out into that other world.

Lily stood watching him go. She watched him step in among the trees. She heard him call out and heard another man's voice reply. She watched as the doorway became a swirl of colours once more. Just before the light faded, it seemed to take the shape of a woman's face—the same woman whose features had been carved into the stone outside the cave, leaves in her hair, leaves spilling from her mouth. Then it was all gone. The cave was dim once more and she was alone.

Lily knelt down by Milo Johnson's paint box and closed the lid, fastened the snaps. Holding it by its handle, she stood up and walked slowly out of the cave.

"Are you there?" she asked later, standing by the Apple Tree Man's tree. "Can you hear me?"

She took a biscuit from her pocket—the one she hadn't left earlier in the day because she'd still been angry for his appearing in her dream last night when he'd been absent from her life for five years. When he'd let her think that her night of magic had been nothing more than a fever dream brought on by a snakebite.

She put the biscuit down among his roots.

"I just wanted you to know that you were probably right," she said. "About my going over to that other place, I mean. Not about how I can't have magic here."

She sat down on the grass and laid the paint box down beside her, her satchel on top of it. Plucking a leaf from the ground, she began to shred it.

"I know, I know," she said. "There's plenty of everyday magic all around me. And I do appreciate it. But I don't know what's so wrong about having a magical friend as well."

There was no reply. No gnarled Apple Tree Man stepping out of his tree. No voice as she'd heard in her dream last night. She hadn't really been expecting anything.

"I'm going to ask Aunt if I can have an acre or so for my own garden," she said. "I'll try growing cane there and sell the molasses at the harvest fair. Maybe put in some berries and make preserves and pies, too. I'll need some real money to buy more paints."

She smiled and looked up into the tree's boughs.

"So you see, I can take advice. Maybe you should give it a try."

She stood up and dusted off her knees, picked up the painting box and her satchel.

"I'll bring you another biscuit tomorrow morning," she said.

Then she started down the hill to Aunt's cabin.

"Thank you," a soft, familiar voice said.

She turned. There was no one there, but the biscuit was gone.

She grinned. "Well, that's a start," she said and continued on home.

Refinerytown

Relationships are confusing. Actually, life is confusing, but the relationships part of it seems particularly so.

When you don't have a boyfriend, all your energy focuses around the idea of having one. Doesn't matter if the last man in your life was some sorry-assed, miserable excuse of a parasitic worm, or if *he* dumped you. Doesn't matter that we know we're supposed to be comfortable in our own lives and expect others to be comfortable with us. The idea of having a boyfriend is forever looming on the periphery of everything we do.

But then you get a boyfriend—a good one, mind you—and the funny thing is, you're still not necessarily content. Because now the boyfriend relationship starts looming over all the other ones in your life. Your relationships with your family, your friends, your art . . .

He talks about having to go away for a bit, and you think, okay, that's sad, but I'll get all this work done. I'll have the chance to gather up the tattered ribbons of semi-suspended friendships and actually spend some time with them.

Except the boyfriend's going away leaves this big hole in your days and everything's still unbalanced.

Like I said. It's confusing.

"So it's just going to be a one-shot," I say. "Unless it really takes off, I guess."

Jilly wheels over to one of the long tables in the greenhouse to put the storyboards I've given her on a flat surface. She's a lot better than she was in the first few months after the accident, but simple things, like holding something large for too long, still aren't possible.

"I like the art," she says as she spreads them out. "It's pretty different from your usual strips. More cartoony."

"That's Nina's influence," I tell her. "She's really into anime— you know, that Japanese animation stuff."

"Who's Nina?" Sophie asks.

"Nina Hoffman. We're collaborating on this comic."

"We met her during the summer," Jilly says. "Remember that book signing you took me to?"

"Oh, her." Sophie grins. "She was fun."

The three of us are in the greenhouse that's attached to the back of Professor Dapple's house. Jilly's been staying with him since she got out of rehab. Sophie moved in to help her out and give her some company. The professor had converted the green-house into an artist's studio years ago, when they were both still in university. In those days Jilly shared the space with our friend Is-abelle and dubbed it the Grumbling Greenhouse Studio after the professor's cranky housekeeper, Goon. Now Sophie's using it to keep up with her own art. She and Jilly spend some mornings and most afternoons in it. Three mornings a week Sophie takes Jilly to her physio appointments.

"We're calling it 'Refinerytown,'" I say. "After those Bor-dertown books by Terri Windling."

Jilly smiles. "I got the reference."

"We were just talking one day—goofing really—but then it all started to click, so we decided to actually do something with it."

"I didn't know Nina wrote comics."

"She helps with the plotting," I say. "And also the back-ground and characters. She originally wanted to pitch it to her

editor at Viking—this wild woman named Sharyn November—
but Sharyn was so totally *not* into it. And this from a woman who
has chicken puppets."

"Really?" Jilly asks. "She has chicken puppets?"

I nod. Trust Jilly to zero in on that.

"Apparently," I tell her. "Three life-sized ones. She's managed to get out of most of her editorial meetings because they
won't let her bring them in with her any more. Nina says she'd
have the head poke up over the edge of the table when someone
was talking and have the chicken yawn, or make faces at
people."

"I think she's putting you on," Sophie says.

"No, it's true. They're like these Muppet chickens."

"I'd love to have a chicken puppet," Jilly says.

Sophie leaves the painting she's working on to look over
Jilly's shoulder at the first few pages of the comic that I've finished so far.

"I notice a complete lack of chickens on these pages," she
says. "Puppet or otherwise."

"No chickens," I agree. "Just oily fairies."

Sophie smiles. "They're really cute. When you first started
talking about fairies that lived in oil refineries . . ." She shoots
me a grin. "Well, I didn't know what to think."

"And those names," Jilly says. "Greasy. Oilpan."

Sophie giggles. "Slick."

"He's my favourite," I tell them. "We're still trying to figure
out what his girlfriend's name should be."

"Diesel," Jilly says.

Sophie shakes her head. "No. Squeaky."

"And there has to be a kind of dumb one called Dipstick."

"Thanks a lot, you guys."

"We're just teasing," Sophie assures me.

"I know." I shrug. "But I don't even know how it's going to
play out. Probably nobody will buy it."

"I'll buy it," Jilly tells me.

"Nobody I *don't* know."

"Oh, *pfft*. What's not to like? They're cute. They live in an oil refinery . . ."

"Exactly. People want their fairies in pastoral, natural settings. Like Brian Froud does. Or Charles Vess."

"People used to like my fairies," Jilly says, "and they just lived in junkyards and alleyways."

"That's because you were a brilliant painter," I say, then my voice trails off as I realize what that must sound like. "Oh, God. I'm sorry. I didn't mean it like that. Like your painting days are forever over."

Ever since the accident, Jilly hasn't been able to paint. Partial paralysis of her drawing arm saw to that. She's been messing around with her left hand, but mostly she just gets frustrated.

"It's okay," she says. "I'm the one who brought it up in the first place."

Sophie walks over to the sink in the corner of the greenhouse and takes three cups down from the low shelf just above it. Filling each with tea out of a thermos, she hands them around to us, then hoists herself up to sit on the worktable beside my drawings.

"So why are you doing this comic?" she asks.

I shrug. "I don't know exactly. I guess I want a shot at something more than just writing about myself all the time. That's where Nina comes in. I can't write about myself if we're collaborating on it."

"All the art we do is about ourselves," Sophie says. "Writing, painting. Songs, dance. You name it. If it means anything, there's a piece of you at the heart of it."

I can't argue with that. "I guess I just want to try something that's not so obviously about me."

"I can see that," Jilly says.

Sophie nods in agreement.

—————

"So how's your werewolf boyfriend?" Jonathan asks.

I'm sitting at the counter in The Half Kaffe Café, sipping a latte, and look up. Jonathan has apparently finished reading the latest copy of *Mojo* and now needs some conversational stimulation. I guess since he's the owner, he doesn't have to look busy when there's nothing to do. He's certainly not overrun with customers at the moment. We have the place to ourselves, except for the dreadlocked student sitting at a window table, hunched over her laptop. The new Pink CD's playing on the sound system, the singer telling her diary that she's been a bad, bad girl. I know that feeling.

"He's not a werewolf," I tell Jonathan. "He's a shapechanger."

"And the difference is?"

"He can choose what he wants to be, when he wants to be. And he doesn't have to go around chewing things up during the full moon."

Jonathan nods sagely. He does cool so well, bless his soul, but I knew him as a nerdy little computer geek, heavy into junk food and techno music. That was back in our art school days. The only art Jonathan does now are Photoshopped notices and menus for the café. But the funny thing is, these days he looks like the Bohemian artist he wanted to be in our college days. Slender in his black jeans and shirt, skin clear, mop of blue-black unruly hair, dark eyes no longer hidden behind his old Buddy Holly glasses. Those only come out late at night now, when his contacts start to bother him.

"How come he never changes in front of us?" Jonathan asks.

I feel like going out and buying him another music magazine, but I'm sure he already has every current one. So I try to answer him instead.

"That'd be like you going out with a stripper and us expecting her to dance for us."

"When did I ever go out with a stripper?"

"I said 'like you.' "

"But what made you think of a stripper?"

"I don't know."

"Because if you know any strippers . . ."

"Oh please. Focus here, would you."

Jonathan smiles. "I'm just making conversation."

"Right."

"So where *is* the wolf man these days, anyway?"

"His name's Lyle."

"Sorry. Where's Lyle?"

"He's out of town. Something to do with his family."

"Which, for him, would be a pack."

"Jonathan," I say, in what I hope's a firm voice. "Would you *please* give it a rest?"

"Okay, okay. I'm resting."

"And for your information, they refer to themselves as clans."

I suppose I should explain this werewolf business.

It's a running joke with my friends—has been ever since I wrote about how Lyle and I met in my comic strip–cum-journal "Spunky Grrl," which appears weekly in *In the City*. I guess every city's got one or more of these weeklies—an alternative press newspaper with show listings, news bits, reviews, and columns. I'm in good company here. *In the City* regularly features Dan Savage's column, strips like Dave Russell's "True Monkey Boy Adventures," and Lynda Berry's ongoing sagas.

Lyle and I met right here in the café on a blind date courtesy of the personals—something I *don't* make a habit of doing, let me add. Though I guess neither of us has to do that anymore anyway.

After a little bit of a rocky start involving a bunch of renegade shapechangers—don't ask, it's way too long a story—we've sort of settled into a nice, relatively normal boyfriend/girlfriend relationship.

The thing is, while regular readers of *In the City* would figure that shapechanger storyline was just me exercising my imagination—of which I've got an excess anyway—my friends all know that only true stuff goes in the strip. Same with "My Life as a Bird," a longer, autobigraphical strip that runs in my own bimonthly comic book, *The Girl Zone*. The real difference is, the pen & ink Mona gets to have the last word—you know, like telling the guy off the way you would have when he dumped you, except you couldn't think of what to say until an hour later. The pen & ink Mona's never at a loss for exactly the right thing to say, though otherwise both strips do faithfully wander through the ongoing parade of my various screwups and mishaps. They have to. Panel after panel of me sitting around drinking coffee with my friends would make for dull reading after awhile.

"If 'Refinerytown' works as well as I think it will," Nina says, "I've got some other fun ideas."

We're talking on the phone about a week after my visit to the Grumbling Greenhouse Studio. It's late at night for me, but still before midnight for her in Eugene, Oregon. Ever since we've started this project there've been any number of e-mails, faxes, and phone calls going back and forth between our houses. Tonight we started talking about the JPEG character design for Slick's girlfriend I sent her an hour or so ago. But our conversations never stay on topic.

"Such as?" I ask.

I'm a little hesitant. Nina's a lovely woman to be sure, but she has the wildest ideas. You should read her books.

"It's about this snake named Pelican Bob," she says. "He wants to have wings, but of course he can't because he's a snake."

"There've been winged snakes."

"Sure. If you're an Aztec god, maybe."

"Dragons are kind of like snakes with wings."

Nina laughs. "Well, of course they are. But I'm talking smaller scale here."

"Ouch."

"Sorry. But you know what I mean. This'll be the small story. Sort of like *The Little Engine That Could*, except it'll be about a snake who can't."

You see what I mean? And she talks like this all the time. Good thing she's a writer and gets to let that stuff out onto the page. Otherwise she might find the men in white coats knocking on her door.

"So have you heard from Lyle?" she asks.

"He called earlier. He says he's bored, but he sounds like he's doing okay."

"You miss him, don't you?"

"Sure. I'm supposed to, aren't I?"

"That's a funny way to put it," she says.

"I'm just confused," I tell her. "Boyfriends make everything so complicated, both when you have them and when you don't."

"Do you love him?"

"It's not that. It's more . . . I have this image of myself as an independent woman and it drives me crazy that all Lyle has to do is call and see if I want to get together, and I'll drop whatever I'm doing, even if I've got a deadline looming, to go off and see him. Before he was in my life I was always mooning about having a boyfriend. Now I'm always mooning *about* my boyfriend."

Nina laughs. "I'm sorry," she says. "I'm not laughing at you. But it's kind of funny, when you think about it."

"Oh, I know. It's all so Marie Antoinette. Having my cake and all."

"Have you talked to Lyle about it?"

I sigh. "It's nothing Lyle's doing. He's actually pretty much the most perfect boyfriend I've had. It's me and the constant story of my life that runs through my head."

"Even in 'Refinerytown'?"

"No. That's why 'Refinerytown' is so important to me right now. It's about the only time I'm not inside my head, trying to make sense of what I'm doing and why I'm doing it."

I guess the way my life goes, I should have expected one of these Refinerytown fairies to show up sooner or later. For real, I mean. The way I had a cantankerous sort-of-dwarf move in on me a few years ago, or find myself going out now with a guy who everybody thinks is a werewolf.

Nina and I settled on Diesel as the name for Slick's girlfriend. She's fun to draw—definitely sexier than any character I've done before, with her hourglass figure and flirty ways. The way the whole story starts is when this trollish guy named Crude who lives under one of the fractionating towers—the place where the crude oil is separated into more useful compounds—thinks that Diesel's interested in him. She's not, of course, but it starts a chain reaction of events that allows us to fill our thirty-two pages of comic book with a fun, rollicking story.

So it's late at night and I'm sitting at the drawing board, laying out the panels for my next page. This is the one where Slick and Oilpan are spying on Diesel to see if she's really going to meet Crude at this midnight rendezvous the way Crude has boasted she is. What they don't know is that Diesel's best friend Ethane is spying on *them* and—

"Ahem."

I sit up with a start at the sound of someone clearing their throat. I look around, but I'm still alone in my studio, which is really just one end of my living room.

"Down here," a strange, small voice says.

My gaze follows its husky timbre to the top of my drawing desk and there she is, sitting on a bottle of Calli ink.

"Whoa," I say. "I've been working way too much on this."

Because standing—well, sitting—there, at a height of no more than eight inches, is Diesel. Not the Diesel I've been drawing. She's got the knee-high motorcycle boots with all the buckles and zippers. The black jeans and the torn T-shirt to show off her midriff. The hourglass figure and the heart-stopping face and the little pointed ears sticking up on either side of her black wool beanie, midnight hair spilling in a tangle of curls down her back. But this is the real thing. The difference between her and the anime Diesel I've been drawing is as profound as it would be between you and the caricature someone might draw of you.

"You're getting it all wrong," she says.

"I think I need a time-out," I tell her.

"That's what the other big-head said."

"Big head? I don't have a big head."

"Oh, relax. It's just what we call you."

"I just think if you're going to insult somebody, you should at least be accurate."

I can't believe I'm arguing with an eight-inch-tall oil fairy about the size of my head.

She stands up, puts a hand on her hip, and glares at me. I've drawn her in that exact same pose, only much more cartoony.

"Oh, but *you* can write whatever you want about *us*," she says. "I can't believe how you're telling the story. I'm goofing with Crude just to get Slick to give me some space."

"But—"

"He's always just so *there*. Sometimes I feel like I can't even breathe."

"I didn't even know you were real," I say. I resist the urge to poke at her with a finger. "Are you real?"

"Of course I'm real."

"And you live in a refinery?"

"Where else would a refinery fairy live?"

She's got me there.

"So where is your refinery?" I ask.

She gives an exaggerated sigh. "Don't you read what you write? It's 'east of wherever, on the far side of dreams.' Like it says on page one."

I lean back in my chair.

"This is going to take some getting used to," I tell her.

"Oh, please. Like you're not dating a werewolf."

"He's not a werewolf, he's a—"

"Canid. I know. A shapechanger. Same difference. He still turns into a wolf."

Though not for me. If I hadn't seen his face . . . *shift* that one time, when the other shapechangers were ready to attack us, I don't know what I'd believe. I asked him once why he doesn't change in front of me and he said he didn't want me to start thinking of him as my pet dog. I'm not a hundred percent sure he was joking.

"So are you going to fix it?" Diesel asks.

"Fix what?"

For a moment I think she's talking about my relationship with Lyle, and there's nothing to fix. At least not on his part. I'm the one with confusion banging around in my head.

"The story," she says. "What else?"

"What did Nina say?" I ask, hoping to buy myself a little time.

"She said I should talk to you."

I'm paying attention to our conversation, really I am, but at the same time I'm so fascinated to see her standing here, this real flesh-and-blood version of something I thought Nina and I had made up. She's got the poutiest lips, and that figure. No wonder half the guys in Refinerytown are so crazy about her.

"Hello, big-head?" Diesel says. "Are you still with me?"

I blink. "My name's Mona," I tell her.

"I know that."

"How can you *be* here?" I ask. "I mean—"

"As in, you and your friend made us up, how can we be real, blah blah blah."

"Well . . . yeah."

She gives me this wicked little grin, which is *just* the way I've drawn her when she's about to say something dazzlingly obvious to Slick or Dipstick.

"Magic," she says.

"Well, if that's not a cop-out, then I don't know what is."

"Look," she says. "The hows and whys of it aren't really important. What's important is that if you're going to tell our story, you have to tell it right."

"You'll help?"

"Well, duh. How else are you going to fix it?"

"Can I take a one-day rain check on . . . what? Interviewing you?"

"Take as long as you want," she says. "Just don't draw any more lies."

"How will I reach you?" I ask.

She gives me that grin again, but this time it's the version that says, I know a secret that you don't.

"Just call my name."

"But how will you hear me all the way over in Refinerytown?"

"What makes you think we're ever any farther than a thought away?"

And then, *phwisht*, she's gone.

I think about what she just said. Great. Another invisible presence in my life. That cranky dwarf who did the home-invasion thing a few years ago and moved in on me? He could do the invisible thing, too. It's just creepy.

"I don't like being spied on," I tell the air where she was standing.

"Welcome to the club," her husky, disembodied voice replies.

"I just had the weirdest conversation," I say when Nina picks up the phone at her end.

"With an eight-inch-tall oil fairy?"

"Bingo."

"I should have called," she says, "but to tell you the truth, I thought I was having an incident."

"What do you mean?

"Seeing things, like this friend of mine does when he forgets to take his medication."

"What are you taking medication for?" I ask.

My amazement at what I've just experienced flees in the face of worry for her.

"Nothing," she assures me. "It was just an analogy."

"A writer thing."

"A writer thing," she agrees. "You know, big words, hidden meanings. All the deep stuff."

She can always make me laugh.

"So what do you think we should do?" I ask.

Nina doesn't even pause to think.

"Tell their story," she says.

"But what if they all start showing up to tell their part?"

Nina laughs. "Well, then you'll have a whole life-sized contingent of models, ready and willing to pose for you. Weren't you telling me that you were having a little trouble with the action scenes?"

I wait a beat, then say. "Remember your story about the snake who wants wings? What was his name again?"

"Pelican Bob."

"Right. You're on your own with that one."

Jilly's by herself when I go over to the professor's house the next day. I come around the back as usual to the greenhouse door and see her through the window. She's sitting in her wheelchair with a laptop computer on the low worktable in front of her. She's got some kind of pen in her hand that she's using on what looks like a fancy mouse pad. When I tap on the glass, she waves me in.

"Hey, you," she says.

"Hey, yourself. What're you doing?"

She gets this cute little proud smile. "Have a look," she says.

When I come stand behind her shoulder, I see that she's using a pen and tablet to input information into the laptop. There's a drawing program window open on the screen showing an incredibly intricate piece of art. Fairies like she used to paint, hovering around an old coffee tin in what looks like an empty lot.

I know she can't draw or paint anymore. I also know that all her fairy paintings were destroyed after the accident. So while this piece is in her style, it can't be hers.

"Very nice," I say. "Where'd it come from?"

"Me," she says.

My gaze drops down to where the hand of her bad arm lies limply on her lap.

"But . . ."

She laughs. "No, I haven't gone all dotty on you. It takes me forever, but I can actually do art again with this program."

"I don't understand. You still have to be able to draw to input the lines."

She nods. "Yes, but you can do it as small as a pixel at a time if you want. So even if I can't get the expression I once could in my lines, I can get the detail again. Here, look."

She shows me how she magnifies a small section of the drawing and then adds some pixels with the pen on the tablet. When she reduces the image again, the fairy to the right of the coffee tin has a little more shading under her eyes.

"This is so cool," I tell her. "How long have you been working like this?"

"It feels like forever. This is only my first one and I started it over a month ago."

"And never told a soul."

She shakes her head. "Except for Sophie. I guess I just wanted to make sure I could actually do it."

"How does it feel—working on a screen like that instead of on paper or canvas?"

"Kind of distancing. I really miss the hands-on part of the process."

I have to smile. Jilly hasn't had paint on her hands or in her hair for over a year. It used to be like jewelry—there was always a speck here, a drop there. Vivid colours creating sudden happy highlights. Sometimes I've wanted to splash some on her, just for old time's sake.

"But at least I can do it again," she adds.

She does something on the tablet and a little window pops up asking her if she wants to save her work. She clicks "save" and then shuts down the computer.

"Sophie left me some tea in the thermos," she says. "I'm sure there's enough for both of us. Do you want some?"

"Sure. Let me—"

But she's already wheeling over to the sink. She reaches for a pair of cups and the thermos, then comes back with them on her lap to where I'm sitting.

"You'd better do the honours," she says, handing me the thermos. "I can do it, but the tea'd probably be cold by the time I'm done."

I pour us both a cup, then close the thermos and set it on the table beside the laptop.

"Is that the professor's?" I ask, nodding at the machine.

"No, it's Goon's. He says he never uses it."

"Grumpy Goon actually lent you his laptop?"

"I know. Go figure." She takes a sip of her tea. "So what brings you down out of your studio? Not that I'm complaining. I'm happy for the company. But I thought you had a deadline."

"I do," I tell her. "It's just that I met Diesel last night."

There's a long pause as she registers that.

"Diesel as in the refinery fairy from your comic?" she finally asks.

"The same. In the flesh. The very tiny flesh. She really is only eight inches tall."

Jilly leans forward, a happy smile curving her lips.

"I think you need to tell me everything," she says.

So I do. I mean if you can't tell Jilly about something like this, then who can you tell?

"She came back again after I got off the phone with Nina," I say, finishing up, "and we talked some more about how she thinks the story should go. But I don't know. I told her I'd have to think about it."

"Because it feels like everything's being pulled out of your hands?"

"Pretty much. I mean, I was expecting to collaborate with Nina. But this . . . it's so weird having the characters tell you what the story should be."

Jilly smiles.

"I tried to convince her to come visit you with me, but she said, and I quote, 'It's not to be.' "

Jilly nods. "I'm not surprised. Fairy visitations are usually very personal. It's in their nature to be secretive."

"But I really wanted you to see her."

"I will. The way everyone will be able to: in your story."

"It's not my story anymore. It's hers. Theirs."

"But isn't that what you wanted?" Jilly asks. "To get away from yourself a little?"

"I suppose I did."

"And besides. This is the way stories are supposed to be. True to themselves, not to how we want them to be."

"Like life, I guess."

Jilly shakes her head. "In life we have to be true to ourselves."

I nod. Jilly's always had this way of stating the obvious so that it feels like a revelation.

"How do you keep the pieces of your life separate from each other?" I ask her.

"What makes you think I do?"

I shrug. "I don't know. You always seem so centered. Even with all that's happened to you."

She looks out of a window for a long moment, gaze focused on something other than the professor's gardens and lawn. Finally she turns to me again.

"Things don't always work out the way we want them to," she says. "I know that, big-time. Not when I was a kid. Not when that car ran me down. So I guess I've learned to make a point of taking charge of whatever parts of my life I *can* control. And really appreciating the aspects that are good. It's like how things are going with Daniel and me."

Daniel's her current beau, this drop-dead gorgeous nurse she met when she was in the ICU, right after the accident.

"I could worry about what he sees in me," she goes on. "You know, he's this active, handsome guy and here's me, the Broken Girl. And I did, at first. But he doesn't see any limitations in our relationship, so why should I go looking for them?"

"So you think I should tell Diesel's story."

She shakes her head. "I think you should do whatever your heart tells you is the right thing to do."

And that, I realize, could as easily apply to every part of my life, not just my refinery fairies comic. If you follow your heart, maybe you don't have to be confused.

"Diesel," I say.

I'm sitting alone in my apartment that night, at the drawing table, a pad of plain paper in front of me, a pencil in my hand. I expect her to immediately pop into sight out of nowhere but it's actually a few moments before she does. She notices the miniature armchair that I've left for her at the top of my drawing table and smiles. I bought it at a toy store on the way home from Jilly's.

"Very nice," she says as she falls into it, lounging with her legs over one arm with the instant ease of a cat.

I lift the pencil I'm holding. "I'm ready to do it your way."

She swings her feet to the table and leans forward to look at me, elbows on her knees, hands propping her head. I'm hardly aware of my own hand bringing the pencil to the paper to capture the pose. She grins and starts to talk.

"Wait a minute," I say when we're five minutes into this convoluted story about the various relationships between herself and the other fairies. "We only have thirty-two pages."

"What do you mean?"

"We can't tell your whole life story in this comic. We have to focus on just one aspect of it, the way I do with my strips."

"But it's all important."

I think about the way I worry when I'm pasting and editing the portions of my life that show up in the strips.

"I know," I tell her. "But we have to work within our space limitations. Maybe if this one does well we can do another, but for now we have to be a little more practical about what we use and what we leave out."

"I don't know how to make a lifetime smaller."

I get this sense that she's about to get up and walk off with that swagger she has, stepping away into nothing and I'll never see her again.

"You don't have to," I tell her. "That's my job—to pick what we use. Why don't you just tell it to me the way you need to tell it and I'll take what I think will fit into a thirty-two-page story. If you can trust me to do it right."

She gives me a long, considering look, then finally nods.

"Of course I trust you," she says. "And if you get it wrong, I can always turn you into a salamander."

"You can do that?"

She just winks.

"Let me tell you how I first met Slick," she says.

Nina and I have been back-and-forthing faxes of notes and rough storyboards, trying to find a way to tell the story in the pages we have without making it seem either rushed or too cram-packed with detail. There are so many things that are killing us to leave out.

Tonight we're on the phone again, both of us with pages spread out in front of us.

"So did we make them up," I say at one point, "or were they always there and we just somehow tuned into them when we started this thing?"

Nina laughs. "Does it matter?"

I suppose maybe it doesn't. How very Zen of us.

Later I'm on the phone with Lyle. He tells me he's been trying to get through all night, but he's just saying it. He doesn't sound impatient or annoyed or anything.

We've been having a moony conversation, the kind you have when you haven't seen each other for a while and the missing part is really kicking in. Somehow we get onto his shapechanging.

"What's so wrong with you being my pet dog?" I say. "I'll be your pet Boho girl. We can take turns being pets. Pets have it good you know. Lots of pampering and treats and tickles behind the ear."

He laughs. "What are you really trying to say here, Mona?"

I surprise myself probably as much as him.

"I think we should live together," I say. "That way our differences will get to know each other better and I won't have this constant confusion following me about. What do you think?"

It kind of comes out all in one breath and then there's this long silence on the other end of the line. My heart goes very still. If my friend Sue were here she'd be shaking her finger at me, telling me something about how girls aren't supposed to be assertive, it just scares guys away. She's really sweet, but she does have some old-fashioned ideas.

But maybe I *have* blown it.

What do *I* know about relationships? It's not like I ever had one that really worked before.

I'm about to say something about how I was just kidding when I swear that I can actually feel his smile coming across the phone lines to me.

"I think I'd like that very much," he says.

Okay. So the confusion didn't really go away. I think maybe it never does. When things become clear in one part of your life, I guess your capacity for confusion just attaches itself to another part. But I'm learning not to focus so much on it, to worry about what this means, or that means. I'm trying to take things at face value instead.

The comic's almost done, though I swear Diesel could try the patience of a saint. I'm starting to have some real sympathy for Slick. Diesel and I argue so much, there are times when I feel like she's really going to turn me into a salamander. Lyle says he'll love me anyway, but I don't know. I think a salamander is really push-ing it.

You want to know the funniest thing? Nina has me half-convinced to do that Pelican Bob story with her when we're done with this one. Remember him? The little snake who wanted wings?

A Crow Girls' Christmas
(with MaryAnn Harris)

"**We have jobs,**" **Maida told** Jilly when she and Zia dropped by
the professor's house for a visit at the end of November.

Zia nodded happily. "Yes, we've become veryvery respectable."

Jilly had to laugh. "I can't imagine either of you ever being
completely respectable."

That comment drew an exaggerated pout from each of the
crow girls, the one more pronounced than the other.

"Not being completely respectable's a good thing," Jilly assured them.

"Yes, well, easy for you to say," Zia said. "You don't have a
cranky uncle always asking when you're going to do something
useful for a change."

Maida nodded. "You just get to wheel around and around in
your chair and not worry about all the very serious things that we
do."

"Such as?" Jilly asked.

Zia shrugged. "Why *don't* pigs fly?"

"Or why is white a colour?" Maida offered.

"Or black."

"Or yellow ochre."

"Yellow ochre is a colour," Jilly said. "Two colours, actually.
And white and black are colours, too. Though I suppose they're
not very *colourful*, are they?"

"Could it be more puzzling?" Zia asked.

Maida simply smiled and held out her tea cup. "May I have a refill, please?"

Jilly pushed the sugar bag over to her. Maida filled her tea cup to the brim with sugar. After a glance at Zia, she filled Zia's tea cup as well.

"Would you like some?" she asked Jilly.

"No, I'm quite full. Besides, too much tea makes me have to pee."

The crow girls giggled.

"So what sort of jobs did you get?" Jilly asked.

Zia lowered her teacup and licked the sugar from her upper lip.

"We're elves!" she said.

Maida nodded happily. "At the mall. We get to help out Santa."

"Not the *real* Santa," Zia explained.

"No, no. He's much too very busy making toys at the North Pole."

"This is sort of a cloned Santa."

"Every mall has one, you know."

"And *we*," Zia announced proudly, "are in charge of handing out the candy canes."

"Oh my," Jilly said, thinking of the havoc that could cause.

"Which makes us very important," Maida said.

"Not to mention useful."

"So pooh to Lucius, who thinks we're not."

"Do they have lots of candy canes in stock?" Jilly asked.

"Mountains," Zia assured her.

"Besides," Maida added. "It's all magic, isn't it? Santa never runs out of candy or toys."

That was before you were put in charge of the candy canes, Jilly thought, but she kept her worry to herself.

Much to everyone's surprise, the crow girls made excellent elves. They began their first daily four-hour shift on December 1, dressed in matching red-and-green outfits that the mall provided: long-sleeved jerseys, short pleated skirts, tights, shoes with exaggerated curling toes, and droopy elf hats with their rowdy black hair poking out from underneath. There were bells on their shoes, bells at the end of their hats, and they each wore brooches made of bells that they'd borrowed from one of the stores in the mall. Because they found it next to impossible to stand still for more than a few seconds at a time, the area around Santa's chair echoed with their constant jingling. Parents waiting in line, not to mention their eager children, were completely enchanted by their happy antics and the ready smiles on their small dark faces.

"I thought they'd last fifteen minutes," their uncle Lucius confided to the professor a few days after the pair had started, "but they've surprised me."

"I don't see why," the professor said. "It seems to me that they'd be perfectly suited for the job. They're about as elfish as you can get without being an elf."

"But they're normally so easily distracted."

The professor nodded. "However, there's candy involved, isn't there? Jilly tells me that they've been put in charge of the candy canes."

"And isn't that a source for pride." Lucius shook his head and smiled. "Trust them to find a way to combine sweets with work."

"They'll be the Easter Bunny's helpers in the spring."

Lucius laughed. "Maybe I can apprentice them to the Tooth Fairy."

The crow girls really were perfectly suited to their job. Unlike many of the tired shoppers that trudged by Santa's chair, they remained enthralled with every aspect of their new environment.

The flashing lights. The jingling bells. The glittering tinsel. The piped-in Christmas music. The shining ornaments.

And, of course, the great abundance of candy canes.

They treated each child's questions and excitement as though that child was the first to have this experience. They talked to those waiting in line, made faces so that the children would laugh happily as they were having their pictures taken, handed out candy canes when the children were lifted down from Santa's lap. They paid rapt attention to every wish expressed and adored hearing about all the wonderful toys available in the shops.

Some children, normally shy about a visit to Santa, returned again and again, completely smitten with the pair.

But mostly, it was all about the candy canes.

The crow girls were extremely generous in handing them out, and equally enthusiastic about their own consumption. They stopped themselves from eating as many as they might have liked, but did consume one little candy cane each for every five minutes they were on the job.

Santa, busy with the children, and also enamored with his cheerful helpers, failed to notice that the sacks of candy canes in the storage area behind his chair were dwindling at an astonishing rate. He never thought to look because it had never been an issue before. There'd always been plenty of candy canes to go around in the past.

On December 19, at the beginning of their noon shift, there were already lines and lines of children waiting excitedly to visit Santa and his crow girl elves. As the photographer was unhooking the cord to let the children in, Maida turned to Zia to ask where the next sack of candy canes was just as Zia asked Maida the very same question. Santa suggested that they'd better hurry up and grab another sack from the storage space.

Trailing the sound of jingling bells, the crow girls went behind his chair.

Zia pulled aside the little curtain.

"Uh-oh," she said.

Maida pushed in beside her to have a look herself. The two girls exchanged worried looks.

"They're all gone," Zia told Santa.

"I'll go to the stockroom for more," Maida offered.

Zia nodded. "Me, too."

"What stockroom?" Santa began.

But then he realized exactly what they were saying. His normally rosy cheeks went as white as his whiskers.

"They're all gone?" he asked. "*All* those bags of candy canes?"

"In a word, yes."

"But where could they all have gone?"

"We give them away," Maida reminded him. "Remember?"

Zia nodded. "We were supposed to."

"So that's what we did."

"Because it's our job."

"And we ate a few," Maida admitted.

"A veryvery few."

Santa frowned. "How many is a few?"

"Hmm," Zia said.

"Good question."

"Let's see."

They both began to count on their fingers as they talked.

"We were veryvery careful not to eat more than twelve an hour."

"Oh so very careful."

"So in four hours—"

"—that would be forty-eight—"

"—times two—"

"—because there are two of us."

They paused for a moment, as though to ascertain that there really were only two of them.

"So that would be . . . um . . ."

"Ninety-six—"

"—times how many days?"

"Eighteen—"

"—not counting today—"

"—because there aren't any today—"

"—which is why we need to go the stockroom to get more."

Santa was adding it all up himself. "That's almost two thousand candy canes you've eaten!"

"Well . . . almost," Maida said.

"One thousand seven hundred and twenty-eight," Zia said.

"If you're keeping count."

"Which is *almost* two thousand, I suppose, but not really."

"Where *is* the candy cane stockroom?" Maida asked.

"There isn't one," Santa told her.

"But—"

"And that means," he added, "that all the children here today won't get any candy canes."

The crow girls looked horrified.

"That means us, too," Zia said.

Maida nodded. "We'll also suffer, you know."

"But we're ever so stoic."

"Ask anybody."

"We'll hardly complain."

"And never where you can hear us."

"Except for now, of course."

Santa buried his face in hands, completely disconcerting the parent approaching his chair, child in hand.

"Don't worry!" Maida cried.

"We have everything under control." Zia looked at Maida. "We do, don't we?"

Maida closed her eyes for a long moment, then opened them wide and grinned.

"Free tinsel for everyone!" she cried.

"I don't want tinsel," the little boy standing in front of Santa with his mother said. "I want a candy cane."

"Oh, you do want tinsel," Maida assured him.

"Why does he want tinsel?" Zia asked.

"Because . . . because . . ."

Maida grabbed two handfuls from the boughs of Santa's Christmas tree. Fluttering the tinsel with both hands over her head, she ran around the small enclosure that housed Santa's chair.

"Because it's so fluttery!" she cried.

Zia immediately understood. "And shiny!" Grinning, she grabbed handfuls of her own.

"Veryvery shiny," Maida agreed.

"And almost as good as candy," Zia assured the little boy as she handed him some. "Though not quite as sugary good."

The little boy took the tinsel with a doubtful look, but then Zia whirled him about in a sudden impromptu dance. Soon he was laughing and waving his tinsel as well. From the line, all the children began to clap.

"We want tinsel, too!" one of them cried.

"Tinsel, tinsel!"

The crow girls got through their shift with great success. They danced and twirled on the spot and did mad acrobatics. They fluttered tinsel, blew kisses, jingled their bells, and told stories so outrageous that no one believed them, but everyone laughed.

By the end of their shift, even Santa had come around to seeing "the great excellent especially good fortune of free tinsel."

Unfortunately, the mall management wasn't so easily appeased and the crow girls left the employ of the Williamson Street Mall that very day, after first having to turn in their red-and-green elf outfits. But on the plus side, they were paid for their nineteen days of work and spent all their money on chocolate and fudge and candy and ice cream.

When they finally toddled out of the mall into the snowy night, they made chubby snow angels on any lawn they could find, all the way back to the Rookery.

"So now we're unemployed," Zia told Jilly when they came over for a visit on the twenty-third, shouting "Happy eve before Christmas eve!" as they trooped into the professor's house.

"I heard," Jilly said.

"It was awful," Maida said.

Jilly nodded. "Losing a job's never fun."

"No, no, no," Zia said. "They ran out of candy canes!"

"Can you imagine?" Maida asked.

Zia shook her head. "Barely. And I was there."

"Well, I'm sorry to hear that," Jilly said.

"Yes, it's a veryvery sorrysome state of affairs," Maida said.

"And we're unemployed, too!"

"Lucius says we're unemployable."

"Because now we have a record."

"A permanent record."

"Of being bad bad candy cane–eating girls."

They both looked so serious and sad that Jilly became worried. But then Zia laughed. And Maida laughed, too.

"What's so funny?" Jilly asked.

Zia started to answer, but she collapsed in giggles and couldn't speak.

Maida giggled, too, but she managed to say, "We sort of like being bad bad candy cane–eating girls."

Zia got her fit of giggles under control. "Because it's like being outlaws."

"Fierce candy cane–eating outlaw girls."

"And that's a good thing?" Jilly asked.

"What do you think?" Maida asked.

"I think it is. Merry Christmas, Maida. Merry Christmas, Zia."

"Merry Christmas to you!" they both cried.

Zia looked at Maida. "Why did you say, 'Merry Christmas toot toot'?"

"I didn't say 'toot toot.' "

"I think maybe you did."

"Didn't."

Zia grinned. "Toot toot!"

"Toot toot!"

They pulled their jingling bell brooches out of their pockets, which they'd forgotten to return to the store where they'd "found" them, and marched around the kitchen singing "Jingle Bells" at the top of their lungs until Goon, the professor's housekeeper, came in and made them stop.

Then they sat at the table with their cups of sugar, on their best behavior, which meant they only took their brooches out every few moments, jingled them, and said "toot toot" very quietly. Then, giggling, they'd put the brooches away again.

Dark Eyes, Faith, and Devotion

I've just finished cleaning the vomit my last fare left in the backseat—his idea of a tip, I guess, since he actually short-changed me a couple of bucks—and I'm back cruising when the woman flags me down on Gracie Street, outside one of those girl-on-girl clubs. I'll tell you, I'm as open-minded as the next guy, but it breaks my heart when I see a looker like this playing for the other team. She's enough to give me sweet dreams for the rest of the week, and this is only Monday night.

She's about five-seven or five-eight and dark-skinned—Hispanic, maybe, or Indian. I can't tell. I just know she's gorgeous. Jet black hair hanging straight down her back and she's all decked out in net stockings, spike heels, and a short black dress that looks like it's been sprayed on and glistens like satin. Somehow she manages to pull it off without looking like a hooker. It's got to be her baby-doll face—made up to a T, but so innocent all you want to do is keep her safe and take care of her. After you've slept with her, mind.

I watch her in the rearview mirror as she gets into the backseat—showing plenty of leg with that short dress of hers and not shy about my seeing it. We both know that's all I'm getting and I'm lucky to get that much. She wrinkles her nose and I can't tell if it's some linger of l'eau de puke or the Lysol I sprayed on the seat after I cleaned up the mess my last fare left behind.

Hell, maybe it's me.

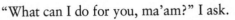

"What can I do for you, ma'am?" I ask.

She's got these big dark eyes and they fix on mine in the rearview mirror, just holding on to my gaze like we're the only two people in the world.

"How far are you willing to go?" she asks.

Dressed like she is, you'd be forgiven for thinking it was a come-on. Hell, that was my first thought anyway, doesn't matter she's playing on that other team. But there's that cherub innocence thing she's got going for her, and, well, take a look at a pug like me and you know the one thing that isn't going to happen is some pretty girl's going to make a play for me from the backseat of my cab.

"I can take you anyplace you need to go," I tell her, playing it safe.

"And if I need something else?" she asks.

I shake my head. "I don't deal with anything that might put me inside."

I almost said "back inside," but that's not something she needs to know. Though maybe she already does. Maybe when I pulled over she saw the prison tattoos on my arms—you know, you put them on with a pin and the ink from a ballpoint so they always come out looking kind of scratchy and blue.

"Someone has stolen my cat," she says. "I was hoping you might help me get her back."

I turn right around in my seat to look at her straight on. I decide she's Hispanic from her accent. I like the Spanish warmth it puts on her words.

"Your cat," I say. "You mean like a pet?"

"Something like that. I really do need someone to help me steal her back."

I laugh. I can't help it.

"So what, you flag down the first cab you see and figure whoever's driving it'll take a short break from cruising for fares to help you creep some joint?"

"Creep?" she asks.

"Break in. But quietly, you know, because you're hoping you won't get caught."

She shakes her head.

"No," she says. "I just thought *you* might."

"And that would be because . . . ?"

"You've got kind eyes."

People have said a lot of things about me over the years, but that's something I've never heard before. It's like telling a wolf he's got a nice smile. I've been told I've got dead eyes, or a hard stare, but no one's ever had anything nice to say about them before. I don't know if it's because of that, or if it's because of that innocence she carries that just makes you want to take care of her, but I find myself nodding.

"Sure," I tell her. "Why not? It's a slow night. Where can we find this cat of yours?"

"First I need to go home and get changed," she says. "I can't go—what was the word you used?" She smiles. "Creep a house wearing this."

Well, she could, I think, and it would sure make it interesting for me if I was hoisting her up to a window, but I just nod again.

"No problem," I tell her. "Where do you live?"

This whole situation would drive Hank crazy.

We did time together a while back—we'd each pulled a stretch and they ran in tandem for a few years. It's all gangs inside now, and since we weren't either of us black or Indian or Hispanic, and we sure as hell weren't going to run with the Aryans, we ended up passing a lot of time with each other. He told me to look him up when I got out and he'd fix me up. A lot of guys say that, but they don't mean it. You're trying to do good and you want some hard case showing up at your home or place of employment? I don't think so.

So I wouldn't have bothered, but Hank never said something unless he meant it, and since I really did want to take a shot at walking the straight and narrow this time out, I took him up on it.

He hooked me up with this guy named Moth who runs a Gypsy cab company out of a junkyard—you know, the wheels aren't licensed but so long as no one looks too hard at the piece of bureaucratic paper stuck on the back of the driver's seat, it's the kind of thing you can get away with. You just make a point of cruising for fares in the parts of town that the legit cabbies prefer to stay out of.

So Hank gave me the break to make good, and Moth laid one piece of advice on me—"Don't get involved with your fares"—and I've been doing okay, keeping my nose clean, making enough to pay for a room in a boardinghouse, even stashing a little extra cash away on the side.

Funny thing is I like this gig. I'm not scared to take the rough fares and I'm big enough that the freaks don't mess with me. Occasionally I even get someone like the woman I picked up on Gracie Street.

None of which explains why I'm parked outside a house across town on Marett Street, getting ready to bust in and rescue a cat.

My partner in crime is sitting in the front with me now. Her name's Luisa Jaramillo. She's changed into a tight black T-shirt with a pair of baggy faded jean overalls, black hightops on her feet. Most of her makeup's gone and her hair's hidden under a baseball cap turned backwards. She still looks gorgeous. Maybe more than she did before.

"What's your cat's name?" I ask.

"Patience."

I shrug. "That's okay. You don't have to tell me."

"No, that's her name," Luisa says. "Patience."

"And this guy that stole her is . . . ?"

"My ex-boyfriend. My very recent ex-boyfriend."

That's what I get for jumping to conclusions, I think. Hell, *I* was cruising Gracie Street. That doesn't automatically put me on the other team either. Only don't get me wrong. I'm not getting my hopes up or anything. I know I'm just a pug and all she's doing is using me for this gig because I'm handy and I said I'd do it. There's not going to be any fairy-tale reward once we get kitty back from her ex. I'll be lucky to get a handshake.

So why am I doing it?

I'll lay it out straight: I'm bored. I've got a head that never stops working. I'm always considering the percentages, making plans. When I said I'd come to enjoy driving a cab, I was telling the truth. I do. But you're talking to a guy who's spent the better part of his life working out deals, and when the deals didn't pan out, he just went in and took what he needed. That's what put me inside.

They don't put a whole lot of innocent people in jail. I'm not saying they aren't biased towards what most people think of as the dregs of society—the homeboys and Indians and white trash I was raised to be—but most of us doing our time, we did the crime.

Creeping some stranger's house gives me a buzz like a junkie getting a fix. I don't get the shakes when I go cold turkey like I've been doing these past couple of months, but the jones is still there. Tonight I'm just cozying it up with a sugar coating of doing the shiny white knight bit, that's all.

I never even stopped to ask her why we were stealing a cat. I just thought, let's do it. But when you think about it, who steals cats? You lose your cat, you just go get another one. We never had pets when I was a kid, so maybe that's why I don't get it. In our house the kids were the pets, only we weren't so well-treated as I guess Luisa's cat is. Somebody ever took one of us, the only thing Ma'd regret is the cut in her check from social services.

You want another reason? I don't often get a chance to hang out with a pretty girl like this.

"So what's the plan?" I ask.

"The man who lives in that house is very powerful," Luisa says.

"Your ex."

She nods.

"So he's what? A politician? A lawyer? A drug dealer?"

"No, no. Much more powerful than that. He's a *brujo*—a witch man. That is not a wrong thing in itself, but his medicine is very bad. He is an evil man."

I give her the same blank look I'm guessing anybody would.

"I can see you don't believe me," she says.

"It's more like I don't understand," I tell her.

"It doesn't matter. I tell you this only so that you won't look into his eyes. No matter what, do not meet his gaze with your own."

"Or what? He'll turn me into a pumpkin?"

"Something worse," she says in all seriousness.

She gets out of the car before I can press her on it, but I'm not about to let it go. I get out my side and join her on the sidewalk. She takes my hand and leads me quickly into the shadows cast by a tall hedge that runs the length of the property, separating her ex's house from its neighbours. I like the feel of her skin against mine. She lets go all too soon.

"What's really going on here?" I ask her. "I mean, I pick you up outside a girl bar on Gracie Street where you're dressed like a hooker, and now we're about to creep some magic guy's house to get your cat back. None of this is making a whole lot of sense."

"And yet you are here."

I give her a slow nod. "Maybe I should never have looked in your eyes," I say.

I'm joking, but she's still all seriousness when she answers.

"I would never do such a thing to another human being," she tells me. "Yes, I went out looking the way I did in hopes of attracting a man such as you, but there was no magic involved."

I focus on the "a man such as you," not sure I like what it says about what she thinks of me. I may not look like much, which translates into a lot of nights spent on my own, but I've never paid for it.

"You looked like a prostitute, trying to pick up a john or some freak."

She actually smiles, her teeth flashing in the shadows, white against her dark skin.

"No, I was searching for a man who would desire me enough to want to be close to me, but who had the heart to listen to my story and the compassion to want to help once he knew the trouble I was in."

"I think you've got the wrong guy," I tell her. "Neither of those are things I'm particularly known for."

"And yet you are here," she says again. "And you shouldn't sell yourself short. Sometimes we don't fulfill our potential only because there is no one in our life to believe in us."

I've got an idea where she's going with that—Hank and Moth have talked about that kind of thing some nights when we're sitting around a campfire in the junkyard, not to mention every damn social worker who's actually trying to do their job—but I don't want to go there with her anymore than I do with them. It's a nice theory, but I've never bought it. Your life doesn't go a certain way just because other people think that's the way it will.

"You were taking a big chance," I say instead. "You could've picked up some freak with a knife who wasn't going to stop to listen."

She shakes her head. "No one would have troubled me."

"But you need my help with your ex."

"That is different. I have looked in his eyes. He has sewn

black threads in my soul and without a champion at my side, I'm afraid he would pull me back under his influence."

This I understand. I've helped a couple of women get out of a bad relationship by pounding a little sense into their ex-boyfriend's head. It's amazing how the threat of more of the same is so much more effective than a restraining order.

"So you're looking for some muscle to pound on your ex."

"I'm hoping that won't be necessary. You wouldn't want him for an enemy."

"Some people say you're judged by your enemies."

"Then you would be considered a powerful man, too," she says.

"So the getup you had on was like a costume."

She nods, but even in the shadows I can see the bitter look that comes into her eyes.

"I have many 'costumes' such as that," she says. "My boyfriend insists I wear them in order to appear attractive. He likes it that men would desire me, but could not have me."

"Boy, what planet is he from?" I say. "You could wear a burlap sack and you'd still be drop-dead gorgeous."

"You did not like the dress?"

I shrug. "What can I say? I'm a guy. Of course I liked it. I'm just saying you don't need it."

"You are very sweet."

Again with the making nice. Funny thing is, I don't want to argue it with her anymore. I find I like the idea that someone'd say these kinds of things to me. But I don't pretend there's a hope in hell that it'll ever go past this. Instead, I focus on the holes in her story. There are things she isn't telling me and I say as much, but while she can't help but look a little guilty, she doesn't share them either.

"Look," I tell her. "It doesn't matter what they are. I just need to know, are they going to get in the way of our getting the job done?"

"I don't think so."

I wait a moment but she's still playing those cards pretty much as close to her vest as she can. I wonder how many of them are wild.

"Okay," I say. "So we'll just do it. But we need to make a slight detour first. Do you think your cat can hold out for another hour or so?"

She nods.

She doesn't ask any questions when I pull up behind a plant nursery over on East Kelly Street. I jimmy the lock on the back door like it's not even there—hey, it's what I do, or at least used to do—and slip inside. It takes me a moment to track down what I'm looking for, using the beam of a cheap key ring flashlight to read labels. Finally, I find the shelf I need.

I cut a hole in a small bag of diatomaceous earth and carefully pour a bit of it into each of my jacket's pockets. When I replace the bag, I leave a five-spot on the shelf beside it as payment. See, I'm learning. Guys back in prison would be laughing their asses off if they ever heard about this, but I don't care. I may still bust into some guy's house to help his ex-girlfriend steal back her cat, but I'm done with taking what I haven't earned.

"You figure he's home?" I ask when we pull back up outside the house on Marett.

She nods. "He would not leave her alone—not so soon after stealing her from me."

"You know where his bedroom is?"

"At the back of the house, on the second floor. He is a light sleeper."

Of course he would be.

"And your cat," I say. "Would she have the run of the house, or would he keep her in a cage?"

"He would have . . . other methods of keeping her docile."

"The magic eyes business."

"His power is not a joking matter," she says.

"I'm taking it seriously," I tell her.

Though I'm drawing the line at magic. Thing is, I know guys who can do things with their eyes. You see it in prison all the time—whole conversations taking place without a word being exchanged. It's all in the eyes. Some guys are like a snake, mesmerizing its prey. The eyes lock on to you and before you know what's going on, he's stuck a shiv in your gut and you're down on the floor, trying to keep your life from leaking out of you, your own blood pouring over your hands.

But I'm pretty good with the thousand-yard stare myself.

I get out of the car and we head for the side door in the carport. I'd have had Luisa stay behind in the cab, except I figure her cat's going to be a lot more docile if she's there to carry it back out again.

I give the door a visual check for an alarm. There's nothing obvious, but that doesn't mean anything, so I ask Luisa about it.

"A man such as he does not need a security system," she tells me.

"The magic thing again."

When she nods, I shrug and take a couple of pairs of surgical gloves out of my back pocket. I hand her one pair and put the other on, then get out my picks.

This door takes a little longer than the one behind the nursery did. For a guy who's got all these magic chops, he's still sprung for a decent lock. That makes me feel a little better. I'm not saying that Luisa's gullible or anything, but with guys like this—doesn't matter what scam they're running, magic mumbo jumbo's not a whole lot different from the threat of a beating—it's the fear factor that keeps people in line. All you need is for your victim to believe that you can do what you say you'll do if they don't toe the line. You don't actually need magic.

The lock gives up with a soft click. I put my picks away and take out a small can of WD-40, spraying each of the hinges before I let the door swing open. Then I lean close to Luisa, my mouth almost touching her ear.

"Where should we start looking?" I say.

My voice is so soft you wouldn't hear me a few steps away. She replies as quietly, her breath warm against my ear. This close to her I realize that a woman like her smells just as good as she looks. That's something I just never had the opportunity to learn before.

"The basement," Luisa says. "If she is not hiding from him there, then he will have her in his bedroom with him. There is a door leading downstairs, just past that cupboard."

I nod and start for the door she pointed to, my sneakers silent on the tiled floor. Luisa whispers along behind me. I do the hinges on this door, too, and I'm cautious on the steps going down, putting my feet close to the sides of the risers where they're less liable to wake a creak.

There was a light switch at the top of the stairs. Once I get to the bottom, I stand silent, listening. There's nothing. I feel along the wall and come across the other switch I was expecting to find.

"Close your eyes," I tell Luisa.

I do the same thing and flick the switch. There's a blast of light behind my closed lids. I crack them slightly and take a quick look around. The basement is furnished, casually, like an upscale rec room. There's an entertainment center against one wall, a wet bar against another. Nice couch set up in front of the TV. I count three doors, all of them slightly ajar. I'm not sure what they lead to. Furnace room, laundry room, workshop. Who knows?

By the time I'm finished looking around my eyes have adjusted to the light. The one thing I don't see is a cat.

"You want to try calling her?" I ask.

Luisa shakes her head. "I can feel her. She is hiding in there." She points to one of the mystery doors. "In the storage room."

I let her go ahead of me, following after. Better the cat see her first than my ugly mug.

We're halfway across the room when someone speaks from behind us.

<I knew you would return,> a man's voice says, speaking Spanish. <And look what you have brought me. A peace offering.>

I turn slowly, not letting on that I know what he's said. I picked up a lot of Spanish on the street, more in jail. So I just look surprised, which isn't a stretch. I can't believe I didn't feel him approach. When I'm creeping a joint I carry a sixth sense inside me that stretches out throughout the place, letting me know when there's a change in the air.

Hell, I should at least have heard him on the stairs.

"I have brought you nothing," Luisa says, speaking English for my benefit, I guess.

<And yet I will have you and your champion. I will make you watch as I strip away his flesh and sharpen my claws on his bones.>

"Please. I ask only for our freedom."

<You can never be free from me.>

I have to admit he's a handsome devil. Same dark hair and complexion as Luisa, but there's no warmth in his eyes.

Oh, I know what Luisa said. Don't look in his eyes. But the thing is, I don't play that game. You learn pretty quickly when you're inside that the one thing you don't do is back down. Show even a hint of weakness and your fellow inmates will be on you like piranha.

So I just put a hand in the pocket of my jacket and look him straight in the eye, give him my best convict stare.

He smiles. "You are a big one, aren't you?" he says. "But your size means nothing in this game we will play."

You ever get into a staring contest? I can see that starting up here, except dark eyes figures he's going to mesmerize me in seconds, he's so confident. The funny thing is, I can feel a pull in that gaze of his. His pupils seem to completely fill my sight. I hear a strange whispering in the back of my head and can feel that thousand-yard stare of mine already starting to fray at the edges.

So maybe he's got some kind of magical power. I don't know and I don't care. I take my hand out of my pocket and I'm holding a handful of that diatomaceous earth I picked up earlier in the nursery.

Truth is, I never thought I'd use it. I picked it up as a backup, nothing more. Like insurance just in case, crazy as it sounded, Luisa really knew what she was talking about. I mean, you hear stories about every damn thing you can think of. I never believe most of what I hear, but a computer's like magic to someone who's never seen one before—you know what I'm saying? The world's big enough and strange enough that pretty much anything can be out there in it, somewhere.

So I've got that diatomaceous earth in my hand and I throw it right in his face, because I'm panicking a little at the way those eyes of his are getting right into my head and starting to shut me down inside.

You know anything about that stuff? It's made of ground-up prehistoric shells and bones that are sharp as glass. Gardeners use it to make barriers for various kinds of insects. The bug crawls over it and gets cut to pieces. It's incredibly fine—so much so that it doesn't come through the latex of my gloves, but eyes don't have that kind of protection.

Imagine what it would do if it got in them.

Tall, dark, and broody over there doesn't have to use his imagination. He lifts his hand as the cloud comes at him, but he's too late. Too late to wave it away. Too late to close his eyes like I've done as I back away from any contact with the stuff.

His eyelids instinctively do what they're supposed to do in a situation like this: they blink rapidly and the pressure cuts his eyes all to hell and back again.

It doesn't help when he reaches up with his hands to try to wipe the crap away.

He starts to make this horrible mewling sound and falls to his knees.

I'm over by the wall now, well out of range of the rapidly settling cloud. Looking at him I start to feel a little queasy, thinking I did an overkill on this. I don't know what went on between him and Luisa—how bad it got, what kind of punishment he deserves—but I think maybe I crossed a line here that I really shouldn't have.

He lifts his bloodied face, sightless eyes pointed in our direction, and manages to say something else. This time he's talking in some language I never heard before, ending with some Spanish that I do understand.

<Be so forever,> he cries.

I'm turning to Luisa just then, so I see what happens.

Well, I see it, but it doesn't register as real. One moment there's this beautiful dark-haired woman standing there, then she vanishes and there's only the heap of her clothes left lying on the carpet. I'm still staring slack-jawed when the clothing moves and a sleek black cat wriggles out from under the overalls and darts into the room where Luisa said *her* cat was.

As I take a step after her, the man starts in with something else in that unrecognizable language. I don't know if it's still aimed at Luisa, or if he's planning to turn me into something, too—hell, I'm a dyed-in-the-wool believer at this point—but I don't take any chances. I take a few quick steps in his direction and give him a kick in the side of the head. When that doesn't completely stop him, I give him a couple more.

He finally goes down and stays down.

I turn back to go after Luisa, but before I can, that black cat comes soft-stepping out of the room once more, this time carrying a kitten in its mouth.

"Luisa?" I find myself saying.

I swear, even with that kitten in its mouth, the cat nods. But I don't even need to see that. I only have to look into her eyes. The cat has Luisa's eyes, there's no question in my mind about that.

"Is this . . . permanent?" I ask.

The cat's response is to trot by me, giving her unconscious ex's body a wide berth as she heads for the stairs.

I stand there, looking at the damage I've done to her ex for a long, unhappy moment, then I follow her up the stairs. She's sitting by the door with the kitten, but I can't leave it like this. I look around the kitchen, not ready to leave yet.

The cat makes a querulous sound, but I ask her to wait and go prowling through the house. I don't know what I'm looking for, something to justify what I did downstairs, I guess. I don't find anything, not really. There are spooky masks and icons and other weird magical-looking artifacts scattered throughout the house, but he's not going to be the first guy who likes to collect that kind of thing. Nothing explains why he needed to have this hold over Luisa and her—I'm not thinking of the kitten as a cat anymore. After what I saw downstairs, I'm sure it's her kid.

I go upstairs and poke through his office, his bedroom. Still nothing. But then it's often like that. Too often the guy you'd never suspect of having a bad thought turns out to beating on his family, or goes postal where he works, or some damn crazy thing.

It really makes you wonder, especially with a guy like Luisa's ex. You find yourself with power like he's got, why wouldn't you use it to put something good into the world?

I know, I know. Look who's talking. But I'm telling you straight, I might have robbed a lot of people, but I never hurt them. Not intentionally. And never a woman or a kid.

I go back downstairs and find the cat still waiting by the kitchen door for me. She's got a paw on the kitten, holding it in place.

"Let's go," I say.

I haven't even started to think about how a woman can be changed into a cat, or when and if and how she'll change back again. I can only deal with one thing at a time.

My first impulse is to burn the place to the ground with him in it, but playing the cowboy like that's just going to put me back inside and it won't prove anything. I figure I've done enough damage and it's not like he's going to call the cops. But the first thing I'm going to do when I get home is change the plates on the cab and dig out the spare set of registration papers that Moth provides for all his vehicles.

For now I follow the cats down the driveway. I open the passenger door to the cab. The mama cat grabs her kitten by the skin at the nape of her neck and jumps in. I close the door and walk around to the driver's side.

I take a last look at the house, remembering the feel of the guy's eyes inside my head, the relief I felt when the diatomaceous earth got in his eyes and cut them all to hell. There was a lot of blood, but I don't know how permanent the damage'll be. Maybe he'll come after us, but I doubt it. Nine out of ten times, a guy like that just folds his hand when someone stands up to him.

Besides, the city's so big, he's never going to find us, even if he does come looking. It's not like we run in the same circles or anything.

So I get in the cab, say something that I hope sounds calming to the cats, and we drive away.

I've got a different place now, a one-bedroom, ground-floor apartment that gives me access to a backyard. It's not much, just a jungle of weeds and flowers gone wild, but the cats seem to like it.

I sit on the back steps sometimes and watch them romp around like, well, like the cats they are, I guess. I know I hurt the man who had them under his power, hurt him bad. And I know I walked into his house with a woman and came out with a cat. But it still feels like a dream.

It's true the cat seems to understand everything I say, and acts smarter than I think a cat would normally act, but what do I know? I never had a pet before. And anybody I talk to seems to think the same thing about their own cat or dog.

I haven't told anybody about any of this, though I did come at it from a different angle, sitting around the fire in the junk-yard with Hank one night. There were a half dozen of us. Moth, Hank's girlfriend Lily, and some of the others from their extended family of choice. The junkyard's in the middle of the city, but it backs onto the Tombs and it gets dark out there. As we sit in deck chairs, nursing beers and coffees, we watch the sparks flicker above the flames in the cut-down steel barrel Moth uses for his fires.

"Did you ever hear any stories about people that can turn into animals?" I ask during a lull in the conversation.

We have those kinds of talks. We can go from carbs and en-gine torques to what's wrong with social services or the best kind of herbal tea for nausea. That'd be ginger tea.

"You mean like a werewolf?" Moth says.

Sitting beside him, Paris grins. She's as dark-haired as Luisa was and her skin's pretty much covered with tattoos that seem to move on their own in the flickering light.

"Nah," she says. "Billy Joe's just looking for a way to turn himself into a raccoon or a monkey so he can get into houses again but without getting caught."

"I gave that up," I tell her.

She smiles at me, eyes still teasing. "I know that. But I still like the picture it puts in my head."

"There are all kinds of stories," Hank says, "and we know one or two. The way they go, the animal people were here first and some of them are still living among us, not looking any different from you or me."

They tell a few then—Hank and Lily and Katy, this pretty red-haired girl who lives on her own in a school bus not far from the junkyard. They all tell the stories like they've actually met the people they're talking about, but Katy's are the best. She's got the real storyteller's gift, makes you hang on to every word until she's done.

"But what about if someone's put a spell on someone?" I say after a few of their stories, because they're mostly about people who were born that way, part-animal, part-human, changing their skins as they please. "You know any stories like that? How it works? How they get changed back?"

I've got a lot of people looking at me after I come out with that.

Nobody has an answer.

Moth gives me a look, but it's curious, not demanding. "Why are you asking?" he says.

I just shrug. I don't know that it's my story to tell. But as the weeks go by I bring it up again and this time I tell them what happened, or at least what I think happened. Funny thing is, they just take me at my word. They start looking in on it for me, but nobody comes up with an answer.

Maybe there isn't one.

So I just drive my cab and spend time with these new families of mine—both the one in the junkyard and the cats I've got back home. I find it gets easier to walk the straight and narrow the longer you do it. Gets so that doing the right thing, the honest thing, comes like second nature to me.

But I never stop wondering about what happened that night. I don't even know if they're really cats who were pretending to be human, or humans that got turned into cats. I guess I'm always going to be waiting to see if they'll change back.

But I don't think about it twenty-four/seven. Mostly I just figure it's my job to make a home for them and keep them safe. And you know what? Turns out I'm pretty good at doing that.

Riding Shotgun

1

I wasn't surprised to learn that my father had died. He would have been seventy-two this winter and he'd always lived hard—I doubted that had changed after I left the farm. What surprised me was that I was in his will. We hadn't spoken in twenty-five years. I hadn't thought of him, except in passing, for maybe half that time. If you'd asked me, I would have said he'd leave his estate to a charity like MADD, considering how it was drunk driving that changed all of our lives.

I missed the funeral. There are a lot of Coes in the phonebook, so it took the lawyers awhile to track me down.

When they told me he'd left everything to me, I authorized them to put the farm up for sale, with the proceeds to be split between MADD and the local animal shelter. Dad never much cared for me, but he always did have a soft spot for strays.

I could have used the money. I'm a half owner of a vintage clothing and thrift shop in Lower Foxville and there always seems to be more money going out than coming in. But I knew it wouldn't be right to keep this unexpected inheritance.

Alessandra was good about it. There are things we argue about, but how we deal with family isn't one of them.

We're not exactly a couple, but we don't see other people either. It's hard to explain. We met in AA and we're good for each other. Neither of us have had a drink in fifteen years—sixteen for me, actually.

We have a pair of bachelor apartments in the same building as the store. Ours isn't a platonic relationship, but neither of us can sleep with someone else. Alessandra gets panic attacks if she wakes and there's someone in bed with her.

For me, it just makes the bad dreams worse.

2

We open late on Mondays, so one fall morning after the farm's sold, but before the closing date, Alessandra and I drive out to have a look at the place. Alessandra wouldn't have come at all, but I don't drive anymore and Newford's public transport system stops at the subdivisions that are still four or five miles south of the farm.

"I haven't been here in twenty-five years," I say as we pull into the lane.

I see the farmhouse ahead, surrounded by elms and maples in their fall colours. The barn and outbuildings lie behind the house, the fields yellow and brown, the hay tall. You know how they say you can never go back, or how everything looks smaller if you do?

As we drive up the lane, everything looks exactly the same.

"I hadn't spoken to him for that long either," I add. "To my father, I mean. Not once."

Alessandra nods. She knows. It's not like we haven't shared war stories a hundred times before. Late at night, when the darkness closes in and a drink seems like the only thing that will let us sleep. Instead we talk.

She pulls up near the house and shuts off the engine.

"So what am I doing here?" I ask. "Why would he want me to have anything?"

"I wouldn't know, Marshall," she says. "I never met your father."

And wished she'd never met her own.

I nod. I wasn't really expecting an answer. The question had been pretty much rhetorical.

"Do you have the key for the house?" she asks.

That makes me smile. I'd forgotten about that. So some things have changed. Back when I lived here, I can't remember us ever locking our doors.

"I think I'll walk around a little outside first," I say.

"Sure. I'll wait in the car."

"I won't be long."

She touches the bag on the seat between us. "Don't worry. I've got a book."

She's always got a book. We pick them up by the boxful at garage and rummage sales, usually for free. You'd be surprised what people will just leave on the curb when the sale's done. Saves them carting it back inside the house and storing it, I guess.

At the rate we read, and considering our income, these books are a real windfall. Reading's another way to go somewhere else and keep the past at bay.

"Don't . . . you know," she says as I'm getting out of the car.

Get all wound up in what you can't change. She doesn't have to say it.

"I'm okay," I tell her.

But I'm not. I don't realize how *not* until about ten minutes later.

If the old man's last will and testament surprised me, what I find behind the barn pretty much takes all the strength from my legs. I find it hard to breathe. It's all I can do just to stand there at the corner of the barn, staring, my hand up on the graying barn wood to keep my balance.

I don't see the rusted junker, sitting in the tall grass on its wheel rims, the tires rotted away, the grill and right fender smashed in, windshield a spiderweb of cracks, side windows gone. I see the car I'd bought in 1977: a 1965 Chevy Impala two-door hardtop, with a 253 V-8 under the hood and 48,000 original miles on it. Black interior, crocus-yellow exterior, whitewalls. That long sleek slope of the rear window.

I'm dizzy looking at it. The wreck it is, the beauty and freedom it represented to the seventeen-year-old who'd worked his ass off for a whole summer and winter to be able to afford it. I see them both for a long time—the car that's there and the one in my head—until it finally settles back into the junker it is and I can breathe again. I push away from the wall, no longer needing it for support.

I had no idea that the old man had retrieved the car after the accident. Or that he'd stored it back here.

I was in police custody for the funeral because there was no one to put up my bail. When I got out of prison after doing my time, the last place I wanted to come was the farm. I wouldn't have been welcome anyway.

I walk over to the car and try the door, but it's rusted shut. I make a trip into the barn and come back with a crowbar to pry the door open. I don't know what all's been nesting in it, but it doesn't smell too bad.

I get in and my foot bangs against a beer bottle. I remember that bottle, and the other half dozen just like it I drank that long-ago afternoon.

I sit and stare at the spiderweb cracks that turn the view through the windshield into something like a finished jigsaw puzzle. My chest tightens again. Up on the dash there's a baseball cap, half-eaten—by mice, I guess. I can make out the insignia. The Newford Hawks, from back when the city had a ball team. I used to listen to the games on a little transistor radio while I was doing my chores.

I'd dream about my car, listen to the games.

After the accident, I had different dreams about this car. About that day. About how it could all have been different.

I still do.

"Let me drive," Billy had said.

"You want to go to the quarry, little brother, you're staying in the shotgun seat."

I'd let him drive before, but I was feeling ornery that day. Too many beers.

Funny.

Alcohol was the problem.

And afterward alcohol was the only thing that had let me forget, allowing me the sweet taste of temporary oblivion. But that wasn't until I'd done my time and was back on the street again. When I was inside, I'd wake up two, three times a night, that afternoon still as fresh in my mind as when it happened.

I reach under my shirt and pull out a key on a string. I can't tell you why I've kept it all these years. I went through a lot of strings, lost pretty much all I ever had before I turned my life around again, but I've hung on to that key through the years.

We've got a jar of old keys in the store and I've thought of tossing it in with the rest, but I never do.

Keys are funny things. They can unlock the cage and let you out, the way it was for me when I finally got that car. And they can lock you up and stand guard so that you'll never be free.

That key was both for me.

The string comes over my head easily and that little flat piece of metal with its cut edge fits into the ignition just the way it's supposed to. I don't know why, but I put my foot on the clutch and turn the key to the right.

Of course nothing happens. It wasn't like I was actually expecting it to start up. But when you have the key that fits the lock, you have to try, right?

Then I turn it to the left. Backwards.

Nothing.

I smile to myself and start to turn it back, but it won't budge. I give it a harder turn, then back and forth, trying to loosen it.

Something like an electric charge runs up my arm.

That arm, my whole right side goes numb. There's a sharp pain in the center of my chest, radiating out. My vision blurs.

I think:

I'm having a heart attack.

No wonder the old man left the place to me in his will, left this old car just waiting for me.

He knew.

He just *knew* this would happen.

Crazy idea, but I'm not exactly thinking straight. And then I realize the pain's on the wrong side of my body for a heart attack.

Then what . . . ?

The sharp hurt doesn't go away, but my vision clears. Vertigo hits me, deep and sudden, but at the same time I'm disassociated from it. I feel like the world's falling away below me only it doesn't seem to concern me. Everything stays in focus. Preternaturally sharp.

I watch the cracks in the windshield disappear. They recede, leaving behind clear, uncracked glass. Weirder still, the view beyond the windshield is a flickering dance of images. It's like watching time-lapse photography. Seasons change. Weeds and scrub trees come and go. Clouds strobe in the sky, here one moment—thick and woolly, or thin and long, or dark and pregnant with rain—gone the next.

And that's when I know I'm dreaming.

Or having some kind of attack.

Heart attack . . . panic attack . . .

It all stops so suddenly it's as if I've suddenly run up against a wall. The last time I felt like that was twenty-five years ago, when the car was just about to hit the tree. When I put my arm out to stop Billy's forward motion, but there was too much momentum. He just about tore my arm out of its socket with the force of his forward motion. Went crashing into the windshield. Cracking it. Spraying blood . . .

The windshield's not cracked anymore.

There's a summer day on the other side of it, not the fall day that's supposed to be there.

"Al . . . aless . . ."

I can't get her name out.

"I'm definitely driving," a voice says from beside me. "You are totally wasted."

I turn so slowly, scared of what I'll see, scared of what I won't see. But he's there. My brother Billy.

Alive.

Alive!

I put out a hand to touch him. To see if he's real.

He can't be real.

He backs away from my hand.

"Whoa," he says. "What's with the groping, Marsh?"

And then I understand. Not how or why. I just understand that I've been given a second chance.

"Are you okay?" Billy asks. "You look a little like Patty Crawford, just before she puked all over the bleachers."

I let my hand drop.

"I . . . I'm okay," I tell him.

My voice sounds like a stranger's in my ears. Distant. No, it's just that its from another time. Funny, I remember so much, a lot of it painstaking detail, but not the sound of his voice. Not that mole, on his neck, right under his ear.

"I'm just feeling a little . . ."

"Out of it?" Billy finishes for me. "How many beers did you have, anyway?"

I look down at my feet. There's an empty bottle there. I don't see any others, but I remember I was starting in on my second half of a twelve-pack. I don't even know why. It's a beautiful summer's day. I'm alive. My *brother*'s alive. Why the hell would I be drinking?

"So can I drive?" Billy asks.

I need to explain something here. Billy was the golden boy in our family. The smart one who knew by the time he was fourteen that he was going to be a doctor. I, on the other hand, was unfocused. I liked cars. I liked girls. I liked to party. I had no idea what I wanted to do with my life beyond get off the farm.

The old man didn't get it—because it was different for his generation, I guess. You figured out what you wanted to be, what you *could* be given your situation in life, and that's what you aimed for. He couldn't understand that not only did I not know, I didn't care.

It was bad enough before Mom died. But after that, the friction between us got worse and worse. I could pretend that he favoured my brother because Billy had Mom's blond hair, that his cherubic features reminded us of her, too. But the truth is, Billy was focused—something the old man could admire. He worked hard in school, aiming for scholarships. The money he got from his part-time jobs went into a college fund, not towards a car.

I couldn't begin to compete.

But the funny thing is, I never resented Billy for that. The old man, sure. But never Billy.

His dying was such a waste. See, that was the real heartbreak when he died. He was going to be somebody. A doctor. He was going to save lives.

I wasn't ever going to be anybody.

But I was the one who survived. The drunk driver. The one with nothing to lose.

Sitting here in my old Impala, looking at Billy, I know it doesn't have to be that way now. I can change what happened. I could just refuse to go anywhere, but Billy'd never let up. He was supposed to be meeting some girl at the quarry. So we have to go.

But so long as I'm not driving, it's not going to end the way it did the first time around.

"Sure," I say. "You can drive."

I open the driver's door and walk around the car while he scoots over to my seat. He grins at me when I get in, makes a show of putting on his seat belt. He wasn't wearing one the last time we did this. He takes off his ball cap and throws it onto the dashboard.

I fasten my seat belt as well and then we're off.

It's funny, considering how much I've thought of that moment, that day, but I can never remember what caused me to lose control of the car. I just know *where* it happened. I tense up as we start into the sharp turn on our local dead man's curve—more than one car's gone skidding off the gravel here. But Billy's got everything under control. He's driving fast, but not too fast.

And then it comes. Something, I still don't know what. A cat, a dog, a rabbit. It doesn't matter. Something small. Brown and fast.

Billy does the same thing I did—brakes and the car starts to slide on the gravel. But he's not drunk and he doesn't panic. He begins to straighten out, but we hit a pothole and it startles him enough to momentarily lose his concentration. The back wheels skid on the gravel. He touches the brakes, remembers he shouldn't, and lifts his foot.

Too late.

We're going sideways.

He tries to straighten us again, touches the gas. The wheels catch on a bare patch of dirt along the side of the road. We shoot forward. Out of the curve, across the road.

We're going fast enough to clear the ditch.

We clear it.

I see the tree coming up. The same oak tree I hit.

We bottom out on the field—the shocks can't absorb this kind of an impact, but it doesn't slow our momentum.

Then we hit the tree and the last thing I remember is my seat belt snapping and my face is heading for the windshield.

3

"Hey, cowboy."

I blink at the unfamiliar voice. Open my eyes. The bright blue of the sky above me hurts too much to look at. It makes my eyes water so I close them again and lie there for a long moment, trying to figure out where I am.

When it comes back to me, it's all in a rush: the crash. The same damn crash that killed Billy twenty-five years ago, repeating itself even though this time I wasn't driving.

And if I'm alive, then that means . . .

I sit up fast and my head spins. I'm lying in tall, summergreen grass. The sky's clear above me, the sun's bright. I can hear the sound of bees and flies and June bugs. I don't hurt anywhere. I turn slowly, take in the big oak tree, the road. There's no car anywhere in sight. No Billy.

That's impossible. I'd think I was dreaming, but if I am, then I haven't stopped, because I'm not back in that old wrecked Impala of mine. I'm here, at the crash site, and it's still summer—not the autumn day when I pried open the Impala's door in back of the old man's barn.

Then I see the girl, the one whose voice brought me out of my blackout. She's standing on the side of the road, one hand on her hip. Her hair's so dark it's black and she's wearing it pulled back in a ponytail. Her features are pretty, if a little hard. She's wearing bell-bottom jeans, fraying at the hems, and a white tube top. Cute little plastic see-through shoes.

"Welcome back to the world," she says. "Or what's left of it for us."

I realize I know her and dredge her name up from my memory. Ginny Burns. She used to live in the trailer park at the edge of town and ran away from home a couple of years ago—at least it was a couple of years ago if I'm still in the past. She was always a little wild and her taking off like that didn't really surprise anybody.

Like about half the kids in school, I had a major crush on her, but she was unattainable. Three years older than me and she didn't date kids.

I'm surprised she's come back.

"Ginny?" I say.

She studies me a little closer. "I know you," she says. "Marshall Coe, right? You've grown up some since the last time I saw you."

I may look like a kid, but I'm a middle-aged man inside this seventeen-year-old boy's body. Still, I feel a flush of pleasure at the thought of her actually knowing my name. I cover it up by standing and brushing the grass and dirt from my jeans.

"So when did you get back?" I ask, trying to be cool.

"What makes you think I ever left?"

"Well, you've been . . . gone."

She gives me a sad smile that softens her features and makes her look even prettier.

"Yeah," she says. "Just like you."

I'm confused for a minute. How could she know I left? Went to jail, moved to the city. That I had this whole life before I found myself back here in my seventeenth year, starting it over again.

"How . . . ?" I start to ask her, but the next thing she says puts a stopper in my mouth that I can't talk around.

"Did I die?" she says. Her face goes hard again. "With a wire around my neck and some freak's dick up my ass."

"I . . ."

I don't know what to say. I'm focused on the word "die."
Then I remember her saying "just like you." And then . . .

"What . . . what do you mean . . . ?"

She comes over to where I'm standing.

"Sit down," she says, then lowers herself to the ground beside me, sitting cross-legged. "I forgot that it takes time for it all to sink in."

"What . . . seriously . . . what are you talking about?"

"The short of it," she says, "is we're dead. And I don't completely know the long of it."

"Dead? And my brother?"

She shrugs. "You're the only one who's been lying here."

"But we were together in the car . . ."

"Look, I know it's confusing, but it gets easier. Just don't try to figure everything out at the same time—it's too much at first."

Easy for her to say.

"So I'm—we're dead."

She nods. "Yeah. It wasn't pretty for me and I guess it wasn't for you either."

"What do you mean?"

"You've been lying here for a few days. Sometimes it takes the soul awhile to wake up again, especially if they died hard."

I give a slow nod. "I guess I did. But all I really remember is that tree coming up on me . . . so fast . . ."

"I wish I *didn't* remember," she says.

I think about the little she's already told me of how she died and it's already too much. Time to change the subject.

"How do you know all this stuff?" I ask.

She shrugs. "Hanging around in boneyards. The dead have all kinds of things to tell you if you're willing to listen."

"So . . . this is it? This is what we get when we die?"

She shakes her head. "No. Most folks go on—don't ask me where, because I don't know and I haven't met anybody yet who can tell me."

"But these ghosts you've talked to . . . ?"

"Well, like I said, most people go on. Then there're those you find in boneyards, or haunting the place they died. They won't accept that they're dead, so they just . . . linger. And finally there's the folks like us."

She paused a moment, but I don't say anything. I'm not so ready to be a part of her "us." I don't know that I'm dead for sure. I don't know anything, really. For all I know, I'm still sitting in that junked out car out behind my dad's barn, dreaming all this up. It would sure explain why I feel so damn calm.

But whether I believe or not, I find myself needing to know more.

"What about—" I still can't say "us," so I settle for "—them?"

"We've still got unfinished business," she says. "We *can't* go on. Not till it's done."

I figure I know what her unfinished business is.

"You're waiting for your killer to be found," I say.

"Hell, no. I'm just waiting for somebody to find my body so that people know I'm dead."

I can't imagine that. Though I guess if I'm dreaming, I'm actually imagining *all* of this.

"I wonder why I'm still here?" I find myself saying.

"I couldn't tell you."

I give a slow nod. "I guess that's something we all have to work out for ourselves."

I look back at the oak tree, take in the fresh scars on its trunk. Ginny said I've been lying here in the field for days. I guess that explains why the car's not here. And why Billy's gone. I'm hoping it's because he got out of it okay. I'm also hoping that he's not going through what I did, but I don't see why he would. I was drunk, with a history of being picked up for one thing or another. Fighting, mostly, and drinking. Joyriding once. Vandalism a couple of times. By the time of the accident, the sheriff was looking for any excuse to put me away, and it's not like the old man ever stood up for me.

But Billy was about as clean-cut as they come. Dad would go his bail. He'd make sure Billy didn't spend an hour in jail, never mind the years in prison I did.

But I have to be sure.

"I need to see that he's all right," I say and stand up.

"Your brother?"

"Yeah."

"Mind if I tag along? It gets lonesome sometimes."

"I don't mind," I say.

I start to walk down the road, back to the farm, and she falls into step beside me.

"So I guess you're stuck around here," I say.

She gives me a puzzled look, then smiles. "No, we can go anywhere we want. But I keep coming back, thinking there's some way I can get someone to notice me—you know, so I can steer them to my grave? People can see us, but not all the time, and not necessarily when we want them to. Pike says it's not impossible to interact with those we left behind, but that it's really hard. They have to be what he calls sensitive. The big problem is that, even if you do make contact, no one seems to get what you're trying to say—it comes out garbled, for some reason, or like a riddle—and it's not like you can write it out for them on a piece of paper, because the thing you can't do is have physical contact with the, you know, physical world."

"Because we're ghosts now."

She nods.

"Who's Pike?" I ask.

"John Pike," she says. "He lived at the end of Connell Road."

And then I remember. He was a real hermit, living in a tar-paper shack at the end of the road. Rumour was he had a fortune in gold stashed away somewhere in that run-down excuse of a house of his, some kind of treasure, for sure. But he also had a couple of mean dogs and a shotgun loaded with salt that he wasn't afraid to use on trespassers. It did a bang-up job of keeping the curious away when he was alive.

"He died back in '75, '76," I say. "I was just a kid then."

"So was I. But I remember his picture in the paper."

I did, too. This scary wild man, long-haired and bearded. Kids used to dare each other to sneak into his place because everybody knew it was haunted.

"So he really was still hanging around," I say. "Like a ghost."

She nods. "At least he was when I died, and didn't that freak me out when I first met him. But he's gone on now."

She talks about it so easily, like still hanging around after you're dead is the most natural thing in the world. But the funny thing is, the longer we're walking along here, talking, the less unbelievable it seems. I mean, considering how this day's already gone for me . . .

"So he said, if we try, we can contact the people we left behind?"

"Yeah," she says. "But that it's really hard. You need a pretty strong connection between yourself and the person you left behind. And like I said, the time's got to be right and there's no way to guess that moment so all you can do is keep trying. The world's not real for us anymore. All we can do is look at it. We can't be part of it anymore."

"It feels pretty real to me."

I scuff my shoe against the gravel and send bits of it flying into the ditch.

"It just feels real because you expect it to," she says. "But nothing really moved and no one can see you. You can't really *affect* anything."

"I just kicked that gravel."

I do it again.

She shakes her head. "No, it just seems like you can. You'll see."

4

"**Want to hear a weird** story?" I say after we've been walking for a while.

She laughs. "What's weirder than the afterlife?"

I think of what happened about fifteen minutes ago when she stepped in front of this pickup that went barrelling by us. How the driver never saw her. How I tried to grab her. How the pickup went right through both of us.

It's taken me most of those fifteen minutes for my legs to stop feeling so rubbery. Except if I'm dead, how come it still feels like I have a body?

"Earth to Marshall," she says.

I blink and give her a confused look.

"You said you had a weird story," she says. "But now you're just being weird."

"Sorry."

So I tell her about it all, my old Impala, how when I was trying to get the key out of the ignition, I found myself here, back in the past.

There's a long silence before she finally asks, "Is this on the level?"

I nod.

"So you're really how old?"

"Forty-three."

"Forty-three," she repeats and she gets a look in her eyes that I can't describe. "Imagine having all those years."

I kind of glossed over the jail time and the years on skid row, and I don't expand on them now, because I know what she means. I might have had some tough times—doesn't matter that I brought them on myself—but at least I had them.

"Anything you'd go back and change if you could?" I ask instead.

She nods. "For starters, I wouldn't have gotten in the car with the freak that killed me. You know I had a funny feeling as soon as I opened his door, but I so wanted that ride. I was *so* ready to get away from here."

She shakes her head and I don't know what to say. And then we're at the lane leading up to my old man's farm and I can't think of anything but Billy and my need to know that he's okay.

She trails along behind as we walk up the lane, the same lane I drove up with Alessandra this morning, except that morning hasn't even happened yet. And I guess the way things have turned out, it never will.

I'm not sure what I expected to find here, but it wasn't the old man sitting on the front porch when he should be out in the back forty with his tractor. He's dressed for work: coveralls over a T-shirt, work boots on his feet, John Deere hat on the table beside him. But he doesn't look like he's ready to go anywhere. He looks deflated—defeated—and I get scared. Not for me, but for Billy. Because I know now: I died in that crash, but so did my brother. There's no other way to explain the old man's grief.

I can barely look at him, sitting there in the rocker, holding a framed picture loosely against his chest, gaze staring right through me as I come onto the porch. Ginny takes a seat on the stairs and doesn't follow me up.

I stand there looking at him for a long time. There's an unfamiliar emotion swelling inside me—unfamiliar so far as it concerns my feelings for the old man. I feel bad. For letting him down. For being such a shit. For not trying to be the man he wanted me to be. But especially for killing the son he loved.

"I . . . I'm so sorry, Dad."

I say the words I never got to say before.

He doesn't hear me, but he shifts in his chair as though he feels something. Then he lays the photo he's been holding against his chest down on his lap and I find myself staring down at a school picture of my own seventeen-year-old self.

It's not Billy he's mourning.

It's me.

I back away and slowly make my way down the stairs until I'm sitting beside Ginny.

"What is it?" she says.

I shake my head. For a long time all I can do is stare out across the fields. Ginny puts a hand on my arm. Turns out we can touch each other. We just can't touch anything in the world we left behind.

"It's me," I finally say. "He's mourning me."

"Well, what did you expect? You're his son."

"No, you don't get it. He hated me. When . . . the other time . . . before I changed how it would turn out . . . when I got drunk and my brother died in the crash . . . he never spoke to me again. He never went my bail. He never tried to see me. He was never in the courtroom . . ."

My voice trails off. It's impossible to catalogue the enormity of the distance that lay between us.

"So what?" Ginny asks. "Now he hates your brother?"

"I . . ."

I realize I don't know.

I go back up the stairs. The front door's open, but the screen door's closed. I reach for the handle, but I can't get a grip on it.

"Just walk through," Ginny says, coming up behind me. "Maybe we can't touch the world, but it can't touch us either. At least not"—she looks at my father, grieving—"physically."

I need to go inside, to find Billy, but the business with the door is freaking me badly. I can't imagine walking through the screen. But I just can't seem to grab hold of the handle.

Ginny steps by me and walks right through the door—screen, wooden crossbars, and all. It's like earlier on the road, when the truck went through us both. She reaches a hand back to me and I take it. I let her lead me inside.

"Which way?" she asks.

I nod down the hallway towards the kitchen and take the lead, ignoring the closed doors of the parlour and the front sitting room. They haven't been used since my mother died.

When we find the kitchen empty, I lead us up the back stairs. My relief is immediate when we find Billy in his room, sitting at his desk, reading a book. I stay in the doorway, content to look at him, to know he's alive, but Ginny slips past me and walks over to the desk.

"Eeuw," she says as she looks at his book.

I join her and see that he's studying graphic black-and-white pictures of an autopsy. He's had that book for a while and it *is* gross—I know, I've flipped through it before, but I can never take more than a few pictures.

"He's going to be a doctor," I tell Ginny. "He needs to know about this stuff."

"Yeah, but morbid much?"

I shrug. "He's always been interested in how people work. You know, muscle tissue and arteries and nerves and stuff."

Ginny nods. "All the things we don't have."

"I guess."

"He's a good-looking kid," she says.

"He takes after our mother."

I put my hand on Billy's head, trying to ruffle his hair, but my fingers go into his skull. I pull my hand back quickly.

It doesn't matter that I can't touch him, I tell myself. All that matters is that he's alive.

But I'd still like to give him a last hug before I go.

I settle for a look—drinking in the familiar sight of him, sitting at his desk and studying—then I leave the room.

"What was she like?" Ginny asks as she follows me out into the hall.

"Our mom? Everything the old man and I'm not: gentle, kind, thoughtful. And beautiful. She was like an angel, and now she's sleeping with them."

I want to hold that thought, but I can't. Not anymore.

"Unless she's like us," I add as we go down the stairs and step back through the screen door. "Trapped in some kind of nonlife, able to see and hear the world go on around us, but unable to interact with it."

"Maybe heaven's where we end up when we go on," Ginny says.

"Maybe," I say, wanting to be convinced.

But Ginny lets my word hang, so if I'm going to believe Mom's safe and happy somewhere, I have to do my own convincing.

I give the old man a last glance before I step off the porch and head back up the lane. There's nothing left for me here now. I don't know what happens next, but at least I've accomplished this much: I've changed the past and made things right again.

But it's funny. I don't feel any better. Truth is, what I really want is a drink. Not a beer, like I was drinking before I died, but a stiff shot of whiskey.

I need some oblivion.

I almost ask Ginny if there's such a thing as ghost whiskey—maybe there's a reason another word for hard liquor is spirits—but I settle on stepping out of my own head and getting Ginny to talk about her life instead.

"What was your mother like?" I ask her.

She shrugs. "I don't know. She left us not long after I was born."

I don't remember that from what I knew of her before, but I guess it's not so surprising. The kids I hung with only ever talked about how hot she was.

"That can't have been easy," I say.

"I never knew it to be any different. My dad was good to me—you know, he did his best. But he wasn't equipped to raise a kid, especially not the girl I turned out to be."

I can guess what she means, but I ask her anyway.

"A girl with a reputation," she explains. She shakes her head. "It's not something I ever asked for or wanted, but I sure as hell had one all the same."

"But you—"

I stop myself from saying it, but she nods and gives me a sad smile.

"Put out all the time, right?"

"It's just . . . I heard . . ."

She cups her hands under her breasts. They're not disproportionately huge, but you can't ignore them either. Not in that tight little tube top.

"I got these the summer I turned twelve," she says, "and by Christmastime, everybody thought I was a slut. I got tired of arguing about it, so after awhile, I just started acting like the trailer trash everybody'd already decided I was. But I'll tell you this, I was still a virgin when I died." Her features cloud over. "Well, right up to those last few minutes, I guess."

"I don't understand. Why would all these guys—"

"Oh, please. Derek Kirkwood was the one who started it—said I'd done it with him under the bleachers during a football game. Now, I *was* down there with him, but only having one of his beers. And maybe I let him kiss me and have a little grope, but we never did it."

"Then why didn't you say something when he started telling people you did?"

"I'd already stopped caring. I had a lot of 'boyfriends,' all right. I was happy to have people take me to dances, to drink their beer and smoke their joints, but the most any of them got was a hand-job." She gives me a sassy grin that never reaches her eyes. "But none of them was going to admit they didn't score when Kirkwood supposedly had. They might not ask me out again, but hell. If I *had* put out, they still probably wouldn't have."

"Jesus."

"If I'd've had any brains, I'd've put a stop to it long before it got to that point. But it was kind of fun at first—flattering that all these guys wanted me. And then it was too late."

We've reached the end of the lane, but neither of us makes a move to step onto the road.

"So that's why I took off," she says. "I wanted a new start. I wanted to go someplace where I could be who I decided I was, instead of letting other people decide it for me." She shakes her head. "And you can see what a good plan that was."

"I feel like a shit," I say.

"Why? Because you wanted to get into my pants as much as those other guys?"

I nod.

"Well, don't. I probably flirted with you like I did with any guy. I had a rep to uphold and all."

"It doesn't seem fair."

She shakes her head. "Nope. And neither does what we've got now, but we're stuck with it all the same."

She looks back down the lane at the farmhouse, then turns to look at me.

"So what are you going to do now, Marshall Coe?" she asks.

"I don't know."

"Ever been to Tibet?"

"I've never been any farther than the city—not in this life or the other one I had."

"So let's do a little traveling. Seeing the sights is about the only option left to us at this point."

Now it's my turn to take a last look at the old farmhouse.

I don't understand how my father could be grieving for me, but it's too late now to find out why he is.

I changed the past so that Billy's alive. Instead of the waste of a life I had, he can go out there and help people, make it a better world. But I can't be a part of that world.

So there's nothing left for me here except for the question of why I didn't go on after I died. Thinking about it, I realize I don't really care.

"Sure," I say when I turn back to her. "Why not?"

5

I think time moves differently when you're dead. You don't eat and you don't sleep, but there's always a little hunger in you that's maybe got nothing to do with food, and while you don't lie down and take a nap, there are holes in your awareness all the same. The days don't seem to follow one after the other so much as jump around—when they don't slide by in a confusing blur.

I guess what I'm trying to say is that I lose track of time. I lose track of everything—the life I had that ended when I tried to start up that old Impala of mine, and the half-day or so of the second one I got.

It all just goes away.

We really do go to Tibet. We go to a lot of different countries, spending most of our time in the wild places. It's not like the big cities aren't interesting—and just as wild in their own way—but it gets old fast when people and vehicles keep going through you because no one knows you're there. That doesn't happen to you in the big empty places. The mountains of Nepal. The Australian outback. Out on the Arctic tundra. Deep in the

Amazon jungles. The red rock canyons of southern Utah. The
Mongolian steppes. The mountains of Peru. The Sahara desert.

Sometimes we're noticed there—by people sensitive to the
spirit world—but we can't communicate with them and we don't
try. The only conversations we have is with the other dead and we
don't spend a lot of time with them either. The ones that stayed behind are mostly a bitter, self-centered group, unable to understand
why the world still goes on after they've died. I know I'm generalizing here, but unless one has unfinished business, why stay?

But the people with unfinished business aren't usually such
great company either. Most of them died hard and unhappy, and
don't seem as resilient as Ginny in how they deal with it. They're
focused on their deaths, determined to get their business done and
move on.

No, that's not true. Most of them are just focused on their
business. They don't even consider what will happen when it's
done.

But they're not all like that, because some people's unfinished
business isn't of a negative nature. Like the mother who's waiting
for her son to graduate. The grandparent waiting for the birth of a
grandchild. The husband waiting for his wife to stop mourning
and fall in love again. They have stories I can appreciate—at least
the first time around. By the third or fourth repetition, I'm ready
to move on.

Ginny's not like that. She's good company, always ready for a
laugh or an adventure, though the longer I get to know her, the
more I'm aware of this streak of melancholy that runs under even
her best moods. I'm also more than half in love with her, and
that's just weird because, well, we're both dead, aren't we?

It's four years before we get back to this part of the world. I only
know that because I remember when I died and, as we're walking by a newsstand, I happen to see the date on a newspaper,

right above a heading that reads "3rd VICTIM FOUND." The headline depresses me. Seems there's some guy running around cutting up young women like they were meat at a butcher's. It's senseless, and horrible, and I feel for the girls.

Ginny's looking in a store window and doesn't notice the headline, so I don't point it out to her. I don't want to remind her of her own terror time, starting out to find a new life and finding only an end in pain and horror.

We don't spend long in the city, but I want to look in on the old man before we head into some new wild place, so we head up into the country. I can't believe how far the city's spread in just four years.

The old man's changed, too. He seems to have aged ten years instead of four. He's still working the farm—on his own now. I check Billy's room, but he's moved out.

It takes me awhile to track him down.

Turns out he made the dream come true. He's in premed at Butler U., on a scholarship, but he's working a job on the side that lets him keep a crummy little bachelor apartment in Lower Foxville, close to the campus. He's taking a shower when we drift into his apartment. I look around at all his books and things, waiting for him to come out when I realize that Ginny's not with me. I find her in the bathroom, checking Billy out.

"Jeez," I say. "Give him a little privacy."

She pulls her head out of the shower curtain and laughs. "We're ghosts, Marsh. What difference does it make what we see? Besides, he's got a nice butt."

I don't want to be having this conversation.

"Get away from there," I say.

But before she can respond, the shower stops and Billy opens the curtain. The first thing I think is, my little brother's all grown up. The second is, where'd he get the black eye?

But a funny thing happens when I see that bruise. It reminds me of . . .

It's like I suddenly wake up from a dream and my thoughts go flying to my other life, the one I had before the old Impala brought me back and put me into this one.

"Alessandra," I say softly.

Ginny turns to me. "What?"

I repeat the name. How could I have forgotten her? The same way I forgot all that other life, I guess.

"Oh, right," Ginny says. "Your old girlfriend."

She was way more than a girlfriend, but I'm not thinking about that right now. I'm thinking about how she was five years younger than me. How right now she'd be fifteen or sixteen, still living at home with her father—the drunk who used her as punching bag.

"I've got to see her," I say.

Ginny starts to say something, but I guess there's a look in my eyes that makes her just shrug instead.

"I'm proud of you, Billy," I tell my brother. "But what the hell are you doing fighting? You're going to be a doctor. You don't have time for crap like that."

He doesn't respond. Why should he? He can't hear me. He doesn't even know that we're here.

Then I lead the way out of his apartment, heading for where Alessandra is living at this time in her life.

"I guess you knew her for a long time," Ginny says when we're standing outside the brownstone where Alessandra and her father live.

I nod. "But not when she was a teenager."

"Then how'd you know to find this place?"

"She took me by here one time. Later, when we were together."

We stand on the pavement for a while, looking at the building. We're at the edge of the sidewalk where it meets the road so that we don't have people walking through us, but there's not much foot traffic anymore. It's almost dinnertime and most people are home by now.

"So are we going in?" Ginny asks.

"I guess."

But I'm reluctant.

For one thing, I'm feeling this enormous guilt at having let all those years Alessandra and I were together just slip away out of my mind like they didn't mean anything. It was just the opposite. They meant everything. *She* meant everything.

For another, I'm nervous about what we'll find. If we've picked a time when her dad's drunk, it'll kill me to have to stand by, unable to step in and help.

"Marsh?" Ginny says.

I turn to look at her.

"You don't have to do this."

I shake my head. "Yeah, I do."

And I move forward, up the steps. Apartment 310, Alessandra told me. We walk through the front door into the foyer—doing this has long since stopped bothering me—and head up to the third floor. We can hear yelling when we come out of the stairwell and it gets louder as we go down the hall. Then there's the sound of breaking glass.

"Is her mother around?" Ginny asks, her voice hushed.

"No. She died when Alessandra was just a kid."

We step through the door, into the apartment. The noise is coming from down the hall, in the kitchen. I don't want to be here. I don't want to bear silent witness to Alessandra's terrors.

But I can't stop myself now.

Alessandra's stories were bad, but it's worse seeing it first-hand. She's lying on the floor, curled into a fetal position and bleeding from a cut on her head. Her father's standing over her, a broken bottle in his hand. That explains the cut.

Alessandra's crying—soundlessly, trying to be invisible. That's how she'd describe it to me. That all she was ever able to do was try to be invisible.

But it never helped.

Her father's yelling something, but I can't make out the words through the red rage that comes over me.

I've hated this man for a long, long time. In another, forgotten life, but it all comes back to me now in a rush. All those nights that Alessandra woke up crying. All those war stories she told, her voice flat, her eyes lost, looking off into the past.

Her father pulls back his foot, and I lose it.

I charge at him, hands flat in front of me.

I don't know what I'm thinking. What good will it do if I go running through him? But I can't do *nothing*.

And then the impossible happens.

My hands meet flesh. The force of my momentum knocks him backward, off balance, and he goes down. The back of his head catches on the edge of the kitchen counter and makes an awful sound. A wet, *cracking* sound.

He twists as he falls. Lands on the floor. On his face.

And he doesn't move.

I stand there, stunned, then slowly step forward. I nudge him with my foot but the toe of my shoes goes right through him.

I turn to Ginny. "What . . . what just happened?"

She shakes her head and we stand in the kitchen for what seems like a very long time. Staring at him, waiting for him to move.

He never does.

But Alessandra gets up. She holds her hand to her head and blood seeps through her fingers. She shuffles over to him, with the look of a scared dog, ready to bolt at a moment's notice. She does what I did, nudges him with a foot. Her shoe makes contact, but her father still doesn't move.

She stares at him, emotions playing across her features. Then she spits on him and slowly backs out of the kitchen.

I'm about to follow her—to do I don't know what—but Ginny grabs my arm.

"Marsh," she says, her voice strained.

I turn to see that the body on the floor has started to glow. Ginny and I exchanged puzzled glances. When we look back, the glow is lifting from the body, separate from, but retaining the body's shape.

It's Alessandra's father. The *spirit* of her father. Sitting up.

Neither of us has ever seen somebody die before. We've never been right there when it happens. We don't know *what's* going to happen.

I'm thinking, I don't want to be here.

The spirit looks around, then pushes itself up from the floor until it's finally standing. Its face turns to us, but before I can tell if we register in its consciousness, if it even has a consciousness at this point, the spirit begins to diminish. I'm not quite sure how to describe it. It's as if there was a tiny pinprick hole in the fabric of the world and the light that makes up the spirit just gets sucked away into it.

The last thing we see is that pinhole, shining a light so fierce that when it abruptly winks out, we have stars flashing in our gazes.

I clear my throat, then manage to say, "I guess it . . . went on."

Ginny gives a slow nod. "I guess."

I remember Alessandra and we go looking for her, but she's left the apartment. I don't know if my killing her father is going to make things better or worse for her. If it's going to stop her slow descent into alcoholism that followed her finally getting away from the man in the life where I knew her, or if it's going to push her into a more radical plunge into I don't know what.

I can only hope she'll be all right.

"Was this my unfinished business?" I say, thinking aloud. "Helping Alessandra—maybe saving her life?"

"You're still here, aren't you?" Ginny says.

There's that.

I reach towards the nearest wall and my hand goes through it. Just like it always has since I died.

"How could I have been able to push him like that?" I say. "I can't even pick up a pencil."

"I don't know. Maybe you just . . ."

"Just what?" I ask when she doesn't finish.

"Really needed to," she says. She seems reluctant. "Maybe if we need to do it badly enough . . . we can. You know, to help somebody or something like that."

I study her for a long moment.

"You've known this all along," I finally say. "Haven't you?"

She nods. "But it's nothing I've ever been able to do. Pike told me about it."

"Why didn't you tell *me*? Why were you so insistent on my believing that we can't affect the real world?"

"I was scared."

"Scared of what?"

"That you'd leave me."

"I don't understand," I say. "You told me that when we first met. You didn't even know me then."

She shrugs. "You just seemed so normal—and you were, too. You are. I'd been so lonely for so long . . ."

I'm beginning to understand.

"You know how to deal with your own unfinished business, don't you?" I say.

She won't meet my gaze, but she nods.

"But you're scared to go on to . . . wherever it is we go next."

"I had so little time to be me," she says. "What happens when we cross over? Do we just disappear like your girlfriend's father did?"

"We don't know what happened to him. Where he went."

"I know. But I don't want to go yet. I'm not ready."

I can tell she hates saying it, because it groups her with all those losers hiding out in their graveyards, able to go on, but refusing to.

"Is there even such a thing as unfinished business?" I ask.

She nods.

"And when we do it—whatever it is—do we just get sucked away like Alessandra's old man did?"

"No. But, you know. You start feeling ... thinner. Like there's nothing keeping you here anymore except your own need to stay."

"Did the graveyard ghosts tell you that?" I ask.

She shakes her head. "No, Pike did."

"Too bad he's not around anymore," I say. "I'd like to have asked him about all of this."

She told me he'd gone on, way back when we first met. But when I look at her now, I see from the expression on her face that that wasn't true either.

"He's still haunting that shack of his, isn't he?"

She nods.

We stand there for a while, neither of us speaking, uncomfortable with what's lying between us and too aware of the dead body in the kitchen, of what we both saw happen to the spirit that rose up from it.

I can't leave it like this.

"I won't leave you behind," I tell her. "When we go, we can go together."

"Promise?"

I nod.

But then everything changes again. Because when we go out looking for Alessandra, we find, instead, the ghost of a broken girl.

6

Her name's Sarah Hooper and I recognize her from the picture in the newspaper that I saw earlier today. She's the third victim of whatever freak it is who's been going around killing young women over the past few weeks. She looks even smaller and frailer in person than she did in the photo. But she didn't go down easy.

"They say you shouldn't fight back," she tells us, "but I didn't care. I guess I knew he was going to kill me and I just wanted to hurt him if I could. I hit him a few times—in the face, where I knew it'd show—but in the end he was just . . . you know . . . too strong . . ."

It's not too hard to figure out what her unfinished business is.

She was pretty messed up when we found her sitting on the ground in an alley not far from Alessandra's apartment, just staring at the brick wall across from her, but she's tougher than she looks.

"So I'm really dead," she says as we bring her up to speed on what she is now, why she's here. "I wasn't sure." She laughs, without any humour. "I know how that sounds, but you don't expect to still be around . . . after, you know? Not like this, where nothing seems any different except you can't touch anything. Nobody can hear or see you."

"Do you think you'd recognize the guy?" Ginny asks.

"Oh, yeah. We have—had a class together at the university. I never really talked to him except for this one time when he asked me out, but he caught me on a bad day and I just shot him down."

Ginny nods. "He gave you the creeps even then."

"Not really. He's just one of those guys with the choirboy good looks and that's never appealed to me. But mostly I guess I was so hard on him because of the way he was always looking at me in class. He was, like, *always* watching me, it seemed."

"Do you know his name?" I ask.

"Coe," she says. "William Coe—don't try to call him Bill, or Billy. I called him Bill when I was turning him down and he set me straight pretty quick."

Everything inside me goes still.

"Are . . . are you sure?" Ginny asks.

Sarah nods. "You don't forget the name of the guy who kills you." Her gaze goes from Ginny to me. "Do you know him?" she asks.

I give a slow nod. "He's my brother."

"Your brother. Jesus." She pauses for a heartbeat, then adds, "So did he kill you, too?"

I start to shake my head, but Ginny speaks up before I can.

"He was driving the car when Marsh died," she says.

I want to say he didn't do it on purpose, but I'm having too much trouble getting my head around the idea that Billy could be responsible for this woman's death. And at least two more.

Billy, who wanted to be a doctor. To help people.

Or maybe just to find out how they work so he'd know the best way to hurt them. To prolong their pain.

Because I'm thinking of that book with all the autopsy photographs in it. Maybe . . . maybe those pictures made him feel good . . .

The idea of it makes me sick.

"So," Sarah's saying, "I just need to find a way to . . . what? Bring him to justice? Get my revenge on him?"

"Something like that," Ginny says.

"And then what?"

"You go on."

"Go on where?"

Ginny shrugs. "We don't know. Nobody on this side does."

Sarah gives a slow nod of her head. "I've got to think about this."

"You don't have to be alone," Ginny says as Sarah starts to walk away.

"Yeah, I do," she says. "I really do."

We watch her walk away, down the alley. Neither of us makes a move to stop her.

"So that's where he got the black eye," I say.

Ginny nods. "I'm so sorry, Marsh."

"You had nothing to do with it."

"I know. But . . ."

"And that damn book of his. It should have been a clue."

"There's no way you could have known."

A deep sadness has settled inside me. But riding on top of it is the same anger I felt a few hours ago when Alessandra's father was beating her. I have that need to hit something and I kick at the nearest garbage bag. It goes flying across the alley and breaks against the far wall, spilling its contents.

"Don't be mad at me," Ginny says.

I know what she's thinking. First she disappointed me, and now my brother's hurt me even worse.

But I'm not mad—not at her. She wasn't deliberately trying to hurt me. She didn't tell me everything only because she was so lonely.

Maybe if I really was the seventeen-year-old I look to be . . . maybe I wouldn't understand. But I've seen things that kid never has and never will. Prison, living on the streets, the life of an alcoholic. I know that people mess up and get messed up by what life hands them.

Ginny had a fucked-up life and a worse death. And then she spent two years as a ghost, unable or unwilling to touch or be touched by anything or anybody. Is it any wonder she's clung to the first person who came along and treated her the way everybody deserves to be treated?

"I'm not mad," I tell her.

"How can you not be mad? I've lied to you about every-thing."

I shake my head. "No, just about the one thing."

"But maybe you could have stopped your brother *before* he started killing those girls."

Girls who died the way she did, alone and hard.

I hadn't even thought of that. That I could have stopped him.

"Maybe," I say. "But probably not. I'd've had to follow him around every day, just to know he was doing it. I'd have to *sus-pect* him first, and why would I do that? He was my little brother. You don't suspect your little brother of being a freak. So I'd've had to catch him in the act—or heard about it the way we just did—to believe."

And maybe that's my unfinished business. I came back and changed the way things were meant to be. Maybe my unfinished business is to fix this second mistake, because it looks like what I thought was my first mistake—drunk driving, killing my own brother—wasn't really a mistake at all.

Ginny's gaze goes to the garbage bag I kicked against the wall, then returns to me. I know what she's thinking. But she says it anyway.

"You have to kill him—like you did your girlfriend's dad."

Don't think I haven't already thought of that. But I shake my head.

"I don't know if I can just kill a person in cold blood," I say.

"What do you call what happened back in your old girl-friend's apartment?"

"An act of passion. Not something I planned to do like this would be." I sigh. "But it's not just that."

"Is it because he's your brother?"

I shake my head again, but I don't have any words for a while. I stare at the spill of garbage across the alley.

Ginny waits. Finally, I turn to look at her.

"I think I probably could do it," I say. "But I just can't stop thinking about the three girls that he's killed. How there might be even more—they just haven't found the other bodies yet."

"And if we don't do something now, he'll kill even more."

"I know. What I'm trying to figure out is a way to undo what I've done so that nobody ever got killed."

Understanding dawns in Ginny's eyes.

"You're going to try to get the car to bring you back again."

I nod.

"You're going to leave me."

I want to say, it's not like that. But we both know it is.

7

The old Impala's still out behind the barn. My dad saved it this time around, just like he did before. It's not in as bad shape as it was in my other life. The front end's still banged in and the windshield's cracked. But it's still got all of its windows and it's not nearly as rusted out. There's not as much scrub and weeds growing around it either.

We get in the car and stare out the through the cracks in the windshield. In this life I don't have a key hanging around my neck. But in this life there's a key still in the ignition.

I put my hand on it but my fingers go right through.

I think about Billy, let the anger come back, but that doesn't help either.

"Maybe all I have to do is wake up," I say after about ten minutes of this. "Maybe all of this really is just a dream—right from when I first stuck that key in the ignition."

"Except I'm here," Ginny says.

I don't want to say that doesn't make a difference. It could still be a dream.

"There's that," I tell her instead.

"You must be doing something wrong," she says.

Now that she's accepted that I'm doing this, or at least that I'm trying, she's been full of useful suggestions. Unfortunately, they aren't helping any more than my own efforts.

"What were you thinking about when it happened before?" she asks. "Were you really concentrating on the day of the crash . . . on your brother . . ."

I shake my head and her voice trails off.

"I wasn't thinking hard about anything," I say. "And for sure I wasn't looking for a way to live it all over again. I spent most of that other life of mine just trying to forget."

"Then I guess we need to go see Pike."

"I guess we do."

The funny thing is, this need of mine to stop Billy . . . I'm not even sure that this is my unfinished business. If I believe that, then I have to believe that life is preordained, and I don't buy that. We make a difference in the world. For good or bad, whether we want to or not, we make a difference. And I think it's our choices that make the difference.

But I'm not really looking for a Frank Capra moment here, though I'd love to wake up from this.

Instead I find myself at what's left of John Pike's ruin of a shack with the crazy-looking old man himself sitting there on a rocker, the ghost of an old blue tick hound asleep at his feet.

"Been awhile," he says to Ginny.

She nods. "I want you to meet my friend," she says and introduces me.

I can't help myself. I have to ask about the treasure, if it really exists.

"Sure, it does," he says. "Have a look inside."

So I do, but there's nothing there. Just a big mess of moldering books and magazines, old newspapers yellowed and chewed up by mice.

"I don't see it," I say.

"It's right in front of you, boy. The books. The *learning*. You won't find a bigger treasure than that."

The kid I look to be would have been disappointed. And I do feel a little twinge of disappointment myself, because like everybody else, I half-believed those stories. But I understand what he means. I learned the worth of books and knowledge over the years. Mind you, I didn't use them to learn so much as to occupy my mind so that I wouldn't think of other things—things I used to wipe out of my mind with alcohol before I went on the wagon.

"We need your advice," Ginny says when I come back out onto the porch.

And then we tell him the whole sorry tale.

"Can't be done," he says when we finish up. "I've got some ideas about how you did it in the first place, but without a body, you're not going to be able to do it again."

"You're sure about that?"

"Sure as I'm dead, and I'm plenty damn sure about that."

I try not to let my frustration show and look out across the scrub brush lot that fronts what's left of his cabin.

"But that doesn't mean there isn't a solution to this problem of yours," he goes on.

I turn back to look at him, trying not to feel too much hope.

"I've heard stories," he says, "of spirits who ride a living person—take them over and make them do the things that are so hard for us ghosts to do. *Physical* things."

"You mean like possess them?"

He nods. "You just slip into their heads and take over. It works best with someone who's empty—you know, he's got nothing going in his life, nothing to look forward to. They're just waiting for any damn thing to come along and fill them up."

I start to understand what he's telling me, but that won't work with Billy. He's got too much to look forward to. All these other girls he's going to kill . . .

"But it also works on someone you were close to when you were alive," Pike adds. "Works better, maybe."

"Like my brother."

He nods. "But the way I heard it, you only get the one shot at riding somebody. You can't just jump from person to person."

"I'd only need the one shot." I hesitate, then add, "Except how do I know I can get the car to take me back again? I don't even know how it worked in the first place."

"It's not the car that's doing it," Pike says. "I think it's the key."

"What do you mean?"

"Sometimes, if you touch something often enough for luck, all those touches gather up inside the thing to become a real charm, the way riverbanks get beaches when sand drifts up in the curve of the watercourse. It's not planned, it just happens. And not all at once, but slowly, over the years."

"You think I made a charm out of that key?"

"Have you got a better explanation?"

I didn't.

"So," Pike goes on, "you just have to hope the key sitting there in the ignition of that car is the same one you carried around with you for all those years."

"It probably is," Ginny says, "because you didn't get to take it away with you this last time."

Because this last time I died.

"And if that's the case," Pike says, "it's probably the same key you brought back with you from that other life of yours."

If, if, if . . .

"There's only way you're going to find out," he tells me.

Taking over Billy's easier than I think it will be. He's sitting in class at the university and I just sidle up to him and slip right in. Then I get up and walk out of the lecture hall, leaving his books behind. Ginny falls in step beside me and I turn to look at her.

"I can still see you," I say.

"I guess once you know how, it doesn't go away."

"You had a funny look on your face just now."

She nods. "I wasn't sure who it was inside."

She reaches a hand to touch my arm, but it goes right through.

"We better get going," I say. "Before Sarah shows up with her own revenge in mind."

When we get outside, I check Billy's wallet. There's enough money in there to take a cab out to the farm, so that's what we do.

The old man's out in the back forty—we can hear his tractor from here—so we know we won't be disturbed. I get in behind the wheel, but I look at Ginny sitting beside me before I touch the key.

"I don't mean to break my promise," I start to say.

She shakes her head. "It's okay. I'm already dead. Saving these girls is way more important."

"I wish I could go back and save you."

"I wouldn't have listened to you anyway. You'd be just this kid, talking weird."

"If this works, I'm going to look for you when I'm done."

She gives me a sad look.

"I won't know who you are," she says. "All of these years that we've been together won't have happened. Not for me."

"I'll remind you."

"Don't make any more promises."

There's no blame in her voice, but it hurts all the same.

"I can't even kiss you goodbye," I say.

She smiles, the sadness deepening in her eyes.

"I wouldn't want you to," she says. "Not looking like . . . him."

I nod. I reach for the key and turn it, waiting. But nothing happens.

"Do whatever you did the last time," Ginny says.

I think about it until it comes back to me. I turn the key right, then left twice, then quickly back and forth, and damned if the electric charge doesn't come rushing up my arm and the world around me starts to do its rewind thing again.

"Goodbye, Marshall Coe," I hear Ginny say. "I'm going to miss you."

Then she's gone and I'm back in time again, Billy and me, sitting in the car on that long ago afternoon.

8

Here's the thing that none of us considered: if I'm riding Billy, who's going to be inside my body?

I find out pretty quick.

I don't come back to the same moment I did before, where Billy was trying to convince me to let him drive. I come back to where he's already in the driver's seat, about to start up the car. I turn to look beside me and I'm sitting there, which, let me tell you, is freaky enough. But even freakier is, it's Billy looking out of my eyes.

"What the hell . . . ?" he says.

His voice is slurred—from all the alcohol in my body that he's not used to, I guess—and he's totally confused. Well, who can blame him? But I don't give him time to adjust. I start up the car and pull out from behind the barn—my third time making this trip.

"Oh, Jesus," Billy says. "Stop the car, Marsh. I . . . I'm . . . something's wrong . . ."

I just keep on driving.

He reaches out a hand to me, but I shove him against the passenger's door. Hard. His head bangs against the door frame.

He's saying something else, voice rising in panic, but I tune him out because I need to work this through. I thought I'd go back to when I arrived the last time, before I let him get behind the wheel. I'd refuse to let him drive and everything'd go back to the way it's supposed to be.

But obviously, I didn't.

It takes me a moment to figure out why I didn't. It's because when I worked the mojo this time, it was his body turning the key. This was the only point we could return to, when he had *his* hand on the key in the ignition.

What I have to do is figure out what happens next.

If the passenger always dies in the crash that's coming up, does that mean he'll die in my body? Or will we switch back and I'll die again?

I can't take that chance. It's not that I'm scared of dying— I've already been there. It's that I can't take the chance that *he'll* survive.

Then I realize what I have to do. I can't let the crash happen. I don't know how I'll stop him from becoming the killer he's going to be, but that's not something I should be trying to work out while driving this car.

On this road.

On this afternoon.

"Jesus Christ, Marsh!" he yells. "Stop the goddamn car!"

We're driving faster than I realized, but he's fumbling with the door handle anyway, trying to get it open. He's still got his seat belt on. But he could take it off. He could fall out. And at this speed, he could kill himself.

I keep one hand on the wheel, and grab at him.

Turn my gaze back to the road.

And realize we're already into the curve.

How'd we get here so fast?

Billy struggles in my grip. I stomp my foot on the brake but he pulls me at just that moment and I hit the gas pedal instead. I see the flash of the little animal darting out onto the road. I don't know if we run over it or not because right then we're leaving the road, heading straight for that damned oak tree again and I realize I screwed it up this time as well.

9

I get to go to the funeral this time.

My own funeral. In Billy's body. How weird is that?

Not half as weird as things are going to get, I guess. I have to deal with my father's grief. Then there's the whole business of being Billy, only I can't be Billy. I can't become the doctor he was going to be. I don't have it in me. I'm having enough trouble just *pretending* to be him these past few days.

To tell you the truth, I don't know how long I can deal with any of this. I mean, I can't even look in a mirror.

So I don't know what's going to happen, how long I'll last, but I know I have to hang on for a while because I still have some unfinished business. For one thing, there's a girl in the city who needs looking after. I have to get Alessandra away from her old man. But I can't just waltz in and sweep her away. She's only twelve or so at the moment.

Hell, I look to be only sixteen myself.

But there's something else I have to do before I deal with any of that.

After the funeral, I go back to the house with my father. He changes like he's going to work in the fields, but instead he takes down that photo of me and goes out and sits on the porch. Holding the photo. Staring across the fields.

I change, too. I walk around behind the barn to where my old Impala sits. I asked the old man why he had it towed here.

"It's all we've got left of him," he told me.

There's no key in the ignition. I found it in my hand after the crash and I put it in my pocket—just like I did the first time around. And just like in that other life, I'm wearing it on a string around my neck.

Don't ask me why. It just seems important.

I look at the car for a while longer, then walk away, across the fields alongside the house until I get to the county road. I follow it to the dead man's curve, leaving the road when I reach the old oak tree.

Anybody seeing me here is going to think I'm mourning my brother, but I'm not. I'm waiting for Ginny to show up.

I've come each afternoon since the crash.

I don't know if I'll be able to see her, but I call her name and I talk out loud, hoping she's around, that she can at least hear and see me, even if I can't see her. I tell the story of the first time we met, and I urge her to stop living a half life. To finish her business here and go on.

I can't tell if she hears me. I can't tell if she follows my advice or not. So I come back each day and do it all over again.

Today's no different. I walk up to the oak tree and lay my hands on the fresh scars that mar its bark. I say Ginny's name. Once. Twice.

And this time a voice answers me.

"Who are you?"

I turn, and there she is, standing on the side of the road, the same way she was the first time I met her.

"You're here," I say.

And I smile. It's the first time I've smiled in three days. It's so good to see her again.

"You can see me," she says. "You're alive and you can see me."

"Yeah, I can."

"And you can hear me."

I nod. "Come down and sit with me, Ginny. We need to talk."

She studies me for a long moment, then slowly comes down from the road and sits down under the oak. She puts out a hand to touch me, but her fingers go through my arm.

"I thought maybe . . ." she says, but she lets her voice trail off.

Something I can't read moves in her eyes and she looks away. I wait, patient, until she turns back to me.

"I know you," she says. "You're Marshall Coe's little brother."

It's such a small thing, but I'm pleased that she remembers me—remembers *me* by name—and not Billy.

"Yeah. Well, sort of."

"What do you mean, 'sort of'?"

"It's a long story," I tell her.

"The one thing I have a lot of is time," she says.

"I know."

"*How* do you know?"

So I start to tell her, right from the beginning, the way I've just told you.

Sweet Forget-Me-Not

"You don't want to get involved with the likes of them."

I turned to see who'd spoken, feeling a little nervous because I was skipping school, but it was only Ernie, the old guy who did odd jobs around the neighbourhood. He had a little apartment in back of the Seafair Theatre, but I guess he didn't spend much time there because you'd see him out in the streets at all hours of the day and night.

I've heard my parents tut-tutting about him, the way lots of people in the neighbourhood do. Everybody seems to think it's a shame that a person can live their life the way he does, day to day, with no ambition. But I don't see a lack of ambition as that bad a personality trait. I mean, what if you don't have this drive to succeed at something? Are you supposed to pretend you do, just to fit in?

My parents would say yes. That's if they could even understand the question.

"Involved with who?" I asked.

I could hear my mom correcting my grammar in my head. Being an immigrant, she was very particular about how we use the language of her adopted country. I know she means well, but it gets old.

"Don't play the fool with me, boy," Ernie said. "I'm talking about that gaggle of girls you've been staring at for the last ten minutes."

"You can see them?"

"Do I look blind?"

I shook my head. "But nobody else seems to notice them."

"That's because most people *are* blind."

They'd have to be.

It was the colour of them that first attracted my attention, and I don't just mean their clothing or their race. There seemed to be around six of them, but I kept losing count. Their hair was a wild tangle of curls ranging in colour from a rich mauve to shocking pinks. The ones with loose pants had tight tops, the ones with baggy shirts wore tights under them, and they all had clunky shoes that didn't seem to cause them the least bit of a problem as they danced and pirouetted about, as light on their feet as acrobats or ballerinas. The colour of their clothes was as wild as their hair— bright yellows, reds, pinks, and greens—and there wasn't much to them. They were just a gang of tall, skinny girls with narrow features and the same Mediterranean cast to their skin that I have.

"So what are they doing?" I asked as we watched them dance about.

They were singing something, too, but I couldn't make out the words. I could tell it had a beat, though. A little hip-hop, a little rhyming set to a finger-snapping beat.

"What do you think?" Ernie said. "They're having fun."

"I thought maybe they were stoned."

He laughed. "They don't need stimulants to have fun."

Well, they looked totally blissed-out to me, but what did I know? I still couldn't figure out how they could be having such a grand time, dancing and goofing around the way they were—and the way they looked—but nobody seemed to notice. I know people get jaded, but you'd think *somebody* would turn and have a look as they walked by the alley where the girls were having their fun, if only to shake their heads and then go on.

But there was only me, turned the wrong way around on a bus stop bench and getting a crick in my neck. And now Ernie.

"Why did you say I shouldn't get involved with them?" I asked.

"Because they only stay around long enough to break your heart."

"What's that supposed to mean?"

"They're gemmin," Ernie said. "Little mobile histories of a place. Kind of like fairies, if you think of them as the spirits of a place."

"Yeah, right."

He shrugged. "You asked, so I'm telling you."

"Fairies."

"Except they're called gemmin. They soak up stories and memories, and then one day they're all full up and off they go."

I couldn't believe this stupid story of his, but I couldn't help wanting to know more at the same time. Because there was the plain fact that *no one* seemed to notice them but us.

"So where do they go?" I asked.

"I don't know. I just know they go and they don't come back. Not the same ones, anyway."

I gave him a look. "What's that supposed to mean?"

"You're pretty full of questions, boy. Don't you have some-place better to be, like school?"

"I don't like school."

"Yeah, well, I'm with you on that." He shakes his head. "When I think of all the crap they expect you to remember—like it's ever going to be any use unless you become a brain surgeon or an accountant."

"No, I don't mind learning," I said. "I kind of like that part of it."

"Sure," he said. "If it's something you *want* to learn, right? But you can get that out of a library."

I shook my head. "No, I find it all pretty interesting."

He shook his head like he thought *I* was the one who was weird. He's not alone. Can you say nerd? That's me.

"Then what's the problem?" he asked.

"I just don't . . . you know, get along with the other kids much."

He nodded. "You telling them stuff they don't want to hear?"

"It's more like them telling me."

He'd been standing beside me on the sidewalk, but now he took a seat on the bench.

"What's your name?" he asked.

"Ahmad Nasrallah."

"Well, what are they ragging you about? You look like a nice, normal kid."

"No, I look like a terrorist."

He studied me for a long moment, then gave me another nod, a slow one this time.

"Because of the colour of your skin," he said.

"Yeah. And my name. But my family's not from Afghanistan or Iraq or whatever. We're Lebanese. We're not even Muslims— although I guess my parents were before they immigrated. But I was born right here in this city."

"There's nothing wrong being Muslim," Ernie said. "There's bad apples in whatever way you want to group people—doesn't matter if it's religious, political, or social. The big mistake is generalizing."

"Doesn't stop them from doing it."

"Yeah, people are like that." He smiled. "And there's another generalization for you."

"So did you have trouble in school, too?" I asked.

"Oh, yeah. I was like a trouble magnet. And opening my mouth didn't help much either."

"So that's what you meant when you asked if I was telling people things they don't want to hear."

He nodded. "I had me a big mouth, no question. But the real problem was I couldn't stop talking about . . . them."

He didn't look at the gemmin, but I knew who he meant.

I couldn't imagine telling anybody at school about them. Why would I give the kids more ammunition?

"Why'd you do it?" I asked. "You had to know they'd make fun of you."

He shrugged. "It started in grade school, when I didn't know any better and the teasing just followed me through the years— long after I'd stopped talking about it. But the thing is, if anybody asked me straight out, I couldn't lie. Not because of who was asking, but because I thought lying would diminish the gemmin." He gave me a sad smile. "Like in *Peter Pan*, you know?"

I shook my head.

"Every time a kid says they don't believe in fairies, another one of them dies."

"Is that true?"

"I don't think so now. But it seemed possible back then. I didn't realize that they weren't dying. It's hard to see from here, but their eyes are the most amazing sapphire blue that turn to violet as they get filled up with the little histories around them. And once they do fill up, they leave."

I thought about that, then asked, "What did you mean about the same ones not coming back? Who does come back?"

"Coming back's not exactly the right way to describe it. You see those bits of colour that seem to spin off them sometimes, when they're dancing really hard?"

I nodded. "I thought they were ribbons or confetti or something."

"I don't know what they are either. But if you watch one long enough, you'll see it kind of disappears into the ground. I don't know what happens underground, out of our sight, but something does. Either a piece of that colour incubates down there, or a bunch of them gather together, but eventually, when the ones we're looking at are gone, some new gemmin will come sprouting up."

He smiled, a faraway look in his eyes.

"They're just like the fairies I remember in the stories I read as a kid," he went on after a moment. "When they're new, I mean. Tiny, perfect little creatures."

"And then they grow up to be like these?"

The ones we were looking at seemed to be in their early to mid-teens, around my age, which was still fifteen. I wouldn't turn sixteen until next month. Unlike a lot of the girls in school who were already all curves and breasts, the gemmin were skinny, flat-chested, and almost hipless. They could almost be boys, except you knew from their faces that they were girls. And though they didn't have a lot of shape to them, they were still hot, like you'd see in some magazine.

I imagined kissing one of them and felt my neck and face get warm.

"They're really . . . sexy, aren't they?" I found myself saying.

Ernie laughed. "Not to me. I just see a bunch of cute kids. But I remember I felt different when I was your age."

"You're not that old."

But then I had to wonder how old he was. I figured he had to be at least forty, which was older than I could ever imagine being. Your life'd pretty much be over by then. I just had to look at my parents and their friends. They never seemed to have any fun, except every once in awhile at a wedding or something, when they'd get a little goofy after having too much wine.

"I'm old enough to be their father," Ernie said. He said it in a certain tone of voice that made me think, for a moment, that he was going to rub my head, the way Uncle Joe does. "I don't rob cradles, Ahmad."

Whatever.

"So do they live here?" I asked. "In this alley?"

Ernie shook his head. "You'll see them all over the city—different little groups of them—but this bunch usually comes back here. They seem to have laid claim to our neighbourhood, and that Dodge in particular."

He was talking about the junked station wagon that had been abandoned at the back of the alley. You see useless cars like that all the time around this part of town. They'll be in an empty lot or behind some building for a few months, slowly getting stripped of useable parts. Eventually somebody in one of the neighbouring buildings gets the city to have it towed away.

"I've lived here all my life," I said, "so how come I've never seen them before?"

"Maybe you never really needed to."

"What's that supposed to mean?"

He shrugged. "How were you feeling when you first sat down on this bench?"

"I was fine."

"No, really. You told me you were skipping school. That the kids there had been ragging on you."

"Okay. So maybe I was a little pissed off."

"And sad? Or at least feeling hurt?"

"Yeah, whatever."

I didn't know where this was going, but it was making me uncomfortable to talk about it.

"And how do you feel now?" he asked.

"I told you, I feel fine."

"Maybe even a little happy?"

Then I realized what he was getting at. If I was going to be honest, I felt a *lot* better now than when I'd first gotten here. Before I'd noticed the gemmin and sat down, I'd been fantasizing about how I could get back at Joey Draves and the Ross brothers—the ones who were riding me the hardest. They weren't alone, but the other kids that gave me a rough time were just echoing Joey and his gang. Trying to show how they were cool, too. It didn't seem to help them much, but they didn't stop either. The only way it'd ever stop was if Joey and the Ross brothers laid off, and that wasn't going to happen any time soon. It was like I'd become a pet project for them.

But the funny thing was, while the fantasy of getting back at them was still a going concern—sitting there somewhere in my head where the stuff you can't get away from does—right now I couldn't really muster up a whole lot of anger towards them.

"Yeah, I guess," I told Ernie. I wasn't looking at him as I spoke, but at the gemmin. It was hard *not* to look at them. "I feel pretty good, actually."

"I've noticed that over the years," Ernie said. "The people who do seem to become aware of them are the ones that need a little help with the load they're carrying. It doesn't seem to work for everybody who's feeling bad. I've seen depressed people walk right through a crowd of gemmin and never notice them. But when people do, it's usually when they're feeling low."

"And then they start feeling better," I said. "Like magic."

Ernie laughed. "Hell, they *are* magic. But it's not some kind of cure-all. It's more like they give you a respite. A bit of time to regroup and take stock of the big picture, you know?"

I looked at him and shook my head.

"No matter how good a reason a person's got for feeling bad," he said, "a change of perspective is sometimes all you need to get back on track again."

"And that's what they're for?" I asked.

He laughed again. "Not likely. I think the feeling good part is just a side effect of being around them. You know, you take in the pure joy that they seem to find in life and you can't help but feeling a little better yourself. But they're not here for us. They just *are*."

"They're something, all right."

"So sometimes," Ernie went on, "when I run across a person who seems to be feeling pretty down, I try to steer them to wherever the nearest gemmin are hanging out—just in case it can help, you know?"

So he did have an ambition—it was just a weird and useless one that you couldn't talk to anyone about, except another loser like me.

"How'd you figure out all of this stuff?" I asked.

"They told me."

I turned to look at the gemmin, still fooling around in the alley. Singing and dancing. I wondered what they'd tell me if I could get up the nerve to talk to them.

"They like meeting people," Ernie said, as though he was reading my mind. Maybe he was just reading my face. "They like making friends. The trouble is—"

I remembered what he'd said before, and finished it for him: "They end up breaking your heart."

"That pretty much sums it up."

There was a look in his eyes that I'd never seen before and I knew that when he talked about a broken heart it had nothing to do with what you hear in the songs on the Top 40. It wasn't even like when Sandy Lohnes broke up with me last spring because she didn't want to be going steady with somebody whose relatives were probably all terrorists. It wasn't anything she ever said, and I didn't think she actually believed it herself, but we both knew that was the reason all the same. It was what people were saying to her—the black cloud hanging over me starting to include her as well.

I carried a lot of anger around when she dumped me. Sadness, too, but it was nothing like what I saw in Ernie's eyes.

"I think I have to go talk to them anyway," I said.

Ernie nodded. "Yeah. I figured as much."

I wanted to explain it to him, but he got up then and gave me a little salute, first finger tipping away from his brow, and headed off down the sidewalk. It was just as well. I wouldn't have been able to find the words anyway.

It took me awhile to get up my nerve, but finally I pushed myself up from the bench. I shoved my hands deep in the pockets of my cargo pants and kind of shuffled over until I could lean up against the wall, close enough to hear what they were singing. Turned out the words weren't in English. Maybe they couldn't speak English and I wasn't about to try Lebanese.

They noticed me, the way girls notice guys on a street corner, or at the mall, sort of not looking at you, but you can tell they're checking you out. They didn't seem to think I was a total loser—I guess they hadn't been talking to Joey Draves—but I was starting to feel like one anyway. They were just so . . . special. And I'm not, except to my Mom and Dad. And most of the time to my sister—when I wasn't bugging her. Nothing major, just the usual kid-brother stuff.

I was trying to think of a way to just do a quick fadeaway when the one with the brightest pink hair and this big baggy yellow shirt came up and leaned against the wall beside me, mimicking the way I was standing. The others started to giggle and I thought, oh great. It's even going to happen to me here. But then she grinned and took my hands, pulling me over to where the others were still dancing.

I tried to hold back—I'm the definition of two left feet—but she was stronger than she looked.

"Come on," she said. "What are you so scared of?"

Everything, I wanted to tell her.

"I'm not so good," I told her instead. "You know, at dancing and stuff."

"Then I'll have to teach you."

"You don't want to do that."

"But I do. You can see us. That means you could be our friend and we like having friends."

"Yeah, but—"

"And friends have to dance together."

One of the other girls started making this kind of bass-y noise with her mouth, setting a beat. The others kept time with their feet, clunky shoes tapping the pavement. One of them chimed in with a kind of *shouka-shouka* counterrhythm and then the one holding my hands began to sway back and forth.

"Just find the rhythm," she said. "Move your hips. Like this."

She was skinny under that baggy shirt, but she was sexy as all get-out. No way I could do what she was doing—not and look good the way she did. But when I started to shake my head, she slipped behind me and put her hands on my hips, showing me how to find the beat.

"What's your name?" she asked.

Her voice was right in my ear and I could smell her breath. It was sweet and spicy at the same time, nothing like any other girl's I'd ever been this close to before, which so far has only been three. And I never did kiss one of them—I mean, real kissing. We didn't touch tongues.

"I'm Troon," she said when I told her my name.

The other girls chorused strange words that I realized were their names:

"Shivy."

"Mita."

"Omal."

"Neenie."

"Alaween."

And never once lost the music they were making while they did it. Their names became part of the music. I heard my own in there, too, made even more exotic by the sound of their sweet, husky voices.

Troon let go of my hips and came around in front of me again, the other girls circling around as we danced. Or while they danced and I tried.

But I have to admit, while dancing's nothing I'd ever done in public, I'd tried it lots in my bedroom in front of the mirror. Mostly it was just me trying to figure out how not to make too big an ass of myself, just in case I ever got up the nerve to go to a school dance again. But I did it for fun, too. I'd even tried belly dancing.

My sister Suha took it up for a while because it seemed like an interesting way of doing aerobics with the added bonus of putting her in touch with a part of our cultural heritage. She said. I think it was just a way to put on a sexy show at weddings and stuff, but in a way that our parents couldn't say was improper.

So anyway, I tried a couple of those moves with the gemmin, and sure enough, they all squealed with laughter and I wished I could disappear into a crack in the pavement. But then I realized they were laughing with me, not at me, and they all started trying to shake their tummies like I'd just done.

That afternoon ended up being the best fun I'd ever had. Troon was the one who'd first got me dancing with them, but the one who really seemed to take a shine to me was Neenie. She was a little shorter than the rest, which made her about my five-six, and had the most perfect sky-blue eyes I've ever seen. Her hair was a tangle of tiny mauve braids and she was wearing big red cargo pants and a tight little pinkish top that showed off her belly button.

And when I finally left to go home for supper, she's the one who came up and gave me a kiss.

"You'll come back, won't you?" she asked.

I was still feeling the press of her body against me and the kiss that was tingling on my lips, and I couldn't find my voice. So I just nodded.

Somebody saw me that afternoon, dancing in the alley with the gemmin, except they didn't see the gemmin, only me. Dancing by myself beside a junked out old stationwagon.

I don't know who it was, but Joey got hold of the story and by noon it was all over the school. I guess it made a change from them calling me "Osama," or, the height of Joey's stupid repartee, "Al Kida," but I didn't feel any better.

We were out in the schoolyard and they were all in a loose circle around me. I just kept trying to walk away, but whatever part of the circle I approached closed tight as soon as I got near it. Then Joey said something about me dancing with some wet dream in my head and I lost it. And I understood what Ernie'd meant about having to tell the truth about the gemmin, because doing otherwise diminished even the idea of them. At least in my head.

I didn't say anything, but I took a swing at Joey. He ducked it easily and gave me a shove that knocked me off my feet. A moment later we were grappling—I was just trying to hold on to him so that he wouldn't be able to hit me—but then we got busted by Mr. Finn and sent to the principal's office.

Once we were there, Mr. Taggart started lecturing us about how they had zero tolerance for violence on school property. I wondered where the zero tolerance was when Joey and his buddies were ragging on me all the time, but I knew there was no point in bringing it up. That's the way it always goes. Guys like Joey *always* get away with it. Mr. Taggart probably agreed with Joey that I should just go back to Afghanistan even though I'd never even been there before.

To get him to shut up, I told Mr. Taggart that I'd started it.

That got me a three-day suspension and I knew my parents were going to kill me. Though maybe that was the least of my worries, since the last thing Joey said as we were walking down the hall—him on his way to class, me going home to face the music—was, "This isn't over, Osama."

And I knew it wasn't. I guess the best thing about the suspension was that I was going to have three days before he beat the crap out of me—five actually, I realized, since today was a Tuesday. The worst thing was that I got grounded for two weeks. My parents were really disappointed in me and Dad was into a major lecture before Suha spoke up for me.

"You should be proud of him for standing up for himself,"

she said, not realizing that this time I'd been standing up for the gemmin. "You should hear the things they call us. Ahmad gets it way worse than me."

"What kind of things?" Dad asked.

I saw him deflate as Suha told him about the whole terrorist business that had been dogging us since 9/11 and realized that he'd probably been the brunt of some of that same crap himself. But then he straightened in his chair.

"Is this true?" he asked me.

I shrugged.

"First thing in the morning," he said, "I'm going to have a talk with that principal of yours."

"Dad, no!" Suha and I cried at the same time.

It took us awhile to convince him that talking to the principal would only make things worse, but finally, he nodded his reluctant agreement.

"Still, fighting's not the answer," he told me. "I want you to remember that."

"I will," I said, wondering what he'd have to say when I came back from school on Monday after Joey'd made good his threat.

"So you're still grounded. And no TV for a week. Suha will get your homework and I expect you to study here at home, just as if you were in school."

The studying part wasn't hard. I wasn't lying to Ernie when I told him that I like learning. But it's hard to do it on your own, all day long. The second day of my suspension I went out and sat on the fire escape that we use as a balcony and stared down the alleyway, wishing I could be with the gemmin. But I knew better than to try to sneak off. One of the neighbours would see me and they'd tell my parents and then who knew how long I'd be grounded.

So I sat there on the steps, feeling sorry for myself, when I

suddenly heard a bang on the metal steps behind me, like something big had just fallen onto them. I turned, my heart pounding
because—don't ask me how he'd get there—I was sure it was
Joey. Except it wasn't. It was Neenie. I don't know how she got
there either, but the noise I'd heard was her jumping on the fire
escape to get my attention.

"You didn't come see us," she said.

"I couldn't."

"But you said you would. I thought you liked me."

"I *do* like you. It's just . . ."

"Complicated," she finished for me and came to sit on the
step with me. "That's the trouble with being a people. *Everything's* complicated."

"It's not for you?"

"No, should it be?"

I shook my head. "No, I'm glad it's simple for you. I wish it
was simple for me."

"Make it simple."

I smiled. "Easier said than done."

"Then say it at least."

It took me a moment, but then I realized she was asking me to
tell her my problems. I remembered what Ernie had said, how the
gemmin collected stories, so I thought, why not? She was probably
the only person I could tell my troubles to that wouldn't have to
feel the weight of them because they didn't touch her life.

When I was done she locked that perfect blue gaze of hers on
me. Then she leaned close and kissed me. Long. Tongue slipping
into my mouth. When we came up for air I was feeling flushed and
had to hold my legs together so that she wouldn't see the growing
bulge in my pants.

Neenie licked her lips. "You taste good," she said.

"You do, too."

She did. All sweet and spicy, like her breath. I guess all the
gemmin were like that. Must be their diet.

"I wish you felt better," she added.

Right now I felt like I was in heaven and I told her so.

She laughed. "Were you ever there?"

"No, but it's supposed to be a place where everything's perfect and that's how I feel right now."

"That's good. I feel heaveny, too."

I don't suppose anyone's ever had a stranger girlfriend, except Ernie, I guess. We spent that afternoon together, moving from the fire escape into my room. I played her some CDs, which she liked a lot, humming along and tapping her toes on the floor. I wondered if it was bothering Mrs. Robins downstairs, but she never came up to complain—and trust me, she would have.

So we listened to music and we necked and we talked and then necked some more. The afternoon went by in a blur. It took her awhile to understand the concept of being grounded, but once she did, she promised she'd come back the next day. And she did. It was harder on the weekend because Suha was in and out of the apartment all day and my parents were home, but she snuck into my room at night and we lay on the bed whispering and kissing until we fell asleep. I never had to worry about anyone catching her in there with me in the morning because nobody but me could see her anyway.

Then came Monday and I had to go to school. Dad reminded me about not fighting and I reminded him that I understood. Mom's eyes were a little misty as she sent us off. She didn't know about Joey's threat, but I guess she didn't like the idea of her kids getting treated badly.

It wasn't so bad for Suha—maybe because she was a girl. She wasn't my idea of pretty—I mean, God, she was my sister—but I knew guys were always totally checking her out. And it helped that her boyfriend threatened to beat the crap out of Joey the first time he tried to do his little game on her.

But I didn't have anyone to stand up for me. The few friends I'd had before all of this started were as small or smaller than me. You couldn't miss us. We were the nerd squad that every school has, and while we all desperately wanted to be part of the cool crowd, we spent most of our time just trying to not be noticed. It was safer that way.

Joey waited until after school to make good on his threat.

Suha went off to the mall with some friends, so I had to walk home by myself. I was just as glad. There was no way to stop this from happening, so I'd rather she wasn't there when it did. Not just because I didn't want her to see me humiliated, but to keep her safe in case things got out of hand. She did ask me if I wanted company on the way home, but I told her no.

"I think he's just going to let it slide," I told her, and conveniently didn't mention the dark looks Joey'd been giving me all day. "He didn't even rag me at lunch."

"Okay. If you think you'll be all right."

"I'll be fine."

So I was alone when they herded me into the empty lot behind that strip of thrift stores and junk shops on Grasso Street. People kept saying condos were going up there, but they'd been saying that for years. I sure wished there were condos now, but I don't suppose it would have mattered. They'd just have gotten me in some other alley instead.

Joey led the festivities, the way he always did. With him were Jack and Marty Ross. Phil Kluge. A couple of other guys. More than enough to really hurt me.

I'm useless in a fight—just look what happened last week— but I wasn't going to go down without a struggle. It's not that I was feeling brave. I was probably more scared than I've ever been. But I was mad, too.

They started shoving me back and forth between them. I took a swing at Marty, but he just grinned and pushed me away. And then I saw the last thing in the world I wanted to see: the gemmin, giggling and laughing as they approached us from the far side of the lot.

"Go away!" I cried.

"Not likely, Osama," Joey said.

But I wasn't talking to him and his friends. I didn't want the gemmin getting hurt. I didn't want Neenie to see me get beat up. But then I remembered, the gemmin were invisible to most people. So they wouldn't get hurt. They'd just see me humiliated.

Well, they wouldn't see me go down without a fight.

I charged Joey, but he stepped aside and stuck out his foot. And down I went.

"You want to lick my shoe, raghead?" Joey asked.

Before I could get up, they all moved in, ready to kick the crap out of me. But suddenly the gemmin were among them.

The thing I hadn't considered was that just because they were invisible to most people didn't mean they weren't there. Neenie bent down behind Joey and Mita gave him a shove. Down *he* went. Troon had a stick in her hand and she whacked it so hard against Phil's knee that the stick broke. Phil went down, too. So did the Ross brothers and the other two guys as Omal and the other girls went after them. And once they were all down, the gemmin kicked them with their clunky shoes. In the side. On the arm and thigh and leg. Hurting them, but not damaging them. Not the way they'd have hurt me.

Shivy and Alaween ran over to me and pulled me to my feet.

"Time to go," Troon said.

And off we went.

That night when Neenie and I sat together on the fire escape, I wondered aloud if my escape was going to make things better or worse. Better would be if they'd all just ignore me and leave me alone. Worse would be if they got me some place where I wasn't about to be rescued and they really went to town.

"They won't bother you," Neenie said. "We told them you were haunted and they had to leave you alone."

"I thought most people couldn't see you."

"They can't. Only the special people like you can do it on your own. But we can be seen if want to be. And we can be heard. We went back and found them in their homes and whispered into their ears." She grinned. "I gave the meanest one a good whack on the back of the head when he wouldn't listen."

"So you guys aren't all fun and dancing," I said.

"Oh, yes, we are."

"But . . ."

She laughed. "We can be fierce, too."

"Lucky for me."

"No," she said, snuggling closer. "Lucky for me. I can't have my boyfriend too bruised to hold me."

I put my other arm around her and pulled her tightly against me.

"Or his lips to sore to kiss me," she added.

So I showed her that wasn't the case at all.

I guess she was right. I went to school the next day feeling about as nervous as I've ever felt, but Joey and his friends wouldn't even look at me, except when they thought I wouldn't notice, and then I saw something in their faces that I'd only ever seen on the faces of their victims: fear.

I'd like to say everything was perfect from there on out, but I guess life just doesn't work that way.

October turned into November and it started to get colder, especially at night. I worried about Neenie and the other gemmin, nesting in their junked car at night, but she assured me that the cold didn't bother them.

"Don't be such a worrywart," she told me. "We're not like you, scared of the cold."

But for all the strange way they lived and the fact that they were invisible to the world at large, it was hard to think of them as not like me.

Neenie gave me a potted flower for my birthday—a little blue forget-me-not. I don't know where she got it, at that time of year.

"It's so you'll think of me," she said.

"I'm *always* thinking about you."

"You're so sweet."

November became December.

Around the middle of the month, Neenie and I were walking up Flood Street after school, when she paused by the Chinese grocery store to eavesdrop on a conversation between Mrs. Li and one of her customers. I kept walking, waiting for Neenie a little farther down the block. Being invisible, she could get away standing beside them while they talked, but I sure couldn't.

When she joined me, tucking her hand in my arm, she lifted her face for a kiss. I was happy to oblige, but then I realized that something had changed about her. It had happened so gradually that I'd never noticed. Those blue-blue eyes of hers were almost violet now and I remembered what Ernie had told me, all those months ago.

Something tightened uncomfortably, deep in my chest.

"You . . . are you going away?" I asked.

"I have to go away," she said. "That's what we do. We're here and then we go away. You do, too."

"But . . ."

"I know. You're here walking around ever so much longer than we are. But it's still the same."

"You . . . die?

She frowned, still looking so pretty. "If you mean, do we move from one world to another, then yes. We do. But we don't think of it like that at all. It's just a part of the whole long story of our lives."

"How . . . how long do we have?"

"We're leaving when the days start to get longer again."

She meant the winter solstice. It was less than two weeks away.

I thought knowing this would change everything, and I did brood about it when we weren't together, but it's impossible to have a heavy heart when you're actually around the gemmin. Ernie was right about that, too.

On the night of the winter solstice, there came a tapping on my window and I looked up to see Neenie's face at my window. I don't know how she got up to a third-floor window, but I hurried over to open it and let her in. A gust of cold wind rushed inside and made me shiver. Neenie leaned in, resting her elbows on the sill.

"We're going," she said. "Come meet me on the roof."

Then she did this sort of Spider-Man swing and went monkeying up the side of my building. I didn't hesitate. I put on a coat and shoes and snuck out of the apartment, heading for the stairs.

I thought we'd said goodbye this afternoon when I saw the group of them in the alley by their car. The parting hadn't been hard—my sadness pushed away by their presence—but I'd spent the evening feeling bleaker and bleaker before she showed up at my window.

She was waiting for me on the roof, standing out of the wind beside the little structure that's up there enclosing the top of the stairs. I shivered in the wind as I stepped out the door and joined her, knowing she'd picked this spot for my sake, not hers. She was still just wearing her baggy pants and that little shirt that showed her stomach. The only tracks in the snow leading to where we stood were mine.

"There's something wrong inside me," she said. "I don't know what it is. It feels big and heavy and sometimes it makes it hard to breathe." She lifted her hand to her eyes. "And tears keep wanting to leak out of my eyes."

I knew exactly what she meant. I'd been feeling that way all night.

"Is this what sadness feels like?" she asked.

"That's what it feels like for me."

"It's funny. I've heard about it in a lot of the stories I've collected, but I never knew what it felt like before." She sighed. "It's so heavy."

"I know."

I put my arms around her and held her close. I'd been trying not to cry all night myself.

"It's weighing me down," she said into my shoulder, her sweet, spicy breath lifting to my nose. "It's so heavy that I don't think I can go."

I felt my heart lift. But then she added:

"The others will have to go on without me."

"But . . ."

I couldn't imagine her on her own. The gemmin were such a close-knit group. Neenie and I had spent a lot of time together, but most of the time we were with the others. I think they needed to be together because I'd noticed that when Neenie and I spent too long a time away from the others, Neenie would start to get quieter and quieter. No less sweet, no less loving. But a stillness would gather around her that became poignant and unfamiliar.

"Troon said you could help me," she said. She lifted her face to look into my eyes. "Is it true? Can you help me feel not so heavy?"

I didn't want to, but I knew what I had to do. I had to let her go.

"I love you, Neenie," I told her. "And I'll always remember you. But you have to go."

"Do you want me to go?"

I shook my head. "But you have to. It's . . ." I had to swallow. "What you do."

"It is, isn't it?" she said in a small voice.

When she looked up, those violet eyes of hers were shiny with tears, reflecting the streetlights from below. I nodded.

"And you really love me, like people do?"

"I do."

"And you'll really remember me forever and ever and always?"

"I really will."

She gave me a small smile. "I still feel sad."

"Yeah, me, too. But . . . I feel glad, too. I would never want to have missed out meeting you and knowing you and loving you. You're the best thing that ever happened to me."

"But now I'm going. Doesn't that take away from the happiness?"

I shook my head. "Nothing can take that away."

We held each other for a long moment, the wind rushing across the roof, but not touching us. Then I felt a presence. I turned and the others were there. Troon and Alaween. Mita and Omal and Shivy.

Troon walked up to me and kissed me on the brow.

"Thank you," Troon said. "We would have missed her so terribly. And she . . . she would have . . ."

"I know," I said.

One by one the others came up and gave me a kiss and a hug. And then there was just my Neenie.

"You think of me, too," I told her.

"Oh, I couldn't not," she said. "You're the biggest part of all the stories I carry inside me."

Then she kissed me, too, long and hard and sweet.

And they were gone.

I stood there, staring across the city, alone except for the wind, then I went back downstairs to my bedroom.

Ernie was wrong, I thought, as I sat at my desk. They don't break your heart. They fill it up and the memory of that never goes away. Not unless you let it.

I took out a pad and a pen and I started to write.

I went to Ernie's apartment on Boxing Day. I brought him a wrapped-up box with some of my mom's baklava in it and his face lit up with pleasure when he took off the wrapping and opened the box.

"I can't remember the last time somebody gave me a Christmas present," he said.

He took me into his kitchen and made us some tea. We talked awhile, about the neighbourhood. Like him, I'd learned to pay attention to all the small stories that ebbed and flowed through its blocks—something we'd learned from the gemmin. It was just a natural part of our lives now.

"They're gone again," he said after awhile.

I nodded. "They left on the solstice."

"Any regrets?"

"Not one. No, maybe one. That I couldn't go with them."

"Yeah, I know that feeling." He hesitated for a moment, then leaned forward across the kitchen table. "Don't end up like me, Ahmad. Don't let this define your life. The neighbourhood doesn't need another guy like me."

"Not even when you're gone?"

"Hey, I'm not that old."

"I know." I looked down at my tea, then back at him. "Just before Christmas break my English teacher gave me this flyer . . . about a workshop that's going to be at the library in the new year."

"What kind of workshop?"

"For people who want to be writers. It's being given by this local writer named Christy Riddell, so I took out a couple of his books from the library, and you know what? He's got a story in one of them about the gemmin. He didn't see them, but a friend of his did and he wrote about it."

"So you're going to be a writer?"

"I don't know. I'm going to try. My parents'll hate the idea. They're pretty set on me being a doctor or a lawyer. Somebody important."

"Maybe they'll surprise you."

"Maybe."

"Are you going to write about the gemmin?"

"I'm going to write about all the things that people don't pay attention to."

Ernie smiled. "So am I going to be in the story?"

"Yeah, but don't worry. I'll change your name."

"Don't," he said. "I'd be proud to be in your story. Only . . ."

"Only what?" I asked when his voice trailed off.

"Could you mention Mixie?"

"Was she the one you fell in love with?"

He nodded. "They're all dear to me—from the first ones I met to every new bunch that comes along. But I think you only ever get that one special connection."

"I'll mention her," I told him.

And I did.

That Was Radio Clash

December 23, 2002

"Why so down?" the bartender asked the girl with the dark blue hair.

She looked up, surprised, maybe, that anyone had even noticed.

At night, the Rhatigan was one of the last decent live jazz clubs in town. The kind of place where you didn't necessarily know the players, but one thing the music always did was swing. There was none of your smooth jazz or other ambient crap here.

But during the day, it was like any other low-end bar, a third full of serious drinkers and no one that looked like her.

"Joe Strummer died yesterday," she said.

Alphonse is a good guy. He used to play the keys until an unpaid debt resulted in some serious damage to his melody hand. He can still play, but where he used to soar, now he just walks along on the everyday side of genius with the rest of us. And while maybe he can't express the way things feel with his music anymore, the heart that made him one of the most generous players you could sit in with is still beating inside that barrel chest of his.

"I'm sorry," he said. "Was he a friend of yours?"

The hint of a smile tugged at the corner of her mouth, but the sadness in her eyes didn't change.

"Hardly," she said. "It's just that he was the heart and soul of the only band that matters and his dying reminds me of how everything that's good eventually fades away."

"The only band that matters," Alphonse repeated, obviously not getting the reference. In his head he was probably running through various Monk or Davis lineups.

"That's what they used to call the Clash."

"Oh, I remember them. What was that hit of theirs?" It took him a moment, but then he half-sang the chorus and title of "Should I Stay or Should I Go."

She nodded. "Except that was more Mick Jones's. Joe's lyrics were the ones with a political agenda."

"I don't much care for politics," Alphonse said.

"Yeah, most people don't. And that's why the world's as fucked up as it is."

Alphonse shrugged and went to serve a customer at the other end of the bar. The blue-haired girl returned her attention to her beer, staring down into the amber liquid.

"Did you ever meet him?" I asked.

She looked up to where I was sitting a couple of bar stools away. Her eyes were as blue as her hair, such a vibrant colour that I figured they must be contacts. She had a pierced eyebrow—the left—and pale skin, but by the middle of winter, most people have pretty much lost their summer colour. She was dressed like she was auditioning for a black-and-white movie: black jersey, cargos and boots, a gray sweater. The only colour was in her hair. And those amazing eyes.

"No," she said. "But I saw them play at the Standish in '84."

I smiled. "And you were what? Five years old?"

"Now you're just sucking up."

And unspoken, but implied in those few words was, You don't have a chance with me.

But I never thought I did. I mean, look at me. A has-been trumpet player who lost his lip. Never touched the glory Alphonse did when he played—not on my own—but I sat in with musicians who did.

But that's not what she'd be seeing. She'd be seeing one more lost soul with haunted eyes, trying to drown old sorrows in a pint of draught. If she was in her teens when she caught the Clash at the Standish, she'd still only be in her mid- to late-thirties now, ten years my junior. But time passes differently for people like her and people like me. I looked half again my age, and shabby. And I knew it.

No, all I was doing here was enjoying the opportunity for a little piece of conversation with someone who wasn't a drunk, or what she thought me to be: on the prowl.

"I knew him in London," I said. "Back in the seventies when we were all living in squats in Camden Town."

"Yeah, right."

I shrugged and went on as though she hadn't spoken. "I remember their energy the most. They'd play these crap gigs with speakers made out of crates and broomstick mike stands. Very punk—lots of noise and big choppy chords." I smiled. "And not a hell of a lot of chords either. But they already had a conscience— not like the Pistols, who were only ever in it for the money. Right from the start they were giving voice to a whole generation that the system had let down."

She studied me for a moment.

"Well, at least you know your stuff," she said. "Are you a musician?"

I nodded. "I used to play the trumpet, but I don't have the lip for it anymore."

"Did you ever play with him?"

"No, I was in an R&B cover band in the seventies, but times were hard and I ended up living in the squats for a while, same as him. The closest I got to playing the punk scene was when I was in a ska band, and later doing some Two Tone. But the music I loved to play the most was always jazz."

"What's your name?"

"Eddie Ramone."

"You're kidding."

I smiled. "No, and before you ask, I got my name honestly— from my dad."

"I'm Sarah Blue."

I glanced at her hair. "So which came first?"

"The name. Like you, it came with the family."

"I guess people who knew you could really say they knew the Blues."

"Ha ha."

"Sorry."

" 'Sokay."

I waited a moment, then asked, "So is there more to your melancholy then the loss of an old favourite musician?"

She shrugged. "It just brought it all home to me, how that night at the Standish was, like, one of those pivotal moments in my life, only I didn't recognize it. Or maybe it's just that that's when I started making a lot of bad choices." She touched her hair. "It's funny, but the first thing I did when I heard he'd died was put the eyebrow piercing back in and dye my hair blue like it was in those days—by way of mourning. But I think I'm mourning the me I lost as much as his passing."

"We can change our lives."

"Well, sure. But we can't change the past. See, that night I hooked up with Brian. I thought he was into all the things I was. I wanted to change the world and make a difference. Through music, but also through activism."

"So you played?"

"Yeah. Guitar—*electric* guitar—and I sang. I wrote songs, too."

"What happened?"

"I pissed it all away. Brian had no ambition except to party hearty, and that whole way of life slipped into mine like a virus. I never even saw the years slide away."

"And Brian?"

"I dumped him after a couple of years, but by then I'd just lost my momentum."

"You could still regain it."

She shook her head. "Music's a young person's game. I do what I can in terms of being an environmental and social activist, but the music was the soul of it for me. It was everything. Whatever I do now, I just feel like I'm going through the motions."

"You don't have to be young to make music."

"Maybe not. But whatever muse I had back in those days pissed off and left me a long time ago. Believe me, I've tried. I used to get home from work and pick up my guitar almost every day, but the spark was just never there. I don't even try anymore."

"I hear you," I said. "I never had the genius—I just saw it in others. And when you know what you *could* be doing, when the music in your head's so far beyond what you can pull out of your instrument . . ."

"Why bother."

I gave a slow nod, then studied her for a moment. "So if you could go back and change something, is that what it would be? You'd go to that night and go your own way instead of hooking up with this Brian guy?"

She laughed. "I guess. Though I'd have to *apply* myself as well."

"I can send you back."

"Yeah, right."

I didn't take my gaze from those blue eyes of hers. I just repeated what I'd said. "I can send you back."

She let me hold her gaze for a couple of heartbeats, then shook her head.

"You almost had me going there," she said.

"I can send you back," I said a third time.

Third time's the charm and she looked uneasy.

"Send me back in time."

I nodded.

"To warn myself."

"No. *You'd* go back, with all you know now. And it's not really back. Time doesn't run in a straight line, it all happens at the same time. Past, present, future. It's like this is you now." I touched my left shoulder. "And this is you then." I touched the end of a finger on my left hand. "If I hold my arm straight, it seems linear, right?"

She gave me a dubious nod.

"But really"—I crooked my left arm so that my finger was touching my shoulder—"the two times are right beside each other. It's not such a big jump."

"And you can send me there?"

I nodded. "On one condition."

"What's that?"

"You come back here on this exact same day and ask for me."

"Why?"

"Because that's how it works."

She shook her head. "This is nuts."

"Nothing to lose, everything to gain."

"I guess . . ."

I knew I almost had her, so I smiled and said, "Should you stay or should you go?"

Her blue gaze held mine again, then she shrugged. Picking up her beer, she chugged the last third down, then set the empty glass on the table.

"What the hell," she said. "How does it work?"

I slipped off my stool and closed the few steps between us.

"You think about that night," I said. "Think about it hard. Then I put two fingers on each of your temples—like this. And then I kiss your third eye."

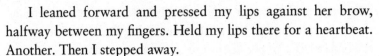

I leaned forward and pressed my lips against her brow, halfway between my fingers. Held my lips there for a heartbeat. Another. Then I stepped away.

She looked at me for a long moment, before standing up. She didn't say a word, but they never do. She just laid a couple of bills on the bar to pay for her drink and walked out the door.

December 23, 2002

"I feel like I should know you," the bartender said when the girl with the dark blue hair walked into the bar and pulled up a stool.

"My name's Sarah Blue. What's yours?"

"Alphonse," he said and grinned. "And you're really Sarah Blue?" He glanced towards the doorway. "I thought you big stars only traveled with an entourage."

"All I've got is a cab waiting outside. And I'm not such a big star."

"Yeah, right. Like 'Take It to the Streets' wasn't the big hit of—when was it? Summer of '89."

"You've got a good memory."

"It was a good song."

"Yeah, it was. I never get tired of playing it. But my hit days were a long time ago. These days I'm just playing theatres and clubs again."

"Nothing wrong with that. So what can I get you?"

"Actually, I was expecting to meet a guy in here today. Do you know an Eddie Ramone?"

"Sure, I do." He shook his head. "I should have remembered."

"Remembered what?"

"Hang on."

He went to a drawer near the cash and pulled out a stack of

envelopes held together with a rubber band. Flipping through them, he returned to where she was sitting and laid one out on the bar in front of her. In an unfamiliar hand was written:

Sarah Blue
December 23, 2002

"Do those all have names and dates on them?" she asked.
"Every one of them."
He showed her the top one. It was addressed to:

Jonathan Block
January 27, 2003

"You think he'll show?" she asked.
"You did."
She shook her head. "What's this all about?"
"Damned if I know. People just drop these off from time to time and sooner or later someone shows up to collect it."
"It's not just Eddie?"
"No. But most of the time it's Eddie."
"And he's not here?"
"Not today. Maybe he tells you why in the letter."
"The letter. Right."
"I'll leave you to it," Alphonse said.
He walked back to where he'd left the drawer open and dropped the envelopes in. When he looked up, she was still watching him.
"You want a drink?" he asked.
"Sure. Whatever's on tap that's dark."
"You've got it."
She returned her attention to the letter, staring at it until Alphonse returned with her beer. She thanked him, had a sip, then slid her finger into the top of the envelope and tore it open. There

was a single sheet inside, written in the same unfamiliar script that was on the envelope. It said:

Hello Sarah,

Well, if you're reading this, I guess you're a believer now. I sure hope your life went where you wanted it to go this time.

Funny thing that might amuse you. I was talking to Joe, back in the Camden Town days, and I asked him if he had any advice for a big fan who'd be devastated when he finally went to the big gig in the sky.

The first thing he said was, "Get bent."

The second was, "You really think we're ever going to make it?"

When I nodded, he thought for a moment, then said, "You tell him or her—it's a her?—tell her it's never about the player, is it? It's always about the music. And the music never dies."

And if she wanted to be a musician? I asked him.

"Tell her that whatever she takes on, stay in for the duration. Maybe you can just bang out a tune or a lyric, maybe it takes you forever. It doesn't matter how you put it together. All that matters is that it means something to you, and you play it like it means something to you. Anything else is just bollocks."

I'm thinking, if you got your life straight this time, you'd probably agree with him.

But now to business. First off, the reason I'm not here to see you is that this isn't the same future I sent you back from. That one still exists, running alongside this one, but it's closed to you because you're living that other life now. And you know there's just no point in us meeting again, because we've done what needed to be done.

At least we did it for you.

If you're in the music biz now, you know there's no such thing as a free ride. What I need you to do is: pass it on. You know how to do it. All you've got to decide is who.

Eddie

Sarah read it twice before she folded the letter up, returned it to the envelope, and stowed it in the pocket of her jacket. She had some more of her beer. Alphonse approached as she was setting her glass back down on the bar top.

"Did that clear it up for you?" he asked.

She shook her head.

"Well, that's Eddie for you. The original man of mystery. He ever start in on his time travel yarns with you?"

She shook her head again, but only because she wasn't ready to admit it to anyone. To do so didn't feel right, and that feeling had made her keep it to herself through all the years.

Alphonse held out his right hand. "He wanted to send me back to the day before I broke this—said I could turn my life around and live it right this time."

"And . . . did you?"

Alphonse laughed. "What does it look like?"

Sarah smiled. Of course, he hadn't. Not in this world. But maybe in one running parallel to it . . .

She thought about that night at the Standish, so long ago. The Clash playing and she was dancing, dancing, so happy, so filled with music. And she was straight, too—no drinks, no drugs that night—but high all the same. On the music. And then right in the middle of a blistering version of "Clampdown," her head just . . . *swelled* with this impossible lifetime that she'd never, she *couldn't* have lived.

But she knew she'd connect with a guy named Brian. And she did.

And she *knew* how it would all go downhill from there, so after the concert, when they were leaving the theatre from a side door, she blew him off. And he got pissed off and gave her a shove that knocked her down. He looked at her, sobered by what he'd done, but she waved him off. He hesitated, then walked away, and she just sat there in the alley, thinking she was going crazy. Wanting to cry.

And then someone reached a hand to her to help her up.

"You okay there?" a voice with a British accent asked.

And she was looking into Joe Strummer's face. The Joe Strummer she'd seen on stage. But superimposed over it, she saw Joe Strummers that were still to come.

The one she'd seen fronting the Pogues in . . . some other life.

The one she'd seen fronting the Mescaleros . . .

The one who'd die of a heart attack at fifty years young . . .

"You want me to call you a cab?" he asked.

"No. No, I'm okay. Great gig."

"Thanks."

On impulse, she gave him a kiss, then stepped back. Away. Out of his life. Into her new one.

She blinked, realizing that Alphonse was still standing by her. How long had she been spaced out?

"Well . . ." she said, looking for something to say. "Eddie seemed like a nice guy to me."

Alphonse nodded. "He's got a big heart. He'll give you the shirt off his back. Hasn't got much of a lip these days, but he still sits in with the band from time to time. You can't say no to a guy like that and he never tries to showboat, like he thinks he plays better than he can. He keeps it simple and puts the heart into what he's playing."

"Maybe I'll come back and catch him one night."

"Door's always open during business hours, Miss Blue."

"Sarah."

"Sarah, then. You come back any time."

He left to serve a new customer and Sarah looked around the bar. No one stood out to her—the way she assumed she had to Eddie—so she'd have to come back.

She put a couple of bills on the bar top to cover the cost of her beer and went out to look for her cab. As she got into the backseat, she found herself hoping that Eddie had made himself at least one world where he'd got his lip back. That was the only reason she could think that he kept passing along the magic of a second chance—paying back his own attempts at getting it right.

It was either that, or he was an angel.

January 27, 2003

Alphonse smiled when she came in. When he started to draw her a draught, she shook her head.

"I'll have a coffee if you've got one," she said.

"We don't get much call for coffee, even at this time of day, so it's kind of grungy. Let me put on a fresh pot."

He busied himself at the coffee machine, throwing out the old grounds, inserting a filter full of new coffee.

"So what brings you in so early?" he asked when he turned back to her.

"I can't get those envelopes out of my head."

"The . . . oh, yeah. They're a bit of a puzzle all right. But I can't let you look at them."

"I'm not asking. But when you were giving me mine, I saw the date on the one on the top of the stack."

"Today's date," Alphonse guessed.

She nodded. "Do you mind if I hang around and wait?"

"Not at all. But it could be a long haul."

" 'Sokay. I've got the time."

She sat chatting with Alphonse for a while, then retired to

one of the booths near the stage with her second cup of coffee. Pulling out her journal, she did some sketches of the bar, the empty stage, Alphonse at work. The sketches were in pictures and words. At some point they might find a melody and swell into a song. Or they might not. It didn't matter to her. Doodling in her journal was just something she always did—a way to occupy time on the road and provide touchstones for her memory.

Jonathan Block didn't show up until that evening, after she'd had a surprisingly good Cajun stew and the band was starting to set up. He looked nothing like what she'd expected—not that she'd had any specific visual in mind. It was just that he looked like a street person. Medium height, gaunt features, a few days worth of stubble and greasy hair, shabby clothes. She'd expected someone more . . . successful.

She waited until he'd collected his envelope and had a chance to read it before approaching him.

"I guess your replay didn't turn out," she said.

He gave her a look that was half wary, half confused.

"What do you mean?" he asked.

She pulled out her own envelope, creased and wrinkled from living in her pocket for over a month, and showed it to him.

"Do you feel like talking?" she asked. "I'll buy you a drink."

He hesitated, then shrugged. "Sure. I'll have a ginger ale."

She got one for him from Alphonse, then led Jonathan back to her booth.

"What did you want to talk about?" he asked.

"You have to ask? I mean, this, all of this . . ." She laid her envelope on the Formica tabletop between them. "It's just so strange."

He gave a slow nod and laid his own down beside his drink.

"But it's real, isn't it?" he said. "The letters prove that."

"What happened to you? Why didn't it work out?"

"What makes you think it didn't?"

"I'm sorry. It's just . . . the way you . . . you know . . ."

"No, I should be the one apologizing. It was a fair question." He looked past her for a moment, then returned his gaze to hers. "It worked for me and it didn't. I just didn't think it through carefully enough. I should have focused on a point in time *before* I got drunk—before I even had a problem with drinking. But I didn't. So when I went back the three years, suddenly I'm in the car again, pissed out of my mind, and I know that the other car's going to come around the corner, and I know I'm going to hit it, and I know it's too late to just pull over."

He wasn't telling her much, but Sarah was able to fill in the details for herself.

"Oh, how horrible," she said.

"Yeah, it wasn't very bright on my part. But hey, who'd have ever thought that a thing like that would even work? When he kissed me on my forehead I thought he was just some freaky guy getting some weird little thrill. I was going to take a swing at him, but then I was there. Back in the car. On that night."

"What happened?"

"Well, the good thing was, even drunk as I was, I knew what was coming and whatever else I might have been, I wasn't a bad guy. Thoughtless as shit, oh yeah, but not bad. So instead of letting myself hit the car, I just drove into a lamppost in the couple of moments I had left. The twelve-year-old girl who would have died—who *did* die the first time around—was spared."

"And you?"

"Serious injuries. I didn't have any medical, so I lost everything paying for the bills. Lost my job. Got charged with drunk driving, and it wasn't the first time, but since I hadn't hurt anybody, they just took away my license. But after that it was pretty much the same slide downhill that it was the first time."

"You don't sound . . ." Sarah wasn't sure how to put it.

"Much broke up about it?"

"Yeah, I guess."

"It's like I told you," he said. "This time the little girl lived. I wasn't any less stupid, but this time no one else had to pay for my stupidity. I've still got a chance to put my life back together. I've been sober since that night. I just need a break, a chance to get cleaned up and back on my feet. I know I can do it."

Sarah nodded. Then she asked the question that troubled her the most.

"Did you ever try to change anything else?" she asked.

"What do you mean?"

"Some disaster where a little forewarning could save a lot of lives."

"You mean like 9/11?"

"Yeah. Or the bombing in Oklahoma."

He shook his head. "It's a funny thing. As soon as I heard about them, it all came back, that I'd been around when they happened the first time and I *remembered*. But the memory just wasn't there until it actually happened."

"Like all we're changing is our own lives."

"Pretty much. And even that's walking blind, the further you get from familiar territory."

Sarah knew exactly what he meant. It had been easy to change things at first, but once she was in a life that was so different from how it had gone the first time, there were no more touchstones and you had to do like everybody did: do what you could and hope for the best.

"I was afraid there was something wrong with me," she said. "That I was so self-centered that I just couldn't be bothered with anything that didn't personally touch my life."

"You don't really believe that."

"How would you know?"

"Well, c'mon. You're Sarah Blue. You're like a poster child for causes."

"I never told you my name."

He smiled and shook his head. "What? Suddenly you're anonymous? Maybe the charts got taken over by all these kids with their bare midriffs, but there was a time not so long ago when you were always on the cover of some magazine or other."

She shrugged, not knowing what to say.

"I don't know what your life was like the first time around," he went on, "but you've been making a difference this time out. So don't be so hard on yourself."

"I guess."

They sat quietly for a moment. Sarah looked around the bar and saw that the clientele had changed. The afternoon booze-hounds had given way to a younger, hipper crowd, though she could still spot a few gray heads. These were the people who'd come for the music, she realized.

"Will you do like it says in the letter?" she asked, turning back to her companion.

"You mean pass it on?"

She nodded.

"First chance I get."

"Me, too," she said. "And I think my go at it should be to help you."

"You haven't passed it on yet?"

She shook her head.

"I don't know if you get a third try," he said.

She shrugged. "If it doesn't work out, I can always front you some money, give you a chance to get back on your feet, and use the whatever-the-hell-it-is on someone else."

"You'd do that for me—just like that?"

"Wouldn't you?"

He gave a slow nod. "Not before. But now, yeah. In a heart-beat." He looked at her for a long moment. "How'd you know I'd be here?"

"I saw your name and the date on your envelope when I was

collecting my own. I just . . . needed to talk to someone about it and Eddie doesn't seem to be available."

"Eddie," he said. "What do you think he is?"

"An angel."

"So you believe in God?"

"I . . . I'm not sure. But I believe in good and evil. I guess I just naturally think of somebody working on the side of good as being an angel."

He nodded. "It's as good a description as any."

"So let's give this a shot," she said. "Only this time—"

"Concentrate on a point in time where I can make the decision not to drink before it's too late."

She nodded.

She gave him a moment, turning her attention back to the bandstand. Looks like tonight they had a keyboard player, a guitarist, a bass player, a drummer, and a guy on saxophones. They were still tuning, adjusting the drum kit, soaking the reeds for the saxes.

She turned back to Jonathan.

"Have you got it?" she asked.

"Yeah. I think I do."

"I'm not going to try to tell you how to live your life, but I think it helps to have something bigger than yourself to believe in."

"Like God?"

She shrugged.

"Or like a cause?" he added.

She smiled. "Like a whatever. Are you ready?"

"Do it," he said. "And thanks."

She leaned over the table, put her hands on his temples and kissed him where Eddie had kissed her, on—what had he called it? Her third eye. She kept her lips pressed against his forehead for a couple of moments, then sat back in her seat.

"Don't forget to come back here on the same day," she said.

But Jonathan only gave her a puzzled look. Without speaking, he got up and left the booth. Sarah tracked him as he made his way through the growing crowd, but he never once looked back.

Weird. How was she even supposed to know if it had worked? But she guessed that in this world, she wouldn't.

Her gaze went to Jonathan's half-drunk ginger ale and she noticed that he'd left his letter behind. There was another puzzle. How did they go from world to world, future to future?

Maybe it had something to do with the Rhatigan itself. Maybe there was something about the bar that made it a crossroads for all these futures.

She thought of asking Alphonse, but got the sense that he didn't know. Or if he knew, he wouldn't be telling. But maybe if she could track down Eddie . . .

He appeared beside her table as though her thoughts had summoned him.

"Never thought about third chances," he said.

He slid a trumpet case onto the booth seat, then sat down beside it, smiling at her from the other side of the table.

"Is—was that against the rules?" she asked.

He shrugged. "What rules? The only thing that's important is for you to come back and get the message to pass it on."

"But what *is* it that we're passing on? Where did this thing come from?"

"Sometimes it's better to just accept that something is, instead of trying to take it apart."

"But—"

"Because when you take it apart, it might not work anymore. You wouldn't want that, would you, Sarah?"

"No. Of course not. But I've got so many questions . . ."

He made a motion with his hands like he was breaking something, then he held out his palms looking down at them with a sad expression.

"Okay, I get the point," she said. "But you've got to understand my curiosity."

"Sure, I do. And all I'm doing is asking you to let it go."

"But . . . can you at least tell me who you are?"

"Eddie Ramone."

"And he's . . . ?"

"Just a guy who's learned how to give a few people the tools to fix a mistake they might have made. Doesn't work on everybody, and not everybody gets it right when they do go back. But I give them another shot. Think of me as a messenger of hope."

Sarah felt as though she was going to burst with the questions that were swelling inside her.

"So'd you bring a guitar?" Eddie asked.

She blinked, then shook her head. "No. But I don't play jazz."

"Take a cue from Norah Jones. Anything can swing, even a song by Hank Williams . . . or Sarah Blue."

She shook her head. "These people didn't come to hear me."

"No, they came to hear music. They don't give a rat's ass who's playing it, just so long as it's real."

"Okay. Maybe." But then she had a thought. "Just answer this one thing for me."

He smiled, waiting.

"In your letter you said that this is a different time line from the one I first met you in."

"That's right, it is."

"So how come you're here and you know me in this one?"

"Something's got to be the connection," he told her.

"But—"

He opened his case and took out his trumpet. Getting up, he reached for her hand.

"C'mon. Jackie'll lend you his guitar for a couple of numbers. All you've got to do is tell us the key."

She gave up and let him lead her to where the other musicians were standing at the side of the stage.

"Oh, and don't forget," Eddie said as they were almost there. "Before you leave the bar, you need to write your own letter to Jonathan."

"I feel like I'm going crazy."

" 'Crazy,' " Eddie said. "Willie Nelson. That'd make a nice start—you know, something everybody knows."

Sarah wanted to bring the conversation back to where she felt she needed it to go, but a look into his eyes gave her a sudden glimpse of a hundred thousand different futures, all banging up against each other in a complex, twisting pattern that gave her a touch of vertigo. So she took a breath instead, shook her head, and just let him introduce her to the other musicians.

Jackie's Gibson semi-hollowbody was a lot like one of her own guitars—it just had a different pickup. She took a seat on the center-stage stool and adjusted the height of the microphone, then started playing the opening chords of "Tony Adams." It took her a moment to find the groove she was looking for, that hip-hop swing that Strummer and the Mescaleros had given the song. By the time she found it, the piano and bass had come in, locking them into the groove.

She glanced at Eddie. He stood on the side of the stage, holding his horn, swaying gently to the rhythm. Smiling, she turned back to the mike and started to sing the first verse.

For Joe Strummer, R.I.P.

The Butter Spirit's Tithe

1

It happened just as we were finishing our first set at the Hole in Tucson, Arizona, running through a blistering version of "The Bucks of Oranmore"—one of the *big* box tunes, so far as I'm concerned. Miki was bouncing so much in her seat that I thought her accordion was going to fly off her knee. I had a cramp in the thumb of my pick hand, but I was damned if that'd stop me from seeing the piece through to the end, no matter how fast she played it.

So of course she picked up the speed again, grinning at me as we kicked into our third run through the tune. I grinned back, adding a flourish of jazzy chords that I shouldn't have had the space to fit in, but I managed all the same. It's the kind of thing that happens when you play live and was nothing I'd be able to duplicate again. Miki raised an eyebrow, suitably impressed.

And then, just as we came up on a big finish, all the strings on my guitar broke, even the bass E. I snapped my head back, which probably saved me from losing an eye, but I got a couple of wicked cuts on my chording hand.

Needless to say, that brought the tune to a ragged finish. Miki stared at me for a long moment, then turned back to her mike.

"We're taking a short break," she said, "while Conn restrings his guitar. Don't go away, and remember to tip your waitress."

I reached over to the PA's board and shut off the sound from the stage, switching the house speakers back to the mix of country and Tex-Mex that the bar got from some satellite feed. Then I sucked at the cuts on my hand. Miki dropped the strap from her accordion and set the instrument on the floor.

"Jesus, Mary, and Joseph," she said, sounding more like her brother than I'd ever tell her. "What the hell just happened?"

I shrugged. "Guess I got a set of bum strings. It happens."

"Yeah, right. Every string breaking at the same time." She paused and studied me for a moment. "Has it happened before?"

I shook my head. I was telling the truth. But other things just as strange had—no more than two or three times a year, but that was two or three times too many.

I set my guitar in its stand and went to the back of the stage where I got my string-winder and a fresh set of strings. Miki was still sitting on her stool when I got back to my own seat. Usually she'd be off the stage by now, mixing with the audience.

"So what aren't you telling me?" she asked.

"What makes you think I'm not telling you something?"

"You've got that look on your face."

"What look?"

"Your 'holding back something juicy' look."

"Well, it *was* strange to have them all break at once like that."

"Try impossible," she said.

"You saw it."

"Yeah, and I still don't quite believe it. So give."

I shook my head.

"It's nothing you want to hear," I told her.

She stood and came over to my side of the stage so that I had to look up at her. Though perhaps "up" was stretching it some since she wasn't much taller than me, and I was still sitting down. Her hair was bright orange this week, short and messy as ever, but it suited her. Truth is, there isn't much that doesn't suit her. She might be too small and compact to ever be hired to walk down the runway at a fashion show, but she could wear anything and make it look better than it ever would on a professional model.

Tonight she was in baggy green cargos and a black Elvis Costello T-shirt that she'd cut the arms off of, but she still looked like a million dollars. She'd kill me if I ever said this in her hearing—because she's probably the best button accordion player I've ever heard; certainly the best I've ever played with—but I'm sure that half the reason we sell out most of our shows is because of her looks. Sort of pixie gamine meets sexy punk. It drew the young crowd, but she was too cute to put off the older listeners. And like I said, she can *play*.

"I just asked, didn't I?" she said.

"Yeah, but . . ."

I'd learned not to talk about certain things around her because it just set her off. I can still remember asking her if she ever read any Yeats—this was in the first week we were out on the road as a duo. She'd given up on fronting a band, because it cost too much to keep the four-piece on the road, and had hired me to be her accompanist in their place.

"Don't get me started on Yeats," she'd said.

"What's wrong with Yeats?"

"Yeats, personally? Nothing, so far as I know. I never met the man. And I'll admit he had a way with the words. What I don't like about him is all that Celtic Twilight shite he was always on about."

I shook my head.

"What?" she said.

I shrugged. "I don't know. It just seems that for a woman born in Ireland, who makes her living playing Celtic music, you don't care much for your own traditions."

"What traditions? I like a good Guinness and play the dance tunes on my box—those are traditions I can appreciate. I can even enjoy a good game of football, if I'm in the mood, which isn't bloody often. What I don't like is when people get into all that mystical shite." She laughed, but without a lot of humour. "And I don't know which is worse, the wannabe Celts or those who think they were born to pass on the great Secret Traditions."

"Which is a good portion of your audience—especially on the concert circuit."

She had a sip of her draught and smiled at me over the brim of her glass. "Well, you know what they say. Doesn't matter what your line of work, there'll always be punters."

This was so Miki, I soon discovered. She was either irrepressibly cheerful and ready to joke about anything, or darkly cynical about the world at large, and the Irish in particular. But she hadn't always been this way.

I didn't know her well before she hired me, but we'd been at a lot of the same sessions and ran with the same crowd, so I already had more than a passing acquaintance with the inimitable Ms. Greer before we started touring together.

Time was she was the definition of good-natured, so much so that a conversation with her could give some people a toothache. It was her brother Donal who was the morose one. But something happened to Donal—I never quite got all the details. I just know he died hard. Overseas, I think. In the Middle East or some place like that. Some desert, anyway. Whatever had happened, Miki took it badly and she hadn't been the same since. Now she was either up or she was down and even her good humour could often have a dark undercurrent to it. Not so much mean, as bitter.

None of which explained her dislike of things Irish, particularly the more mystical side of the Celtic tradition. I could understand her distancing herself from her roots—I might, too, if I'd been brought up the way she had by a drunken father, eventually living on the streets with Donal, the two of them barely in their teens. But while my background's Irish, I grew up in the Green, what they used to call the Irish section of Tyson before it got taken over, first by the bohemians, and then more recently by the new waves of immigrants from countries whose names I can barely pronounce.

The families living in the Green were dirt-poor—some of us still didn't have hot water and electricity in the fifties—but we looked after each other. There was a sense of community in the Green that Miki never got to experience. I'm not saying everyone was an angel. Our fathers worked long hours and drank hard. There were fights in and outside of the bars every night. But if you lost your job, your neighbours would step in and see you through. No one had to go on relief. And my dad, at least, never took out his hardships on his family the way Miki's did.

There was magic in the Green, too. It lay waiting for you in the stories told around the kitchen stoves, in the songs sung in the parlours. I grew up on great heaps of Miki's "Celtic Twilight shite," except it was less airy, more down-to-earth. Stories of leprechauns and banshees and strange black dogs that followed a man home.

And, at least according to my dad, not all of it was just stories.

"Well?" Miki said.

"Well, what?"

"Do you need a bang on the ear to get you going?"

"It's a long story," I said.

She looked at her watch. "Then you better get started, because we're back on in twenty minutes."

I sighed. But as I restrung my guitar, I told her about it.

2

I remember my dad took me aside the day I was leaving home. We stood on the stoop outside our tenement building, hands in our pockets, looking down the street to the traffic going by at the far end of the block, across the way to where the Cassidy girls were playing hopscotch, anywhere but at each other.

"If it was just a need for work, Conn," he finally said, trying one more time to understand. "But this talk of having to find yourself . . ."

How to explain? With four sisters and three brothers, I felt smothered. Especially since each and every one of them knew exactly what they wanted out of life. They had it all mapped out—the jobs, the marriages, the children, the life here in the Green. There were no unknown territories for them.

I only had the music, and while it was respected in our family, it wasn't considered a career option. It was what we did in the evenings, around our kitchen table and those of our neighbours.

I'd tried to put it into words before today, but it always came out sounding like I was turning my back on them, and that wasn't the case. I just needed to find a place in the world that I could make my own. A way to make a living without the help of an uncle or a cousin. It might not be music. But with a limited education, and the even more limited interest in furthering what I did have, music seemed the best option I had.

Besides, I lived and breathed music.

"I know you don't understand," I said. "But it's what I need to do. I'm only going to Newford and I won't be gone forever."

"But wouldn't it be easier on you to live with us while you . . . while you try this?"

I'll give them this: my parents didn't understand, but they were supportive, nevertheless.

I shook my head. "I need the space, Dad. And there aren't the venues here like there are in the city."

He gave a slow nod. And maybe he even understood.

"When you do find yourself a place," he said, "make peace with its spirits."

I guess you might find that an odd thing for him to say, but we O'Neills are a superstitious lot. "Everything has a spirit,"

Dad would tell us when we were growing up. "So give every-thing its proper respect or you'll be bringing the bad luck down upon yourself."

The presence of spirits wasn't something we talked about a lot—and certainly not in the mystical way people do now, where it's all about communicating with energy patterns through crys-tals, candles, or whatever. It was just accepted that the spirits were here, all around us, sharing the world with us: Ghosts and sheerie. Merrow, skeaghshee, and butter spirits. All kinds.

"I will," I told him.

He pressed a folded twenty into my hand—a lot of money for us in those days—then embraced me in a powerful hug. I'd already said my other goodbyes inside.

"There'll always be room for you here," he said.

I nodded, my throat suddenly too thick to speak. I'd wanted and planned for this for months and suddenly I was tottering on the edge of giving it all up and going to work at the factory with my brothers. But I hoisted my duffel bag in one hand, my home-made guitar case in the other. It was made of scavenged plywood and weighed more than the instrument did.

"Thanks, Dad," I said. "Just . . . thanks."

We both knew that simple word encompassed far more than the twenty dollars he'd just given me and the reminder that I'd al-ways have a home to return to.

He clapped me on the shoulder and then I turned and headed down the street where I had an appointment with a Newford-bound bus.

Things didn't go as planned.

I'd set up a few gigs before I left home, but my act didn't go over all that well. I'm not a strong singer, so I need the audience to actually be listening to me for them to appreciate the songs.

But people don't have that kind of patience in a bar. Or maybe it's simply a lack of interest. They've gone out to drink and have fun with their friends and the music's only supposed to be background.

"You're a brilliant guitarist," the owner of the bar I played on the second weekend told me. "But it's wasted on this lot. You should hook up with a fiddler, or somebody with a bigger presence. You know, something to grab their attention and hold it."

In other words, I wasn't much of a front person. As though to punctuate the point, he didn't book me for another gig.

Worse, I knew he was right. I didn't like being up there on those little stages by myself, and even though I knew nobody was really listening, I could barely mumble my way through my introductions. It was different sitting around the kitchen at home, or in a session. I loved backing up the fiddlers and pipers, the flute and box players. And when I did sing a song, people listened.

So I put the word out that I was available as an accompanist, but all the decent players already had their own and the people who did contact me weren't much good. It was so frustrating. I ended up taking gigs with some of them anyway, but they didn't challenge me musically or help my bank balance—my bank being the left front pocket of my cargo pants, which I could at least button closed.

I ended up busking a lot—in the market, at subway entrances, down by Fitzhenry Park—but since I didn't have enough presence on stage where I had the benefit of a sound system, I sure didn't have what it took to grab the attention of passersby on the street, where I was competing with all the traffic and city noise as well as audience indifference. My take after playing was never more than a few dollars. By the end of a month I was out of money and had to leave the boardinghouse where I was staying. I ended up in Squatland, sleeping in one of the many abandoned buildings there with the other homeless people, keeping my busking money for food.

I could have gone home, I guess. But I was too proud. Though not too proud to find another way to make a living.

I finally found a job as a janitor at the Sovereign Building on Flood Street. I got the gig through Joey Bennett, this cabdriver I met when I was busking at the gates of Fitzhenry Park. He'd stand outside his cab, arms folded across his chest, listening to me while he waited for a fare. He was a jazz buff, but we got to talking on my breaks. When he heard I was looking for work, it turned out he knew a lawyer who had an office in the Sovereign and the lawyer got me the job.

I guess it wasn't much different from getting a job through an uncle or cousin, except Joey and the lawyer were my connections. I'd done this on my own.

I didn't mind the job that much. I like seeing things put to order and kept clean, and it's very meditative being in a big building like that, pretty much on my own. There are other cleaners, but we each have our own floors and we don't really see each other except at break time.

Now here's the thing.

I'd paid my respects to the spirits at the boardinghouse, and later my squat—feeling a little foolish while I talked into thin air to do so. No one answered and I didn't expect them to. But I never thought about doing it at work. So when I saw the kid tracking muddy footprints down the hall I'd just spent a half hour mopping down, I wasn't thinking of house spirits and respect. I just told him off.

When he turned in my direction, I saw that he wasn't really a kid—more a kid-sized little man with brown skin and hair that looked like Rasta dreadlocks. He was wearing a dark green cap and shirt, brown-green trousers, and was barefoot—unless you counted the mud on them as footwear. Over his shoulder, he had a coil of rope with a grappling hook fastened to one end. In his hand, he carried a small cloth bag that bulged with whatever it was holding.

It was raining outside, so it wasn't hard to figure out where the mud had come from. How he'd gotten *into* the building was a whole other story. Used the grappling hook to get up the side of the wall, I suppose, and then forced a window.

He glared at me when I yelled at him, dark eyes flashing.

"How'd you get in here, anyway?" I demanded.

He pointed a gnarled finger at me.

"I give you seven years," he said in this gravelly voice that felt like it should have come from a much larger person.

"Yeah, well, I'll give you thirty seconds to get out of here," I told him.

"Do you know who I am?"

Until he said that, I hadn't actually considered it. Not after my first impression when I thought he was just some kid, nor when I realized that he was this weird little man who'd somehow found his way into this locked office building. But as soon as he asked, I knew. And my heart sank. I'd done the very thing my dad had always warned us against.

Though I'll tell you, while I grew up with his stories of fairies and such, accepting them the way you do things that are spoken of in your family, I'd never really believed in them. It was like any other superstition—spilling salt, walking under ladders, that kind of thing. Most people don't believe, but they avoid such situations all the same, just in case. Which is why I'd paid my respects to invisible presences in the boardinghouse and my squat. Just in case.

"Listen," I began, "I didn't realize who—"

But he cut me off.

"Seven years," he repeated.

"Seven years and what?"

"You'll be my tithe to the Grey Man."

My dad had stories about this as well. How the brolaghan known as Old Boneless was like a Mafia don to the smaller fairies, offering them his protection in return for a tithe—the main protection he offered being that he himself wouldn't hurt them. The tithe could be anything from tasty morsels, beer or whiskey, to pilfered knickknacks and even changelings. It just had to be something stolen from the human world.

Dad's stories didn't say what the Grey Man did with any of these things. Being a creature of mist and fog, you wouldn't think he'd have any use for material items. Maybe they helped make him more substantial.

I certainly didn't want to find out firsthand.

"Wait a sec'," I said. "All I did was—"

"Disrespect me. And just to remind you of my displeasure," he added.

He pointed that gnarled finger at me again and my pants came undone, falling down around my ankles. By the time I'd stooped to pull them up, he was gone. I zipped up my fly and re-did my belt.

They came undone and my pants fell down once more.

I suppose that's what really convinced me that I'd just had an encounter with a genuine fairy man. No matter how often I tried, I couldn't get my pants to stay up. Finally, I sat down there in the hall holding them in place with one hand while I tried to figure out what to do.

Nothing came to mind.

And the worst thing about it, there was this totally cute girl named Nita Singh that I'd been spending my breaks with. She worked the floor below mine and while I hadn't quite figured out yet if she was seeing anybody, she was friendly enough to give me hope that maybe she wasn't. She certainly seemed to return my interest.

So of course she had to come up looking for me when I didn't come down at break time.

"Are you okay?" she asked as she came down the hall from the stairwell.

Nita was almost as tall as me, with shoulder-length, straight dark brown hair tied back in a ponytail. Like all of us, she was wearing grubby jeans and a T-shirt, but they looked much better on her.

"Oh sure," I said. "I'm just . . . you know, having a rest."

She leaned her back against the wall, then slid down until she was sitting beside me. She glanced at how I was holding my jeans and grinned.

"Having some trouble with your pants?"

I shrugged. "I think my zipper's broken."

From the first night I'd met her, all I'd ever wanted was to be close to her. Now I just wanted her to go away.

"Maybe I can fix it," she said.

In any other circumstance, could this have played out any better?

"I don't think so," I told her.

I couldn't believe I had to say that. She was going to think I was such a dork, but instead she gave me a knowing look.

"Had a run-in with the local butter spirit, did you?" she asked.

Butter spirits were supposed to be a kind of house fairy related to leprechauns, but much more thieving and malicious. Back home they especially enjoyed fresh butter and would draw the "good" of the milk before it was churned.

I blinked in surprise. "How do you know about that kind of thing?"

"Daddy-ji's Indian," she said, "but my mum's Irish. There was a big to-do when they hooked up. You know, son disowned, the whole bit."

"I'm sorry."

She shrugged. "Not your fault. Anyway, Mum was forever telling stories about the little people."

"My dad did, too."

"I just never thought they were more than stories."

"But you do now? Have you seen him?"

She nodded. "Not up close. But I've caught glimpses of him and his little grappling hook that he uses to clamber up the out-side walls. I think he pilfers food and drink from the bars and restaurants in Chinatown. I've seen him leave empty-handed, but return with a bag full of something or other."

"You never said anything before."

"What was I going to say? I thought you'd be telling me about him soon enough. And if you didn't, what would you think of me, telling you stories like that?"

"Has anyone else seen him?"

She laughed. "How do you think you got this job?"

"I don't understand."

"I've been working here for almost nine months and you've lasted the longest of anybody who's worked this floor in all that time. How long have you been here?"

"Almost a month."

"Most people don't last a week. There's almost always an opening for the job on this floor. Management tries to shift some of us to it, but we just threaten to quit when they do."

"So that's why it was so dirty when I first came on."

She nodded.

"And it's the butter spirit that scares people off?"

"Most people just think this floor is haunted, but you and I know better."

"They got on the wrong side of him," I said. "Like I just did."

"Don't worry," she told me. "Whatever he's done—"

"Fixed it so my pants won't stay up."

She grinned. "It doesn't last."

"Well, I can work in my boxers, but I don't know how I'm going to get home."

"If it's not gone by then, we'll see if we can rustle up a long coat for you to wear."

3

"**So I'm assuming it wore** off," Miki said when I was done.

I nodded. "Before I left the building at the end of my shift."

"Then what was tonight all about?"

"He likes to remind me that the tithe is still coming due."

Miki got a hard look. "You see what I mean about how this is all shite?"

She looked off the stage, trying to see if the little bogle man was in view, I assumed. He wasn't. Or at least he wasn't visible. I knew, because I'd already checked.

"It's not shite," I said. "It's real."

"I know. It's shite because it does no one any good. There's a reason the Queen of the Fairies gave Yeats that warning."

"What warning?"

"He was seeing this medium and through her, the Fairy Queen told him, 'Be careful, and do not seek to know too much about us.' But do any of the punters listen?"

"I wasn't trying to find out anything about them."

She nodded. "I got that. My point is, any contact with them is a sure recipe for heartache and trouble."

She had that much right.

"You don't seem any more surprised by this than Nita was," I said.

"I'm not. Messing about with shite like this is what got Donal killed."

"I didn't know."

"Well, it's not something I'm going to shout out to the world." She paused a moment, then added, "So what happened with Nita? She sounded nice from what you had to say about her."

"She's wonderful. But that little bugger made her allergic to me and *that* spell hasn't worn off yet. Whenever she gets physically near to me, her nose starts running and she breaks out in hives. Sometimes her throat just closes down and she can't breathe."

I finished tightening my last string, dropped the string-winder under my stool, and plugged my guitar into my electronic tuner.

"We seem to still be able to talk on the phone," I added.

"Is that who you're always calling?"

I nodded. I didn't have a better friend in the world than Nita. And at one time, we'd been far more than that. But the butter spirit thought making her allergic to me would be a good joke, especially when he didn't let the enchantment wear off. Talking on the phone was all we had now.

"I always thought it was one of your brothers or sisters," Miki said.

"Nita's *like* a sister now," I told her, unable to keep the hurt from my voice.

Miki gave me a sympathetic look.

"So it's not just breaking guitar strings and pulling your pants down," she said.

"Christ, that's the least of it. Mostly things happen in private. Shutting off the hot water on me when I'm having a shower. Or fixing it so that the electricity doesn't work—but only in the room where I am. It's the big jokes that I dread. Once I was in a coffee shop and he curdled all the dairy products just as I was halfway through a latte. There were people puking on the tables that day and I was one of them."

Miki grimaced.

"And then there was the time I was downtown and he vanished all the stitches and buttons in what I was wearing. It's the middle of a snowstorm, and suddenly I'm standing there trying to cover myself with all these pieces of cloth that once were clothes."

"And you've never said anything about it."

I gave her a humourless smile. "Well, it's not something I want to shout out to the world either."

"Good point," she said. She paused for a moment, then added, "We're just going to have to find a way to turn the little bugger off."

I didn't want to feel the hope that rose at her words, but I couldn't help it.

"Do you know a way to do it?" I asked.

She shook her head and my frail surge of hope fled. But this was Miki. Determined, tough.

"Only that doesn't mean we can't find out," she said. "You wouldn't know this butter spirit's name, would you?"

I shook my head.

"Too bad, but I suppose that would have been too easy."

"What use would his name be?"

"There's power in names," she said. "Don't you pay attention to the stories? Just because it's all shite doesn't mean it isn't true."

"Right."

I was having trouble relating to this conversation. I mean, to be having it with Miki, of all people. Who knew that behind her disdain she was such an expert?

"When's the tithe due?" she asked.

"April thirtieth."

She gave a slow nod. "Cally Berry's night."

"You've lost me."

"They call her the Old Woman of Gloominess. She's the blue-skinned daughter of the sun and she rules the world between Halloween and Beltane. On the last day of April she throws her ruling staff away and turns into stone for the next half of the year—why do you think there are so many stone goddess images louting about in Ireland? But on that night, when she gives up her rule to the Summer Goddess, the fairies run free—like they do on Halloween. Babies are stolen and changelings left in their cribs. Debts and tithes are paid."

"Lovely."

"Mmm. I wonder if we have a gig that night . . ."

She took out her Palm Pilot and looked up our schedule.

"Of course we do," she said. "We're in Harnett's Point at the Harp & Tankard, from the Wednesday through Saturday. Close enough to Newford for trouble, though I guess distance doesn't seem to be a problem with him, does it?"

I shook my head. We were halfway across the country in Arizona at the moment and that hadn't stopped him.

"Actually, that can work to our advantage," she went on. "I know some people living close to Harnett's Point who might be able to help. We'll put together some smudge sticks . . . let's see . . . rosemary, rue, blackthorn, and hemlock. That'll be pungent to burn indoors, but it'll keep him off you."

"You really think you can stop him?" I asked. "I mean, it's not just the butter spirit. There's the Grey Man, too."

She nodded. "Old Boneless. Another of those damned hard men that we Irish seem to be so good at conjuring up, both in our fairies and ourselves. But I have a special fondness for the bashing of hard men, Conn, you'll see. Now tell me, how intimate were you and Nita?"

"Jeez, that's hardly—"

She held up a hand before I could finish. "I'm not prying. I just need to know if you have a bond of flesh or just words."

"We were . . . very intimate. Until he pulled this allergy business."

She gave me another one of her thoughtful nods.

"What are you thinking?" I asked.

"Nothing. Not yet. I'm just putting together the pieces in my head. Setting them up against what I know and what I have to find out."

"Not that I'm ungrateful," I said, "but you seem awfully familiar with this kind of thing for someone so dead set against it."

The grin she gave me was empty of humour. It was a wolf's grin. Feral.

"It's the first rule of war," she told me. "Know your enemy."

War, I thought. When did this become a war? But maybe for her it was. Maybe it should be that way for me.

"So what's Nita doing these days?" Miki asked.

"She's a social worker. She was working on her degree when I met her at the Sovereign Building."

"Is she with the city?"

I nodded.

"And you still love her? She still loves you?"

"Well, we're not celibate—I mean, it's been six and a half years now. We had six months together before the butter spirit conjured up this allergy, but . . ." I shrugged. "So, yes, we still love each other, but we see other people." I paused, then added, "And you need to know this because?"

"I need to know everything I can about the situation. You do want me to help, don't you?"

"I'll take any help I can get."

"Good man. So, are you all tuned up yet?" she asked, abruptly shifting conversational gears. When I nodded, she added, "Then I think it's time to start playing again."

I was going to have to fight the tuning of my guitar for the rest of the night as this new set of strings stretched. But better that—better to lose myself in the mechanics of playing and tuning and the spirit of the music—than to have to think about that damned butter spirit for the next hour or so.

Except I never did get him out of my head. At the very least, throughout the set, I carried the worry of my strings snapping on me again.

4

Miki wasn't at all forthcoming about her plan to deal with the butter spirit. The first time I pressed her harder for details— "Hello," I told her. "This concerns me, you know."—she just said something about the walls having ears and if she spoke her plan aloud, she might as well write it out and hand it over to the enemy.

"Trust me, Conn," she said.

So I did. She might get broody. She might carry a hard, dark anger around inside her. But it was never directed at me and I knew I could trust her with my life. Which was a good thing because if the Grey Man ever did get hold of me, it was my life that was forfeit.

The month went by quickly.

We finished up our gigs in the Southwest, did a week that took us up through Berkeley and Portland, and then we were back in Newford and it was time to start the two-hour drive out to Harnett's Point for our opening night at the Harp & Tankard.

Harnett's Point used to be a real backwoods village, its population evenly divided between the remnants of back-to-the-earth hippies who tended organic farms west of the city and locals who made their living off the tourists that swelled the village in the summer. But it had changed in the last decade, becoming, like so many of the other small villages around Newford, a satellite community for those who could afford the ever pricier real estate and didn't mind the two-hour commute to their jobs.

And where once it had only the one Irish bar—Murphy's, a log and plaster-covered concrete affair near the water that was a real roadhouse—now it sported a half-dozen, including the Tankard & Horn where we were playing tonight.

Have you ever noticed how there seems to be an Irish pub on almost every corner these days? They're as bad as coffee shops. I can remember a time when the only place you could get a decent Guinness was in Ireland, and as for the music, forget it. "Traditional music" was all that Irish-American twaddle popularized by groups like the Irish Rovers. Some of them were lovely songs, once, but they'd been reduced to noisy bar jokes by the time I got into the music professionally. And then there were the folks who'd demand "some real Irish songs" like "The Unicorn," and would get all affronted when, first, you wouldn't play it for them, and second, you told them it was actually written by Shel Silverstein, the same Jewish songwriter responsible for hits like Dr. Hook & the Medicine Show's "Cover of the Rolling Stone."

Miki and I played an even mix of bars, small theatres, colleges, and festivals, and I usually liked the bars the least—probably a holdover from when I was first trying to get into the music in a professional capacity. But Miki loved them. It made no sense to me why she kept taking these bookings—she could easily fill any medium-sized hall—but they kept her honest, she liked to say. "And besides," she'd add, "music and the drink, they just go together."

When we got to the Tankard & Horn that afternoon we were met out back where we parked our van by a Native American fellow. Miki introduced him to me as Tommy. I thought he was with the bar—after all, he helped us bring in our gear and set up, then settled behind the soundboard while we did our soundcheck—but he turned out to be a friend of hers and in on her secret plan. After we got the sound right, he lit a pair of smudge sticks and then he and Miki waved them around the stage until the area reeked. They weren't sweetgrass or sage, but made of the herbs and twigs that Miki had told me about back at the Hole: rosemary and rue, blackthorn and hemlock.

The smell lingered long after they were done—which was the whole point, I suppose—and didn't make it particularly pleasant to be up here in it. I wasn't the only one to feel that way. I noticed as the audience started to take their seats that people would come up to the front tables, then retreat to ones farther back after a few moments. It was only when the back of the room was full that the closer tables filled up.

The audience was part yuppies, part the local holdover hippies, with a few of the longtime residents of the area standing in the back by the bar. You could tell them by their plaid flannel shirts and baseball caps. There were also a number of older Native women scattered throughout the room and I wondered why they didn't sit together. I could tell that they knew each other— or at least they all knew Tommy, since before he got back to the soundboard, he made a point of stopping and chatting with each of them.

"Do you know the song 'Tam Lin'?" Miki asked.

Tommy was back on the board now and we were getting ready to start the first set.

"Sure. It's in A minor, right?"

"Not the tune—the ballad."

I shook my head. "I know it to hear it, but I've never actually sat down and learned it."

"Still you know the story."

"Yeah. Why—"

"Keep it in mind for later," she told me.

Her mysteriousness was beginning to get on my nerves. No, that wasn't entirely fair. What had me on edge was the knowledge that tonight was the night the butter spirit meant to make me his tithe to Old Boneless.

"Don't forget now," she said.

"I won't."

Though what "Tam Lin" had to do with anything, I had no idea. I tried to remember the story as I checked my foot pedals and finished tuning my guitar. It involved a love triangle between the knight Tam Lin, the Queen of the Fairies, and a mortal woman named Janet, or sometimes Jennet. Janet loved Tam Lin and he loved her, but the Fairy Queen stole him away and took him back with her to Fairyland. To win him back, Janet had to pull him down from his horse during a fairy rade on Halloween and then hold on to him while the Fairy Queen turned him into all sorts of different kinds of animals.

It was hard, but Janet proved true, and the Queen had to go back to Fairyland empty-handed.

Fair enough. But what did any of that have to do with my butter spirit and him planning to make me his tithe to Old Boneless?

Apparently, Miki wasn't going to tell me because she just called out the key of the first number and off she went, blasting out a tune on her accordion. In a moment, the pub was full of bobbing heads and tapping feet and I was too busy keeping up with Miki to be worrying about the relevance of old traditional ballads.

Miki was in a mood tonight. The tunes were all fast and furious, one after the other, with no time to catch a breath in between. Most of the time, when we got to the end of one of our regular sets, she'd simply call out a key signature and jump directly into the next set.

I didn't really think of it as peculiar to this particular night. Once she got on stage, you never knew where Miki would let the muse take her. Having a long-standing fondness for jazz tenor sax solos, as well as a newfound love for Mexican conjunto music that she'd picked up on our tours through Texas and the Southwest, she could as easily slide from whatever Irish tune we might be playing into a Ben Webster solo, or some *norteño* piece she'd picked up from a Flaco Jimenez album.

But tonight it was all hard-driving reels and we didn't come up for air until just before the end of our first set. I took the momentary respite to kill the volume on my guitar and give it a proper retuning, not really listening to what Miki was telling the audience. But I did note that they all had the same, slightly stunned expression that I was sure I was wearing. Miki in full tear on her box could do it to anyone, and even playing on stage with her, I wasn't immune.

I got the last string in tune, then suddenly realized what Miki was telling the audience.

". . . have to ask yourselves, why these stories persist," she was saying. "We've always had them and we still do. I mean, alien abductions—that's just a new twist on the old tale of people getting taken away by the fairies, isn't it? Now, I don't want to go all woo-woo on you here, but tonight's one of the two nights of the year that these little buggers are given complete free rein to cause what havoc they can for us mortals. The other's on Halloween.

"Anyway," she went on, smiling brightly at the audience in that way she had that immediately made you have to smile back, "whether you believe or not, it can't hurt to wish a bit of good luck our way, right? So while we're playing this next tune, I want you to think about how everybody here should be kept safe from the influence and malice of these so-called Good Neighbours. What do you think?"

She cocked her head and gave them a goofy look, which got her a round of laughter and applause.

"Key of D," she told me and launched into "The Fairies' Hornpipe."

"Remember," she said over the opening bars, directing her attention back to the audience. "Fairies bad. Us good."

I looked out at the crowd as I backed Miki up. People were still smiling, some of them clapping along to the simple rhythm of the tune. And I'd bet more than half of them were doing what she'd said, thinking protective thoughts for everybody here inside the pub.

This was Miki's big plan? I found myself thinking.

Don't get me wrong. I appreciated whatever effort she might have made to solve my problem, but this didn't seem like it would be all that effectual. And I sure didn't see the connection to the old ballad "Tam Lin."

But then I realized that the Native women I'd noted earlier were all standing up now, backs against the various walls. One after the other, they lit smudgesticks and soon that pungent scent of herbs and twigs was drifting through the pub, only this time, except for me, nobody seemed to notice.

And then I realized something else. While the audience continued to clap and stomp away to the music, while I could still *hear* the music, I wasn't playing my guitar anymore. I looked over at Miki and there seemed to be two of her, superimposed over each other. One still playing away on that old box of hers—she'd switched to a tune that I recognized as "The Fairy Reel"; the other regarding me with a serious expression in her eyes.

The sound of her playing and the crowd was muted. Actually, my sight felt muted, too, like there was a thin gauze hanging in front of my eyes.

"It's up to you now," the Miki who wasn't playing said. "Go outside and deal with him."

"What . . . where *are* we?"

"In between. Not quite in the world, not quite in the otherworld where the spirits are stronger."

"I don't understand. How did you bring us here?"

"I didn't," she said. "They did."

I didn't have to ask who she meant. It was the Native women, with their smudge sticks and something else. I heard a low, rhythmical drumming, under the music, under the noise of the crowd. Mixed with it were the sounds of rattles and flutes, keeping time to Miki's tune, but following their own rhythm at the same time. I couldn't see the players.

More spirits, I guessed. But Native ones.

"And I'm not really with you," Miki added. "You're on your own."

"I don't understand—" I began, but she cut me off.

"There's not a big window of time here, Conn. Get a move on. And remember what I told you."

"I know. Think of the ballad. Why can't you just *tell* me what you've got planned?"

She smiled, but there was no humour in it. Only a kind of sadness.

"You'll know what to do when the time comes," she said. "One way or another, you can finish this business tonight."

You know how in a dream you find yourself doing things that don't make sense in retrospect, but in the dream they're perfectly logical? That's what this felt like. I got up and put my guitar in its stand, then made my way down from the stage and through the tables to the front door of the pub. No one paid the slightest attention to me except for Tommy, who gave me a smile and a thumb's-up as I passed the soundboard where he was sitting.

I thought of stopping to see if he could tell me what was going on, but then I remembered Miki saying something about there not being a lot of time, so I continued on to the door. Considering how weird everything else had gotten, I didn't really expect Harnett's Point to be still waiting for me outside. But it was. And that wasn't all that was waiting for me.

I stepped out into the parking lot, then stopped dead in my tracks. Nita stood there, waiting in an open parking spot between an SUV and a Volvo stationwagon. She looked as gorgeous as ever and my heartbeat did a little skip of happiness before my chest went tight with anxiety. I looked to the left and right, searching for some sign of the butter spirit, but so far as I could tell we were alone. Which I knew meant nothing.

"Nita . . ." I said, stepping closer to her. "What are you *doing* here?"

The smile she'd been wearing faltered. "Your friend Miki . . .

she asked me to come. She said we had to do this and then every-thing would be all right."

I shook my head. *What* had Miki been thinking?

In the light from the bar's signage behind me I could see that her eyes were already getting puffy and her nose was beginning to run—her allergy to me kicking in.

"I shouldn't have come, should I?" Nita said. "I can tell. You don't really want me here."

The sadness I saw rising up in her broke my heart.

"No, it's not that," I told her. "It's just . . . oh, Christ, Miki couldn't have picked a worse night to have you come."

She started to say something, but a voice to the side spoke first.

"Using words like that will just make it worse on you, Conn O'Neill."

I turned and this time I spotted him. He was perched on the roof of an old Chev two-door, one car over from the Volvo. The butter spirit with his hair like dreads and that glare in his eyes.

"I'm not afraid," Nita told me. "Miki told me all about it."

"I wish she'd told me," I said.

The butter spirit jumped onto the roof of the Volvo and grinned down at me.

"Don't know what you've got planned here, my wee boyo," he said. "I just know it's too late."

Nita and I both felt it then, a sudden coldness in the air. Looking over her shoulder, I was the first to see him: a fog lifting from the pavement of the parking lot that became the figure of a man with a cloak of wreathing mist that swirled about him. The Grey Man, his features sharp and pale, framed by long gray hair. Old Boneless himself. He didn't seem completely solid and I re-membered my dad telling me how he sustained himself on the smoke from chimneys and factories, on the exhaust from cars and other machines. That had never made sense until now.

His gaze had none of the butter spirit's meanness. Instead, he appeared completely indifferent, and in him, that struck me as far more dangerous.

"Get away, girl," the butter spirit told Nita. "Or you'll suffer the same fate as your boyo."

Nita ignored him. She moved closer to me.

"H-hold me," she said.

She could barely get the words out, her allergy to me closing up her throat.

"But—" I began, but couldn't finish.

She tried to speak, only she didn't have the breath anymore. Swaying, she would have fallen if I hadn't stepped forward and taken her into my arms. I lowered her to the pavement and knelt there, holding her tight, my heart filling with hopelessness and despair.

"Let her go," the butter spirit said.

I wanted to. I knew I should get as far away from her as I could so that she could recover from this allergy attack. But Nita still had the strength to grip my arm and she wouldn't let go. I knew what she was trying to tell me. So I looked down into her face and I kissed her instead.

Her skin changed under my lips. When I lifted my head, I found myself holding a corpse. Nita's lovely brown skin had gone pallid and cold and her gaze was flat. Empty. Her lips moved and then a maggot crept out of the corner of her mouth.

I might have pushed her aside and scrambled to my feet in horror, except somehow I managed to remember Miki's cryptic reminders about the old ballad. So I held her closer. Even when the flesh fell apart in my grip and all I held were bones, attached to each other by bits of dried muscle and sinew. I held her even closer then, tenderly cradling the skull against my chest. Wisps of what had once been her thick brown hair tickled my hand.

I still didn't really see the connection between the ballad and our situation. I was the one in peril with fairy, not her. I should be the one changing shapes. But I knew I wouldn't let her go, never mind the gender-switch from the ballad.

None of this made much sense anyway, from the butter spirit's first taking affront to me, through the years of petty torment to this night, when the tithe he owed the Grey Man was due. None of it seemed real. It was all part and parcel of that same dreamlike state I felt I'd entered back on the stage inside the pub. I suppose that was what let me continue to kneel here, holding the apparent remains of Nita in my arms, and still function.

"This man is yours," I heard the butter spirit say. "My tithe to you."

Before the Grey Man could do whatever it was he was going to do, I lifted my head and met his flat, expressionless gaze. I still felt disconnected, reality floundering all around me, but I knew what I needed to do. It wasn't Miki's advice I needed to take, but my dad's.

"I'm honoured to make your acquaintance, sir," I said, falling back on the formal speech patterns I remembered from dad's stories.

For the first time since he arrived, I saw a flicker of interest in the Grey Man's gaze.

"Are you now?" he said.

His voice was a voice from the grave, deep and husky, filled with cold air.

I gave a slow nod in response. I was no longer trying to figure out what Miki's plan had been. Instead, I concentrated on the stories from my dad, how in them, no matter how malevolent or kind the fairy spirit might seem to be, the one thing they all demanded of us mortals was respect.

"I am, sir," I said. "It's a rare privilege to be able to look upon one so grand as yourself."

"Even when I am here to eat your soul?"

"Even, then, sir."

"What game are you playing at?" he demanded.

"No game, sir. Though in all fairness, I feel I should tell you that your butter spirit actually has no claim to my soul. That being the case, it puzzles me how he can offer me up as his tithe to you. It seems to me—if you'll pardon my speaking out of turn like this—rather disrespectful."

The Grey Man turned that dark gaze of his to the butter spirit. "Is this true, Fardoragh Og?"

The butter spirit spat at me. "Lies, my lord. Everything he says is a lie."

"Then tell me, how did you gain a lien on his soul?"

The butter spirit couldn't find the words he needed.

"Well?"

"He . . . I . . ."

"If I might speak, sir?" I asked.

The butter spirit wanted to protest—that was easy to see—but he kept his mouth shut when the Grey Man nodded. I explained the circumstances of the butter spirit's enmity to me, and how when I'd realized my mistake, I'd tried to apologize.

"And where in this sorry tale," the Grey Man asked the butter spirit, "did you acquire the lien on this man's soul?"

"I . . ."

"Do you know what would have happened if I had taken it in these circumstances?"

"N-no, my lord."

"For the wrongful murder of their son, I would have been in debt to his family for eternity."

"I . . . I didn't . . . I never thought, my lord . . ."

"Come here, little man."

With great reluctance, the butter spirit shuffled to where the tall figure of the Grey Man stood. I didn't know what was coming next, but I knew that if I could get Nita and myself safely out of this, the last thing we'd need would be the continued enmity of the butter spirit, magnified by who knew how much after tonight's ordeal?

"Sir?" I said. "May I speak?"

The Grey Man's gaze touched me and I shivered. "Go ahead."

"It's just . . . this all seems to have been a series of unfortunate misunderstandings, sir. Couldn't we, perhaps, simply put it all behind us and carry on with our lives?"

"You ask for clemency toward your enemy?"

"I don't really think of him as an enemy, sir. Truly, it was just a misunderstanding that grew out proportion in the heat of the moment. And I should never have disrespected him in the first place."

The butter spirit actually gave me a grateful look, but the Grey Man appeared unmoved. He grabbed the butter spirit by the scruff of his neck.

"You offer a commendable sentiment," he told me, "but I care only for the danger he put me in. It's not something I can afford to have repeated."

With that, he pulled the little man towards him. I thought, how odd that he would embrace the butter spirit in a moment such as this. But the Grey Man didn't draw him close for an embrace, so much as to devour him. The butter spirit gave a shriek as the foggy drapes of the cloak folded over him. And then he was gone, swallowed in the cloak of fog, with only the fading echo of his cry remaining before it, too, was gone.

"Now there is only one last problem," the Grey Man said, his dark gaze returning to me.

I swallowed hard.

"I am still owed a tithe from your world," he said. "Some human artifact or spirit. But I stand before you empty-handed."

I didn't reply. What was I going to say?

"I can only think of one solution," he went on. "Will you swear fealty to me?"

I had to be careful now.

"Gladly, sir," I told him. "So long as my doing so causes no harm to any other being."

"You think I would have you do evil things?"

"Sir, I have no idea what you would want from me. I'm only being honest with you."

For a long moment the Grey Man stood there, considering me.

"I owe you a favour," he finally said. "I know you spoke up only to save your own skin, but by doing so, you prevented me from an eternity of servitude to your family."

"Sir, it was never my intention to—"

He cut me off with a sharp gesture of his hand. "Enough! You've made your point. You're very respectful. Now give it a rest." He sighed, then added, "Burn a candle for me from time to time, and we'll leave it at that."

I knew he was about to go.

"Sir," I said before he could leave. "My friend . . ."

He looked down at the bundle of bones in my arms, held together with sinew and dried muscle.

"It's only a glamour," he said. "Seen by you, felt by her."

And then he was gone in a swirl of fog.

I'd managed to keep my soul. The butter spirit would no longer be tormenting me. But I still knelt there with bones in my arms where Nita should be.

At that moment there came a roar of applause from inside the bar. I turned in the direction of the door. It seemed so inappropriate that they would be cheering the Grey Man's departure, but then I realized that it was only that Miki had ended her set.

I started to get to my feet, not an easy process because those bones weighed more than you'd think they would. But I refused to put them down.

I was still trying to stand when the door opened and one of those tall Native women I'd seen inside the bar came out into the parking lot. A moment later and the others followed her, one by one, nine of them in all. The last of them was an old, old woman with eyes as dark as the Grey Man's. When her gaze settled on me, I felt as nervous as I had under his attention.

"You did well," one of the younger women said—younger meaning she was in her forties. I couldn't tell how old the oldest of them was. She seemed ageless.

When they started to walk across the parking lot, I called out after them.

"Please! Can you help me with my friend?"

The old woman was the closest. She reached into her pocket and tossed what looked like a handful of pollen into the air, then blew it in my direction. I sneezed. Once. Twice. A third time. Blinked to clear my eyes.

By the time I was done, the Native women were gone. But Nita was in my arms—the real Nita, seemingly unaffected by allergies. Her eyelids fluttered and then she was looking up at me. A small smile touched her lips.

"I had the strangest dream," she said.

"It's okay. It's all over now."

"Did . . . did we win?" she asked.

I wouldn't call it winning. I don't know what I'd call it. But at least it seemed we were free.

"Yeah," I told her, settling on the easiest reply. "We won."

5

Strong whiskey was the order of the day when we got back inside, because Lord, did I need a drink. Jameson's in glass tumblers, no ice. I had the waitress leave the bottle at the table where Nita and I sat with Miki and her friend Tommy. We still had a half hour before Miki and I had to start our next set.

"I can't believe you let me go into that so blind," I told Miki.

"Shut up and drink your whiskey."

"No, really."

"I told you why. It was so the butter spirit wouldn't get a hint of what I had planned."

"But how could you know the Grey Man would swallow him and let me go?"

Miki shrugged. "I listened to your story, and then I talked to Nita about it. I knew the butter spirit didn't have a hold on you except for his malice. He couldn't offer you as a tithe. But if I'd mentioned it to you, he could have heard and made a different plan."

I was only half-listening, my attention now focused on the other thing that had been so troubling to me.

"And I can't believe you put Nita in that danger," I told her.

"I had to make sure you were both free of his spells. She had to be here for that. Besides, although you won't get them to admit it most of the time, the spirits are big on courage and true love. I figured with the two of you there, you'd show both."

"It's okay," Nita said, putting her hand over mine and giving it a squeeze. "Once she told me how it would go, I agreed to it."

I shook my head and used my free hand to have another sip of the whiskey. I knew I'd be playing very simple chords when we got back on stage for the next set.

"I don't even know how she got hold of you," I said.

"Oh, that was dead simple," Miki told me. "Once I knew she worked for the city's social services, it was easy to get her number."

I glanced across the table at Tommy. Of the four of us, he was the only one not drinking the whiskey. He had a ginger ale on the table in front of him.

"You don't seem much surprised by any of this," I said to him.

That seemed to be the tagline for this whole sorry affair.

Maybe I should have been more surprised by people not taking it all at face value.

He shrugged. "I grew up on the rez with the aunts. There's not much that surprises me anymore."

"I never got to thank them."

"I'll pass it on for you."

"So, are you happy?" Miki asked.

She looked from me to Nita, beaming with the look of someone who'd not only got the job done, but got it done well.

"Very," Nita assured her.

"And will you be together now?" Miki asked.

I met Nita's gaze and saw the love shining in her eyes, just as I knew it was in my own.

"Of course you are," Miki went on before we could answer. "Lord, I love a happy ending. I should go back to Ireland and take up matchmaking. It's a respectable profession there, you know," she told Tommy.

"Yeah," he said. "I saw the movie."

"What movie?"

"*The Matchmaker.*"

"Oh, please."

I gave Nita's hand a little tug and we left the two of them to go on at each other while we went outside to get a breath of air. It was a gorgeous night, the sky so full of stars that even the electric aura of the lights of Harnett's Point couldn't put a damper on them.

"It's hard to believe we're finally free of that little bugger," I said. "I didn't think we'd ever be able to do anything but talk on the phone."

"Stop wasting time," Nita told me.

Then she wrapped her arms around my neck and drew me down for a long, deep kiss.

Da Slockit Light

Da Slockit Light ("The Putting Out of the Light") is
a Shetland fiddle tune composed by Tom Anderson.

"Hey!" the boy cried.

She wasn't quick enough to stop his hand from darting in
and out of her purse, but she managed to snag him by the collar
of his shirt before he could get away. She almost hauled him off
his feet as she pulled him back towards her. Her wallet fell from
his hand. The soft slap as it hit the pavement was lost in the sound
of the traffic going by on Lakeside Drive.

"Well, now," Meran Kelledy said, studying her captive.

The boy struggled ineffectively. For all her slenderness, her
fingers had an iron grip.

"What have we got here?"

Not much, if looks were anything to go by. He was a homely,
undersized boy in oversized skater's jeans and a plain white T-shirt
that was also too big. One running shoe had a grubby toenail poking through its toe, its mate was held together with twine. His hair
was an unkempt, brown thatch; his eyes too old.

He couldn't have been much more than twelve or thirteen. If
that.

"Lemme go," he demanded.

Retaining her hold on the collar of his shirt, Meran stooped
to retrieve her wallet. She flipped it open as she straightened, letting its contents flutter to the pavement.

"Here's what you were stealing," she said.

The boy gave her a look that plainly put her on a level of intelligence just a step up from a slug as he stared at what had fallen from her wallet. Pressed leaves and bits of paper with what looked like verses scribbled on them; a carefully folded candy-wrapper; a red balloon and a yellowed newspaper clipping. The only currency was a pair of copper pennies that winked up at them from amongst the detritus.

"That's just crap," he said.

Meran smiled. "Then why did you want to steal it?"

"I . . ."

Confusion washed across his face, then he spat at her. As she dodged the phlegm, he kicked out at her. The toe of the twine-wrapped runner connected with her shin. Her grip loosened momentarily on his collar and he was off, scurrying down the street, shouting a string of obscenities behind him.

Meran was half-inclined to chase after him, but settled on simply watching until he rounded a corner and was lost from her view.

He was so young. . . .

She stooped once more, this time to retrieve the contents of her wallet, carefully replacing each item.

"Louie Felden," a voice said.

Meran looked up to find a young woman standing close by. She had a face shaped like a heart, short blond hair, and pale blue eyes. Her trim figure was lost in a pair of baggy black jean overalls under which she wore a man's dress shirt. A red canvas knapsack hung from her shoulder by one strap, the thumb of her right hand hooked into the bottom of the strap's loop.

"I beg your pardon?" Meran said.

The woman nodded down the street with her chin.

"The boy," she said. "His name's Louie Felden. He does that a lot. Usually he gets away with it."

Meran straightened up. "But he's only a child."

"He's actually around sixteen," the woman said. "But he does look a lot younger." She held out her hand. "My name's Lisa—Lisa Hooper. I used to be his family's social worker. But when his mother died and his father went to prison, he and his brother took to the streets and we couldn't help them. Every time we found a home for them, they'd run away. He'll still talk to me from time to time, when he wants to cadge a meal. But since his brother Bobby died, this is the closest I usually get to him—seeing the back of his head as he runs away."

"I see," Meran said, though she didn't at all.

"Did he get away with anything?"

Meran stowed her wallet back into her purse and shook her head.

"Odd kinds of things to be carrying around in a wallet," Lisa said.

She spoke as though she was trying to keep the conversation going, but wasn't quite ready to get to the point.

"Memories," Meran said.

"Treasure."

They both smiled and Meran decided she liked this woman.

"I saw your concert at the Standish on the weekend," Lisa went on. "You and your husband. I love that kind of music."

"We've been playing it for a very long time."

"And you do it very well."

"Thank you."

"I . . ."

As Lisa hesitated, Meran knew that she was finally coming to the point of her conversation. She gave Lisa an encouraging smile.

"Working on the street as I do," Lisa went on finally, "I've heard about you and your husband. How you sometimes help people. . . ."

Meran raised an eyebrow.

"I could really use some help," Lisa said.

Meran tucked her hand into the crook of the woman's arm.

"Well, why don't we find someplace quiet," she said, "and you can tell me about it."

It was a short walk up Battersfield Road to Kathryn's Café in the heart of Lower Crowsea. Like the area itself, with its narrow streets and old stone buildings, Kathryn's had an old-world feel about it—from the dark wood paneling and hand-carved chair backs to the small round tables with their checkered tablecloths, fat glass condiment containers, and straw-wrapped wine bottles used as candleholders. The music piped in over the house sound system was timeless. Telemann and Vivaldi, Bill Evans and Clifford Brown.

But if the atmosphere was Old World, the clientele were definitely contemporary. Situated so close to Butler University, Kathryn's had been a favourite haunt of the university students since it first opened in the early sixties as a coffeehouse. Though much had changed from those early days, there was still live music played on its small stage on Friday and Saturday nights, as well as poetry recitations on Wednesdays and Sunday-morning storytelling sessions.

Meran and Lisa sat by a window, fair-trade coffee and homemade banana muffins set out on the table in front of them.

"How much do you know of Newford history?" Lisa asked after she'd stirred her coffee for the third time.

"Well, I don't follow politics."

"But you've heard of Old City?"

Meran nodded. Old City was part of the original heart of Newford. It lay underneath the subway tunnels—dropped there in the late eighteen hundreds during the great quake. The present city, including its sewers and underground transportation tunnels, had been built above the ruins of the old. There'd been talk in the early seventies of renovating the ruins as a tourist attraction—as had been done in Seattle—but Old City lay too far underground for easy access, and after numerous studies on the project, the city council had decided that it simply wouldn't be cost-effective.

"There've always been stories about people living down there," Lisa went on. "You know, skells—winos and bag ladies and the like. But now I keep hearing rumours on the streets that if you're lost and hurt and nobody cares about you, you can find a haven in Old City." Lisa gave Meran a wan smile. "You know . . . like on that old TV show with the cat guy."

Meran shook her head. "We've never had a television."

"Oh." Lisa blinked, as though the concept of not owning a set was utterly foreign to her. "Well, it's supposed to be a kind of utopia. Dry and warm. You don't have to worry about food, or police, or parents. . . ."

Her voice trailed off.

"And?" Meran prompted her after a few moments of silence.

"I don't believe in benevolent utopias," Lisa said, "but I do believe that something's going on down there and it can't be good. Street people are disappearing. *Kids* are disappearing. It's not in the papers, because the press hasn't caught on to it yet, but I hear the talk around the office. I'm not the only one whose caseload has suddenly lightened. Everybody I work with has heard these new stories about Old City."

"So why don't you go to the papers?"

Lisa shook her head. "And tell them what? Even a rag like *The Examiner* is going to want more than the say-so of a few social workers."

"Well, then, how about the police?"

"We're talking street people and poverty-level families that are probably relieved to have one mouth less to feed."

"I can't believe that," Meran said.

Though what she really meant was, she didn't want to believe it.

"I've seen parents sell their own kids," Lisa said. A bleakness settled in her eyes. "I'm not saying they're all like that, but there are people out there with children who shouldn't be entrusted with the responsibility of caring for a goldfish, little say a child. In a city this big you're going to get all kinds—and that includes the dregs."

"Still, the police—"

"Missing person reports have been filed, but they're all caught up in paperwork."

Meran sighed and looked out the window. Across the street, two children were playing ball in an alleyway.

"What did you want me to do?" she asked finally.

Lisa shook her head. "I don't know. I just heard you could fix things. I thought maybe you could look into it. I just want to know that they're . . . okay."

"What makes you think they're not?"

"They don't come back."

"I see," Meran said. "I'll talk to my husband. And we'll see what we can do."

"Here's my card," Lisa said. "Call me if you need anything."

Meran turned the card over and over in her hands, her gaze drifting across the street again to where the children played. A prickle of uneasiness fingered her spine.

"We'll do what we can," she said softly.

When she got home, Meran followed the sound of harping through the house until she came to the narrow, windowless room on the second floor that her husband used for his music. It was just large enough for a few comforts and necessities: a Morris chair with a reading lamp standing behind it; a barrister's bookcase that stood five stacks high, the middle shelf of which had a wooden front that folded out to make a small desk; and his roseharp, Teleynros, standing near the straight-backed chair he sat in when he played. The bookcases were stuffed with music folios, mostly written in his hand. More lay in stacks on the floor, or balanced precariously from the ledge of his music stand.

There were many rooms in this big rambling house of theirs, rooms with tall ceilings and wonderful acoustics, with windows that overlooked the gardens along the sides and back, or the grove of oak trees in front. But for some reason, this was the room Cerin preferred.

He looked up when she reached the doorway.

"That's the tune you taught Alan, isn't it?"

Cerin nodded. " 'Eliz Iza.' He plays it so simply, yet I can't seem to capture the poetry he puts into it."

"Different hearts make different music."

He smiled.

"I was talking to a social worker today," Meran said.

"One of Angel's people?"

"No. Her name's Lisa and she works for the city. She was telling me about this community of homeless people and run-aways that's living in Old City."

"There've always been stories of people living down there and in the abandoned subway tunnels."

Meran nodded. "But for that many people to be down there, they'll have started to encroach—"

"On goblin territory. What does Christy call them?"

"Skookin," Meran said with a smile.

"That's it. And our friend Bramley's butler is their king, isn't he? I'm surprised he'd let any more than a few stragglers take refuge down there."

Notoriously bad-tempered, Olaf Goonasekara was not known for either his generosity or patience.

"The problem," Meran went on, "is that the people going down there don't seem to be coming back."

"Maybe I'll take a walk down there. I'll see if Lucius feels like going for a stroll."

While her husband didn't have Goon's unfortunate temperament, he could be infuriatingly protective. He grinned now at the look on her face.

"It's for simple reconnaissance," he said. "There'd be nothing strange about a couple of odd birds like Lucius and myself wandering about down there. We do that kind of thing all the time. But a lady such as yourself, who loves the woods and the open air? What would they make of your wandering about in that dark Goblinburg? If there is anything suspicious, your appearance would immediately raise an alarm."

"I suppose . . ."

"And considering your history . . ." he added.

"Yes, well . . ."

"Not to mention that Old Town's under the ground."

Meran nodded. She rode the subway as rarely as possible, preferring streetcars and buses, and she hated basements. It was the being underground. In her father's forest, their trees sent roots deep into the earth, wandering happily down there in the dirt and rocks, but the people lived aboveground. She felt more kinship to the boughs that reached skyward, and the leaves that exchanged their gossips with the wind.

"But it's not like I *can't* go underground," she said.

"I know. Only why go if you don't need to?"

So she agreed to stay home, and the two of them went down into Old City, her tall harper husband and Lucius Portsmouth, a large black Buddha of a man with pure raven blood and such a brood of relatives, it was impossible to keep track of them all.

And they didn't come back.

Meran was looking through the vegetable drawer in the fridge to see if she had enough for a stir-fry, when her flute came scampering in. It wasn't in flute form when it was mobile like this, of course, but rather in its bodach shape: Wee Jack, skinny as a stick figure with a narrow head and large eyes.

"Mistress, mistress!" the little man called. "The goblins have himself."

The big rambling Kelledy house was home to dozens of bodachs and other fairy folk. They loved to tease Meran, but kept out of her husband's way, since they believed his harping could lock them into an inanimate form. A superstitious bunch, they wouldn't even use his name in conversation, referring to Cerin as "himself" instead.

Meran looked up from her inventory.

"What did you say?"

"I'm sorry, I'm sorry," Wee Jack said, "but I heard it from Caperdrum, who heard it from the Church Street wrens, who heard a pair of goblins talking about it not a half hour ago."

Meran banged the fridge door shut and ran up the stairs to Cerin's music room to check on the roseharp. She already feared the worst because, now that she was listening for it, she realized that the instrument's usual murmuring had gone still. That never happened. No matter where Cerin was, there was a bond between himself and his harp that kept the strings of the instrument trembling, if not actually playing some soft tune—no matter where or how far away Cerin might have gone.

But it was silent now.

She walked slowly up to the harp and put a hand on its support beam, close to where the rose was carved out of the joint. Against her palm, the wood felt cool, rather than the warmth of an instrument in use.

Wee Jack stood miserable in the doorway, unwilling, as most of the house's uninvited inhabitants would be, to actually enter the master's private room.

"Oh, what will we do?" he asked.

Meran regarded him with dark eyes.

"Pay a visit to Old City," she said.

Wee Jack gave her a look as though he thought she'd gone mad.

"But if they've captured himself and Mr. Raven . . ."

Meran gave a slow nod. Old as time, the pair had more magic in a little finger than an oak maid might in her whole tree, just saying she even had a tree anymore. If the goblins had found a way to render them captive, they'd make even quicker work of her.

"Then maybe we should pay a visit to their king," she said.

Wee Jack shivered, but this time he made no argument.

"Is Goon here?" Meran demanded when the door to the professor's house opened at her knock.

Jilly Coppercorn stood in the doorway, leaning on a pair of canes, and smiled at her.

"And hello to you, too," she said.

It took Meran a moment to shift from fierce mode.

"I'm sorry," she said. "It's just that his goblins have done something to Cerin and Lucius."

Jilly's eyes widened with concern. Using her canes, she shuffled to one side as quickly as she could make herself move.

"He's in the kitchen," she said.

Meran thanked her, then swept down the hall, with a little fairy man at her heels. The little man waved to Jilly as he hurried along behind his mistress, leaving Jilly blinking and not entirely sure she'd even seen him. By the time she got to the kitchen, Meran had the professor's butler backed up against one of the kitchen's counters.

"Did you forget who we were?" Meran was saying in a grim voice that Jilly had never heard her use before. "Do you think I wouldn't be able to remember the word that will unmake you?"

Jilly had grown so used to thinking of the professor's friends as people she just sat around with, sharing a cup of tea and some gossip, she'd forgotten that so many of them had truly exotic origins. Meran was a dryad from the Otherworld, her husband an ageless harper. Goon—properly Olaf Goonasekara, though no one called him that—was the king of the skookin who lived under the streets of Newford in Old City. Lucius was the Raven who'd called the world into being, though he himself didn't remember that. He had that in common with the crow girls, who were almost never aware of being anything other than a pair of rambunctious teenage girls.

But Jilly hadn't realized that Meran Kelledy had a temper or could be so grim, because in all the time Jilly had known her, Meran had only ever been kind and sweet-mannered. Such wasn't the case now. Today she was in full mother-bear mode, protecting those she loved.

"I have nothing to do with the world down under," Goon protested.

In place of his usual curmudgeonly demeanor, he actually looked alarmed. Jilly didn't blame him. She was feeling a bit worried herself, and Meran's attention wasn't even on her.

"It's common knowledge that you rule in Goblinburg," Meran said.

"Then it should be equally common knowledge that my throne was taken from me and Cornig Fairnswanter sits on it in my place."

"You abdicated?"

Goon shrugged. He was regaining some of the normal sour look that he normally wore.

"As much as, I suppose," he said. "By choosing to live here with Bramley, rather than down under."

Meran's shoulders lost their stiff resolve and drooped.

"And this Fairnswanter," she said. "How did he become so powerful that he could trap both Cerin and Lucius?"

Goon shook his head. "The Fairnswanter I knew couldn't have. He's nothing more than a little pissant with a couple of drops of royal Goonasekara blood from a few generations back."

"They're changing human folk into goblins down there," a small voice piped up.

Jilly tracked it to its source and saw the little man who'd come in with Meran standing on one of the kitchen chairs. Meran's gaze followed Jilly's.

"Where did you hear that?" Meran asked.

The little man shrugged. "It's just something everybody knows."

"And you never told me?"

"I thought you knew, Mistress. I thought everybody knew."

"I didn't," Goon said.

"Oh, it's all darkness and trouble down below," the little man said. "No one goes there now—not among my folk."

"None of this was my doing," Goon said.

Meran nodded. "I can see that now."

"I don't particularly like humans, but—"

"Then again, you don't like anyone," Meran finished for him.

Goon gave her a haughty look.

"I was going to say, I don't agree with reshaping of any kind, simply on principal. Alchemy's best left in the box with all the other perils men have inflicted on the world."

"What makes you think this is alchemy?" Meran asked.

"Human into skookin's no different than iron into gold. What would you call it?"

Jilly made her way to the table and carefully lowered herself into one of the free chairs. She leaned her canes up against the table and rubbed her right arm. It was tingling from the strain of using the cane, all the way from her shoulder to the tips of her fingers.

"I don't suppose anyone wants to tell me what's going on?" she asked.

Three heads turned in her direction. For a moment, Jilly thought no one was going to answer, but then Meran pulled out a chair. Sitting down, she told what had happened, frowning at Goon when she got to the part about what Wee Jack had heard.

"I've been down below twice before," she said, finishing up. "Once with you, Jilly, to bring back that drum you'd inadvertently borrowed, and once to get back a hair comb that had been borrowed from me." That earned Goon another dark look. "But on neither trip did I see or hear of anything with enough power down there to capture both my husband *and* Lucius."

"Neither have I," Goon said, "and I know the secrets of Old City. Something new has taken up residence there."

"And been welcomed by your people," Meran said.

"Or has bent them to its will." Goon turned to Wee Jack. "And you say they're swelling goblin ranks with human changelings?"

The little man nodded.

"I don't understand," Meran said. "What would be the point? Surely they don't think they could raise an army against the human world?"

"I doubt it," Goon said. "But there hasn't been a child born down below in over fifty years. There was always talk—even when I lived down below—of how to find new blood to replace those who have died."

"Well, it appears that now they have."

"Indeed."

Meran straightened in her chair. "And I suppose now I'll have to go and find out what."

"You can't," Goon said. "If they took the other two so easily—"

"We don't know how easily they were taken."

"—then they will take you, too. And your old words of power will be of no use to you down below. Speak one of them there and you'll bring the new city down upon the old, and upon your own head as well."

"Can you go?" Meran asked.

Goon shook his head. "I'm too well known, and probably less welcome. What we need is a thief. Someone to creep in and snoop about for us. Until we know *what* we're dealing with, we can't make any plans."

He and Meran both turned to Wee Jack.

"Why are you looking at me?" he asked.

"Because," Goon said, "sneaky thief is the very definition of a bodach."

"Oh, unlike a skookin, who's the soul of good manners and means no one any harm."

"I thought skookin was a word Christy or the professor made up," Jilly said, hoping to forestall an argument between the two.

"Where *is* Bramley?" Meran asked before either Goon or Wee Jack could speak.

"Delivering a paper on his Bigfoot theories at some conference in Anchorage," Jilly told her.

Goon snorted. "It's not a conference. It's one of those sci-fi conventions where people dress up like spacemen or—"

"Ill-mannered skookin," Wee Jack offered.

"Better that than a cowardly bodach."

"I'm not cowardly," Wee Jack said. He turned to Meran. "Am I, Mistress?"

"Not in the least."

"It's just, if there's dark magic afoot, they'll sniff me out in the down below. We always know when there's other fairy about, so the skookin will, too."

"That's true," Goon had to admit.

"I know a thief," Meran said. "A human one. Just tell me what he needs to look for, where he needs to go."

If Louie Felden felt any surprise at Meran tracking him down in his Tombs squat, it didn't show in his features. He didn't get up when she stepped over the litter in the doorway and entered his room. The only furnishings were a pile of trash in one corner, the duffel bag he was using as a pillow, and the bedding on which he sat.

"Did you bring the police?" he asked.

"No. Should I have?"

He shrugged. "I'm not going anywhere with you, if that's what you're thinking. I'm not going to be anybody's project. I'm not something you can fix."

"Actually, I'm here to avail myself of your expertise."

"Say what?"

"I want to know if you'll do a job for me."

He gave her a considering look and followed it with another shrug.

"What do you want me to steal?" he asked.

"Nothing. It's more like a scouting expedition."

He sat up straighter, interested despite himself. "To where?"

"Old City."

"Ah. You've been talking to Lisa."

"I have," Meran agreed. "But not about this."

He lounged back against his duffel bag.

"Maybe," he said, "people just like it better down there and that's why they're not coming back."

Meran nodded. "And maybe something's keeping them down there against their will. Maybe they're being . . . changed."

"Maybe, but why should you care? There's all kinds of homeless people who aren't going down into Old City who'd be happy to become your personal charity cases. Want me to point out a few of them to you?"

"My husband's down there," Meran told him.

Louie shook his head. "You don't look the type to have a wino for an old man, but then I guess it doesn't matter how high and mighty a person might be before they find themselves on the streets—you hit the bottom just the same."

"It's not like that."

"Look at me," he said. "This is where I live. You've already seen how I make my living. You don't have to be embarrassed in front of someone like me. Shit happens. Whatever he's done with his life, it's not necessarily your fault."

"I know. But it really isn't like that. Someone is keeping him down there."

"And you want me to bring him back?"

"I doubt that would be possible, and I wouldn't ask you to get so involved. I just want you to go down there and snoop around, see if you can find out what's happening."

"And then?" he asked.

"You come back and tell me."

He studied her for a long moment, then shook his head.

"Nah, I don't think so," he told her. "You seem like a nice lady, but I try not to get involved in other people's problems. There's nothing in it for me."

"I'll give you a hundred dollars to go down. More when you get back and bring me something useful."

"A hundred dollars?"

She nodded.

"Right now—*before* I go?"

When she nodded again, he just laughed.

"What's to stop me from just taking your money and blowing you off?" he asked.

"I'd find you and get it back."

"Yeah, right."

"I found you here, didn't I?"

He frowned. "How did you track me down?"

Meran nodded to the window.

"The gargoyle across the street told me you were here," she said.

He laughed again. "Oh, right. The gargoyle."

But he got up and had a look out the window. The abandoned structure across the street from his squat had once been an office building and there *was* a gargoyle pushing out from its roof gutter that had a direct view into his window. There were, in fact, three of them along the gutter, each a little more grotesque than the next.

He was still smiling when he turned back to Meran. She returned his smile and pulled a hundred-dollar bill from her pocket and offered it to him.

"You're awfully trusting," he said. "I could just roll you for whatever else you're carrying."

"Try me," she said.

He tried to stare her down, but he couldn't hold her gaze as long as she could his.

"Whatever," he said.

Walking over from the window, he plucked the bill from her hand.

"So how do I get in touch with you?" he asked.

"Call my name aloud three times. Someone will hear and tell me."

"Ho-kay."

"Thank you, Louie," she said, then picked her way back over the litter in his doorway and returned the way she'd come.

Louie stood in his squat, turning the hundred-dollar bill over in his hands. Then something occurred to him. He went to the door to call down the hall that she hadn't told him her name.

But she was already gone.

An hour later, Louie was in Jimmy's Billiards at the corner of Vine and Palm, halfway to doubling his money in a game with three college kids too green to realize they were being sharked by what they thought was some dumb little kid. Jimmy'd been letting him hang around the pool hall for years, even though he was underage. They had an understanding. Louie could play the tables, but if he so much as tried to have a sip from anybody's drink, he was out on his ass.

Seemed fair to Louie. He didn't like the taste of beer anyway. What he liked was this: playing the game, sinking the impossible shots.

He was about to take a complicated cross-side when a strong hand clapped onto his shoulder.

"The fuck?" he said.

He slipped out of the grip and turned, trying to get the room to bring his pool cue into play and give whoever this was a lesson in manners, except it was only her. That weird woman who'd tracked him down in his squat.

"I meant do it immediately," she said.

"Okay, this is getting creepy," he told her. "How'd you—"

She stepped in close to him. "Or you can just give me my money back."

"Lady, you need to back off," he said and started to give her a push.

He didn't get to touch her. She caught his wrist before his hand could reach her shoulder, and just like that, he couldn't move his arm.

"I'm disappointed," she said. "I thought you were a man of your word."

He pulled back, but he couldn't get his wrist free until she decided to let it go. The college kids were watching all of this with big eyes. Hell, everybody in Jimmy's was watching him be humiliated. But that didn't make him feel as bad as what she'd said. He wanted to tell her that you only kept your word to your brothers and sisters on the street, not some chump woman like her. Except he knew that wasn't true. Your word was your word. And she wasn't a chump. He didn't know what the hell she was, but she wasn't some mark ready to be fleeced.

"I . . . I didn't know you were in such a big hurry," he said.

"I am."

He tried to hold her gaze and again he was the first to look away.

"Whatever," he said.

He peeled off a few bills from his winnings and tossed them on the green velvet to cover the table.

"Some other time, guys," he said. "Duty calls."

One of the college boys—the one who'd come in with the lettered jacket—laughed.

"Yeah," he said. "You wouldn't want to keep Mommy waiting for that little dick of yours."

His friends began to laugh with them until Meran turned in their direction and fixed them with her dark gaze.

Crap, Louie thought. Now it was going to get messy, because he was going to have to hit that loudmouth, just on general principle.

Except before he could step in, Jimmy himself was standing at the side of the table, a half-smoked cigar stuck out of the corner of his mouth.

"These guys bothering you, Meran?" he asked the woman.

"Oh, I don't think they're going to be any trouble—are you, boys?"

Here and there in the pool room, dark-skinned men were stepping back from their tables, or standing up from the benches where they'd been drinking beer and watching the various games.

The college boys were green, but they weren't entirely stupid.

"Sorry, ma'am," the one who'd spoken up first said. "I didn't mean anything by that."

"You see, Jimmy?" the woman said. "Everything's fine."

The college boys beat a hasty retreat. Jimmy returned to his stool behind the bar. The men who'd displayed such a sudden interest were back doing what they'd been doing as though they'd never interrupted their activities.

Louie suppressed a shiver. There was something seriously *weird* going on here.

When the woman started for the door, Louie followed her.

"So how do you know Jimmy?" he asked as they walked down the stairs to the street.

"Oh, Jimmy knows everybody," she said over her shoulder.

"Yeah, I guess he does." Though how would he know someone like *you*, Louie wanted to ask. Instead he said, "And all those guys who seemed so interested?"

She stopped on the sidewalk and gave him a guileless look.

"Oh, you know how it is," she said. "Sometimes people just get protective."

Yeah, but not toughs like that. He'd seen some of those same guys just sit there and watch somebody get beat half to death without lifting a hand to stop it.

"So," the woman went on. "*Do* we still have a bargain?"

"Yeah, sure."

"Then, please," she said. "Would you get to it?"

And then she walked off down the street.

Louie stood there for a long moment, watching her go.

You owe me some explanations, lady, he thought.

But he turned and headed for the Grasso Street subway station. There was a steel door in its east tunnel that led down into Old City. There were probably other ways down, but that was the only one he knew.

And that was how Louie found himself skulking around through the rubbled streets of Old City, wondering what exactly he was doing down here. It had started with a hundred bucks, but it wasn't about the money anymore. Now it was about keeping his word, and what was up with that?

He'd only been down here a couple of times before, just to

check it out, but he'd never stayed. This was where the real losers came, the people with no hope at all. It wasn't particularly great, squatting in the abandoned buildings of the Tombs, but you could still pretend you were seminormal. You could drift out of the ruined blocks of old tenements, factories, and office buildings and take your tithe from the normal citizens who had real homes to go to. A little panhandling, some wallet snatching, pool sharking if you had enough cash to stake you to a game.

Old City was where you went when you just gave up.

The door from the subway station opened into what had once been a four-story building before the quake dropped it underground. Louie made his way down a stairwell that years of previous visitors had cleaned up enough so that the route was relatively clear. When he stepped out of the building, he was on the ruin of an old lost street.

Which was really more weirdness, when you thought about it.

Louie looked around himself.

How come he'd never thought about this the other times he'd been here? He was deep underground, but it wasn't completely dark like it should be. Once your eyes adjusted, you could make out the buildings, the rubble on the street around you. And what was a street doing here? How come the buildings still stood? How come everything wasn't just buried and swallowed away in the dirt?

He craned his neck and stared up into the dark, but he couldn't see a roof. Couldn't see anything up there.

He shrugged. Whatever. And started off down the street.

There weren't a lot of people living down here, but after a couple of blocks, he was surprised that he hadn't run into anybody. The other times, he'd seen people huddled in doorways, ducking out of sight in windows, scurrying down narrow alleys. Today there was nothing.

He'd walked for about ten minutes before he saw the glow of

a fire ahead. He quickened his pace until he was close enough to see that the fire was in an old oil drum. Some guy stood by it, warming his hands.

Louie looked around himself, blinking at the afterimages the fire had put in his gaze. The guy seemed to be on his own, so Louie approached him, walking easy, hands in his pockets, one wrapped around the handle of the flick-knife he kept in his right jacket pocket.

What a weird-looking little guy, Louie thought. He had a big round head and a bigger rounded body, with not much of a neck in between, so he looked like two-thirds of a snowman. His arms and legs, in sharp contrast, were thin as twigs. But he seemed friendly enough, smiling as Louie approached.

"Got any food?" the guy asked.

Louie pulled a chocolate bar from his left pocket and passed it over.

"Thanks, kid."

"No problem." He looked around himself. "So, where is everybody?"

"This is Old City, kid," the guy told him around a mouthful of chocolate. "You don't exactly get crowds around here."

"Yeah, but I haven't seen a soul. Usually there's somebody around."

"I'm here, ain't I? Stadell Froome, at your service."

"You know what I mean," Louie said.

Froome nodded with his head, indicating where the city went on.

"Folks have been taking to heading on," he said, "and they don't come back."

"Something happening to them?"

"I guess you could say that. There's a bunch living down there that can fix people so they're more comfortable living here below. Use a thing they've got called da slockit light to get the job done."

"That supposed to mean something?"

Froome nodded. "It's a thing that puts out the light we carry inside us—you know, like your soul?—but you don't die the way you normally would when you lose that light. You just get changed."

"Changed into what?"

"Like I said: into something that's more comfortable living down here."

Louie shook his head. "Why would anybody want to do a thing like that?"

"You've got a lot of questions, kid."

Louie shrugged. "I'm just curious. Curiosity's the only thing I haven't lost yet, I guess."

"People come down here, they don't have *anything* left."

"Yeah, well, I'm not planning to move in. I'm just snooping around. I've got no home, no job, and no money, so bumming around and snooping into weird-ass shit's pretty much all that's left to fill my day."

Froome laughed. "Guess you've got a point, kid."

"So how do the people find out about this thing that can change them? They just go wandering around until they stumble onto it?"

"Nah. There's these guys come up through here from time to time. They talk it up, offer to show anybody who's interested how they can partake of it their own selves."

Louie smiled. "These guys look anything like you?"

"Now that you mention it, maybe they do. I could show you, if you're interested. I owe you a favour, after all, for that very tasty chocolate bar that was freely given."

There was something about the way he said "freely given" that set off a little warning bell in Louie's head. It was the same one that went off when he was setting up a pool game and he realized the other player was playing him.

"I don't think showing me anything's worth the favour

you owe me," he said. "Not when it's something you'd do anyway."

Something flickered in Froome's eyes, but it was gone before Louie could read it.

"Got me there, kid," he said. "You want to see it anyway?"

"What? This socket light?"

Froome shook his head. "That's 'slockit light' and it's all got to do with the light you've got inside you. The thing we've got back there can put it out for you. Stop the hurting, you know? Up above"—he nodded with his head—"no one gives a crap about what happens to you. They don't get the pain that won't go away, because they're snug in their perfect little lives."

"Everybody feels pain," Louie said.

"Sure, but not everybody's got the nice meal, or the pretty toys, or the soft bed, or the family and friends to help make it go away."

Louie nodded. "You've got a point."

"Course I do, kid. You wouldn't be here if I didn't."

"So what's in it for you?"

Froome looked genuinely puzzled. "What do you mean?"

"Well, you're helping all these people into these new lives of theirs where they can forget about the dark hole in their heads and just be happy down here, right?"

"Right."

"So what do you get out of it?"

"Company," Froome said.

"Just that."

Froome nodded. "What else? It's not like these people have anything else to offer."

The funny thing was, Louie believed him. Everybody had an angle, he knew that—some way they came out ahead—but Froome seemed to be the exception.

"Cool," he said.

Froome smiled. "So do you want come see how it's done?"

This was the point where he should go back to the woman—what had Jimmy called her? Something like . . . Marion.

What he should be doing is go back aboveground and tell Marion what he'd learned. Show her that he could keep his word, earn his hundred dollars.

But he found himself wanting to do more.

Marion was a woman who obviously knew a lot of other people who could have done this for her. She knew Jimmy. She knew the toughs that hung around the pool hall. But she'd come to him. He'd tried to lift her wallet, but she'd still come to him and offered him good money to do a job for her.

She didn't look at him like he was some little useless kid. She'd looked at him like he was a person. Like he could do this for her. Like he could give his word and keep it.

That hadn't happened in a long, long time.

Most people just wanted to fix him up, like he was broken. He knew he was small for his age—he looked about twelve, but he was actually sixteen now. And he was a homely kid, that was about the kindest way you could put it. "Ugly as sin" was how his old man used to describe him. Sure, he lived on the streets, but he made do. He didn't peddle his ass like Bobby had before he'd ODed. And it wasn't like he really hurt anybody. People could afford what he took. And even when he lifted a wallet, he didn't try to peddle the ID or the credit cards. He just took the cash and dropped the wallet in the nearest mailbox.

So he wasn't an angel. But that didn't mean he had nothing to give.

He could do this thing: find out what was going on, maybe track down Marion's husband for her, too.

Not to be the hero.

Just to show that he was worth his word, and maybe more. Because he couldn't remember anybody ever having any kind of faith in him before.

"Well?" Froome asked.

Louie shrugged. "Sure, why not? I've come this far; I might as well check this thing out."

Meran decided she needed to go home, and Jilly thought she shouldn't be on her own. In the end, they all made the trek from the professor's house with Goon pushing Jilly's wheelchair and Wee Jack riding on her lap.

"How come nobody else seems to see him?" Jilly asked when they were on Stanton Street and had passed yet another person oblivious to the little bodach.

"They do," Meran told her. "They just see him in his other form."

Jilly looked down and for a moment she thought there was a wooden flute lying on her lap instead of a little man riding there. Then it was Wee Jack again, grinning up at her.

"He's . . ."

"My flute, yes," Meran said.

Jilly grinned. "I just love magic."

"We don't," a voice said from above.

Jilly looked up to see the crow girls—two skinny, dark-haired girls perched in the branches of one of Stanton's tall old oak trees. They dropped lightly to the ground and gave Goon fierce looks.

"Magic's just trouble," Maida said.

Zia nodded. "Like goblins stealing away your uncle."

"We're going down there right now."

"We'll set things right."

"We'll bang them with sticks."

Zia waved the twig she had in her hand. "Except I need a bigger stick."

"You can't go down there," Goon said.

Maida stuck out her tongue at him. "We don't have to listen to you."

"No, you're just a goblin yourself."

Zia slapped her twig against the palm of her hand.

"Maybe we'll just bang *you* with sticks," she added.

"As soon as we get bigger ones," Maida said.

"Much bigger ones."

"Please don't," Meran said.

She explained how, if there was something down below that could render both Cerin and Lucius helpless, then a frontal attack, even by two such brave crow girls, probably wasn't the best idea.

"We're not afraid," Zia said.

"Not one bit."

"Not even a bit of a bit."

"Not even—"

"I know you're not," Meran said. "But I'm asking you to wait. Will you do that for me?"

The crow girls gave Goon another pair of fierce scowls, but they nodded in agreement.

"Maybe you could ask your cousins if there's any news," Meran added.

Looking ahead, Jilly saw that the oaks surrounding the Kelledy house were full of crows. They were making a terrible racket, as though they were all talking at the same time. As she watched, new ones arrived, while others flew off.

"We can do that," Zia said and the two of them ran off ahead.

Meran turned to Goon. "You're lucky they don't remember how powerful they really are."

"I know," Goon said. "I'd be skookin jelly on the sidewalk."

"What do you mean?" Jilly asked.

"The crow girls were already here when Raven made the world," Meran explained. "They're the oldest and most powerful of all, but it's not something they remember."

"Why not?"

"I'm not sure. I think it's got something to do with how remembering something like . . . well, I think it would be too much for anyone to hold on to and still stay sane."

"I'd hardly call that pair sane," Goon muttered.

"I like them," Jilly said.

"You would."

"But why," Jilly asked Meran, "don't you let them go down below? If they're so powerful . . ."

"There's a story," Meran said, "that if the crow girls ever fully wake and remember who they are, they will return the world to the state it was in before Raven made it."

"That doesn't make any sense. If there was no world until Raven made it . . . oh, I get it. There'd just be nothing."

Meran nodded.

"Nothing," Goon said, "and the crow girls. *If* those stories are true."

"But they've been fierce before," Jilly said. "I've heard stories of them helping people out of some pretty rough situations."

"That's like you or me, turning in our sleep because of a restless dream. On those occasions you're referring to, I doubt they actually woke up."

Jilly slowly shook her head. "The world really is a complicated place, isn't it?"

"Or a very simple one," Meran said.

She seemed about to say more, but just then the crow girls came racing back, shrieking as raucously as their cousins in the trees above.

"There's news, there's news!" Zia cried.

"But the news is there's no news!" Maida added.

Meran sighed and Jilly's heart went out to her.

Froome led Louie deeper into Old City. After awhile, the rubble-strewn streets gave way to tidier avenues as though city work crews had been down here, cleaning up and maintaining the area. Louie still didn't see anyone about, but now he got the sense that they were no longer alone. That they were being watched from the buildings, even though he could never actually catch a single soul in the act.

Finally they came to a small park. Dead trees were the only vegetation left. In the middle of the park was what looked like a stone table, and on it, a lantern stood amongst a clutter of smaller objects that he couldn't make out from where he was. The lantern itself gave off a strange red light—it made Louie uncomfortable, but it also quickened his pulse.

He wasn't sure he wanted to get any closer to that light, but he followed Froome all the same, his gaze locked onto the lantern's glow until he was distracted by a life-sized stone statue lying on its back not far from the table. He stepped closer and looked down on it. It was a little hard to tell because of the way it was lying there, but it appeared to be a rendering of a man who, if the statue had been set upright, would have been crouching down and looking at something terribly interesting. On his shoulder was a raven. The workmanship was amazing—so much detail. You could make out every feather of the raven's wings, every hair on the man's head.

"Cool statue," Louie said.

He put a hand on the knee closest to him and suddenly heard a voice in his head.

Who's there?

It was a day for strangeness, Louie thought, no question about it. Strangest of all, maybe, was how he didn't question the way he was just going along with each new surprise that came his way.

He'd never been particularly imaginative. Oh, he could scheme and plot and work out the finest details of a scam, no problem. But he hadn't had fairy tales read to him as a kid, hadn't really *had* a childhood. So he didn't know how to use his mind for the make-believe that would allow a person to imagine there to be more to the world than what you could see. For Louie, everything just was what it was. He didn't care about its story, just whether it could be of use to him or not. Truth was, he'd never had much of an interest in any kind of story until this strange day came along and woke a hunger in him.

Now he wanted to know the story behind Marion and Jimmy and the dark-skinned men in the pool hall. He wanted to know the story behind Froome and his need to turn the hopeless and the lost into odd little people, just like him. And most of all, at this moment, he wanted to know the story behind the voice in his head which, he had the crazy idea, was coming from the statue his hand was resting upon.

Can you hear me? he asked, shaping the words in his head.

Yes. Who are you?

Nobody. But I guess I could be a friend. How can I help you?

Break the—

Louie lost the connection to the voice when Froome grabbed his arm and jerked him back from the statue.

"What are you doing?" Froome wanted to know.

"Nothing," Louie said. "It's just a really interesting statue."

He wanted to put his hand on it again, but Froome was standing between him and the statue now.

"Where did it come from?" he asked Froome.

"Nowhere. It's always been here. It must have been part of the world above and came down when everything else did."

Oh yeah? Louie thought. Then why is it lying on its back when everything else around here has been tidied up and set right?

But all he said was, "I guess. But don't you wonder if—"

He started to reach for the statue again—"Break what?" he wanted to ask the voice—but Froome pushed him away.

"Don't bother with that nosy old thing," Froome said and steered him towards the stone table. "This is what you really came to see."

Louie let himself be led over to the table. This close, the lantern made him more than uncomfortable. The dull red light, like the fading embers in a fire, started a pulsing between his temples. Nausea filled the pit of his stomach like sour milk. He wanted to put his hands on the lantern and let the light run over his skin. At the same time, he wanted to run as far from it as he could. To pay his couple of bucks at the Y and scrub himself in the showers for as long as he could, never mind the creepy guys who hung out in there looking to prey on the little kid he seemed to be.

He forced himself to look away, turning his attention to the junk that was piled around the lantern. The weirdest thing for sure was the mummified hand that gripped the lantern's handle, but the rest of the stuff wasn't exactly treasure. Bottle caps and rats' skulls. Lengths of ribbon, coins and a bird's nest. Feathers, twigs, and shoelaces. Screw bits and empty pop cans. Smoothed pebbles, balls of tinfoil, and tangles of rubberbands.

"What is all this crap?" he asked.

Froome shrugged. "People carry around the strangest things, especially those who end up down below. But after the change, they don't seem to need those things anymore."

Like anybody ever would, Louie thought.

Reluctantly, his gaze went back to the lantern. He remembered what the voice in his head had started to say.

Break the . . .

It seemed pretty obvious what it had been trying to tell him to do.

Break the frigging lantern.

Louie didn't have a problem with that. He just had to figure out how to do it before Froome could stop him. He had the feeling the little man was a lot faster and stronger than you'd think.

"Did you hear that?" Meran asked.

The others shook their heads from where they sat around the kitchen table in the Kelledy's house.

"Hear what?" Jilly asked.

Meran was smiling. "The roseharp. It played for a moment."

"Does that mean something?" Goon asked.

"It means the master's still alive!" Wee Jack cried and he jumped down from his chair and did a circuit of cartwheels all around the table.

The crow girls got up, too, and danced about, though for their part they weren't so much celebrating as using the news as an excuse to not have to sit still.

"When it was so silent," Meran told Jilly and Goon through the hubbub, "I feared the worst."

Jilly cocked an ear, but she couldn't hear anything above the tumult of the bodach and the crow girls.

"But now you can hear it," she said.

Meran shook her head. "No, but *having* heard it I know that Cerin and Lucius have just been taken away. They're not dead." She looked down the hall. "Oh, I wish Louie would finish so that we can know what we're up against."

"It's been awhile now," Goon said.

"I know," Meran said.

"He could be far away with your money."

Meran nodded. "Except we know that he went down under and the crows haven't seen him come out yet."

"I don't envy him being down there," Jilly said.

"No," Meran said. "Neither do I."

"So how does it work?" Louie asked. "You know, how does it change people?"

Froome didn't answer. He was studying Louie, a strange look in his eyes.

"He doesn't trust you," he told Louie.

Louie looked around. So far as he could tell, they were still alone. Except for the statue, lying on its back, and he didn't think that was who Froome meant.

"Who doesn't?" he asked.

"Father."

Louie nodded, still looking around them.

"Who's invisible?" he asked.

Froome glared at him, the lantern's light giving his eyes a wicked glow. Or had that glow been there all along and he'd just managed to not notice it? Because other things were changing with Froome. He didn't seem quite so *human* anymore.

"You're another spy!" Froome cried.

He lunged for Louie, but Louie had been expecting something like that and was already in motion. He darted around the table and grabbed the lantern. The texture was horrible—like holding something alive instead of metal and glass. And that stupid mummified hand still clung to the handle.

"Back off," he warned, "or I'll break this."

He was planning to do it anyway, since that was what the statue had seemed to be trying to tell him, and whatever else the statue was, at least it looked human. But he was hoping to find a way to do it that would also give himself a chance to escape.

"You'll set them all free, will you?" Froome asked. He didn't try to grab Louie. Instead, he stood there now, smiling. "All those poor trapped souls. Did they tell you you'd be a hero?"

Louie caught movement from the corner of his eyes. He looked away for a moment to see that dozens of little pumpkin-bodied men and women were filling the park, all moving toward the stone table. He returned his attention to Froome.

"I'm no hero," he said.

"Oh, that's obvious, kid."

"But I will break this."

"Go ahead."

Great, Louie thought. He looked at the rest of the junk on the stone tabletop. There was probably something else he was supposed to break, but how was he supposed to figure out what it was? It was all just weird-ass crap.

He supposed that the fleshy feel of the lantern should have

been a giveaway. It probably wouldn't break even if he threw it against the table.

What he did know was that just holding it was giving him a serious case of the creeps.

"What makes you think you're the good guy, anyway?" Froome asked him.

The others were close now, too close. They stayed maybe ten, twelve feet back, but they made a circle about seven people deep and growing.

"Why is what we're doing here automatically evil?" Froome went on. "I told you no lies. The ones who were changed did so of their own free will. No one was forced. No evil army is being amassed. We *are* simply making unhappy lives content. Holding out the hand of friendship to those who have nothing. Who have less than nothing."

At the words "free will," Louie remembered Froome's odd reaction earlier when the business of favours had come up.

"Then what's the deal with that statue?" he asked. "Who made it? Who's it supposed to be and what do you have against the guy?"

"That's none of your business."

"Remember that chocolate bar and the favour you say you owe me?"

Froome glowered at him. "What of it?"

"Do me a favour," Louie said, "and explain the statue to me."

An unhappy murmur arose from the crowd around them.

"You're all the same," Froome said. "Meddlers who all think you know what's better for us than we do."

"Hey," Louie said. "I know all about that kind of thing. Up above, I've always got somebody trying to fix my life for me. They think they know best, but I don't buy it."

"Then you should be sympathetic to us."

"I never said I wasn't. It's just . . . what's the deal with the statue? I put my hand on it and it talked to me. You know, in my head. It asked me for help."

"So of course you would give it to them, the meddlers, rather than stand with us."

Them? Louie thought, glancing at the statue. There was only one figure lying there. Did this crazy little guy think that the man the statue was based on had a bird, and the bird was after him, too? Hello, paranoid much?

"So this is a statue of someone who was spying on you?" he asked.

"They weren't always statues," Froome told him. "Father turned them to stone."

"Whoa. People don't just get turned into stone."

"No? But they can give up their soul's light and change from human to us? And statues can speak to you in your head. How is the one any less possible than the other?"

"It's just . . ."

His voice trailed off. He realized two things. The first was . . .

"Yes," Froome said. "Father thinks you'll make a fine statue."

And the second was, that maybe the statue hadn't meant for him to break the lantern. Unless Froome was a better player than Louie thought he was, Froome really didn't care if the lantern was broken or not. So maybe the statue had been trying to tell him to break the contact between the lantern and the mummified hand. Because of all the weird things on that stone table, the withered hand clutching the lantern's handle was definitely the weirdest.

So he grabbed at it with his free hand.

He was almost too late. He could feel an impossible weight spreading through his limbs. Flesh turning to stone, bowing him down.

But he was able to grasp the hand.

And almost jerked his hand away when it began to wriggle in his grip.

But he held on. He ripped it away from the handle.

And was blinded by the flare of light that burst from the candle.

He dropped the lantern, but managed to keep his grip on the squirming, mummified hand. Blinded, he stumbled against the stone table, his body still feeling heavy . . . so heavy . . .

He heard the crowd wailing. Froome screeching.

And then he heard the sound of a harp and he figured he'd died and somehow managed to luck his way into Heaven, because where else did you hear harps?

"I am not happy," a deep, resonating voice said.

Uh-oh, Louie thought. They figured out that I'm not supposed to be here in Heaven.

He cracked his eyes open and pushed himself upright from the table. He was still holding the hand, but it was limp in his grip now. He saw Froome, trembling with fear. The crowd was backing away.

From him?

No, he realized. From something behind him. He turned to see two men standing where the statue had been. One looked just like the statue, a tall, white guy with long hair and a thin beard. The other was a bald black man and maybe the biggest person Louie had ever seen.

He could still hear the harp playing, but couldn't see where it was coming from, or who was playing it.

"What will we do with them?" the guy who'd been the statue said.

"Teach them a lesson," the black man said. "Meddling, were we? Let them see what true meddling is."

"Wait a sec," Louie said.

He held up his hand to get their attention, realized it was the one with the mummified hand, and brought it quickly down again. But it had gotten the result. The two men were both looking at him.

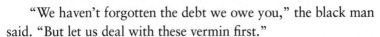

"We haven't forgotten the debt we owe you," the black man said. "But let us deal with these vermin first."

Louie swallowed. This was all so not his business, except he'd made it his business, hadn't he?

"It's about your dealing with them," he said.

"What are you trying to say?" the black man's companion asked.

When Louie turned his attention to him, he saw that the guy's fingers were moving at his sides, moving in the same tempo as the harping.

"Well, they didn't do anything wrong," Louie said.

"They turned us into stone."

"And stole the souls of the helpless," the black man added.

"Well, yeah," Louie said. "They turned you into stone. But that's only because you were interfering. Nobody's soul got stolen. They all chose to be changed."

The harper—Louie had to think of him as that, the way his fingers called up harp music from the air—shook his head.

"They preyed on the hopeless and the helpless," he said. "People too far gone to make a decision on their own."

"How do you know?" Louie asked. "Have you been where they were?"

"No, but I—"

"And what makes the life they'd have here so much worse than what they had before?"

Louie was thinking of Froome, the look on his face when he said the people who came to them provided company.

"They're part of a community down here," he went on. "They're looking after each other. So they're not human—so what? I'm getting the idea that neither of you are either. But tell me this: what gives you the right to decide what they should or shouldn't be?"

There was a long moment of silence.

"They still attacked us for no reason," the black man finally said.

"Is that true?" Louie asked Froome.

The little guy still looked scared, but Louie's defense seemed to be giving him some courage.

"Technically, I suppose they're right, kid," he said. "But they've been down here before—if not them, then their kind. Big old powerful spirits who decide how things are going to be. Father knew that if we didn't take them by surprise, then we'd be helpless before them."

"You keep saying 'father,' " Louie said. "Where is he?"

"You're holding all that's left of him in this world. He can only be with us when he holds da slockit light. Then he has the power to change one thing into another. We knew there'd be problems when we found the lantern and put the two of them together, but the chance to make things a little better down here seemed worth it."

Louie turned back to the harper and his companion.

"Are you seeing what I am here?" he asked.

Both men shook their heads.

"Well, I think it's pretty obvious," Louie said. "You came down here, with your minds made up that Froome and his people are all evil, and they assumed the worst of you as well. Sort of like willful misunderstandings, because I guess all of you have history, am I right? Seems to me, the best thing for everybody is for us to go back where we came from and leave the people down here alone to mind their own business."

The black man frowned, but the harper gave a slow nod.

"He's right, Lucius," he told his companion.

Lucius nodded. "I know. But it rankles."

"So can I give this back?" Louie asked, holding up the hand.

The harper's gaze went to Froome. "And when Father has his power back?"

"You go free," Froome said. "You have my word on that.

Just as you have my word that no one joins us except of their own free will."

"The word of a goblin," Lucius muttered.

"But no less his word," the harper said. "Except you don't rule down here, do you? Goonasekara is your king."

"Not anymore. Cornig Fairnswanter holds that title—or at least we let him think he does. Our true king is Father, who returned to us from beyond the grave in our time of need."

"And do we have his word?"

Froome nodded. "I can speak for him. The real question is, do we have your word that we will be left alone?"

The harper stilled the movement of his fingers and the music faded.

"You have our word," he said.

Louie walked over to Froome and gave him the hand.

"No hard feelings, right?" he said.

"None at all. They would have kept coming and we would have ended up with a park full of statues until one of them finally got through our defenses and destroyed our world."

Louie blinked at him. "Uh, right. Whatever."

He started to turn, but Froome held out a hand.

"I meant, thank you," he said as he and Louie shook.

Louie paused and looked at the debris on the stone table.

"Hey, can I have this?" he asked, picking up a small shiny object.

"Of course."

"Thanks."

When he turned, the crowd parted, making an avenue for him and the two men to walk down.

"What brought you here?" the harper asked Louie once they'd left the crowd behind.

"This woman named Marion asked me to scout things out for her. Either one of you her husband?"

"If you mean Meran, then that would be me," the harper

said. He smiled and elbowed Lucius. "Trust her to be bring the voice of reason even into Goblinburg."

"We did let things get out of hand," Lucius said.

"But we had to be careful," the harper said. "We couldn't just walk in and demand an answer."

Lucius nodded. "We had no choice. We had to scout things out first."

Walking beside them, Louie smiled to himself. They might be these old powerful spirits, but right now they just sounded like they were working up their excuses for when they had to tell Meran how things had gotten so out of hand.

"Here," Louie said. "I brought you something."

He'd come to the big house on Stanton Street at the insistence of his companions, but he hadn't wanted to go in, so Meran had come out onto the porch to thank him. He opened his hand now and offered her the sliver of mica that he'd taken from the stone table.

"It's for that weird-ass wallet of yours," he said.

Meran smiled. "It's perfect," she said. "Thank you."

Louie blushed, then blushed more when she leaned forward and kissed his cheek.

"Can I ask you something?" Louie asked.

"Of course."

"Why'd you come to me? I saw those guys in Jimmy's. I bet any one of them would have done it for you."

She nodded. "But I needed someone human."

Louie blinked. "So what? You're telling me they're not?"

"Not everything is what it appears," she said.

"You're telling me. I guess you don't know any actual, um, humans, right?"

Meran laughed. "I know hundreds."

"So when you asked me . . ."

"I suppose there are others I could have asked," she said, "but I knew you could do it. And I was right. You did it and more."

"I guess. Do you think people will leave them alone—the ones that choose to stay below and be . . . um . . ."

"Goblins?"

"Is that what they are?"

"Pretty much."

"So will they?" Louie asked.

"I know Cerin and Lucius will," Meran told him.

She reached into her pocket and pulled out some money.

"No, it's okay," Louie said. "I didn't do it for the money—not in the end."

"Will you at least come back to visit? The house isn't always full of the noise and confusion you see here today."

"Don't take this wrong," Louie told her, "but I'm like those goblins down below. I don't want to be anybody's salvage project."

"How about being somebody's friend?"

Louie looked at her for a long moment. He didn't see that look in her eyes, the weighing of the damage, the deciding how much work it would take to fix up the poor little kid he looked to be.

"Yeah," he said, dropping his gaze to the ground. "I guess I could do that."

"Don't think I won't hold you to it," she said.

The Hour Before Dawn

Newford, September 1957

Let me tell you about the real witching hour: the hour before dawn when uninvited spirits come visiting. Ghosts, demons, any bodiless thing can come sliding into your dreams right about then. It's got something to do with it being the last dream of the night, but I'm not big on the details of the how or why. All I know for sure is, I don't much appreciate it. Personally, if I want to talk to some dead guy, I'd rather call him up on my own dime. Pick the time and place, make sure I'm ready for the encounter, because I purely do hate surprises.

But the dead don't especially have much consideration for those of us who happen to not be deceased ourselves. Everybody gets visits from them, only most people don't remember like I do. And maybe the dead don't come to me every night—or at least I don't remember them coming every night—but I wake up far too often with the sour ache that they leave in my heart.

All of which is to explain why I wasn't particularly overjoyed at having a pleasant roll in the hay with Ginger Maloney be interrupted by the ghost of my ex-wife's sister-in-law.

Hell, I didn't even know Ina Bell had died.

Alive, she was no pretty thing; dead, she makes my skin crawl.

Imagine a woman about as wide as she is tall, hair like thin straw, two little dark eyes that get lost in the vast expanse of her piggy face. Now I know looks aren't everything. I've been with big women and they're not so different from the skinny ones. There's just more of them to hold. The real measure of a woman is what she's got inside and that's where Ina truly comes up short. She was about as self-centered and bitter as they come. Nobody ever did right by her—not in her book. If she ever had a kind word for anyone, I never heard it.

"Kind of pathetic," she says, once she's chased Ginger out of my head. "Making time with the widow of your own dead partner."

"It was a dream," I tell her. "You don't plan them. You just lie back and enjoy it and worry about the guilt later."

"Can't see you worrying about much of anything."

"Yeah, well, there's a lot you don't know."

"When it comes to you, I consider that a blessing."

I decide politeness has run its course.

"What do you want from me?" I ask.

"I want to know why I'm dead."

"How's that my problem?"

"You won't help?"

"Why should I?"

She shrugs. "It's the charitable thing to do? For old times' sake? Simple curiosity? Take your pick."

"You know, I never much cared for you when you were alive, and dead's not turning out to be much of an improvement."

"I guess that'd be a no."

"You'd be guessing right."

She gives me a slow nod. "Then it looks like you'll be seeing a lot more of me, Jack Daniels. Every morning, right around this time. You think about that."

"Now wait a minute—"

But she's already gone, the alarm clock's ringing, and I wake up on the sofa in my office with a bad taste in my mouth and that sour ache in my heart. I don't have any mouthwash, but I do have a pack of gum. I shove a stick in my mouth and chew until my mouth feels as clean as the magazine ads claim it should. Then I light up a cigarette and make a waste of all that chewing.

Making a waste of things is pretty much my specialty.

It's the reason I'm sleeping in my office. Couldn't hold my marriage together, but I don't make enough as a private dick to pay rent on more than my ex's apartment and this place, so I sleep here when office hours are over.

Right now, I don't have the stamina to call Ella and ask her about her sister-in-law, not without fortifying myself first. It's too early, even for me, to open the bottom drawer of my desk and have a nip from the bottle with my namesake on the label. Instead, I grab the kettle and head down the hall to the public washroom. I have a leak, shave, and splash some water on my face. I'll go to the Y later for a shower.

Filling the kettle, I bring it back to my office and put it on the hot plate. Not until I have a cup of instant coffee and another cigarette going do I pick up the phone and dial the number of my old apartment.

"Yeah?" Ella answers with her usual charm.

Time was she was the sweetest thing, but then once upon a time, things were different for all of us. Tom was still alive and Korea hadn't left its mark on either of us. Ella had her own troubles, but she never talked about them, and I never asked, which I guess tells you everything you need to know about why our marriage took a nosedive and never recovered. Ginger's the only one who didn't change so much, though after Tom died, a sadness slipped into her eyes and it just never went away.

The guilt I told Ina I'd be feeling shows up right about then, but I manage to put it aside. The dead that come visiting me in my dreams might be real, but nothing else.

"I just heard about Ina," I say to my ex.

"Funeral's over, and so's the wake. So you're going to have to look somewhere else for free booze."

"Nice."

"Hey, I didn't drink *my* way out of a job."

I didn't mean to, I want to say. I just needed something to get the damn voices in my head to shut up. Turned out I really needed to listen to them instead.

"I didn't call to fight," I tell her.

"That's new. So why did you call?"

"I wanted to find out what happened to Ina."

She sighs. "Jesus, Jack. Why do you even pretend to care?"

"I don't . . . I mean . . ."

My voice trails off and I can imagine the look on her face from the cold silence that falls between us.

"I don't ask for them to come to me," I say.

"Course you don't."

"It's just—"

"What you need to do is go see a shrink," she says. "But I guess that's too much to ask from a big tough guy like you."

"All a shrink's going to do is . . ."

I don't bother to finish because she's already hung up on me. I drop the handle onto the receiver and go downstairs to the newsstand to get myself a paper and some breakfast at Nick's Diner down the block. I hardly have time to sit down in a booth before Judy's coming over with a plate of bacon and eggs and a cup of joe. She's another of those big women, but unlike Ina, she's got a smile and kind word for everyone.

I spread the paper out on the table. The front page has more on the mess in Little Rock. Faubus has gone ahead and sent in the National Guard to stop nine Negro kids from entering the city's Central High School. I just shake my head.

About the one thing I brought back from Korea was the realization that it doesn't matter what we look like. Under our skin, we're all the same. We all bleed the same red blood.

The paper doesn't say what Ike's going to do, but the ball's in his court now and I sure as hell hope he doesn't fumble it.

I turn to the local pages and then the obits as I eat my breakfast. I don't really expect to find anything about Ina in there—if she's already in the ground, any news on how she died would have been reported earlier. I'm just wondering if anybody else I know's kicked the bucket. I don't see any familiar names.

Thinking about Ina reminds me how there was nothing much when Tom died either. But that's the way it is with the little people. Unless we go out in a particularly spectacular way, it's not news. It doesn't mean anything, except to those of us left behind to pick up the ruin of our lives.

Why'd Tom eat his gun? Nobody seems to have an answer, but I know.

He was always talking about the state of the world. I remember not long before he went into the garage and put his old service pistol in his mouth, he told me, "I can't stop thinking how the world's such an ugly place. And every time you're sure that this is as bad as it's going to get, things just seem to get worse."

I knew he was really talking about Korea, about what we did there, the killing. About what was done to us. About what the killing made of us.

I don't think anybody who goes to war can ever really let it go. Those first few weeks you're home, they treat you like a hero. But eventually you have to live with the memories you've got sitting in your head.

And what good did we really do? It wasn't over. War's never over. It sits on the borders of civilization, hungry and waiting. The Ruskies sure as hell aren't going to back down. The Cold War's going to heat up—anybody can see it coming. Next time it'll be atomic bombs and what little we've still got that's good in the world will all be destroyed.

That's why Tom ate his gun. But how do you tell his widow that? How do you tell anyone? Nobody wants to hear that kind of stuff. We're supposed to deal with what the world throws at us. Only cowards take the easy way out.

Except I think it's more complicated than that. Hell, I know it is. I've got the stories the dead tell to back me up, but people *really* don't want to hear about that.

I finish my breakfast and head off to the Y for my shower, then I ride the streetcar to Upper Foxville.

I'm chasing down a bail-jumper for Tony Vario who runs a bail bond office out of a storefront on Palm Street. He's got a regular crew to collect the no-shows, but every once in awhile he throws me a bone. He figures he owes me for saving his kid back in Korea. It's something I would have done anyway, but these days I don't turn down the work.

Joseph Miller's not hard to track down. I find him at his mother's place on MacNeil and he only puts up a token fight. He doesn't really want to get into it—we've got the same height, but he's a stringbean and I'm at least twice his size. But he's got his pride, I guess.

I drop him off at the Crowsea precinct, fill in the paperwork, and I'm done until later tonight when I have a husband to follow.

It's kind of funny. I got screwed over by the courts, but here I am all the same, collecting evidence that'll put some other poor chump in the same boat. Except I never cheated on Ella. I just agreed to the divorce because it was easier than arguing with her about it.

With time on my hands, I decide to drop in on Frank Bell, Ina's husband. Or I guess I should say widower now.

Frank meets me at the front door of the little clapboard house he and Ina bought back in '49 before the prices started going up. He looks smaller than I remember. I offer him my hand.

"I only just heard about Ina," I say. "I wanted to come by and give you my condolences."

Frank doesn't speak, but his eyes well with tears and the next thing you know, the tears are streaming down his cheeks. He just stands there, shoulders drooping, crying.

I don't know what to do. What are you supposed to do when a guy just starts crying on you? But I know I have to do something. So I pat him awkwardly on the shoulder and then steer him back into the house, closing the door behind us.

I make us coffee and sit through a couple of smokes while he gets himself together.

"It's hard," he finally says. "I don't know what to do without her." He lifts his gaze to mine. "I guess . . . I guess the hardest thing is how people think I should just be . . . relieved. Like living with Ina was some kind of hardship."

I try to think of a diplomatic way to put it and settle for, "She didn't exactly go out of her way to make people comfortable."

That actually gets the hint of a smile twitching on his lips.

"Yeah," he says, "she was a spitfire, all right."

"So what happened?" I ask.

"She died in her sleep. I just woke up and . . . she was gone."

"Jesus."

Tears well in his eyes again, but this time he holds them back.

Neither of us say anything for a long moment. I'm trying to work my way around what he's just told me. I know enough from the visits that the dead pay me to know that they're usually aware of how they died, so there's no big mystery here for Ina. Why'd she die? It just happened. Her time was up.

"Do you think she had, you know, any unfinished business?" I ask.

Frank gives me a puzzled look. "What do you mean?"

"I don't know. Sometimes when people go before their time, there are important things that they've left undone. Things that were important to them, anyway."

"I'd guess everybody must leave unfinished business, then," Frank says. "But with Ina . . . well, she wasn't shy about letting people know where they stood in her esteem, so I guess she'd be about as ready as any of us when our time comes."

I nod.

"I'll tell you a mean thought I've had since she died," Frank says. "I wish it'd been me that went first so I didn't have to feel this pain. But then I think of Ina on her own, and I can't really wish this hurt on her."

"You got along well?"

He looks surprised. "We were soul mates, Jack."

I need to work through that as well. It's something you tend to forget: everybody's got someone who loves them, even if it's only their mother.

"Why are you asking about unfinished business?" Frank wants to know.

I shrug and try to think of a way to answer his question without having to get into Ina's visit this morning. But he seems to be way ahead of me.

"She came to you, didn't she?" he says. "She's been one of your morning visitors."

I just look at him.

"They used to come to Ina, too," he explains, "except she couldn't do much to help them. Not the way she said you do—you know, working out their leftover problems for them and everything. All she could do was give them a sympathetic ear."

"You don't think this is crazy?" I have to ask. "Ella thinks I should be seeing a shrink about it."

He shakes his head. "It's what Ina told me, and she'd never lie to me—not about this. Not about anything. Like I said, we were close."

"And you're okay with the idea of the dead hanging around like this?"

"I don't know that I'd like it happening to me—not unless it was Ina coming to visit."

Yeah, well, dead, she's no charmer, I want to tell him. But then for him, that probably wouldn't be true.

"You get used to it," I say.

"So what did she say to you?"

He's so eager, I hate to let him down.

"Not a lot. She just wants me to find out why she's dead."

"I'd like to know that myself," he says.

I nod, though I hadn't taken her asking to be particularly philosophical. I'd figured there was some question as to how she'd died, like she'd been murdered, but never got to see who did it. But now that I've talked to Frank, I really don't know what she wants. Just to bring me some misery, I suppose.

I stand up.

"Well, if I figure it out," I tell Frank, "I'll let you know."

"Tell her I love her."

"From what you've told me, I'm sure she knows that."

"Tell her anyway. It's not something you can hear too often."

"I will," I say.

Turns out the husband I follow that night is definitely cheating on his wife. I want to give him a break—go up to him and tell him not to screw this up—but I need the money and it's not like anyone's forcing him to do it. So I take my pictures and drop the film round to Eddie's. He'll have a full set of glossies for me by tomorrow afternoon that I can give to the wife, along with my invoice.

I'm tempted to stop in at the corner bar when I leave Eddie's, but I go back to the office instead. I turn on the radio and listen to Benny Goodman playing at a ballroom somewhere, where people are out having fun instead of lying on the sofa in their office, staring up at the ceiling and smoking cigarettes. I think about the bottle in the bottom drawer of my desk, but I don't touch it either.

I'm feeling virtuous, if lonely as hell, when I finally fall asleep.

Right before dawn, Ina shows up again. This time I'm not dreaming of Ginger. I'm just standing under an awning, watching the rain come down on the street in front of me, when she appears beside me, taking up way too much space.

"So," she says. "You learn anything, or is our meeting like this every morning going to be a regular habit?"

"Face it, Ina," I tell her. "The only why to your being dead is that the world just got sick of all your bitching and moaning and pulled the plug on you."

But I'm only mouthing the words out of habit. After my visit with Frank, I don't feel the same annoyance towards her anymore. I figure, anybody who can have such a close and loving relationship with their husband . . . well, they've got more good points going for them than maybe I can see.

I turn to look at her. "There's no mystery to it, no unfinished business. Your number just came up."

"So you were talking to Frank?"

I nod.

"How's he doing?"

"He misses you. Asked me to tell you he loves you."

Ina sighs. "I miss him, too."

"He told me the dead used to come see you."

"Yeah, but I could never do much for them, so I used to send them to people like you."

"Thanks a lot."

"You've got what it takes to help them," she says.

I shake my head. "Why do you think that is? Why do they come to me?"

"You're like a light—somebody they know is going to pay attention and maybe even help them deal with whatever leftover crap that's keeping them from moving on. They all talk about you, over here on the other side."

"Yeah? How come Tom never came to me?"

"I'm guessing he didn't have any unfinished business."

"Not like you."

She smiles. "What makes you think I came back for me? Maybe I came back for you."

"What the hell's that supposed to mean?"

"Look what you've done with your life, Jack. You're no more alive than Tom is."

That hit too close to home.

"Yeah? Why should you care?"

"Why shouldn't I?"

"Oh, for—"

"We never got along," Ina says, interrupting, "and that's okay. I didn't make it easy for you. But I don't make it easy for anybody. So maybe I didn't show it, but I always liked you, Jack."

"Right. That's why we got along so well."

"I told you, that's just the way I was. But see, I've got to give you this, Jack. Any hard words you had for me had nothing to do with the way I looked. And more important, to me, you never ragged on Frank for 'marrying that fat ugly mountain,' as his own father told him one time."

"I always liked Frank," I tell her, just to be saying something. "Don't know how he put up with that mouth of yours, but I figured it was his business."

Ina grins. "That mouth's what kept me sane. Best defense is offense."

"I suppose."

"Christ, Jack. Look at me. Nobody was going to buy sweetness and light coming out of something like me."

"I think you're selling yourself short."

"You didn't grow up being me."

I nod. "But the folks who treated you hard, they weren't worth knowing anyway."

"Even my own family?"

"Even your own family," I tell her. "Maybe especially them, since they should've stood by you instead of jumping on the bandwagon. But maybe you could have laid back a little on the harsh words—you might've made some friends."

"And you'd be first in line, I suppose."

"Why not?"

"Maybe . . . hell, you're probably right. And if I'll admit to that, will you at least think about what I've been saying?"

"Sure. Am I going to see you again?"

"That all depends on you, Jack."

And then she's gone, and so is the rainy street. I'm back in my office again and I hear somebody unlocking the front door.

Damn, I forgot it was Saturday.

I sit up quick. I run a comb through my hair, try to straighten my shirt, but there's no way I can disguise that I was sleeping in my clothes and that I'm just waking up.

And in walks Ginger.

Back when Tom was still alive, when we still ran the agency together, Ginger would come in on Saturdays and work on some of the paperwork that had built up over the week—filing, receipts, invoices. We weren't taking advantage of her—she got a salary, the same as us. But after Tom died and my marriage went down the tubes, there wasn't enough work and I couldn't afford even the little I was paying her, so I had to let her go. Except she keeps coming in anyway, over my protests. Every Saturday, regular as clockwork.

There were long silences at first—not because of any bad feelings between us. We just didn't have anything to talk about that didn't leave one or the other feeling sad or angry. Then, slowly, we started talking again—but never about personal stuff. She pretends not to notice that I'm living here in the office. She doesn't say anything about how I've let the business slide, how now I'm working on making a complete ruin of the rest of my life. She doesn't have to. I know all too well what's happening.

The problem is, I can't seem to stop it. When I get a job, I do it, and I do it well. But I'm not hustling for work, and when I'm not working, most of the time I just sit here in the office and stare at the walls. I don't think about eating my gun. Truth is, I don't think about much of anything at all. I listen to the big bands on the radio. I smoke my cigarettes. I drink my instant coffee. I go out to eat when I've got some money. When I don't, I heat something on the hot plate and eat it out of the can.

Ina's right. It's not living. But knowing you've got a problem and knowing how to fix it are two different beasts.

Ginger smiles at me when she comes in.

"Good morning, John," she says.

She's the only one who calls me by my given name. When I was a kid, some wag thought it was funny to call me Jack to go with the whiskey, and the nickname's pretty much stuck to me ever since.

"Morning," I say. "There wasn't much business this week, so there's not really anything to file."

I've long since given up trying to talk her out of these weekly visits. I mean, I feel bad having her come in, do some tidying and filing and I can't even pay her, but to tell you the honest-to-God truth, her showing up here every Saturday morning's pretty much the only thing I've got to look forward to. And isn't that a god-damned sorry state of affairs?

"That's all right," she says. "It gets me out of the apartment."

I nod. I wish I could say something to her, something personal, something that would let us connect, but all I can do is grab my shaving kit and ask her to excuse me for a minute.

I shave, wash up. By the time I get back, she's made us each a cup of coffee. She's sitting in the straight-backed wooden chair by the desk where clients do when I actually have them. We chat a little about the business in Little Rock, how Ike's sent in federal troops to deal with the mob of white agitators that had gathered outside the school. I like that she's up on current events. She can talk arts, too, but I keep my mouth shut then because what do I know about art? But I like to listen to her, the sound of her voice, and we have the same tastes in music—definitely jazz.

All too soon it's twelve o'clock and she's leaving. I almost ask her if she wants to go grab some lunch, but I stop myself. Ina's visit has my head churning with crazy thoughts, thinking I should reach out, start living. But who are we kidding? I wouldn't wish myself on anybody—especially not Ginger—so I let her leave without saying anything.

After she's gone, I walk over to the diner for a late breakfast, then pick up the photos from Eddie's. They're crisp and clear, showing the poor chump on his way into a motel room with his arm around this gal in a tight skirt. By the time Mrs. John Wellington arrives at my office to pick them and my report up I'm in a bad enough mood that I don't even feel sorry for the husband. Mrs. Wellington is older than the woman in my pictures, but she's still a looker with a nice way about her and her husband's an idiot for having an affair.

I have supper at the diner, alone. I think of going to a bar, maybe catch some music at one of the clubs on Grasso Street, but instead I head over to Jimmy's Billiards on Palm and shoot a few games before coming back to the office and falling asleep to the sounds of Lester Young on the radio.

I'm standing on the Kelly Street Bridge, looking down at the water, when Ina shows up and I realize I'm dreaming. And before you ask, no, I wasn't thinking of taking a dive. I just like watching the movement of water. I've spent whole afternoons sitting on a bench on the boardwalk by the Pier, just watching the lake, the ferries crossing over to Wolf Island.

"That the best you can do with Ginger?" she asks. "Talk about the civil rights movement and Bud Powell?"

I don't even turn to look at her.

"Why don't you go visit Frank," I say.

"I do. Every morning since I died. But he never remembers when he wakes up."

"How's that make you feel?"

She laughs. "What are you now, a shrink?"

"I think maybe Ella's right. Maybe I could use one."

"You're not crazy, Jack."

"Tell that to Ella."

"You just didn't talk about this with the right person."

I think about my conversation yesterday with Frank.

"When did you first start talking to the dead?" I ask her.

She shrugs. "It feels like all my life, but I guess it started in high school."

"For me it was after I got back from Korea—when I joined the NPD."

"That's right," she says. "You were a cop before you went into business with Tom."

I nod. "And then he upped and killed himself."

"Everybody dies," she says. "Just like everybody gets to talk to the dead. It's only that most people don't remember when they wake up in the morning."

"I wonder how we got picked."

Ina shrugs. "Who knows?"

"And you never told anybody but Frank?"

"Who was I supposed to tell? I never had any friends. No one likes to spend time with the ugly fat girl. Was I supposed to add crazy to my job description?"

"But Frank was okay with it? He didn't think you were nuts?"

She shakes her head. "We trusted each other. Completely. If I said something was happening . . . when I told him what I was dreaming, and how I knew the dreams were true, he believed me."

I nod. "I didn't really believe it myself until I first helped one of the dead. This guy just kept bugging me, morning after morning, until I finally went to the *Journal*'s morgue and looked up his story, and sure enough, everything he said was true, but I'd never met him before in my life. Never even heard of him before."

"So you fixed his problem."

"Yeah. It wasn't a big deal. He had some bonds stashed away in his garage and he wanted to make sure his wife got them." I smile, remembering. "It felt pretty good, helping them out. Both of them—the living and the dead."

"I couldn't do much for them except listen to their stories," Ina says. "Looking like I do, it wasn't so easy to get around or talk to people."

"Not to mention how you'd tear a strip off anybody who happened to open his mouth around you."

"You need to let that go," she says. "I'm not in your world anymore, so none of that matters."

"Except if you'd talked to people the way you're talking to me right now, maybe you'd have made some friends."

"Sure," Ina says. "So I was a bitch and you've got no life. Can we move on?"

But it was just such a goddamn waste, I want to say. Because I find myself genuinely liking her now, like I never did when she was alive. Get her smiling, get that pissed-off look out of her eyes, and it turns out she's got a sweetness to her that I never got to see before. But she's right. There's no point in going on about it. She's dead and the chance to live differently is gone, too.

"So you only ever talked to Ella about it?" Ina asks.

I shake my head. "I told Tom, too. Not that I thought they were real—just that I was having these dreams."

"What did he have to say?"

"Nothing much. I guess he was too busy dealing with his own demons."

"Yeah, and we saw where that took him."

"What's that supposed to mean?"

"Nothing," she says. "Except you might as well have stuck

the end of a pistol in your own mouth because you haven't really been living since then either."

"I thought we agreed to let that go."

She smiles. "No, we're just not talking about what-might-a-beens when it comes to me. My time is done. But you're still breathing, even if you're not living. You've still got a chance to turn things around."

"How'd you ever find out about the dead coming to me anyway?"

"Ella talked about it to Frank when you first told her."

"And he told you."

"We didn't have any secrets between us," Ina says.

"Yeah, well, look how well that worked with Ella and me."

"You just need the right person to confide your secrets to."

"Like you."

She shakes her head. "No, somebody living. Somebody you care about and who cares about you."

"That animal doesn't exist in my world."

"So now Ginger's an animal?"

"Jesus, Ina," I say. "Ginger's the last person I'd tell."

"And why's that?"

"She's already witness to how I've screwed up my life. I don't want her thinking I'm crazy on top of that."

"Except maybe knowing will explain to her how a still young, good-looking guy like you feels he's got to push the world away."

"Yeah, and maybe it won't."

"You won't know unless you try," Ina says. "What've you got to lose?"

"Everything."

Ina laughs. Not meanly, but it cuts all the same.

"If what you've got is everything," she says, "then you're even worse off than I thought."

And then she's gone and I'm waking up on the sofa in my office.

Ina's got me so frustrated, I feel like hitting something. Instead, I bundle up some clean clothes and head down to the Y. When I leave the Y, I'm freshly scrubbed, wearing a suit, white shirt, and tie. The suit's a little wrinkled, but it's the best I've got. I stop back at the office and drop off my old clothes, then take the streetcar to Lewis Street. By the time I'm standing in the hall outside Ginger's apartment, I've got this shaky feeling in the pit of my stomach that I haven't felt since Korea.

If Ginger's surprised to find me standing there when she answers the door, she doesn't show it. She invites me in and asks if I'd like a coffee. We make small talk while the coffee percolates in this little aluminum pot she puts on the stove. I get up and pour us each a mug when it's done its job. I add a splash of milk to hers, then sit back down at the kitchen table. Finally, I light another cigarette and start to talk.

I tell her about how the dead come to me in dreams; how they showed up after Tom and I got back from Korea and I joined the NPD while he started the agency that's now mine; how I found if I drank enough they'd stay away and I wouldn't hear the echo of their voices inside my head all day; how the combination of telling Ella about my dreams, the drinking, and losing my job on the force killed our marriage; how after Tom took me in as a partner, I figured out that the dead were real and I could help them.

I run out of steam around then and light a cigarette from the butt of the one I'm smoking. I grind the butt out in the saucer we're using as an ashtray.

"Did Tom see them, too?" Ginger asks. "These dead people?"

I shake my head. "I don't think so. At least not so's he ever told me."

"That's one thing you're both good at," she says. "Not talking."

I don't know how to respond to that so I don't say anything, which proves her point, I guess.

"Why are you telling me this now?" she asks.

"I . . . I just thought you should know."

"But why now? Why wait four years to talk about this? Did it never occur to you how it'd be for me, watching you flush your life down the toilet like this?"

"I told Ella," I say, "and look where that got me. She thinks I should be seeing a shrink."

"I'm not Ella."

"Jesus, I know that."

"And I don't think you're crazy."

"You don't?"

She shakes her head. "No. It explains a lot. I always knew there was something going on with you, something strange. I could just never figure out what."

"Well, now you know my sorry secret."

"I guess I do," she says and then she sighs. "I thought we were close," she adds, her voice soft. "Sometimes I thought . . . that maybe we could be more than friends."

"That's why I'm telling you."

She gives a slow nod. That sad look Tom left in her eyes looks deeper than ever. She leans across the table and then before I can stop her, she slaps me hard in the face.

I jerk back.

"Jesus!" I say. "What was that for?"

"For waiting until now to talk to me about all of this."

"But—"

"And now I think you should leave."

"Come on, Ginger."

She's looking down at the table and shakes her head.

"Please," she says, refusing to lift her gaze. "Just go."

So I do.

I get as far as the hall outside her apartment and then I lean on the door. I feel about as bad as I've ever felt. Through the door, I can hear Ginger crying. I feel like crying myself, but I push away from the door and shuffle down the hall.

I want a drink bad, but I just walk the streets for a long time instead.

I have an appointment in the morning with a dead woman. To keep it, I need to be sober.

I'm waiting for Ina in my office at the hour before dawn. I've never been able to do this before, never knew I could: choose where I'll be when I'm dreaming. Be waiting for the ghost to show up.

I don't see her arrive. I just hear the weight of her settling into my client's chair and lift my gaze from my desk to find her sitting there, looking at me.

"That was a nice piece of advice you gave me," I tell her.

It's funny. I've been pissed off at her all night, but now that she's sitting here in front of me, I don't have it in me to tell her off like I was planning to. Guess you need a heart for that, but I left mine broken in the hall outside of Ginger's apartment. Or maybe I dropped it on one of the streets I was out walking last night.

"What happened?" she asks.

I tell her and she shakes her head the way you do when you've heard something so dumb, you can't believe you heard it.

"Did you tell her you were sorry?" she asks.

"Sure, I explained how—"

"Did you actually use the words 'I'm sorry'?"

"I don't know. I must have. But she—"

"Listen to me, Jack," she says. "Nobody wants to hear excuses and explanations. All they want is for you to admit you screwed up, for you to say you're sorry and it won't happen again. All that other crap can wait for another time."

"But—"

"Trust me on this, Jack. If you honestly believe you messed

up, just tell her that. Tell her you're sorry and it won't happen again. And then shut your mouth."

"She already told me she doesn't want to see me again."

"Really? I thought she just asked you to leave."

"What's the difference?"

"Don't be more of an idiot than you already are," Ina says. "You go back to her and tell her you're sorry. Bring her some flowers—there should still be asters growing in my garden. Pick a bunch for her. And tell Frank I'm getting ready to move on, but I plan to be waiting for him wherever it is we go to next."

"Just like that," I say.

"Oh, it won't be easy. Saying you're sorry and meaning it— that's never easy, Jack. But if the other person means anything to you, it's worth it."

"What if she won't talk to me?"

"You won't find that out sleeping on your sofa, talking to some dead woman."

"I guess." I wait a beat, then ask, "You're really heading on?"

She nods. "I've done all I can here."

"You've . . . ?"

"The dead aren't always looking for somebody to help them," she says. "Sometimes we stick around because there's someone *we* can help."

And then she's gone again.

Ginger works at the First Newford Bank on Williamson. She gets off around four. She's usually home by four-thirty, quarter to.

I've been sitting on the front steps of her apartment building since ten past four, holding a bouquet of the little purple flowers I picked in Ina's yard, when I finally see her coming down the street, blond-red hair bobbing, that little sway in her hips when she walks. She stops on the pavement in front of me, but she doesn't say a word.

I stand up and offer her the flowers.

"I'm sorry," I tell her. "I've been an idiot and I'm truly sorry."

She holds my gaze with hers, searching.

I feel explanations and excuses pushing around in my brain, desperate to get out.

But, "And no matter what," I say, "I promise it won't happen again."

She makes me wait another long moment until finally the ghost of a smile twitches at the corner of her mouth. She takes the flowers and then my hand.

"Come on," she says and starts up the stairs, giving my hand a tug. "Let's see what we can put together for supper."

Newford Spook Squad

Now . . .

We haven't had any rain for the past few weeks, so the water level in the storm drains isn't high—a trickle in most places, though occasionally it comes up to our ankles. But not having to slosh though heavy storm water doesn't make it any more pleasant to be down here. Our flashlights cut a series of crisscrossing beams into the darkness ahead of us. The air has a musky scent and I keep hearing things scuttling away from us in the darkness.

Rats, I guess. Nothing big. Not what we're looking for, but then who knows what the hell we're really looking for? All I know for sure is three workers from the Water & Sewer Department have gone missing down here and no one knows what happened to them.

"What's that up ahead?" Hellboy asks.

The beam from his flashlight plays on a side tunnel. Waller checks the screen of his PDA. He downloaded the specs for this tunnel system before we left headquarters.

"It's a dead end," he says.

When we reach the branching tunnel, Hellboy plays his flashlight down its length.

"A dead end?" he asks.

"That's what's showing up on my schematic," Waller tells him.

"Then how come I can feel a breeze?"

He's right. There's a draft coming down the tunnel towards us.

I step around him and move farther in, the beam of my flashlight showing nothing but damp stone walls as far as it will reach. The passage slopes away from us at a slight angle. After ten feet, it makes a turn to the left. There's no telling how far it goes.

I start to take another step, but Hellboy catches my arm.

"Wait," he says. "Hear that?"

I shake my head.

"There's something . . ." he begins.

But then we all hear it. Hell, we *feel* it. A sudden pressure in the tunnel, a sound like something's shifting deep underground. Something *big*. The stone underfoot sends tremors up our legs and right through our bones.

I look at Hellboy and he grins.

"Now it's getting interesting," he says.

He sets off down the tunnel, his partner, Agent Sherman, on his heels. Waller and I exchange glances. He looks as uneasy about all of this as I'm feeling.

"Crap," I say.

I don't want to go, and neither does Waller. The hair on the back of my neck is standing up.

But we follow them into the tunnel all the same.

Then . . .

My name's Sam Cray.

One week ago I was a detective for the Newford Police Department's Special Investigations Squad.

Six days ago I was put in charge of the NPD's new Paranormal Investigations Task Force.

No matter what I've been told, I figure I must have really pissed someone off to get the transfer.

"Tell me you're kidding," I say to Bill Sweet when he gives me the news in one of the downtown conference rooms.

Bill's the chief of police now, but we go way back. We came up together from the Academy and even our rabbis were partners. We both made detective around the same time, but Bill was always more ambitious than me. Right from the start, he had a leaning towards the politics of the job, while I just wanted to be on the street, putting away the bad guys. I'm not saying one's better than the other, just that we're different. And it's worked out well, because at least we have a chief who actually knows the job from the bottom up.

Yeah, he knows my job, but at times like this, I can't believe what's involved with his.

"You can't do this to me," I tell him.

Bill shakes his head. "The mayor insists on it."

"And there's room in your budget for something like this?"

"No. The task force is being funded by an anonymous group of concerned citizens."

"Who expect to get what out of it?"

"Nothing, Sam. In case you haven't been paying attention, a lot of seriously *weird* things go down in our city—not just once or twice, but *all* the time. These people are worried about its effect on real estate values, on the tourist trade, on their ability to lure new businesses to town. So it's not like they're being particularly charitable here. But that's fine, because no matter how self-serving their motivations might be, it still gives *us* the budget to actually help the people who are being affected by this."

It's a good speech, but I don't buy it.

"This is bullshit," I tell him. "What exactly am I supposed to do? Track down monsters and spooks and things that go bump in the night?"

"If necessary. If that's what comes up."

He says this with such a straight face it makes me glad I never played poker with him.

"Seriously," I say. "What'd I ever do to piss you off like this?"

"This is a compliment to your abilities, Sam. Simply put, you're the best man for the job. I went to every precinct with this and only your captain was against you being offered the position."

"Really? Well, at least Monroe's not trying to screw me."

"Don't be an idiot," Bill says. "He just doesn't want to lose you to the task force."

"I can't believe you're even calling it a task force. I'm going to be a laughingstock when this gets out. Jesus."

Bill shakes his head. "This task force won't officially exist, so no one's going to know."

Like that ever stopped information from getting around before. I swear, cops are worse than little old ladies when it comes to gossip.

"And you don't answer to anyone but me," Bill finishes.

"A task force," I say. "On the paranormal. Do you have any idea how that sounds?"

"Last week we had a rain of frogs inside the Williamson Street Mall," he tells me. "Monday a complaint was filed about something that looked like a cross between an eagle and a lion flying off with some guy's Doberman. Just this morning two female joggers reported a fishman rooting through a garbage bin who dove into the lake at their approach and never surfaced. Do you need any more? Because I've got stacks of them."

"Look," I say. "I'll admit this city seems to have more than its fair share of nutcases, but that doesn't mean we should start believing what they tell us."

"The guy who lost his dog," Bill says, "is the president of the

Newford First National Bank. One of the joggers sits on the city council; her friend is VP of Human Resources at McCutcheon & Grambs."

Doesn't mean they're not loopy, I think, but I say, "Okay, so I'm supposed to do what? How is anybody supposed to figure out who's responsible for this crap? Come *on*, Bill. You can't arrest smoke and shadows and hearsay."

But he's shaking his head. "It's not a lot different from what you're already doing, except instead of collecting data on gangs and subversives and extremists, you're going to be investigating the weird things that go on in this city. Hopefully, you'll get to the point where you'll be able to identify and prevent the incidents from occurring in the first place."

"I don't know the first thing about the paranormal."

"That's why we brought together those advisers for you."

He's talking about the collection of misfits he's got waiting for us in the room on the other side of the one-way mirror where we're having our meeting. Like the idea of working with them would even remotely boost my confidence.

"You get to pick your own team," Bill says. "No strings, no PC processes. Choose whomever you want, and if they agree to the transfer, they're yours."

"Plus that bunch of bozos," I say, pointing to the group waiting on the other side of the mirror.

"These people can be useful, Sam. They know things we can't guess at."

Because we still have the full use of our senses, I think. Or at least I know I do. I'm not so sure about Bill anymore, because these people . . .

I recognize some of them—mostly from pulling them in on various charges when I was still walking a beat. There's the alcoholic priest who thinks he talks to angels and demons. The owner of The Good Serpent Club in Upper Foxville who claims to be a voodoo priestess. At least two of the people Bill's brought in do the phony oracle shtick in Fitzhenry Park, or down on the Pier.

I also recognize the writer, but not from a rap sheet. I've just seen his mug in the paper when they're reviewing his books.

"Whose the old guy beside Christy Riddell?" I ask.

"Dr. Bramley Dapple. He's got a couple of PhDs, but the one that interests us is in mythology and folklore. He's supposed to be a world-renowned expert in his field."

"And he's got time for this?"

"He thinks it's important and long overdue," Bill says. "As do I."

"You're not asking me to head up a task force," I say. "You're asking me to babysit a pack of charlatans and lunatics." I turn to look at Bill. "I have to work in an office with these people?"

He shakes his head. "This is just a meet and greet to let you all put faces to each other's names. I want you to go in, introduce yourself to them, thank them for being a part of this. That's all."

"I don't do this well," I warn Bill.

"I know. Just be nice and get it over with. After this, you'll only speak to them when you need their expertise on a particular case. And you don't even need to do that yourself. You can delegate one of your people to be the liaison."

I shake my head. Now I've got people.

"Let's get this over with," I tell Bill.

Now . . .

"Is he always like this?" I ask Hellboy's partner when Waller and I catch up with her.

I can see the light from Hellboy's flashlight a good twenty yards farther down the tunnel from us.

Agent Sherman smiles. "We spend a lot of downtime, back at headquarters, twiddling our thumbs. Which is a good thing, of course, because it means there isn't some big crisis that needs looking after. But Hellboy likes it best when he's in the thick of the action."

"What's his real name?"

"That's it. Just Hellboy."

Okay, I think. Be like that.

"I've read the stories," I say. "Saw that *Life* magazine cover back when. But I always figured it was mostly image stuff, PR, all that. So what, was he caught in a fire or something when he was a kid?"

She gives me a look that's beyond cold. There's anger in it and ice, and just the hint of old ghosts. It stops me in my tracks and Waller bumps into me, but she just keeps walking, back stiff, long red hair bouncing against her back.

I turn to Waller. "What'd I say?"

He shrugs. "Who knows? But I wouldn't bring it up again. Maybe it's like asking if my skin's so brown because I fell down a crapper."

"Who's going to say something that stupid?"

"I don't know. Maybe some kid back when I was in high school—just before I broke his nose."

"Christ, so now I'm a racist?"

Waller smiles. "Not that I can see. Seriously, though. You think the guy's a fake? Somebody's going to pretend they're a demon? Big media hoax? Who'd do that?"

"Stranger things happen. Maybe you should ask Agent Sherman?"

Waller shakes his head. "Nah, I think I'd rather give myself an enema with a fire hose. Man, if I didn't know better, I'd think she'd done time, because she's sure got that thousand-yard stare down pat."

I grin in agreement and we quicken our pace, rubber boots splashing in the few inches of water we've got underfoot. But just because I'm in better humour doesn't mean I'm not checking out the walls and tunnel roof for cracks or fissures. That sound we heard earlier, I figure it came from a piece of the roof falling in somewhere down a ways, and I don't plan on getting stuck down here.

Then . . .

Chad Waller is my first choice for this task force I'm putting together. He's got experience, he's tough, and at six-foot, two-twenty, he can hold his own. I've seen him in action. He can look like a street thug, and he's played the part in the past, though he can't go undercover again—not since he put away most of the Taggart Street Runners, along with their main man, Frankie Chestnut. Waller's also smart as hell, but more important, he's a guy I can get along with. If I'm stuck with this job—if I'm going to have "people"—at least they're going to be people I like.

Waller grins at me when I walk up to his desk at the 12th Precinct.

"If you're here to ask me if I want to join up with your Spook Squad—" he starts.

"Jesus, who's calling it that?" I say, before he can finish.

"Everybody. Come on, what did you expect?"

"Well, I knew no matter what the chief said, it was going to get out. I just didn't think it'd be this fast."

"Or that somebody'd come up with such a cute name," Waller says.

"That, too."

"Anyway," he goes on, "I'm in. Unless you're here to ask me to go for a beer, and then I'm going to be seriously embarrassed."

"Why would you want in?" I have to ask.

"Are you kidding me? This is the gig of a lifetime. I mean,

think about it for a minute: they're willing to actually pay us to investigate all this weird stuff that goes down in the city. Which reminds me, do I get a raise?"

"Put it on your list of demands."

"I get to make a list of demands? Sweet. I'm putting in for a Ferrari. Maybe that'll finally get me some respect in the old 'hood."

I laugh. "But seriously," I say. "When did you get into the weird stuff?"

"Living here, how can you not? It drives me crazy trying to figure out what's really what."

"You're beginning to sound like Ricker."

"Oh, crap. You're not bringing him on board, are you?'

Alfred Ricker's been collecting data on unexplained phenomena for about as long as anyone can remember and everybody avoids him because he's got a hundred theories and he's not afraid of sharing them with you. At great and tedious length. The only way you can get him to stop is to just walk away.

He'd probably add a lot to the team—if he didn't drive us all insane first. I'm surprised Bill didn't put him on my board of advisers, considering some of the other winners that are there.

"No," I assure Waller. "I'm asking Rameriz next."

"Judita's good," he says. "I heard she once stood down a swarm of fifteen or twenty kids going after a couple of Arab boys outside the Williamson Street Mall. Just her on her own, no backup. Knowing her, she stopped them dead with the sheer force of her will."

I nod, wait a beat, then ask, "So is she a believer, too?"

Waller gives me a puzzled look. "I don't know. Why do you ask?"

"It's just . . . everybody's treating this so damn seriously."

"And you don't," Waller says.

It's not a question, but I can see he's just figuring it out now. The Looney Tunes crap the task force is being put together to investigate isn't something the two of us have ever really discussed before. You want to know the truth, I don't like to talk about it with anybody.

"Which really makes me wonder why they've got me heading up the task force," I say.

"You're a good cop."

"I try. But this stuff . . ."

"Maybe they want someone in charge who's going to stop and ask questions instead of just running with the weirdness of the moment."

"I guess . . ."

Waller doesn't say anything for a long moment. He just sits there, studying my face—hesitating, I realize, when he finally does speak.

"This have anything to do with Lela?" he asks.

It's been three years but I still feel the ground disappear under my feet at the mention of her name. Lela Searle. We were supposed to be married. She was going to leave the Job, become a civilian, raise our family. Instead, she got torn apart by a pack of dogs set on her by a crack dealer in Butler University Common. Except the whisper in the NPD is that it wasn't dogs. The whisper says it was the dealer himself, Bobby Cairns. That he goes all Wolfman three nights of the month. That she wasn't paying attention to the lunar cycle when she went to make her bust because otherwise she'd still be alive.

All of which seriously pisses me off. Lela was a good cop. Maybe she shouldn't have been out on the common at night without backup, but those kinds of situations happen on the job. In the heat of the chase, you make the judgment call. It was bad luck Cairns had those dogs. It wasn't supernatural. And if we ever pull in the murdering son of a bitch, I'll go a few rounds with him and prove he's just a lowlife with a freak for fighting dogs.

I hate the fact the whisper says she was killed by bad mojo. I want the world to know it was a man that got the drop on her, not some monster. If we buy into monsters, then what do we have left? What good are we against monsters? I mean think about it. If there really are these wolfmen and vampires and crap out there in the dark, how are we supposed to protect the public against them? We're as helpless against that kind of thing as the average joe.

Sure, there's weird shit on the street. But the point is, you get the facts, you take the incidents apart, and you don't find monsters—at least not like in some freak show. We've got plenty of human monsters as it is. We don't need to make up storybook ones.

Lela's death has to mean something. She was a good cop. She died doing her job. She didn't die because some random boogeyman stepped out of the shadows and tore her apart. She died trying to bring down Bobby Cairns, a crack dealer, end of story. Accepting anything else diminishes her death.

"No," I tell him. "I don't buy this crap for a lot more reasons than that."

"And if it turns out to be true?"

I shrug. "Then I'll buy myself some silver bullets for when I finally track down Cairns."

Now . . .

When I was a kid, my friends and I were fascinated with the idea that the bedrock underneath the city was supposed to be honeycombed with caverns, some so big you couldn't see from one side to the other. Discussing the possibility of their existence was a big deal for us. We'd sit around for hours planning all these Tom Sawyer in the caves/*Journey to the Center of the Earth* expeditions that never got further than the neighbourhood storm sewer, though it wasn't for want of trying. We could just never find the secret entrances.

You put that kind of thing behind you once you grow up and find other interests—like, hello, girls—but it stays there in your subconscious. Every once in awhile I'd remember. Maybe I'd be on a stakeout and the steam coming up from a manhole cover would remind me. Or I'd read in the paper about the fire department rescuing some kid from a storm sewer.

The city's got an underground history, too. Everybody knows about Old City—that section of Newford that got dropped underground during the big 'quake at the beginning of the last century—but nobody goes there except for the homeless. They say there are still buildings standing down there in some subterranean cavern—that's what happened during the 'quake: the roof of one of those caverns collapsed and Old City got swallowed up, buildings, streets, and all.

I'm thinking about that now as Waller and I follow Hellboy and his partner down the storm sewer, pretty sure that what we heard and felt was a cavern roof falling in. But then we get to where the other two are standing, their flashlights playing over what appears to be a large body of water. I can't see the far end. There's no longer concrete or brickwork underfoot or on the walls. There's just bedrock, with a bunch of loose boulders and stones along the edge of this underground lake.

If my childhood pals could see me now . . .

"How deep are we?" I ask Waller.

He shrugs. "Hard to tell, with all the ups and downs and turns we took."

"Probably the equivalent of a ten-story building," Sherman says.

Her voice is completely normal, like she didn't give me the big ice-stare two minutes ago.

I shine my light across the water and wonder what its range is.

"There's something moving in there," Hellboy says.

He's shining his light into the water but it's so murky I can't make out a damn thing.

"Something big," he adds.

It's like he calls it to us, whatever the hell it is. I'm just aware of some large shape that comes out of the water like a whale, before the waters close over it again. The motion sends waves towards us, lapping at the tops of our boots.

"Jesus," Waller says. "What the hell was that thing?"

Hellboy grins. "It looked like a kraken."

"Yeah," I say. "You'd have to be on crack to make sense out of something like this."

Hellboy shakes his head. "I said 'kraken.' It's a kind of sea monster."

"In the city sewers?"

"It's a small one," Agent Sherman says. "But you're right, it is puzzling. I didn't think they could survive in fresh water."

"Hey, the water down here's anything but fresh," I put in.

Hellboy smiles at me, then turns back to his partner. "Remember Nazas, in '88? We had a pair of them."

Sherman shakes her head. "You were with Abe that time." She pauses a moment, then adds, "I thought they were Nessies."

"What the hell are you people talking about?" I ask.

"Do you remember those Ray Harryhausen movies with the giant octopi?"

"Sure. But what's that got—"

"They were actually kraken, which is like a giant cuttlefish or squid."

Waller grins. "Man, I knew this was going to be an interesting gig."

They're all nuts, so far as I can see. And then Hellboy, as though to drive the point home, strips off his trenchcoat. He unbuckles his belt and lays that oversized handgun of his down on top of it, but he keeps the big glove on. I'm starting to think maybe the hand inside is deformed—you know, like he's got elephantitis, which would maybe explain his size and colouring, too, but I'm no doctor. And the thing is, his hand works fine. It's just big.

"What're you doing?" I ask.

"Going to have some fun," he says.

He turns to the lake and that's when I see it. A red tail. He's got a freaking tail.

I'm still trying to register the fact when he dives in.

I take a step into the water, but his partner calls me back.

"I wouldn't try to follow," she says. "Not unless you can hold your breath for five minutes or so."

"And Hellboy can?"

"He's kind of bigger than life in a lot of ways," she says.

Waller laughs. "No kidding."

"He's got a tail," I say. I turn to Waller. "Jesus, did you see it?"

Waller only shrugs and I make myself calm down. Okay, so he's got a tail. I guess it should have sunk in by now that he's not exactly like you or me.

Agent Sherman sits down on one of the nearby boulders and rummages around in her pocket. She comes up with a pack of smokes.

I step out of the water and sit on a rock near her, pretending a nonchalance I don't really feel. But I figure if she's not concerned about her partner, I'm not going to be either. At least I won't let on that I am.

"Look," I say. "About what happened earlier. I didn't mean—"

She waves me off before I can finish.

"That was my fault," she says. "It's a touchy subject for me. I lost some people close to me in a fire."

She snaps her fingers and damned if a little flame doesn't appear, hovering there between her fingers long enough for her to get her cigarette lit. She offers it to me, but I shake my head. Waller accepts it, though, and I watch in fascination as she lights herself another.

"Nice trick," I say.

She nods, but doesn't explain. I guess she holds to that magician's code where you never reveal how you did the trick, though she did do it twice. Didn't help me much. I couldn't figure it out either time.

I turn to look back at the water, then check my watch. It's been almost three minutes and there's still no sign of Sherman's partner.

Then . . .

So Bill has one more surprise for me. I'm six days on the job, and the task force is just settling into our new offices at police head-quarters, when he drops by with agents from something called the Bureau for Paranormal Research and Defense. Turns out the Feds have their own full-time investigative task force.

"These are agents Hal Jones and Liz Sherman," Bill says as he ushers them in.

The man is just a nondescript suit, but the woman is a real looker. Great figure, pretty face. Long red hair falling past her shoulders. Cool, blue-gray eyes. But attractive as she is, she can't hold my attention once the third member of their team comes through the door.

"And this is Hellboy," Bill finishes.

The third team member has to duck his head coming through the door because he's got to be seven feet tall. I put his weight at close to four hundred pounds, but even with the trenchcoat, you can tell there's not an ounce of fat on him. So his size grabs you right off the bat, but then there's his skin: bright red, like a cooked lobster. Weirder still, he's got a couple of disks stuck to his forehead—wood, bone, I'm not sure what. Except they look like they're growing there. Like maybe he had some kind of growths and they were cut off, which makes no sense at all. What the hell would anybody have growing out of their head like that? But then I don't know anybody who has his size or skin colouring either.

I can't tell the caliber of the gun he's got holstered at his hip.

I just know it's the biggest damn handgun I've ever seen. And then there's this glove he's wearing on his right, doubling the size of his hand. The cloth has a texture that makes it look like stone.

For the first time since I took this gig, I'm ready to think maybe it's not all bogus. Because looking at him, it's like looking at something not quite human. And he's supposed to be one of us, one of the good guys, for Christ's sake.

I guess I've been staring, but he doesn't seem to take offense. He smiles, like he's used to it. Like I'm an idiot for staring. So I turn it around and focus on the strangeness of him.

"That's a seriously bad sunburn you've got there, buddy," I tell him.

The monster laughs and turns to Agent Sherman.

"I already like him," he says to her.

"Now that we've established that we all like each other," Bill says, "maybe we can get down to the business at hand."

"I'm all business," Hellboy assures him, but he winks at me.

It's a friendly gesture—brothers-in-arms bonding and all that—but something goes pit-patting up my spine all the same.

Bill lays it out for us once we're in his office. A worker from the Water & Sewer Department went missing on a regular maintenance recon down in the storm sewers earlier this morning, so they sent in two more to look for him. They haven't come back either, but one of the men did make a cell call just before Water & Sewer lost contact with them. There was screaming on his end of the line, screaming so bad that the receptionist who took the call was being treated for shock at the hospital as we spoke.

"What makes it our case?" I ask.

"Stafford at Water & Sewer says his men have been talking about weird sounds coming from down in the lower sewer levels," Bill says. "Says it's been going on for some time now."

I nod, wondering if this is how it's going to be. If every time someone gets some little whiff of the weird they're going to call in the Spook Squad.

"I know you and your people only came down to introduce yourselves to my men," Bill is saying to Agent Jones, "but seeing how this will be their first active case in the field . . ."

"No problem," Jones says before Bill can finish. "Hellboy and Agent Sherman will be happy to assist."

Great, I think. So now I'll have the Feds breathing down my neck while dealing with my first case.

There's a little more talk between Bill and Jones, but I tune them out. It's all bureaucratic doublespeak, making nice, we'll work together, share resources, yadda yadda. Instead, I concentrate on what I need to do once I get out of Bill's office. I'll take Waller and Rameriz. Waller to come down into the sewers with me—and won't he love that—Rameriz to set up a command post at the entrance. We'll have to grab a couple of uniforms. I'm trying to decide what the closest precinct is when I realize the meeting's come to an end.

"So what do you think we're looking at?" Hellboy says as we're walking back to the Spook Squad offices. "Giant albino crocs? Mutant rats?"

I look at him, then at his partner.

"Is he for real?" I ask.

"If this is your first time out on something like this," she says, "I guess it can seem a little over the top. But . . ."

She shrugs.

"Wait a sec," I say. "You guys have seen crap like that?"

"I just hope it's not zombies," Hellboy says. "I hate zombies. It takes forever to wash the stink of them away."

Now . . .

I just about have a heart attack when my radio squawks, but it's only Rameriz at the command post, checking in.

"No, we're good," I tell her. "We just found this lake and

Hellboy's gone for a swim looking for some giant octopus or something."

There's a moment's silence before Rameriz says, "You're kidding me, right?"

"I wish I was."

"But—"

"I'll get back to you, Judita."

I cut the connection, still staring at the water.

"How long's it been?" I ask.

"Four minutes," Waller says.

I turn to Agent Sherman, but before I can ask if we shouldn't be starting to worry, something explodes out of the water. No, not something. It's Hellboy. The beam from Waller's flashlight follows his trajectory as he sails maybe fifteen feet above the water before smashing against the wall to our right. When he lands, he lies still, but we don't have time to see to him, because there's something else coming out of the lake.

Now, I heard what the BPRD agents were telling me earlier about giant squids and crap, but it didn't really register. By which, I guess, what I really mean is, it was just too stupid to take seriously. But this . . . this thing . . .

Stupid, impossible, what*ever*—I can't deny what I'm seeing.

The water churns and this monster the size of a small car rises up out of the lake. We play our flashlights on it, but there's no way their beams can take the whole of it in at once. I freeze when my light illuminates one huge eye along the side of its head because there's . . . not exactly intelligence, but certainly a cunning that's more than animal in the look it gives me.

Tentacles . . . arms . . . these appendages thick as tree trunks come whipping out of the water and then things get even weirder.

Turns out Agent Sherman's trick with lighting a cigarette is just the tip of the iceberg when it comes to her talents. She puts her hands together and when she moves them apart, a ball of fire forms in between.

I don't know what she plans to do with it, because she doesn't get the time. One of those tentacles comes ripping out of the water and knocks her flying. The flame ball lands in the water and splutters out. She lies still.

I manage to duck as the tentacle comes for me—I don't know how, I'm just a gibbering idiot at this point. It's like everything's closing up inside me and I can't even remember how to breathe. I've been a cop for over fifteen years and I've been in situations before. Serious situations. I've seen shit nobody should have to take home from work. But this *thing* does what nothing else in my experience ever has. It just shuts me down.

So I don't know how I manage to duck. I just do.

Waller isn't as lucky.

He's standing there like me, frozen, just staring at the thing. He starts to move when the tentacle comes for him, but he's not quick enough. It wraps around him and tugs him up into the air.

I know I couldn't have done this for myself. I just didn't have what it would take in what was left of me. But on the job, your partner's a sacred trust. That's the first thing my rabbi taught me when he took me under his wing. No matter *what*, you watch your partner's back. You stand by him and take the bullet for him if that's how it plays out.

So seeing that the monster's got Waller is what makes me move. I know my .38's not going to do a damn thing against this creature, but we've got something else down here that might.

I take the few quick steps over to where Hellboy dropped his gear and tug that oversized handgun of his out of its holster. Turns out it's not so much a handgun as a small mortar cannon with a handle, and the damn thing weighs a ton. I need both hands to hold it, to aim. I squeeze the trigger and the blast pretty much deafens me. The gun bucks in my hand and I feel a snap as my shoulder dislocates. The gun falls from my hand, back onto Hellboy's coat.

But I hit the monster.

Didn't kill it, I don't think, but I did enough damage that it shrieks with pain and drops Waller into the lake. Those arms of its are churning the water into a froth. My gaze goes from the gun to Waller. I don't think I can lift the gun again, even if I had another shot for it, but I don't know that I can get out there to Waller either.

Then a big shape looms up beside me and I don't have to decide.

Hellboy stoops and picks up his gun. He cracks it open, knocks out the spent shell, and inserts another that he gets from the pocket of his coat.

"I'm impressed," he says. "I haven't met many guys who can fire this and actually hit anything."

He holds the gun with one hand and fires off a round, reloads and fires again. The first goes deep into the oily skin on the monster's side. The second hits it in the eye. Bam, bam. Just like that, and the creature's falling back into the water, dead. The impact of its body sets up a wave that brings Waller in close enough that I can wade in and pull him back to shore with my good arm.

He coughs up some water, but otherwise he's okay.

I find my flashlight. I play its beam over the body and we just stand there staring at the damn thing floating in the water. Then I think of Agent Sherman. I turn to find that Hellboy's already seen to her. She seems to be shook up, but okay.

I remember the fireball she made in her hands.

I turn again to look at the impossible monster floating in this underground lake.

"Everybody okay over here?" Hellboy asks as he walks up to us.

Waller nods.

"I think your damn gun dislocated my shoulder," I tell him.

"Yeah, it's got a kick. Here, let me fix it."

"No, it's okay. I can wait to see a—"

I don't get the chance to say "medic" before he's already

grabbed my arm and popped my shoulder back into place. The pain goes through me like a white heat.

"Th-thanks," I manage.

"What happened to you down there?" Waller asks.

Hellboy shrugs. "I couldn't get a grip on its skin—it was too slick."

Agent Sherman joins us. She lights a cigarette and I don't even blink at her not using a lighter.

"We were lucky," I say.

Hellboy shakes his head. "The hell we were. We're better than the monsters. We're smarter and we never give up. That's why we're always going to come out on top at the end."

"I guess . . ."

"I'm serious," Hellboy says. "You want to survive in this business, you need to remember that. The monsters are strong and they're mean and they can scare the crap out of you. But we can stand up to them. We can put them down. It's what we do."

Agent Sherman smiles. "Make the world a safer place, yadda yadda."

"But it's true," Hellboy says.

"I know it is," she tells him.

Hellboy works a kink out of his neck, then bends down to get his coat and holster.

"You know what I need?" he says, looking at us.

Waller and I shake our heads.

Hellboy grins. "I need a cigar, a beer, and some Peking ravioli."

There's paperwork and debriefings to go through, but here's the good thing about having the Feds at your back: you can put it off until tomorrow on their say-so. We take Hellboy and Agent Sherman to Cassidy's, a cop bar on Palm Street, and make sure Hellboy gets both his cigar and his beer. Hell, he earned them.

"So you still think the boogeyman's all a load of crap?" Waller asks later when we're walking back to our car.

I shake my head. "I just don't get how we don't hear more about it. You'd think the papers and TV crews would be all over this stuff. You'd think there'd be federal task forces with their scientists dissecting these things right down to the cellular level. But there's nada."

"Well, we don't know about the scientists," Waller starts.

"What do you mean?"

He shrugs. "Someone's going to go down there and take that monster away."

"I guess you're right. They're just going to keep a lid on it."

"Everything's need-to-know," Waller says.

"But what about the ordinary joes who get caught up in this kind of thing?"

"I figure it's a kind of consensual denial, you know? It's easier to let it just be something that never happened. Human beings, we're good at that."

I nod. "I suppose we are."

It's another half-block to where we found a parking spot earlier and we cover the distance in silence.

"Do you think the armory carries silver bullets?" I ask when we reach our car.

"I don't know. Why?"

"It's a full moon next week. I thought I might go hunt me a werewolf."

"Bobby Cairns," Waller says.

"Since I can't find him as a human, maybe I'll have better luck tracking him down as a creature of the night."

I can't believe I just said "creature of the night" in all seriousness. I guess I'll have to get used to it on this job.

"You doing this for Lela," Waller asks, "or for the safety of the public?"

I have to think about that for a moment. I know what my

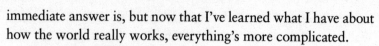

immediate answer is, but now that I've learned what I have about how the world really works, everything's more complicated.

"Bit of both," I finally tell him.

He nods. "Either way, let me know when you're going out. I'll watch your back."

In Sight

I don't know when it was that people first started dropping into the Rainbow Tavern Grill after their gigs. They've been doing it for longer than I've been in the biz, and I've been making music since the late seventies, when "folk" was a four-letter word in more ways than one. Around two a.m., when the late-night crowd starts to drift in, Stan shuts off the outside lights and the place is officially closed for business. He keeps the kitchen open and he'll still serve beer and drinks, but the alcohol's all on a tab now. You can't pay until regular business hours.

If it ever went to court, I guess it would be a fine point for the lawyers to argue, but until someone lodges a complaint, the cops leave Stan alone. They know he's not running some speakeasy. After hours at the Rainbow really is a social club. No one gets too drunk and there aren't any fights, though I've seen feuding couples shoot looks that could kill across the room.

If you don't have a gig, and your apartment's getting to feel claustro, the Rainbow's a great place to just hang out at any time. People bring instruments and sit in the booths or around the tables and swap songs. I've seen it used as a rehearsal hall during the day, and sometimes in the evening a band'll set up their whole kit and jam with whoever wants to sit in.

So it can get a little noisy, but in a musical way, and with everything nearby closed at six, there's no one to bother. And sure there's a pecking order—all you need is three or more people together and social politics take over—but here, it's not such a big deal. The Rainbow's a cool place to hang, but it's also a bit of a dive, so there aren't too many of the really big egos coming out to be seen. What's the point? It'll only be other musicians, and it takes more than a record deal or a hit song to impress most of us. And besides, it's big enough inside so that if you don't like what's going down on one side of the room, you can just find a seat on the other.

I spend a lot of time here—more than I should, maybe, but it's a way to get out of my apartment and be social without actually having to participate much if I don't want to. Company without obligations.

I had a gig at the Casement tonight, which is why I'm here early. Rubin always starts his shows right at eight with an open mike—three performers, each gets fifteen minutes—then the headliner's on at nine. By eleven you're packing your gear, collecting your check from Rubin or his sister Justine, and you can be on your way home. Or do like I did and come by the Rainbow.

There was a girl at the open mike tonight that I took a shine to. I invited her to meet me here after the show, and since she stayed through both my sets, I figured she was coming. But by the time I got packed up and paid, she was gone. I chalked it up to the usual: I'm never the person people think I'm going to be.

There's something about a black woman playing folk music that just doesn't make sense for most people. At least not the kind of folk music I play. There aren't any blues, or soul, or R&B influences. No African rhythms or hip-hop street cred. There's just me and my guitar, doing our Joni Mitchell thing.

I've had criticisms leveled at me—usually in reviews, but sometimes in person—about how I shouldn't be ignoring my heritage, but I don't know what that's supposed to mean. Growing up, I never knew anything about the projects or the streets. Woodforest was a mostly white, middle-class suburb. Maybe I was lucky, or maybe I just had real people as neighbours, but I never had any personal experience with racism until I moved to the city.

I grew up listening to people like Joan Baez and Judy Collins and Joni Mitchell—hell, I wanted to be Joni Mitchell. When I started to play guitar, I wasn't looking to learn Bessie Smith's blues riffs or those soulful renditions of old folk and blues songs that Odetta does. I was trying to figure out Joni's weird tunings.

But people see a black woman with an acoustic guitar and they figure they already know what I'm all about. Even my name works against me. Ruthie Blue. Right off, they're thinking twelve-bars. It was hard at first, let me tell you. But later on, Tracy Chapman opened a lot of doors in the folk field for people like me—just like Charlie Pride did in the country field—but you still didn't see many blacks just playing folk music. And now . . . well, somehow I missed the boat on the whole Lilith Fair phenom. So I do what I've done all along: work at the library four days a week, play around town on the weekends, and make the odd self-produced low-fi recording to sell at shows.

I'm not complaining. Maybe I never hit the big time—I came close, just before the seventies ended, which gets me a footnote in the history books—but at least I'm still getting gigs and people will pay to see me. And with the Internet, my CD sales are up. If I had the nerve to quit my day job, I could probably get by on a low-scale tour. I've seen it work for others, using their Websites to build up the interest for the actual gigs, even if most of them would be house concerts. If I was doing it, I know it would be under the media radar—like pretty much anyone who doesn't sing with *American Idol* pyrotechnics—but I could maybe make a living.

Except I don't have the nerve, so I play it safe. Not so much in what I write—I'm always trying to push the boundaries with my music—but definitely in how I live my life. It's a young person's game, anyway. I'm in my mid-forties now, and unless menopause sends me spinning out of control the way it has some of my friends, I'll be doing this for pretty much as long as I can. And you know what? It's not so bad being a medium-sized fish in a small pond. When I play in the Newford area, I get the headline gigs.

I glance at my watch and decide to stay a little longer, so I go to the bar, get another Corona from Stan, then return to my booth. It's not busy yet so no one's complaining about me taking up this much prime real estate. Later on I'll be sharing the booth—if I stay after this beer. I haven't decided yet. It's a slow night. Someone's playing with a keyboard at a table by the door—got a funky little rhythm going, pulled from the on-board styles, and he's trading sampled trumpet riffs with a girl picking a beautiful Archtop Gibson. It's so quiet I can hear every note.

I look out the window, my foot tapping to the music.

It's too bad Tina didn't show. That was the blond at Rubin's open mike tonight—Tina Wallace. A tiny little thing with the kind of translucent white skin that'll never take a tan. She was sitting at a table by herself, guitar at her feet, when I got to the Casement for my gig. I checked in with Rubin, talked with Billy the soundman, and did a quick soundcheck—that's a luxury the headliner gets; the opening acts get their sound adjusted through their first song, though it's not as bad as it sounds. Billy's aces with his board, and really, how hard is it to get a good mix on a guitar and a voice in a room you probably know better than your own apartment? Because I swear Billy lives in the Casement.

I had time to kill after my soundcheck, so I went and sat down with Tina because she looked a little lost and nervous and I can still remember how that feels.

"Are you playing tonight?" I asked.

She nodded. "They tell me I was lucky to get on the list."

"You were," I told her. "This is a good place to showcase your stuff. You never know who's going to show up." I waited a beat, then added, "Belinda Samms got her start here."

Everybody knows Belinda now, thanks to her getting songs on a couple of good soundtracks that she's managed to parlay into a more than decent career. But back then she was just another young songwriter starting out, trying to downplay a bad case of the jitters.

Tina smiled and introduced herself before asking, "So are there any big-shot Hollywood directors in the house tonight?"

"Not that I can see. Just folks with a love for acoustic music. Don't worry about playing for them. The Casement gets crowds that are big on supporting anybody who shows she's serious about what she's doing."

"I don't know if that makes me more nervous or less," Tina said. "I'm used to playing in bars where nobody's really listening."

"Around here?"

She shook her head. "Mostly up the line. I'm from Hazard originally, but we moved to Tyson when I was twelve."

Which meant she'd played the county seat and pretty much every little town between it and Newford.

We talked some more, me working at putting her at her ease, her grateful for the distraction from her nervousness, though, once she played, I didn't see what she had to be nervous about. She had a big voice—I mean a *big* voice—and played her guitar like she'd been born with it in her hand.

The funny thing was, looking at the two of us, she should have been doing my material and I should have been doing hers— if somebody was into stereotypes, that is. Because her music was nothing like mine. It wasn't quite like anything I'd heard before: a kind of funky hip-hop folk, liberally spiced with jazz chords and happy ska beats. The verses were spoken rhymes, the choruses these seriously hooky melodies, like something from an old Motown record.

She had a sound and she was going far, and I told her as

much after her fifteen-minute set. I felt sorry for the guy who was up after her—she was a hard act to follow. Truth is, I felt a little sorry for myself, because while the new guy was playing, bits and pieces of her songs were still stuck in my head, the hooks were that good.

I'd already told her about the Rainbow, and I repeated it before I got up to do my first set. She told me she'd come by—all she had was a room at the Y to go back to tonight—but like I said, by the time I was ready to leave the Casement, she was gone and now I'm sitting here by myself with a half-empty bottle of Corona for company.

I'm just trying to decide whether to get myself another beer or go home when Tina slides her guitar into the booth, and then follows suit herself.

"Hey," she says and smiles.

Just that, with no word of explanation, but then I guess we don't know each other well enough for one to be needed.

"Hey, yourself," I tell her. "You want a beer?"

"Sure. But let me get this round."

Before I can say anything, she fetches a couple of Coronas from Stan and brings them back to the booth. She pushes one of the beers across to me, the bottle leaving a streak of condensation behind it.

"So tell me," she says. "Were you coming on to me back at the Casement, or were you just being friendly to someone who looked way out of place?"

Was that the reason she took so long to show up?

I decide to focus on the last part of what she said.

"You didn't look out of place," I tell her. "Any venue that offers up great music, that's where you belong."

She takes a pull from her Corona, but doesn't say anything.

"And I'm not gay," I add.

I get the sense that wasn't the answer she was hoping to hear.

"So you're just nice," she says.

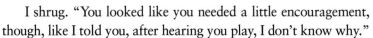

I shrug. "You looked like you needed a little encouragement, though, like I told you, after hearing you play, I don't know why."

"Oh, I needed it," she tells me. "The idea of opening for you . . . I was sure I'd get up there and not remember a single word or even how to play my guitar."

"Now you're being a shameless flatterer."

Not to mention a little flirty.

I'm surprised to find that I kind of like it, but maybe that's because I haven't been out with a guy for a couple of months. I know, musicians are all supposed to lead this wonderfully promiscuous life—in your dreams. For my part, I think the brothers don't know what to make of me, those that actually show up to hear me doing my introspective thing at the kinds of places I play, while the white boys . . . well, I'm guessing they're expecting someone hotter—you know, where it's all about the booty—and I disappoint them, too. I'm tall, black, and big enough in the right places, but I speak softly and I'm a conservative dresser. It must be the librarian in me, though some of my coworkers can party heartier than any clubber half their age.

"No, it's true," Tina says. "I have all your CDs."

I smile. "Even *The Bedroom Demos*?"

"That's one of my favourites. I love 'Valentino.' And that early version of 'Rock Czar' is way better than the one that came out later on *Pointed Interludes*. I think some of the tracks on that album were a little overproduced. You have such a beautiful voice and occasionally it got lost behind the synthesizers."

"It *was* the eighties," I say.

Though I have to admit I agree with her. It was an experiment I didn't repeat.

"Oh, I know. And I didn't mean to sound critical. I don't think you could write a bad song if you tried."

I have to shake my head. "Careful, you're edging into stalker territory."

But I smile to let her know I'm not serious and she smiles back.

"Did you ever think that people were supposed to meet?" she asks.

I'm about to reconsider the stalker angle, but I give her the benefit of the doubt. After all, I'm the one who invited her to meet me here.

"I'm not sure what you mean," I say.

"Well, back at the Casement. I really *was* nervous. It was getting so bad I actually considered leaving before it was time for me to go up on stage. But then you came over and talked to me and all my nervousness went away. You'd never even heard of me before, but you were still so supportive."

"Well, I'm not into being competitive. And seriously, the people who come to a venue like the Casement, they're rooting for you. They want you to be good. Some of the people only show up for the open-stage segment, looking to run across their next personal discovery."

Tina grinned. "I know. While you were packing up, this A&R guy from a local label came up and gave me his card. He wants to meet with me tomorrow." Her grin widened. "I can't believe I just got to say 'meet with me' and it wasn't a joke."

"That's terrific news," I tell her. "And having heard you, I'm not surprised."

And I have to admit, if only to myself, that I'm pleased that it was something so important that had her arriving late. It's getting to the point where you can't much count on anybody, though I suppose that's asking a lot from a total stranger. Call me old-fashioned, but I just think you should do what you say you will, no matter who you're talking to. If you're going to blow somebody off, don't tell them you're going to show up.

"But, see," Tina's saying. "That's what I mean. If you hadn't taken the time to encourage me, I might have left and it never would have happened."

"Don't make more of it than it was. Any serious interest you get in your music is because of what you're putting into it, not because of anybody else."

She shakes her head. "No, I think everything we do depends on the people around us. How we connect to where we are and who we're with."

"Well, I hope it works out for you—your meeting tomorrow."

"Me, too."

She cocks her head, then asks the really hard question that I can't answer to other people's satisfaction, never mind my own.

"You were kind of a star on the rise at one point," she says.

I have to smile to myself. When she was in diapers.

"So why did you put your career on hold?"

"I didn't. I just redefined my priorities."

"You didn't like touring? Because I love the idea of going to new places, meeting new people."

"It has a surface appeal," I tell her, "but it didn't click for me. I could get the gigs—small, but steady—and I did do some touring in the late seventies, early eighties. Maybe it's different now, but I didn't enjoy it at the time. It's hard enough being a woman alone on the road, without being black as well. I guess I had a sheltered childhood because being black was never a problem growing up. Moving downtown from the suburbs was when I got my first inkling of how it could be, and later, when I did travel . . ." I shrug. "I just had too many bad experiences."

"That sucks."

"And now I'm too set in my ways. I like working at the library and my cat would hate me if I abandoned him to go touring."

"What kind of cat?"

"A very needy one."

I smile, thinking of Crosby. Right now he'll be perched in the front window of my ground-floor apartment, studying the street for me to come home. These days he's the only man in my life.

"What would make you happy?" Tina asks.

I just look at her. I wonder if the way she jumps around in a conversation is some particular facet of her personality, or just comes from her youthful energy—she's part of the generation that grew up with the five-second sound bite, after all.

"World peace," I say.

It's always a safe answer.

"No, I mean you personally."

"Where are you going with this?" I have to ask her.

"Well, it's just that you know how in fairy tales people are always being rewarded for their selfless kind acts, so I was just wondering, if you could have anything, what would it be?"

"I don't want any reward and I really didn't do anything."

"But that's the beauty of it. It doesn't come because you want it, or expect it. It's because you did something kind—because that's just the sort of person you are. So you help the old lady, or the talking spoon, and the next thing you know, they're turning straw into gold for you, or teaching you the language of birds."

"I take back what I said about your going far," I tell her, smiling. "I just don't see much of a future for a girl who thinks she's a piece of cutlery."

She laughs. "I know, I know. It all sounds silly, but work with me here. What would you wish for if you could?"

"Now you're a genie offering me a wish?"

"It's not about me granting wishes. It's just what my gran taught me how you have to articulate things and put them out into the universe to give them the chance to happen."

"And now I feel like I'm trapped in the New Age section of the library."

"Come on," she says. "Humour me."

"Okay. If I could have anything I wanted? I guess it'd be to write a song that'll still be around long after I'm gone."

"You've already done that," she says.

She starts listing songs, counting them on the fingers of one hand. The funny thing is, all the ones she picks are among my own favourites.

"Try again," she tells me.

I don't say anything for a long moment.

Did this ever happen to you? You're still in high school, or maybe you're at college, and people start talking about whether or not you have a soul. Then somebody pulls out a twenty, lays it on the table, and offers to buy the soul of whoever's protesting loudest that we don't have one.

Nine out of ten times, they won't do it. They won't take the twenty to sell something they don't even believe they have in the first place, and you can't get them to tell you why either. But I know. It's because their assurance in how the world works has suddenly been gripped by a niggling little "what if?" that they can't shake.

That's what happens to me, sitting across the table from Tina. Her eyes are so blue and serious, with just the hint of a twinkle. That humour isn't coming from her pulling a fast one on me. It's coming from a shared joke, even if she's the only one who gets it so far.

So I think about wishes.

What if, what if . . .

I think about impossible things that could be done. Or un-done.

"When I was on the road," I finally say, "before I settled down here with my job at the library, I picked up this teenage hitchhiker. This was down South, in the early eighties. She was in pretty bad shape—not physically, so much, or at least not that I could see. But inside she was warring with demons. It was in her eyes, in the way her hands trembled where she had them folded on her lap.

"I asked her where I could take her and she wanted to go

home, but she said it in a way that told me it was the last place she wanted to be. I tried to talk her into letting me take her to a shelter instead, but she wasn't very responsive to the idea and I didn't try very hard. In the end I just drove her home and went off to my gig."

I can remember it like it happened this afternoon.

"What happened?" Tina asks.

"I got a room in a motel on the edge of town and went to play my gig. The next morning the TV's on while I'm getting ready to head back on the road and the face of my hitchhiker from the day before appears on the screen. She was shot by her brother, who also killed her sister and her mother, before turning the gun on himself."

Tina doesn't say anything for a long moment.

"So you'd go back and fix that?" she asks when I don't go on.

I shrug. "I don't know. How do you fix something like that? Yeah, it would have been great if I could have gotten her to a shelter, but her sister and mother would still have died."

"Then what would you do?"

"I'd like to know why—*really* know why—people do this kind of thing to one another, and then figure out a way to stop it before they hurt themselves or anybody else." I hold her gaze. "Can you do that?"

It's a stupid question. Of course she can't. But she's put me in this funny mood where it feels like anything is possible. As though, if I can just say the right thing, she can make it happen.

She shakes her head. "No, I'm sorry. That's like world peace—too big an issue." Then she adds, "Why didn't you become a social worker instead of a librarian?"

"A librarian is a kind of social worker, sometimes," I tell her. "We have homeless people coming in. Kids needing a safe place. Lonely, messed up people just looking for some kind of company because they don't get it anywhere else in their lives. And we do what we can while we go about our work. A kind word here. Maybe spot them a snack or a drink from the vending machine. Recommend books that'll maybe help them, or at least let them forget what's going on in their lives for a few hours."

"Books change everything," Tina sang softly, quoting from my song "These Books Do."

"They changed my life," I tell her.

"For me it was music."

"Okay, books and music."

"But I know what you mean about libraries being safe places," she says. "I knew a girl back home who used it to get a breathing space. Her parents were awful to her and the kids on the street seemed to have made it their personal duty to torment her whenever they could. The library was the only place she could be okay."

"We get too many kids like that."

I look past her. The tavern's filling up. I recognize a lot of faces and nod when Sid, the bass player for this retro band called The Everlasting First, gives me a wave.

"I thought about social work," I go on, looking back at Tina, "but I didn't think I'd have the stamina for it. I'd just be part of the lives of too many people I couldn't help. *Really* help, I mean. So I write songs for them instead."

"That's what I'm talking about," Tina says.

I give her a puzzled look.

But instead of explaining, she asks, "What would you say if I told you that there are people who hold the gift of possibilities and that I'm one of them?"

"What do you mean?"

"If someone wants something enough, I can give them the possibility of making it happen."

"You mean like . . . magic?"

She shrugs. "You do it with your songs—is that magic? When a song changes somebody's life?"

"I guess . . ."

"So that's what I can do, except it's more direct. It's the face-to-face promise that it can and will happen. They just have to decide what it's going to be."

"So you just walk around giving people wishes?"

Now I'm wondering what kind of drugs she's on. I mean, she seems sweet, and I doubt she's dangerous, but, come on, really?

"Not exactly," she says. "They need to be worthy of the gift. It doesn't work on the big scale, and it's got to be about putting something good into the world. Also, I can't do it all the time. The ability to do it just comes and goes at its own whim. It kind of sleeps inside me until I meet the right person."

"I don't know, Tina. This sounds—"

"Crazy. I know. But you don't have to make up your mind right this moment. Just humour me and think about it."

"And when I decide, you'll know?"

She shakes her head. "No, you will." She leans her elbows on the table. "So tell me. What should I be looking out for when I talk to this guy tomorrow?"

It takes me a moment to shift gears. How can she be so spacey and so practical, basically at the same time?

"I think I need another beer," I tell her. "Do you want one?"

"Only if you promise to walk me back to the Y after, because I've already pretty much had my limit."

"We don't have to drink beer."

"I'll have a coffee then—regular, not decaf."

"It doesn't keep you up?"

"Just the opposite. Caffeine calms me down."

I start to get up, but pause to say, "You can stay at my place if you like."

She raises her eyebrows.

"No, I'm still not gay."

"Too bad. You should try it."

I smile. "It's been long enough since I've been with a guy that I'm finding it hard to remember what it's like, but I'm definitely into them, no question."

She toasts me with her empty beer bottle.

"To whatever turns us on," she says.

"Let me get our beverages and I'll drink to that."

Later, Tina's curled up in the bed I've made up for her on my couch, sleeping the sleep of the innocent, while I'm lying awake in my own bed, staring at the ceiling. I don't have anything to feel guilty about—at least nothing that I know of—but any kind of sleep seems to be eluding me, innocent or otherwise.

Crosby jumps onto the bed and settles in beside me. I put my hand on him and rub the hair around his chin. His purr is loud in the quiet of my bedroom.

I think about something Tina said when our conversation briefly returned to this gift of possibilities business of hers.

"It's not what we know," she said. "It's how well we share it with each other."

She was talking about how communication gets so messed up between people because half the time we're talking different languages. The kindest thing can be misinterpreted. And instead of taking what people say at face value, we spend too much time trying to guess what we think they really mean.

It happens with songs all the time, which is both good and bad. It's great that a song can mean so many different things to different people. But sometimes the things they get out of a song are so diametrically opposed to the songwriter's intent it's like they're living on different planets.

Like this song I wrote about the confusion of staying in an abusive relationship, how the woman still has all this love mixed up with the hurt she's being dealt on a daily basis. It seemed pretty clear to me, and I worked hard to just tell it as a story, not a diatribe. And it touched a lot of people. But then I had a guy e-mail me, thanking me for writing a song that shows how screwed up women are and why sometimes they needed to be slapped around a little, just to knock a little sense into their heads.

I sit up against the headboard and Crosby makes a complaining sound, but quiets as soon as I start to stroke his fur again.

Think about it, Tina had said.

I don't know if she had this in mind when she said that, but it's what works for me. And it just goes to show you that wisdom doesn't necessarily come from the old wise woman, like some of the authors and singers I turn to for inspiration. It can also come from a twenty-something kid who seems more suited to a career that will be lauded by MTV than the folk festival circuit.

Because if the gift of possibilities is real, then I want people to get exactly what I mean from what I say, whether it's in conversation or song. I want my communication to be clear.

I smile. Which is pretty much what everybody wants, isn't it? Everybody wants to be understood. Not to simply speak clearly—we all think we do that anyway—but to actually be understood.

And that would invest a person with so much responsibility. You'd always have to speak the truth. And if you couldn't, you'd have to keep your own counsel, which is something all of us should probably be doing anyway. Who needs to know what you think, if it's going to be hurtful? Maybe if you want to change some injustice, but it's not relevant in our day-to-day lives. Thumper's mother's advice—echoed by my own, when I was growing up—is always going to hold true: if you can't say something nice . . .

Life's full of unhappiness and disappointment. It's so easy to be brokenhearted by the atrocities, the stupidity, the greed—all the things that fuel the endless litany of bad news that scrolls across the bottom of the screen on the news channel.

So yeah, if you had a voice that was always going to be understood—and maybe even believed—it would be important to speak out about that. But it would also be important to *generate* some happiness, on however small a scale it happens to be. Even if that means shutting up at times.

I can do this, I think.

No, not that magic of being understood. That belongs in the fairy tales Tina was talking about earlier. But doing something more with my life. Using the communication tools I have to make the world a better place—not just in songs, but in my everyday life.

I realize this is something I've been struggling with for a while, I just wasn't able to articulate it to myself in a way that I could do something about it. I've been going through my days without direction, and I'm the kind of person who needs a direction if I'm going to do anything meaningful.

I wouldn't call it magic. It's just insight, which, when it clicks for you—when it finally does come *in sight*—feels like magic.

I get up from the bed, generating another cranky response from Crosby.

"I'll be right back," I tell him.

I know Tina's asleep, and I'm not planning to wake her, but I just want to . . . I don't know. Look at her, I suppose. Make sure she's real.

But the couch is empty. Her duffel bag is gone. Her guitar isn't by the door.

I know she didn't leave, because I would have heard her. And that means . . .

I guess I was expecting this all along.

Strangers don't come offering insight out of the blue. Not in real life. In real life we have to create that kind of a situation in our imagination.

It's funny. I don't think I'm crazy. But I am curious as to whether I generated the whole thing in my head, or if there was some modicum of truth in my having met her.

Did she play at the Casement, or did this little fantasy of mine start there?

If she did play the Casement, did she ever come to the tavern?

If she came to the tavern, did I walk her to the Y and leave her there?

I turn on my computer and Google her name. If she's real, if she's gigging around, she might have a Website or a MySpace page—everybody does, these days.

But the first link that comes up is about a tragic death last year in Tyson. I click on the link, but I don't read the story. I just look at the picture of the victim. It's Tina, with that blond hair and those blue eyes of hers that seem to know so much, but haven't forgotten how to smile.

"Of all the people in the world," I ask the image on my computer screen, "why did you pick me?"

Though maybe she didn't just pick me. Maybe her spirit just goes around, randomly bringing a bit of fairy-tale wisdom into the lives of those she meets.

Bits and pieces from our conversation back at the tavern return to me:

Did you ever think that people were supposed to meet?

I'd never thought about it before, but I guess in this case, she was right. I *needed* to meet her at this time of my life, to get me thinking about all of this.

And when I decide, you'll know? I'd asked her.

She'd shaken her head then, saying, *No, you will.*

And I do.

"Thank you," I tell the image.

Then I close the browser window, turn off my computer, and go back to bed. Tomorrow's the first day of the rest of your life, as the cliché goes.

But you know what? It's true.

And I'm going to make it count.

The World in a Box

Somewhere in the world there is a box, and if you open that box, inside it you'll find the world.

What does that mean? I don't know. I think it's like one of those Zen riddles that you're not really supposed to figure out. It's just supposed to make you think—you know, the whole *it's the journey that's important* thing, not the destination.

I can't even remember where I heard it. It was probably one of those late-night, slightly inebriated conversations you can get into, especially when you're young and weighing in on all the great mysteries of the universe. Like, why are we here and where do we go when we die? Or, what if this world is all a dream and one of us is the dreamer? Or, do things exist only because we expect them to?

Man, if I knew now what I thought I did then, I'd be a very wise man.

Looking back, you have to smile. The meaning of life. Omnipotent dreamers. The world hidden in a box.

Except one day I found that box.

I was working part-time at the Antiques Market Mall, looking after my downstairs neighbour Lizzie's booth in the weekday afternoons so that she could stay home with her two daughters and not have to pay for a babysitter. Money was tight. Money's always tight, but it was a little more so than usual that December.

As a musician, I work evenings anyway—when I have a gig—so it was no big deal for me to help out. I just didn't want to have to get up too early in the morning. There are limits to what we'll do for our friends. I could have stayed home and taken on the role of babysitter, but much as I like her kids, after ten minutes I run out of ways to amuse them. And they *don't* amuse themselves. Trust me. I found that out the hard way.

They're great when Lizzie's around, but when she's not, they can sense my general helplessness and act like their attention spans are only three seconds long. I know that's not true. When Lizzie's at home, it's at least five minutes.

So anyway, I look after the booth.

It's not hard work. Because I don't own it, I don't have to worry about prettying up the displays or where I'm going to get new stock. I just go in with a book and catch up on my reading, or wander around some of the nearby booths and shoot the breeze with whoever's working that day while I keep an eye on Lizzie's space.

She believes the stuff should sell itself—she prides herself on her merchandise and even claims the coolest stuff somehow appears to find her—so I'm not expected to pitch her wares. I wouldn't be much good at it anyway since her stock is mostly vintage clothing, jewellery, and collectibles. What do I know about any of that beyond what I've learned helping her out? Now, if she were selling vintage guitars, that'd be a whole other story.

My favourite customers are the teenage girls and the twenty-somethings because they just get so excited about finding this top or that necklace. When they come in two or three at a time, their enthusiasm ricochets off each other until they get totally giddy and you can't help smiling with them.

My least favourite are out-of-town dealers or the local "experts" that you also run into at every garage sale, church bazaar, or flea market. They just know too much, are more than willing to share that knowledge at great length, and always expect some impossible deal that I can't give them and Lizzie shouldn't.

But a customer's a customer, so I smile and am polite to all of them, even the ones that need a bang on the ear. Because it's Lizzie's rep that's under scrutiny here, not mine.

People often wonder if Lizzie and I are a couple, but really we're just friends who like to hang out together. Sometimes it's easier to do things with a friendly neighbour than to try to work your way through the morass of the dating scene. You'd think a musician would have a better chance at hooking up with someone than most, but you'd be wrong. And as a single, working mom, Lizzie often says that she simply doesn't have time to play the whole dating game, just saying she ever found a guy that wasn't a jerk, "present company excepted," she'll add to me.

She doesn't have to. I can be as much of an idiot as the next guy. But I try not to be mean. You know, set up false expectations, or treat somebody crappy just because its not working out.

Maybe Lizzie and I are just lazy, but it's kind of nice to be able to rent a DVD on a night off and have someone to watch it with. Or to share a dinner because, let's face it—in my case—cooking for one sucks. Come my turn, I'm not as adventurous as Lizzie is, but sometimes the tried-and-true works just fine. When I serve up macaroni and cheese, I'm like a hero to Lizzie's girls. And Lizzie, well, she's just happy to have someone else cook, so there are no complaints from her on those nights either.

I suppose the downside is that you get used to how things are going and you stop making any effort to find that real significant other who might be waiting for you somewhere out there in the big old world. Truth is, I don't go looking at all anymore and probably wouldn't know her unless she came up to me wearing a big sign around her neck saying, "It's me, stupid."

It's like what you find on the shelves of the various booths here in the antique mall. Every once in awhile I've gone with

Lizzie on her rounds—mostly to keep the girls out of mischief—
and I walk by tables of crap where she and the other dealers find
treasure. I guess you need the eye for it. It doesn't look like much
to me until I see it on a shelf here with a jacked-up price tag on
it and then it's, of course, that candelabra is worth fifty bucks.
It's gorgeous. But the dealer who bought it at a yard sale found it
in a box under a table, nestled in a tangle of wires, and got it for
three dollars.

And don't they love to talk about those finds.

But I don't mind. I get a kick out of listening to them go on
about their hits and misses and all the arcane knowledge they have
about pretty much anything you can think of. It's interesting—
if not particularly useful to me otherwise—to learn how to tell
the difference between amber and yellow glass, or a true Victorian
desk and a 1940s knockoff. But then I've always been a magpie
for trivia, not limited to, but particularly the tidbits that are relevant to my own field of reference. Don't get me started on the
background of resonator guitars or the original source of some old
Tex-Mex tune.

Mind you, the dealers also love to gossip, and that's not so
interesting. Everybody in here has something to say about everybody else, but I don't take sides or make alliances. I follow
Lizzie's lead and accept everybody at face value, don't make fast
friends, and while it's not in my nature to automatically distrust
anybody, I keep a healthy dose of skepticism on hand with everyone I meet there.

It was early December when I came across the box in Trevor's
booth, which is two over from Lizzie's. It was just a little wooden
three-dimensional square with a fitted lid, small enough to nestle
in the palm of your hand. Walnut, maybe. Or butternut. I know
next to nothing about that kind of thing unless we're talking
about the tops of guitars or neck stocks.

Trevor had a customer, a feisty old woman who also comes by Lizzie's booth regularly, haggling fiercely over every purchase, but never getting obnoxious about it. It was funny seeing the two of them at it. Trevor's a big man, over six feet tall with a lot of weight on his frame, but he doesn't look fat. Just seriously substantial. Big beard and bald head. The top of Grace's head barely reaches Trevor's chin. Small and delicately boned like a bird, she held her own in the bargaining and had a salty tongue that always made me laugh.

"Oh please," she was saying to him. "Your prices are getting higher than a giraffe's balls."

Trevor tried to keep a straight face. He looked away, turning in my direction where I was already grinning, and then he lost it.

Once we'd all finished laughing, I went back to browsing his shelves and they started bargaining again. That's when I spied the little wooden box, sitting in between an old pair of opera glasses with mother of pearl inlay and a little brass statue of Joan of Arc that was missing the tip of its little sword. I turned the box over in my hands, attracted to it for no reason that I could fathom. I'd like to say that I had a flash of premonition at that moment, a forewarning that my perception of everything was about to change, but the truth is all I felt was a mild curiosity.

The wood had been oiled, bringing out the grain, and the sides had been put together with dovetailed joints—hand-carved ones rather than machined, which meant it was probably from the 1800s and explained the twenty-five-dollar price tag. There were no hinges. The lid simply lifted off, which I proceeded to do.

And then it seemed the world went still all around me.

You know those photographs of the earth taken from one of the space shuttles, the ones that show this beautiful green and blue sphere just floating there in the black velvet reaches of outer space? That's what was inside the box—not a photograph, but a tiny replica of the earth floating there in space.

I held it closer to my eye, trying to figure out the illusion. But it wasn't. An illusion, I mean. Impossible as it should be, somehow there really seemed to be a tiny planet hovering there in the middle of the box.

"Pretty little thing, isn't it?"

I almost dropped the box, but I managed to keep my grip on it as I turned to Trevor.

"It's from the 1800s," he said. "Probably a snuffbox. Or maybe something to keep stamps in. See this?"

He reached out a hand and reluctantly I passed the box over to him. I almost had a heart attack when he stuck his finger inside, the better to hold it as he showed me the joints.

"Hand-carved," he said. "And look how snugly the lid still fits on it. I picked it up at an estate sale last week." His gaze lifted to mine. "I could let you have it for twenty."

It was an automatic spiel, but it surprised me because, after my first few days of booth-sitting, nobody in here ever tried to sell me anything because I didn't buy anything. But mostly I couldn't understand how he obviously couldn't—or at least didn't—see the world slowly spinning inside.

He handed it back to me and I looked inside.

The little planet was still there.

"Sure," I found myself saying as I reached into my pocket with my free hand for the money. "I'll take it."

We might have exchanged a few more words, but I don't remember. I just took my purchase back to Lizzie's booth and sat there staring inside it until I realized that Trevor was giving me a puzzled look. Well, I guess it must have seemed weird, me sitting there, mesmerized by the box the way I was.

I caught his gaze before he could turn away and gave him a shrug and a smile. Putting the lid back on, I set it on the counter in front of me.

I desperately wanted to ask him what he saw when he looked

inside the box, but managed not to. Obviously, he didn't see anything or he'd have kept it. Or sold it for a lot more than twenty
dollars.

Unless I had just imagined it.

I popped the lid and had another quick look.

Still there.

Or I was still imagining it.

I closed the lid again.

But if I wasn't imagining it, then what *was* it?

Lizzie came in just before closing time with a faux fur coat she'd
picked up at the Sally Ann. She was alone, so I assumed the girls
were playing with the Rodriguez twins who lived next door to
our house.

It must have started snowing again because that thick auburn
mane of Lizzie's hair sparkled with melted flakes. She had a rosy
flush to her cheeks.

I've never understood why her ex left her and the girls. What
could he have been thinking? Lizzie's everything a guy could want
in a woman: she's smart, funny, pretty as anything, even-tempered,
and just a little mischievous. And yes, Sophie and Emaline are a
handful, but they're a good-natured, happy handful, not a couple
of surly kids. And they do know how to take a time-out.

"How's it been today?" she asked.

"Slow."

"How slow?"

"I sold a twelve-dollar brooch for ten bucks."

She sighed, then shook her head, determined not to let it get
her down. The past couple of weeks had been particularly bad.
Yesterday she hadn't had even a single sale.

"Oh well," she said. "Everybody says it'll pick up after
Christmas."

I nodded. Apparently, people didn't buy used goods to give as presents, even if they were high-priced and classy like what you could find here in the antiques mall.

"What do you have there?" she asked.

"Just a little box I got from Trevor."

She grinned. "Don't tell me you're finally getting the fever."

"Hardly." I handed it over to her so she could have a look at it. "I just liked it."

I realized I was holding my breath as she turned it over in her hands and then opened it.

"It's pretty," she said. "You can use it to hold your guitar picks."

I nodded, trying not to show my disappointment. I'd wanted her to see the planet, too. It would have, oh, I don't know, been this little shared secret known only to the two of us, and I'd have liked that. Instead, I'd just paid twenty dollars for an admittedly pretty little box in which I imagined I could see a piece of magic.

"What's the matter?" Lizzie asked. "You have the funniest look on your face."

"It's nothing. I guess I just overpaid Trevor for it."

"How much was it?"

"Twenty-five. But he gave it to me for twenty."

Lizzie shook her head. "Well, it *is* very pretty . . ."

"And it's from the 1800s," I said, adding silently to myself, not to mention that it holds the illusion of a miniature earth floating in space.

"He'd probably take it back if you asked. Do you want me to?"

"No," I said as she returned the box to me. "I still like it. And I do need something to keep my picks in."

I peeked inside. The planet was still there.

I didn't have a gig that night, but Lizzie actually had a date with this guy she'd met at her friend Cathy's café earlier in the day.

"I'm as surprised as you that I said yes," she said as we walked home from the antiques mall. "But he seemed nice and what the heck, right? I can't let myself turn into a complete spinster."

"You'd never be a spinster," I told her.

The girls were sleeping overnight at the twins' house next door, so once I heard Lizzie's front door close downstairs, I knew the building was empty except for myself. Mine's the smaller of the two apartments that make up the house because the ground floor has an extra bedroom tacked on at the back. But I have plenty of room since I only have myself and my instruments to worry about. I love to read, but I don't keep books when I'm done. Instead, I trade them back in at the second-hand shop and get a bunch of new ones.

My gear—that's another story. I can't seem to let a guitar or an amp, or even a pedal, leave my possession, but I can't stop picking up new ones either. Mostly used, because like a guy I used to play with once said, "The only thing a guitarist should buy new are strings and picks." There's something to be said about an instrument that's got a little history to it, no question. But you get enough of them and they really start to fill up the place. Lizzie says my apartment looks like an instrument shop, except nothing's for sale.

What can I say? It's true.

I opened a can of pea soup and put it on the stove to warm. No shared meal tonight because Lizzie was eating out with her date. While I waited for the soup to heat up, I took the box out of my pocket and removed the lid. The miniature version of the earth was still floating inside.

This must be how God sees the world, I thought as I looked down on it.

I got so caught up in staring at it that my soup almost boiled over.

———

I had flying dreams that night.

Not the kind I've had before, where I'm skimming over the rooftops and trees and lampposts, looking down on the city below, but it's all close enough to make out details. In these dreams I was floating somewhere in space, out among the stars, and the earth was far, far below me, a sphere of blues and greens the size of a marble because of my perspective. It was so tiny. Like the world in the box I'd bought from Trevor.

That's all I did. I just floated there, looking down at it.

When I woke, I couldn't remember having had a more restful night.

Later that morning I sat at my kitchen table, nursing a coffee and staring out at the snowy streets while I tried to remember where I'd first run across the odd concept of the world in a box. The memory took awhile to come back to me. It was when I was touring with Jenny Wray, back in her cowpunk phase. She does cabaret now with a jazz combo—piano, bass, and drums. She decided she only wanted the trio when she made the switch from her country show, so she had to let me go, no hard feelings.

I didn't have any. You could run out of gigs quickly if you burned your bridges every time things didn't go the way you wanted them to. But I'd liked playing with her. For one thing, she was a great person to spend time with on the road. For another, any excuse to bring out my lap steel was good enough for me. I can never get enough country gigs.

That's what I do: I'm a sideman. I had ambitions once of fronting a band, writing my own music, singing my own songs, but I don't have what it takes. I have nothing to say, or at least nothing that I can put in lyrics and music that a hundred others writers haven't already done, and done better. And I don't have the presence, the charisma to be the front man.

I can sing good harmony and play pretty much any style of

guitar you want. Electric, acoustic. Blues, rock, folk, country, and even a little of that Nouveau Flamenco, but I'm mostly faking the Latin stuff. I have the theory and chops for flamenco, but I don't have the feel. I could never get the rhythms for Celtic music either, but I'm more of a lead player anyway.

Gigging with Jenny, I pretty much got to exercise all my enthusiasms, but especially the country. And Jenny was a blast to play with. Smart, funny, and deadly serious about her music, even when she was doing that goofy cowpunk stuff, which was sort of like the Clash channeling Tammy Wynette. And she treated her sidemen with respect, which is rarer than you might think in this business. Doesn't make much sense not to, because a lot of the time we're what make the singers sound as good as they do. But there are a lot of divas out there. Though maybe I'm just biased.

I knew Jenny was in town from seeing her face looking back at me from flyers on various telephone poles and the like, advertising an upcoming gig, so I tried calling her at the apartment she still keeps in the city.

We spent awhile catching up before I brought up the whole business with the world in a box.

She laughed. "God, you don't forget anything, do you?"

"Well, it was a weird story—the kind of thing that stays with you."

"I guess."

"I was wondering where you first heard about it."

I could sense her smiling on the other end of the line. "You mean what wise man, hidden far away from the eyes of the world, first revealed these great truths to me?"

I laughed. "Something like that."

"I made it up," she said.

I was holding the box and looked down into it at the earth floating there, suspended in the center of the space in a way that just didn't seem possible, but it was happening all the same.

"Did you now," I said.

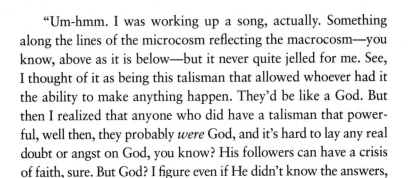

"Um-hmm. I was working up a song, actually. Something along the lines of the microcosm reflecting the macrocosm—you know, above as it is below—but it never quite jelled for me. See, I thought of it as being this talisman that allowed whoever had it the ability to make anything happen. They'd be like a God. But then I realized that anyone who did have a talisman that powerful, well then, they probably *were* God, and it's hard to lay any real doubt or angst on God, you know? His followers can have a crisis of faith, sure. But God? I figure even if He didn't know the answers, He'd let on that He did."

"And being God," I put in, "so it would come to pass."

She laughed. "Something like that. Why are you so interested in this, anyway?"

"Oh, I don't know," I lied. "It's just one of those things that came into my head like an advertising jingle and I haven't been able to get it out again."

"I hate when that happens. Especially when you're sitting down to write something yourself and all you've got in your head is some cheesy oom-pah-pah ditty from a used-car lot."

"It wasn't quite that bad," I told her. "Besides, it gave me an excuse to give you a call."

"Now you need an excuse?"

"You know what I mean."

"Sadly, I do," she said. "Where *does* all the time go? I keep meaning to look up friends whenever I get back to town, but it seems like no sooner do I open the door of my apartment, than I'm already packing my bags and hitting the road again without having made one call."

"The price of success."

"Of steady work anyway. Are you coming to the show on Saturday? I can put your name on the guest list."

We talked a little more, then finally said our goodbyes with promises to get together soon.

It had started to snow again while I was on the phone, which was a good thing. It's always a trade off in the winter. When you get a clear, sunny day, it's usually bitter cold. Snow brings its own challenges, but at least you're not freezing your butt off when you venture outdoors and I had to walk to the antiques mall soon. And I don't mind shoveling because all we've got is the porch and the walkway to the street.

I looked away from the window and studied the box some more, thinking of what Jenny had said.

The person holding it could make anything happen.

Okay, so it was just an idea she came up with for a song that never went anywhere, but it was in my hand now, as real as the kitchen around me, even if I was the only one who could see it.

Maybe I was making it happen. Maybe I was crazy. But there was one way to find out.

Anything, I thought.

I picked something small.

It had been dead in the antiques market for a couple weeks now. None of the dealers were doing well, but poor Lizzie seemed particularly hard hit. I don't think she'd grossed more than forty dollars so far this week and it was already Wednesday.

So let her have a good day, I told the world, floating there in the wooden box I held in my hand.

Let her have an amazing day.

I got to the booth just before one o'clock when I was supposed to take over from her and it was . . . it was just weird. She had three or four people trying to give her money for stuff they'd already chosen to buy, with another couple looking in the display cabinet with the really pricey jewellery.

When she looked up and caught my eye, I could see the relief in her gaze.

"Thank God you're here," she said. "It's been crazy all morning."

I stuffed my coat under one of the tables and started taking money, wrapping up purchases, and generally making myself useful. It was like when Lizzie did the weekend shows, before she got the booth here. Those one-off shows had always been so successful that it had seemed like a no-brainer to get a permanent place to sell her stuff.

It hadn't been bad the first few months, but this recent run of bad luck had been making her seriously reconsider the feasibility of keeping the booth.

Closing wasn't even a consideration today.

It didn't quiet down until past three, and even then there was never a time when there wasn't somebody looking at the clothing racks or peering into the display cabinets. Lizzie'd had to phone the twins' mother and ask her to pick up the girls from school because she couldn't possibly have gotten away to do it herself.

"Wow," she said. "I guess Peter really did bring me good luck."

"Peter?"

"Peter Hendel—my date from last night. The last thing he said after he kissed me goodnight was, 'That one's to bring you luck tomorrow,' which made me feel a little bad because I guess I was going on a bit too much about how lousy business has been."

No, I wanted to tell her. I brought you this luck—me and the world in my little wooden box that no one can see.

Because don't think I hadn't been thinking about it as we dealt with the press of people wanting to buy things. I'd made the wish, and it had come true, just like that. What made it really obvious was how we were the only booth in the mall doing such a bang-up trade today.

I wasn't about to tell Lizzie that, but it annoyed me that this Peter guy was getting the credit for it, just as it annoyed me more when she went on to tell me what a great time she'd had on her date. I don't know why that was. It's not like she hasn't gone out with other guys since I've known her, and it never bothered me those times. We don't have some kind of *When Harry Met Sally* thing happening here—you know, we're right for each other but we just don't know it.

Okay, I'm lying. I'm crazy about her and I know she doesn't feel the same way about me. I haven't exactly asked her, but you pick up on these things and, while I can tell she likes me really well as a friend, I don't get the feeling she's ever considered me in any other light. I've had enough women come on to me at gigs to know when someone's attracted to you, and Lizzie doesn't even flirt with me, so there you go.

But I was good with it. At least, that's what I've always told myself. Except there was something about the sparkle in her eye when she was talking about this guy, not to mention the way he'd stolen my thunder with his damned "good-luck kiss," that just ticked me off today. Ticked me off enough that I found myself in a cubicle in the washroom with the box open in my hand saying something along the lines of how whatever else might happen, a relationship with Peter just wasn't going to work out. It wasn't even going to get started.

Okay, I'm not exactly proud of doing it. But it's not like I tried to work up some mojo to make Lizzie want me instead. And even with the increased business at the booth, and that weird little phenomenon of the world suspended in its wooden box, I hadn't totally bought into the magic being real anyway.

But Peter never called Lizzie like he'd promised he would.

By Friday it was still so busy at Lizzie's booth that we were both working there. We'd probably been in each other's company more in the past few days than we ever had—two full days at the booth, sharing dinner and pricing stock in the evenings. It was lucky that I didn't have a gig either night so I could help out, though I did have one tonight.

Our being together hadn't been like some romantic thing.

We were both too busy trying to get everything done. The girls were great, helping out where they could, amusing themselves and keeping out of the way when they couldn't.

But we weren't so busy that I didn't notice Lizzie getting more and more depressed and it didn't take any great genius to figure out why.

"I don't get it," she said as we were restocking her booth before opening on Friday morning. "We hit it off amazingly well, so why hasn't he called like he said he would?"

She looked at me like I had the answer.

And of course I did. But it was the last thing I could tell her.

"Maybe he just got called away on business," I said.

"I suppose. But they don't have phones where he had to go? I hate it when people promise they're going to do something and then they don't. It makes me feel so pathetic, eagerly awaiting some stupid phone call that's never going to come."

I could have gotten mad at Peter for treating her so bad, but it wasn't his fault, was it?

Truth is, this magic business was trickier than I thought. What I hadn't realized was the whole concept of cause and effect that came into play when you used it. It seemed that if you made something happen in one place, then it took away the possibility of it happening elsewhere. Like all these people buying stuff from Lizzie. Because I'd made them come to her, nobody was shopping at the other booths and you could feel the resentment from the other dealers. Or by keeping Peter away from Lizzie. All I'd done was leave her feeling progressively more miserable, even with all her recent financial success in the past few days.

I excused myself before the store opened and went back to the washroom. I told the world in its box to let whatever was going to happen between Peter and Lizzie play itself out. And to tone down the buying frenzy.

If I hadn't believed that the magic worked before, I had to now.

When the doors opened, there was no rush like there had been the past few days. And it stayed relatively quiet throughout the day. But even though our sales had died down, everybody else's picked up.

And then, just around noon, this good-looking guy came up to the booth with a sheepish look and a bouquet of roses. I didn't have to ask if it was Peter. All I had to do was look at Lizzie's face as he made his apologies. The booth was so small that I couldn't help but overhear what he was saying.

His mom had fallen sick. Flew out immediately to see her. No chance to call, everything was so crazy. Just got back this morning. Yes, she was fine now. A false alarm, thank God.

No, thank me, I thought.

"It's pretty quiet," I told Lizzie. "Why don't you guys go have some lunch or something."

Her beaming smile made me feel even smaller for what I'd done.

"I owe you one," she said.

"You don't owe me a thing," I told her. "Go have some fun."

I watched them walk away, then turned to help a customer who was hemming and hawing over whether to buy a five-dollar brooch.

Yup, things had changed, all right.

My gig didn't go so well that night. The singer who'd hired us kept straying from the set list of stuff we'd worked on, which wasn't a huge problem. The musicians were all professionals. We could keep up. But the music didn't sound tight like it had in rehearsal, and when the singer started to give us a hard time about it after the first set, I wanted to whack him on the head with my guitar.

Or maybe speak a few words into the wooden box that was

in the pocket of my winter coat draped across my gear bag on the side of the stage.

But I did neither. The band soldiered on and the gig came to an end the way every gig does, the good ones and the bad ones. We got paid and I went home.

I was surprised to see the lights on in Lizzie's place.

I tried to be quiet, but it's hard with a guitar case, amplifier, and gig bag of cables and pedals. I was on the landing, halfway up the stairs, when I heard Lizzie's door open.

"Sorry," I started to say.

I didn't finish. Lizzie was crying and her face looked bruised.

I left my gear on the landing and hurried back down the stairs. She looked worse up close. Black eye, with a cut on the brow above it. A bruised cheek. Her lips were swollen, the lower one split.

"God, Lizzie! What happened?"

"I . . . I don't even know for sure . . ."

She let me steer her back into her apartment. Luckily the kids were next door—they were going to think they lived there pretty soon. I sat Lizzie at the kitchen table, then put a kettle on and took a box of herbal tea down from the cupboard. My hands were shaking as I got a couple of teabags out and rinsed the teapot with hot water.

"Who did this to you?" I asked her because I was going to kill whoever had done it.

"It . . . it was Peter," she said.

My anger deflated into a sick guilt.

Peter.

Oh, God. *I'd* done this to her, or I might as well have, because I'd worked the little mojo with my world in a box that had brought him back to her this afternoon.

The water started to boil. I emptied the teapot, dropped the teabags in, and poured the boiling water over them. Covering it with a cozy, I brought it and a couple of mugs to the table.

"Do you want to talk about it?" I asked.

She shook her head and just reached a hand across the table. I hesitated a moment, then took her hand, stroking the top of it in helpless comfort. I don't know how long we sat there, but after awhile she began to tell me what happened.

They'd gone for lunch, were just hitting it off so well. They came back here, put the roses in water, and made arrangements for the girls to stay next door. Then it was off to dinner, followed by what was supposed to be just a few drinks at a jazz bar, except Peter had gone way over any acceptable limit.

"I was a little tipsy, too," she said. "Enough that I knew we should be taking a cab from the club. But he insisted he was fine to drive. Said he'd been drinking water as well, though I don't remember that. I don't know why I got into that car with him. I just didn't want him to think I was pushy, I guess, and how stupid was that?

"Anyway, he lost control running a red light and the next thing I knew we were smashing into a parked car, which is how I got my lovely new facial. I look like the Frankenstein monster."

"You couldn't look ugly if you tried," I told her.

She shook her head. "You always have something nice to say, don't you?"

Maybe not, because right then I didn't have a single response. When she fell silent, I poured tea for us one-handedly. She gave me the sense that she was never going to let go of my other hand. That it was her only anchor to the normal world.

"When you first said Peter'd done this to you, I thought . . ." I began, but then let my voice trail off.

But she picked up on where I'd been going with that.

"Oh, God. That would have been even more horrible. It's bad enough that he had such disregard for our lives. And what if he'd hit somebody?" She shook her head. "Well, I won't be seeing him again, unless it goes to court and I'm asked to testify and you can bet I'll tell the whole truth."

I nodded. I hated drunk drivers. One of my friends had been killed by one back when I was in high school. So far as I was concerned, there was no excuse to get behind the wheel if you were over the limit. Better yet, if you were planning to drive, abstain completely. But some people didn't see it that way. It was all trying to get one past the police, with no consideration for the innocent people that might be hurt.

After a time, Lizzie got tired enough that I could put her to bed. I just took off her shoes and got her to stretch out on her bed, then covered her up with a blanket. She caught my arm before I could go.

"Could you . . . don't leave me alone . . ."

"I won't," I told her. "I'll make up a bed for myself on the couch. I just need to get my gear out of the hall first."

She fell asleep at my promise and didn't hear the rest of what I'd said.

I slipped out of the bedroom and brought my guitar and gear up to my apartment. It took me only a couple of minutes and then I was back in her place. I closed the door and checked in on her. She was still sleeping. I picked up my coat from where I'd dropped it coming into the apartment earlier. Taking the wooden box out of its pocket, I went and sat down on the couch.

I tried to compose myself, but all I could think of was how that man had endangered Lizzie.

Peter Hendel.

Peter Hendel needed some serious Old Testament eye for an eye, something to hurt him as much as he'd hurt Lizzie, and I was just the guy to bring it down upon him in biblical proportions. I had the means, right here in my hands. And I had the will.

The trouble was, every time I'd done something with the world in its wooden box, it had gone wrong.

I knew why, too.

It was because I wasn't omnipotent. I couldn't see all the ramifications of even the simplest wish.

And maybe that was the problem. Not just that I couldn't see how making one thing happen would cause unforeseen consequences. I'd been thinking in terms of wishes.

The world didn't work on wishes. There were no free rides.

I'd been generous at first, helping Lizzie with her slumping sales. But that had taken prosperity from others.

Then I'd been selfish and that had only resulted in making Lizzie miserable.

So I tried to do the right thing, and that had made things even worse.

I had the feeling it would always work out like that.

I could bring rain to some drought-stricken part of the world, but it would only take that rain away from somewhere else and perhaps cause a worse drought there.

I could try to bring peace to parts of the world where there was war. I could stop all the car bombings and acts of terrorism. But bottling it all up would probably make it explode even worse somewhere else.

And right here, on a more personal level, I could bring retribution to Peter Hendel—and God, did I want to—but what ramifications would that have elsewhere in the world?

The box was open in my hand and I had been staring at the small sphere suspended there inside it as all of this was going through my head.

Slowly, I took the lid and put it back on.

Wishes and magic weren't a solution.

I don't know that there are ever real solutions to anything. Not easy ones, at any rate. Mostly, we just seem to muddle through our lives, and maybe that's what we're supposed to do. Learn what we can as we live our lives and make sure that we bring what goodness we can into the world at our individual level as we try to win back the darkness one little bit at a time.

The journey, not the destination.

I moved the box back and forth from one hand to another.

So maybe I'd learned something from this, but I'll tell you now, I wish I'd never found the damn thing.

And what was I supposed to do with it now?

What Lizzie really needed to help her heal was her girls. They were what would remind her that there was still light in the world. They were the best reason to be brave and to carry on that I could think of. She gave a slow nod in agreement and the first touch of a smile since she'd called to me in the hall last night.

We told them that their mom had been in a car accident and left it at that. I went in to work the booth so that Lizzie could have the day with them and wouldn't have to endure the gossip of all the dealers as they checked out her bruises and cuts.

When the antiques market closed at the end of an average day of sales, I went to the club where Jenny was playing and got lucky because they were just finishing their sound check. After exchanging hellos with her band, Jenny and I went and sat at the bar to have a coffee. She never drinks before a show and I wasn't in the mood for a beer—not with Lizzie's story still fresh in my mind. Jenny was still in jeans and a sweater, her straight blond hair tied back in a ponytail. It made her look younger than I knew she was. Tonight, at the show, she'd be wearing the heels and black cocktail dress, her hair pinned up in a loose coil, her makeup just right.

I took out the box and put it on the bar in front of her.

"What's this?" she said.

"The world in a box."

She laughed. "Really?"

"If you want it to be."

"My, aren't you being mysterious."

She picked up the box and admired it for a moment before taking off the lid and looking inside.

"There's no world," she said.

"Then I guess you'll need to find one to put in it."

I was relieved. So she didn't see it either. I don't know why I could and no one else, but I didn't want the responsibility of taking care of it anymore. I also didn't want it to fall into the wrong hands—which were those belonging to anyone who could see that little earth suspended inside, I'd decided.

Jenny was a safe bet. She was sentimental and would keep it safe. And since she couldn't see the world, everything else would be safe, too. Or at least as safe as things can be in a world where wishes actually work.

"Are you staying for the show?" she asked.

I shook my head. Lizzie had called before I left the antiques mall, asking if I wanted to come over for dinner and a movie tonight. There had been something different in her voice. Not the understandable anxiety I'd heard last night. Not the sadness from last week, either, or even a promise. Just something different. Maybe I was only imagining it.

But when I heard her voice I realized that I needed to depend even less on wishes and what-ifs than I had before I found the box. I had to make an effort so that the days to come might go the way I wanted them to, because they weren't just going to come to me.

I had a journey to take, after all.

And I didn't want to take it alone.